TWO COINS

WOMAN OF DETERMINATION AND COURAGE

Two Coins: A Biographical Novel / Sandra Wagner-Wright. – 1st ed.
ISBN 978-0-9963845-4-4 (print)
ISBN 978-0-9963845-3-7 (eBook)

TWO COINS

WOMAN OF DETERMINATION AND COUARGE

Sandra Wagner-Wright

Wagner-Wright Enterprises

WAGNER
WRIGHT
ENTERPRISES

"What are human beings
That you are mindful of them?
Mortals, that you care for them?"
—Psalm 8: 4

Table of Contents

Chapter 1
"I Remove My Own Boots"

CALCUTTA
January 1879
The Reverend William Hastie
Incoming Principal, Scottish College

I adjust my sun hat. *Topi* they call it. Got it at Aden. Most of the passengers went to the nearest shop, but I found mine in a gentleman's store. The clerk said it was the highest quality. I'm not sure I believe him, but it's certainly better than what my fellow passengers procured.

It's been a wonderful passage. The Suez Canal is a marvel of engineering, even if it was built by the French. And nearby is the route Pharaoh took when he pursued the Children of Israel. It's sand and arid desert on either side of the sea, and I've seen the mountains that forced the Hebrews to turn south. No wonder they wandered for forty years. It would take that long to get around the mountains.

That's not the point, of course. The point is no one thwarts God's plan. Pharaoh thought he had the Hebrews until God parted the Red Sea. And now we cross it in ease and comfort. I look forward to my posting in Calcutta. I'm sure the experience will prove invaluable when I return home and take a university position.

A few weeks later, I have my first view of British India. We travel to Calcutta along the coast of the Hugli River. I've read that the people think the river holy, because it's part of the Ganges. Ridiculous to think the British have been in India a hundred years and still haven't taught the people that goddesses don't live in rivers.

The city of Calcutta emerges out of the verdant countryside like a precious jewel unwrapping itself from the green foliage. Looking through crowded shipping lanes, I spy proper buildings peeking out over the water, and a city square. When we arrive at the quay, the illusion is spoilt. There's a line of oxcarts with semi-dressed men sitting on the drivers' benches. Cattle and dogs wander everywhere. When the gangway is secured, I see a welcoming committee from Scottish College. I gaze at the motley assembly of shabby missionary teachers and scruffy students. The College has been without leadership for over a year. Now God has sent me to restore order and lead the entire Scottish missionary enterprise into a new day. I adjust my *topi* and stride down the gangplank.

Mary Pigot
Lady Superintendent
Ladies' Association Female Mission

Mr. Wilson, Acting Superintendent of Scottish College, paces near my desk in the anteroom of the Female Mission. He wanted to speak with me alone, to tell me that he'll lead the delegation to greet The Reverend Hastie on the pier. How he can do that—greet the man—I don't know. I would have fought Mr. Hastie's appointment, demanded that the Foreign Mission Committee recognize everything I'd accomplished. But that's not Mr. Wilson's way. He's always in the background serving others. I know he must leave for the pier, but I keep remonstrating with him.

"Miss Pigot, you must accept Mr. Hastie," he says to me. "I don't have the educational qualifications for the position. Please, for my sake, welcome Mr. Hastie."

Mr. Wilson takes off his spectacles and rubs the space on his nose. He wipes the lenses with his handkerchief and puts them back on, his pale blue eyes suddenly larger.

I pout. "You're the one who raised standards after you took on the job. Your students are the best in Calcutta. Your education has nothing to do with your ability. Besides, everyone is equal before God."

Mr. Wilson shakes his head sadly. "That may be, Miss Pigot, but they aren't equal in the Church of Scotland. I'm an ordinary person. I do a good job, but I'm not fit to be Head of the College. Besides, once the new man arrives I can go home on furlough and see my family."

I stop myself from reaching for his hand. "But you'll come back?" I blink back a tear. I can't bear to think of life without his friendship.

"I hope to, if my health holds out and if the Church sends me. The new man may not want me," Mr. Wilson responds.

"I hate him already," I say, which is hardly fair since I've yet to meet Mr. Hastie. But I don't know how I'll cope without Mr. Wilson's support and advice. Mr. Wilson squeezes my hand.

"You must accept the situation. Mr. Hastie is now God's man in Calcutta." Mr. Wilson moves his head to the side and shrugs. "I understand Mr. Hastie is a great speaker and well-trained. He'll be an asset to the Scottish Mission."

"But he isn't you," I sigh and pick at a piece of lint on my sensible gray dress.

"I think that's the point," Mr. Wilson says. "I'm a simple man from a small town in Scotland. I can't engage in philosophy. I'm not the man for the job. I never was."

"But you're my friend."

"You must make him your friend as well, Miss Pigot. Why don't you invite him to view the Mohurrum Procession? The Female Mission's on the route. Now, if you'll excuse me, I have to get to the pier so I can make a good first impression."

I escort Mr. Wilson to his *gharry,* our local horse-drawn carriage, in the courtyard. As I watch the vehicle drive onto the road, I wonder what the illustrious Mr. Hastie is like.

James Wilson
Senior Lay Missionary, Scottish College

Miss Pigot is correct. I should have been named Principal of Scottish College. I've lived in Calcutta for sixteen years. I know the local culture. I know students, and I know the curriculum. I've served as Acting Principal for two years. Two years! And all for nothing. The Foreign Missionary Committee wants a university man and an ordained minister. And I shall soon lead the delegation to greet him.

When I arrive at the pier, students and teaching staff stand away from the bullock carts and drivers waiting to pick up cargo. I greet Mr. Edwards, another missionary from Scottish College, and turn to the senior students who came to welcome the new principal. All are dressed in dark European suits and some have their hair clipped close to their heads. I'm proud of them. Mr. Hastie won't find any fault with their preparation or manners.

The steamship's horn sounds. We turn to see the gangplank is down. A man of medium height strides down the gangplank with aplomb. I presume this is Mr. Hastie. He wears a brown three-piece suit and an extravagant *topi* that he'll have to trade for one in the missionary style. In Calcutta, the *topi* indicates one's social standing, and his is more suitable for a successful merchant.

"Come, gentlemen. It's time to greet our new principal." Staff and students fan out behind me. I swallow hard. We proceed around the bullock carts and walk towards my replacement.

Mary Pigot

Today I will meet Mr. Hastie for the first time. He's been in Calcutta a week but hasn't called at the Female Mission. This surprises me, since the Scottish mission community is a small one. However, Scottish College and the Female Mission are two separate institutions. The Church of Scotland Foreign Mission Committee supervises Scottish College. My Female Mission is supervised by the Ladies' Association in Edinburgh.

I sent Mr. Hastie and Mr. Wilson invitations to the Female Mission to observe the Mohurrum procession. Mohurrum commemorates the death of Mohamed's grandson. The procession begins at dawn at the nearby Tipu Sultan Mosque in North Calcutta. The route goes past our orphanage and school at 125 Bow Bazar. In preparation for the new principal, I have the groom and groundskeeper sweep the school courtyard at first light and put three cane chairs and a small table under the tamarind tree. No sooner do we finish, then the *gharry* arrives.

"Mr. Wilson, you've brought our new principal." I smile broadly and extend my hands.

"Allow me to introduce The Reverend Mr. William Hastie." Mr. Wilson gestures toward a man of medium height wearing a full suit, including a waistcoat.

He's a handsome man with a medium brown beard and mustache and brown eyes. His *topi* looks painfully new. He must have bought it at Aden; most new arrivals do. Mr. Hastie looks around our courtyard, smiles, and extends his hand. I grab it in both of mine, remembering Mr. Wilson's advice.

"We're so excited to have you with us," I say. "Come, I've arranged some refreshments until the procession comes by."

Mr. Hastie steps back and breaks contact with my hands. *Am I too familiar?* He looks around before selecting the chair with full arms.

I pick up a tasseled blue silk pillow. "Mr. Hastie? Do you require a cushion?"

"Not at the moment." I put the pillow on my own chair.

"A wise choice, sir," Mr. Wilson comments. "Although the morning fog is chilly, the air becomes close when the sun rises. Oh, I almost forgot. Miss Pigot, Mr. Steele sent along this packet of coffee."

"That's so thoughtful. Sajiva," I call.

Sajiva emerges from the veranda without making a sound. He's my most valued servant, always watching for what's needed. "Yes, Mem." His voice is both soft and musical. Sajiva stands with a questioning look.

"Take this coffee and be careful with it. Tell the *khansama* to prepare it with the refreshments. Be sure nothing is taken or wasted," I order. The cook is a good man, but he doesn't always pay attention to what he's doing. Coffee is too precious to waste.

"Yes, Mem," Sajiva replies. He takes the coffee and proceeds into the house.

Mr. Hastie raises his left eyebrow. "I'm surprised to see servants at a mission. I thought you trained your students in housewifery."

I ignore Mr. Hastie's presumption about our curriculum. "A house in India can't be run without servants. We don't have many. No gatekeeper, as you notice. Sajiva is the *durwan*. He organizes everything. Without him, I couldn't do my job. Isn't that true, Mr. Wilson?"

"I would have thought..." Mr. Hastie begins.

Is he criticizing me? "Every house has servants," I interrupt him. "Even the College, doesn't it, Mr. Wilson?"

Mr. Wilson spreads his hands in a calming motion. "Living in Calcutta is... challenging. Take a few weeks to get your bearings and see how things are done here. You're staying with Mr. Steele. I'm sure you'll notice his servants."

"More than seems strictly necessary. They forever sneak up on one," Mr. Hastie replies.

"I assure you, Mr. Steele is careful with money. He doesn't engage extra servants. By Calcutta standards, he lives simply," Mr. Wilson says.

"Well, it's hardly my place to comment." I catch a look of slight disgust cross Mr. Hastie's face and flinch at the implied criticism. Mr. Wilson's lips twitch. He nods at me to change the subject.

"So, Mr. Hastie, did Mr. Wilson tell you anything about this morning's procession?" I ask hastily. "The Hindus have countless gods and festivals to take their attention from other things. The Mohammedans don't do as many public events."

"Why invite me to view a heathen festival?" Mr. Hastie asks. "How could—"

"It's unique," Mr. Wilson comes to my aid. "Mohurrum is the second most important festival on the Mohammedan calendar."

"It's a lunar calendar, you know," I interject.

"I'm not ignorant of world religions." Mr. Hastie clears his throat as he speaks.

Sajiva comes out with a tray and offers each of us a cup of fruit juice. I savor the pungent guava flavor as I gather my thoughts. Mr. Hastie doesn't converse so much as judge.

"I thought you'd find the procession interesting," I offer. "It passes our compound."

Mr. Hastie sips his juice. He glances up as the children begin to chatter from the school veranda above us.

"I allow the children to watch. They can't do anything else with all the noise."

Mr. Hastie's eyes narrow as the sun's rays reach our seats. "Miss Pigot, allowing the children to watch is the same as letting them participate."

"I'm not sure what you mean. We're surrounded by festivals of every kind. It's impossible to ignore them." I can't understand why Mr. Hastie is being so rude, as if he thinks I'm beneath him.

"You must insist they keep their minds on their studies," Mr. Hastie continues.

As if on cue, the sound of drumming fills the air.

"Mr. Hastie, will you stand at the gateway or do you prefer to go upstairs to the veranda?"

"I'm certainly not standing in the street." As the dust kicks up, he holds a handkerchief over his mouth.

"Then follow me up the outside stairway."

Mr. Hastie watches the marchers from the veranda rail with a sour look on his face. I forget about him as men dressed in black march, blow horns, and beat drums. Some hoist black or red flags. It takes them about half an hour to pass our house.

"Such a somber festival. Just drums and horns," I comment. "I prefer happy events. It's over now. Let's go inside to the drawing room and have our coffee."

"Miss Pigot, why did you invite me here?" Mr. Hastie asks again.

"To see the procession. There's a festival somewhere almost every day. Since this one comes by our house, I thought you'd like to see it. That's all. Come, or the coffee will be spoilt."

I lead everyone into the house. The drawing room is dim compared to the bright morning sun, but not dim enough to disguise the dust motes. Ahead of us, Sajiva quickly wipes the lounge and chair cushions. As soon as everyone is seated, Sajiva serves the coffee with the small biscuits I keep for special guests. The biscuits are a bit stale. Mr. Wilson winks at me and talks to Mr. Hastie about students at the College. I catch his eye as I drink, and nod. The sooner we have coffee, the sooner Mr. Hastie will leave.

The following Sunday I drive my *gharry* from Bow Bazaar to the European sector with its open spaces and gardens, an artificial world plopped into the middle of Calcutta. I make this journey at least once a week, passing the English church at St. John's Cathedral where I was baptized. I haven't attended since I started working for the Church of Scotland. The Scots have their own church, St. Andrew's Kirk. It's like their churches at home. In Scotland the churches don't have heat, and here St. Andrew's doesn't catch a breeze. The furnishings are plain, the walls whitewashed, and the organ in questionable tune. In our climate, it's impossible to keep any instrument in tune very long.

St. Andrew's Kirk held its first service sixty years ago. Like all structures in the European sector, the church has no connection to local culture. The nave is an oval shape with a gallery above for extra seating. The roof supports are fat Doric columns. The chairs are mahogany with cane seats for ventilation.

I don't usually attend St. Andrew's. The Scottish merchants and professionals are too busy congratulating themselves to worry much about the rest of us. But today is different. The Reverend Mr. Hastie will preach his first sermon. The gallery and main floor will be full of people ready to be impressed by this paragon from Scotland. After spending time with him yesterday, I'm less enchanted, but still curious.

I nod to the usher and take a place at the back underneath the gallery. All the wood gleams with polish, and the floor must have been scrubbed just before people began arriving. By the time we leave, the dust will be back. I see The Reverend Mr. Gillan at the front, deep in conversation with Mr. Hastie. Mr. Gillan is my sworn enemy. He opposed my appointment as Lady Superintendent because I didn't come out directly from Scotland. Everyone from the home country calls people born and raised in Calcutta, like me, Eurasians. It's not a nice term.

Mr. Gillan seats Mr. Hastie in the center of the formal desk, then takes his seat to Mr. Hastie's right. The Reverend Mr. Thomson, who recommended my appointment, sits at the other end.

Sounds emanate from the organ in its place at the end of the gallery above the lectern. It's out of tune, and some of the keys don't sound. I open my Psalter to today's Psalm and join in singing the first few verses from Psalm 116. I don't see why we can't have something more cheerful. It's only January, and Lent doesn't start until March. This psalm is all supplications and sacrifices of thanksgiving.

Mr. Gillan rises to read the Scripture, John 13: 1-17. He has a flat-sounding voice, but it carries to the back. Mr. Thomson's voice is too soft now.

"He riseth from supper and laid aside his garments; and took a towel and girded himself.

After that he poureth water into a basin and began to wash the disciples' feet."

When Mr. Gillan finishes reading, even I feel a thrill of anticipation. Everyone says Mr. Hastie is a great orator. I settle back to listen.

Mr. Hastie climbs the steps with their plain wooden bannister. From the lectern, he looks over the room silently for what seems a long time but is probably only a minute or so. From my seat at the back, it feels like he's looking down upon the congregation. It must be strange to look down on the lectern from the gallery. I see Mr. Wilson and Mr. Edwards keep the younger boys in the first row quiet.

Finally, Mr. Hastie begins speaking. A hush falls over the room. I sense everyone leaning forward. Mr. Hastie doesn't refer to notes or raise his voice, yet I hear every word. When he speaks of Jesus knowing his hour had come, I shiver despite the heat.

"When you come in after a long, hot day, do you remove your boots or does someone assist you?" Mr. Hastie asks the congregation. "And if so, is it a family member or a servant? And if there's no servant, would you want a family member to pull off your dirty boot? I think not."

My mind wanders. My father told me that when he supervised indigo plantations he had a servant who took off his boots for him and cleaned them for the next day. I didn't see the point since the boots would only get dirty again. But my father said it was important to start each day fresh, which is what I always try to do.

"In this example," Mr. Hastie expounds, "Jesus washes the disciples' feet. In essence he pulls off our boots. No wonder Peter protests. I would do the same. But Jesus tells us to serve one another.

"I'm here as your servant, because Jesus came to me as a servant and washed my sins away forever. Mine and yours, so we may do that for others."

Humpf. Mr. Hastie didn't act like a servant yesterday.

"The Scots came to Calcutta to serve home and country. To uplift, educate and civilize the people around us."

Mr. Hastie continues for about an hour. It was foolish for me to think a man like Mr. Hastie would be interested in a local festival—that it would be fun to talk about how the Mohammedans celebrate Mohurrum. I now realize he sees us as beneath him. Less educated. Less cultured. I understand now why Mr. Wilson said he wasn't qualified to lead the College. The Church leaders don't want someone who cares about the students. They appointed an intellectual man who expects others to remove his boots.

Finally, Mr. Hastie finishes his speech and returns to his seat. Mr. Thomson gives the benediction from Corinthians.

"The grace of the Lord Jesus Christ, and the love of God, and the communion of the Holy Ghost be with you all. Amen."

Usually these words give me a sense of peace. Today they feel like dust in my throat because I make my own way without assistance, remove my own boots, and never turn my back on people in need.

Life at the Female Mission is hectic. We have forty-six girls of all ages in the orphanage. Then there are the two high schools, the day schools, and of course the *zenana* students, those women and girls confined to their homes. And I built all of it. Well, not entirely. But I'm the one who expanded the mission's presence.

The following Tuesday, I'm reviewing our orphans' financial support. An individual or Sunday School class sponsors each child, and I send reports on their progress. As I write about the student we call Louisa, Sajiva enters the room and hands me a note from Mr. Steele. Sajiva waits as I open the stiff paper and read Mr. Steele's dramatic handwriting, which covers the page. Sajiva stands with a questioning look, far too discreet to ask about the note's contents.

"It appears Mr. Hastie has cholera."

"Yes, Mem." Sajiva cocks his head.

"Call for the *gharry*."

It's very bad luck for Mr. Hastie to contract the disease so soon after his arrival. He seemed perfectly fine on Sunday, but disease strikes people down quickly here. We don't keep a long mourning period in Calcutta as they do in Scotland.

Sajiva helps me into the *gharry* and hands me my *topi*. The man is a treasure.

When I arrive at Mr. Steele's house, he isn't home. Mr. Steele has a substantial house with four stories and two courtyards. I climb the steps to the porch. The *durwan* meets me at the door, escorts me to Mr. Steele's nicely appointed drawing room, and tells me to wait for the doctor. When I ask after Mr. Hastie, the *durwan* moves his head to the side and departs. One of the *ayahs*, a maidservant, brings a silver tea service into the room.

"How is the *sahib*?" I ask. "Is he very ill?"

The girl looks at me, her dark eyes concerned. "They say his flux smells like fish, Mem. I hope we don't get sick, Mem."

"No one else will get sick." I assure her. "We'll do what the doctor tells us."

"Yes, Mem." The girl closes the door softly as she leaves the room. I don't think she believes me.

I gaze out the window at the grass Mr. Steele's gardener manages to grow during the Cold Weather. It's easy to grow grass this time of year, but once the Hot Weather arrives in March, the grass withers and blows away. I don't bother with it, but Mr. Steele upholds Scottish standards. If Mr. Hastie recovers, I wonder if he'll try to grow grass at the College.

About twenty minutes after I arrive, Mr. Wilson comes into the room looking more disheveled than usual. Mr. Wilson and his wife are my dearest friends, always ready to listen and offer sound advice. Katy Wilson ran the Female Mission before me and left for home shortly after I took up my position. Since then Mr. Wilson, with his thinning fair hair and cheerful smile, has been my strongest support, willing to help me in any task. I take advantage of his good nature to keep my correspondence and accounts current. I don't know which of us is more surprised to see the other. Obviously, Mr. Steele sent notes to both of us.

"Miss Pigot, I didn't expect to see you. Where's Mr. Steele?" Mr. Wilson asks. "And what's Mr. Hastie's condition?"

"The *ayah* says his flux smells like fish, so it must be cholera. Dr. Charles is with him."

"My God." Mr. Wilson begins pacing while he rubs the back of his neck.

Why all this fuss? Mr. Hastie will either recover or die. I don't like to think of him dead. But if he goes home, Mr. Wilson will stay. Naturally, I'll pray for Mr. Hastie's recovery. It's my duty as a Christian. But surely God will send him home to recover fully. Then Mr. Wilson can take over the College.

Dr. Charles comes in with his stethoscope still around his neck, his round face grave and dripping sweat.

"Ah, Miss Pigot. Mr. Wilson. I'm glad you're both here. I won't have to repeat myself. Mr. Hastie is gravely ill."

"Cholera?" I ask.

"All the symptoms are there. The important thing is to keep him cool and get him to take as much fluid as possible. Allow me to introduce Nurse Briggs. She will remain until the matter is settled." Dr. Charles pulls out a handkerchief and wipes his face.

What kind of nurse will she be? She doesn't know the patient. I don't either, but at least I'm part of the community. If anyone should have charge of Mr. Hastie, it should be me. It's my duty, however inconvenient, not some outsider's.

"Dr. Charles, I thought Mr. Steele summoned me to nurse Mr. Hastie."

"Miss Pigot, I want you to relieve Nurse Briggs during the night. A tired nurse is of little use, after all."

You could have given me the day shift and had an ayah sit with Mr. Hastie at night. Perhaps Mr. Steele wants the community to think he spares no expense. Only qualified nurses for Mr. Hastie. Never mind, this way Mr. Hastie will see a familiar face if he wakes during the night.

I pick up my things. "What time shall I take over?"

"Have your evening meal first, Miss Pigot. Good luck," Dr. Charles says.

I wonder if Mr. Steele's paying Mr. Hastie's expenses. Probably. So, of course, he doesn't want to pay for two nurses when he can get my services without cost. That must be the reason I'm on night duty. The important thing is for Mr. Hastie to recover as quickly as possible.

"Mr. Wilson, can I give you a lift?" I ask. "I'm going back to the orphanage."

"Mr. Steele told me to stay until the crisis passes."

"To what purpose?" I ask.

"I suppose so I can make any necessary arrangements."

When I ask if he expects to be called upon, Mr. Wilson shakes his head.

When I arrive at Mr. Steele's house after dinner, I find there isn't much for me to do in the sickroom. I make sure the mosquito netting stays in place. Watch for restlessness. Call Nurse if matters deteriorate. Mainly, I am here so Mr. Hastie won't be alone in a strange place. When I open the door to the sickroom, I see Nurse Briggs standing at the dresser, measuring something.

"Have you eaten?" I ask.

"Not yet. I'm preparing the patient's medicine," Nurse Briggs says.

"Where shall I put my things?"

Nurse Briggs shrugs, so I hang my hat and shawl on a hook near the door. The bed stands in the room's center, each leg in a saucer of water to keep white ants from creeping up. The cane lounge near the end of the bed also has saucer feet. There's a small table by the lounge with a kerosene lamp. A soft light flickers off the walls.

I watch Nurse Briggs. "What are you giving him?"

"Cholera pills," Nurse Briggs says.

"Do you know what's in them? I've always wondered."

Nurse Briggs shrugs again. She's a substantial woman. I step back from her gaze.

"Doesn't make a lot of difference what's in 'em," Nurse Briggs says. "Sometimes they work. Sometimes they don't. Probably opium. Patients always calm down after a dose. I'm giving him a bit extra. He's been restless. You shouldn't have to do anything much. Just call me if you need me. I'm a light sleeper."

Nurse Briggs walks over to the bed.

"Help raise him up a bit," she directs.

I put my arm under Mr. Hastie's back to lift him. Nurse holds his head. Mr. Hastie's bedclothes are damp; his skin clammy.

"Mr. Hastie," Nurse Briggs whispers. "Swallow these pills I'm putting in your mouth and take some juice."

The patient opens his eyes slightly. I smell his sour breath. Nurse closes his lips over the pills.

"Swallow. Swallow again," she orders, holding the cup to his lips, forcing them open. "Drink. You must drink the entire cup."

"Noooo," the patient moans.

"Yes, sir. You must. I won't leave you be 'til you do," Nurse Briggs says.

Nurse Briggs keeps the glass at his lips. She's oddly patient in her annoyance. Glub. Glub. Glub. The cup slowly empties.

"Very good, sir. Lay him back. That's alright, then."

I dampen a cloth and wipe Mr. Hastie's brow. He's a handsome man, more so when he isn't talking. His beard is neatly trimmed and he seems younger than one would expect for such a senior position. But then, he's only just arrived.

"Call if you need me," Nurse Briggs reminds me.

Sitting up with a sick person isn't very interesting. I thumb through the prayer book I brought with me, looking for the section with prayers for the sick. I hear a light tap on the open door.

"Mr. Wilson, how lovely to see you." I smile. "Please, come sit on the lounge."

"How's the patient?" he asks.

"Resting. Nurse gave him cholera pills. I didn't see you when I arrived earlier."

"I dined with Mr. Steele and then took a walk to clear my head. In future, Mr. Steele invites you to join us for dinner at eight o'clock before you take up your duties."

"I'd like that," I say. "I'm trying to find an appropriate prayer. But they all seem to expect the patient to expire. I can't pray for that."

"I'm not sure what you mean," Mr. Wilson says.

"Well, for one thing, this prayer takes up almost five pages. The patient could pass over from boredom."

Mr. Wilson's face has a funny expression before he bursts into a coughing fit. I pound his back.

"Please excuse me," he gasps, and leaves the room.

What was that about? I thought Mr. Wilson was about to say something before he choked. I decide to make up my own prayer for the patient's speedy and comfortable recovery. As the night deepens and the room grows cooler, I wrap up in my silk shawl. But I don't put my feet up for fear I'll fall asleep. As the hours pass, I listen to Nurse Briggs snore from her small room on the veranda and think the night will never end. Early morning fog is just seeping into the room when there's another tap at the door.

"Good morning, Mr. Wilson."

"I came to see how you're getting on. How's the patient?" Mr. Wilson asks.

We stand by the bed and I move the net. "He seems peaceful," I say. "Do you think his fever has broken? I prayed for him. I'm sure he's better."

Nurse Briggs comes in from the veranda wearing a white gown with a wrapper. Her steel grey hair falls at the side of her head in a braid.

"What's this? Why're you here, Mr. Wilson?" Nurse Briggs asks, sharply, her eyebrows drawn together.

"I came to check on the patient," Mr. Wilson explains.

"Let me see." Nurse Briggs marches toward the bed. We step back and watch her feel Mr. Hastie's forehead and smooth the sheets. Then, she abruptly turns to face us.

"Mr. Wilson, there's no need for you to be here at this hour. And you, Miss Pigot, shouldn't have admitted him."

"That's ridiculous," I snap. "He's here at Mr. Steele's request."

"Not at this hour," Nurse Briggs scolds as she begins to leave the room. "Miss Pigot, you may go as soon as I change."

In a few short minutes, Nurse reappears wearing a plain grey dress and an apron that might have been white once. "I'll see you this evening," she grunts, dismissing me as if I work for her. I raise my eyebrows and look for Mr. Wilson, but he's gone. I gather my things and go downstairs.

I arrive home about eight o'clock in the morning, so tired I don't know what to do with myself. Mrs. Tremearne meets me at the door and helps me into bed. Instead of closing my eyes, I count the plaster cracks in the wall. I have a large room with a canopied bed in the center. Sleep eludes me. The room is hot. I inhale dust coming in with the slight breeze. When my yellow song birds start dancing in their cage near my bedroom window, I get up.

"Poor little birds. I'll feed you. Mrs. Tremearne should've thought of that, but it's my fault. I told her never to touch you. There, there, I'm here now." I dip some seed into the cage and sit by the window. Dear Mrs. Tremearne. She'll do anything for me, but she overfed my last birds. I scolded her when they died and told her never to touch my birds again. She hasn't, which leaves me to clean out the cage.

I dress in loose clothing and move to the veranda where I doze all day, trying to avoid one of my frequent headaches. At dusk, I go inside to wash and put on suitable clothing. I look forward to dining at Mr. Steele's. He keeps a fine table. Far better than the poor missionary fare I usually eat. When I arrive at seven o'clock, Mr. Wilson and Mr. Steele are in the drawing room. Unfortunately, one can't just knock on the door and immediately proceed to the dining table. Instead, one has to arrive early for drinks and conversation. More's the pity.

"Miss Pigot, so good of you to join us," Mr. Steele says in his thick Glasgow accent. "We need a pretty face to break the gloom."

Mr. Steele looks surprisingly complacent considering he's host to someone at death's door. Still, he's a great supporter of the Female Mission, often taking my side against Mr. Gillan. The *durwan* comes into the room and begins preparing pegs of brandy and soda water.

Mr. Steele winks at me as if I'm a favorite daughter. "Would you prefer whiskey?"

"I've no preference," I say.

"And you, Mr. Wilson?"

"You're generous to ask, sir. Brandy is fine."

"We'll have whiskey after dinner then," Mr. Steele says. "Miss Pigot, you'll be about your duties, I'm sorry to say."

"The pleasure of joining you for dinner is more than sufficient." I smile and feel my stomach grumble in anticipation.

"It's a simple meal in view of the circumstances. Soup, vegetables, a bit of tinned beef. Shall we go through?" Mr. Steele asks.

Beef? I can't remember the last time I had beef.

The dining room is immaculate with a mahogany table and side boards, though I'm not sure insect saucers are good for mahogany. Mr. Steele's tablecloths are always snowy and soft. I don't know how he makes that happen. Maybe he purchases new ones every week. I'm not being unkind. He can well afford it.

After dinner the *ayah* gives me a lamp to take upstairs. I tap at the door and enter the sick room. Nurse Briggs turns away from Mr. Hastie's bed.

"How's Mr. Hastie?" I ask.

"Dr. Charles is pleased. Not out of danger though. You'll have to keep a close eye on him."

"Have you finished for the day?" I pointedly glance at the watch on my bodice.

"Just have to settle Mr. Hastie. Then I'm off to my little room on the veranda." Nurse Briggs gives me a tight smile and turns to smooth the sheets and pillows. They look softer than the tablecloth downstairs. I settle myself on the lounge and begin leafing through my prayer book.

After about ten minutes, Nurse Briggs and I look up to see Mr. Wilson standing in the doorway.

"Miss Pigot, I thought I'd keep you company for a bit."

"Wonderful." I pat the seat beside me on the lounge.

"Have you found any new prayers for the patient?" he asks.

I nod "I think simple is best. Shall we?"

We sit close together, heads bowed and hands folded. I find the page and start: "*Good God, Lord and Father; Creator and Conserver, we pray unto Thee that it would please Thine infinite goodness to have a blessing upon this Thy poor creature, whom Thou hast bound and tied to the bed by most grievous sickness. Receive him into Thy protection.*"

Nurse Briggs looks toward the lounge with a disapproving expression. *Has she never heard a prayer before?*

"Amen," I pronounce for her benefit.

"I'm leaving now," Nurse Briggs says as she rubs her hands on her apron, removes it and hangs it on a peg. "Call me if anything's amiss." She looks over her shoulder and shakes her head as she leaves the room.

In the silence, Mr. Wilson and I sit for a moment. Then, suddenly, Mr. Wilson jumps up and rushes out of the room.

James Wilson

I stand on the downstairs veranda taking deep breaths. I should never have gone into the sickroom. Under normal circumstances I'm at the Female Mission two or three times a week to assist Miss Pigot. With my

29

wife in Scotland, I look forward to visiting a sympathetic friend. But I have no reason to be in the sickroom and put myself and Miss Pigot in a compromising position.

Miss Pigot is so artless. She has no comprehension of how someone like Nurse Briggs views a married man and an unmarried woman in close proximity, even if Miss Pigot is in her forties. But I know how quickly tongues can wag. I should never have gone to the sickroom, let alone accepted Miss Pigot's invitation to sit beside her. I can hear my wife Katy admonishing me. "Ye be a foolish man," she would say. "Have a care what you're about."

Chapter 2
"Such Proximity Could Be Considered Intimate"

William Hastie

Cholera. Poor people get it all the time, but not people like me, a man who climbs Scottish hills in all weather, a man in excellent health. I am a man of God. The Lord is purifying my soul for the work ahead. I admit that at one point, I thought He might be calling me to my true home, but I quickly realized He was merely testing my resolve.

My bed is in the middle of the room surrounded by ridiculous netting. I'd rather take my chances with the mosquitos than be swathed in white gauze.

"Mr. Hastie, are you awake?" Nurse Briggs with her raspy voice disturbs my thoughts.

I don't like Nurse Briggs. She's a big woman with a dirty cap and a rough manner. But the night nurse, Miss Pigot, well, she's an angel. Her light touch and gentle voice have guided me through my fever these past few days.

"Dr. Charles is here," Nurse Briggs says.

Why? All he does is poke, prod, and check my breathing.

He comes to the bed and talks to the nurse. "How is the patient?" he asks Nurse Briggs.

Well I'm sick, obviously. Nurse Briggs reports that I'm restless. *Of course, I'm restless. I want to get out of this bed.* I turn to watch the doctor and become instantly dizzy. Dr. Charles takes no notice and continues to prod and cluck.

"You need more liquids," he says sternly.

"Dr. Charles," Nurse Briggs says in her sweetest tone. "I'm sorry to say that I won't be able to continue."

"What's the problem, Nurse Briggs?" the doctor asks as he takes my pulse.

"It's the night nurse."

My angel?

"What about her?"

"The woman is rude. And her behavior inappropriate. I'm a decent woman. I can't remain," Nurse Briggs says.

Inappropriate? How?

Dr. Charles turns away from me to face the nurse. "Would you care to explain?"

"I don't like to speak ill of people," she continues.

"And I don't listen to gossip. Miss Pigot is a respected member of the Scottish community. What possible complaint could you have with her?"

"Doctor, Mr. Hastie. It's her and that Mr. Wilson." Nurse Briggs flushes. "The two of 'em sit on the lounge with their heads together. They think I don't notice, but how could I not? They behave as if they're married. They speak loudly, which isn't allowed in a sickroom. And she touches him. And they laugh. I'm going."

I have to say something, or the woman will leave before I'm on my feet.

"Please," I croak. "Nurse, don't go."

"I'm sorry, Mr. Hastie. I know you're ill. But I must."

"Please," I say. "I can't think about this. Please don't say anything more." The room spins around with the dust motes.

"Nurse, you're upsetting the patient with your gossip. Surely you can stay a few more days. I won't give a reference if you walk out."

"Very well. But I tell you, Mr. Hastie, as soon as you put your feet on the floor, I'm gone. I won't countenance such behavior."

I'm not sure what happens next except that at some point Nurse Briggs and Dr. Charles leave the room together, and then Miss Pigot arrives to be my night nurse. I hear her praying over me. She has such a light voice. That she would take the trouble and interest to intercede for me with the Almighty—it touches my heart.

Nurse Briggs leaves a day or so later still mumbling about Miss Pigot's rude behavior. I can scarcely credit it. I admire Miss Pigot for her care and nursing skills. When I recover, I send her a book of Walter Scott's poetry and inscribe it with a quotation that aptly describes her service.

> "O woman! In our hours of ease,
> Uncertain, coy, and hard to please,
> And variable as the shade
> By the light quivering aspen made
> When pain and anguish wring the brow
> A ministering angel thou."

Miss Pigot sets me right soon enough. She returns the book with a callous letter saying she nursed me out of duty to the church. She writes it would be unpleasant for her to retain any acknowledgement of her service and some other nonsense that it's inappropriate for her to accept a personal gift from a colleague. Who is she to reject a simple thank you gift?

Fully recovered, I resume my introduction to Calcutta life at the end of the week. Mr. Steele offers me the use of his open carriage so I can attend my first meeting of the Corresponding Board. No doubt they'll defer to my judgment. Mr. Wilson rides with me.

"It seems the sun never stops shining in Calcutta," I remark. "Day after day after day."

"You'll miss it when the rains come," Mr. Wilson says with a knowing smile.

Peddlers trot alongside our carriage in various states of dress. They look like children and are painfully thin. They have all sorts of trinkets, shell necklaces, small idols. I don't like being surrounded.

"Away with you!" I shout.

The peddlers keep offering ribbons, shells. One has birds in a cage. A few even have small snakes in baskets.

"Mr. Wilson, I implore you. Get rid of them."

Mr. Wilson waves his arms and shouts something incomprehensible.

"What did you babble to them?"

Mr. Wilson nods his head to the side.

"Tell me what you said."

"I said if they didn't stop chasing us, I'd call a policeman." Mr. Wilson smiles. "Actually, I told them if they went to the College, we'd give them food. I neglected to say there'd be a Bible lesson with the meal."

"So, you bribed them?" I question. Mr. Wilson nods again.

"Mr. Wilson, please stop moving your head about. It's most disconcerting."

"Sorry. I don't realize I'm doing it. How are you feeling, by the way?" Mr. Wilson asks.

"Glad we'll finally be able to evict Mr. Robson," I say. "Why did you let him stay at the College after he left the faculty? His conversion to the

Free Church and departure after the trouble and expense of sending him to Calcutta is an insult."

Mr. Wilson clears his throat. "As Acting Principal, I didn't have authority to evict him. Miss Pigot and I suggested he find other accommodation, but he declined."

"What does Miss Pigot have to do with the College?"

"Nothing. But she's friendly with Mr. Robson. Ah, there's St. Andrew's," Mr. Wilson says with a note of relief in his voice.

I let him deflect the conversation since there isn't time to pursue it. St. Andrew's Kirk is an attractive church. To look at it, you might think you were at home in Scotland, except for the dirt and squalor surrounding the grounds. Most buildings seem dim, but St. Andrew's has a number of windows letting in sunlight. I take off my *topi* as Mr. Wilson leads the way to the meeting room. Mr. Gillan stands at the door holding his watch.

I know most of the faces around the table, but Mr. Wilson gives me a brief introduction.

"Dr. Charles is our Chairman," he says as my doctor stands to extend his hand.

"It's good to see you up and around. I was a bit worried about you," Dr. Charles smiles as he offers his hand, "but you came through with flying colors."

I take the man's moist hand. "Apparently the Almighty has other plans for me," I say.

"I think you met almost everyone else," Mr. Wilson says looks around. "Ah, a few more. This is Mr. Broughton from the high school." We nod to each other. "Mr. Edwards you know from the College; Mr. Gillan, our host; Mr. Wetherill, the Board secretary; and of course, Mr. Steele. These gentlemen oversee Scottish College and are here to support your work."

I shake hands with everyone, assure them of my gratitude for their interest and support.

"How do you find the College accommodations, Mr. Hastie?" Mr. Steele asks.

"Adequate. Not so comfortable as your house, of course.

"Of course," Mr. Steele says complacently.

"We're just waiting for..." Mr. Gillan begins to speak but is interrupted as Miss Pigot rushes into the room, her face flushed. "I'm sorry to be late. I was writing reports and lost track of time."

"Miss Pigot, what brings you here?" I ask. "Surely you're not involved with Scottish College?"

"Mr. Hastie, it's good to see you looking so well. I represent the Female Mission," she says removing her *topi*.

"Do sit down, Miss Pigot," Mr. Gillan says. "Shall we convene? We're here to discuss Mr. Robson's resignation. When did Mr. Robson arrive?"

"He's been here about a year. December 1877 was the date of his arrival, and..." Mr. Wilson shuffles some paper, "he submitted his resignation last month."

"I thought the normal assignment was two years," I say. "He can't be allowed to resign early."

Dr. Charles steeples his hands. "We've never had this situation before. But since he joined the Free Church, it's just as well for him to sever all ties with the Church of Scotland. As I understand the procedure, if someone resigns early, it's customary to give six months' notice and reimburse the Mission for expenses.

"Our present dilemma is that Mr. Robson resigned with immediate effect, continued to live at the College, and..."

Mr. Steele interrupts. "And failed to repay the Mission for funds expended on his behalf. As long as he stays at the College, we continue to pay his expenses. He must leave the property immediately, and we should pursue all means to collect the funds we advanced him."

"But, Mr. Steele," Miss Pigot breaks in, "there's plenty of room at the College. How can you begrudge a fellow Christian our hospitality?"

Is Miss Pigot really so ignorant? Charity is for those who deserve it, not self-serving men who desert their post leaving others to pick up their work.

Mr. Steele glares at Miss Pigot in a way that makes the room seem more cramped than it already is. "That's not the point, Miss Pigot," he growls. "It's a matter of honor, and Mr. Robson's lack of it."

"But surely we can extend Christian charity to him?" she continues.

"No, Miss Pigot. He's doesn't deserve charity. He quit without notice and took a position at Hugli College," Mr. Steele responds. "We're under no obligation to support his defection."

"Only because the Board was so harsh when he started attending the Free Church," Miss Pigot reminds the group.

What's wrong with the woman? Can't she see that Mr. Steele is adamant in his position?

Mr. Steele looks apoplectic. "Miss Pigot, Mr. Robson accepted a position at a Church of Scotland institution. We cannot countenance his defection."

"Mr. Steele. Miss Pigot. We're losing sight of our purpose," Dr. Charles interjects sternly. "This isn't about the division between the Church of Scotland and the Free Church, or whether Mr. Robson deserves any level of charity." He looks around the table, daring anyone to interrupt him.

"The issue is Mr. Robson's decision to leave Scottish College without notice and our lack of instruction from the Foreign Mission Committee regarding his housing. I have a letter from Mr. Robson. He proposes to assist with teaching at the College for the next two months in lieu of giving proper notice. What do you think of his proposal?"

"Does he expect us to pay him?" Mr. Steele demands.

I reach for the letter. "He doesn't mention payment," I reply calmly.

"He probably expects to stay at the College," Mr. Steele speaks in a normal tone, though his complexion retains a reddish hue from his earlier outburst.

"Most likely," Mr. Wilson concurs.

"But why shouldn't he stay at the College, if he's teaching there?"

I wince inwardly. Mr. Steele looks like he's going to explode.

"Miss Pigot," Mr. Steele says, his temper clearly rising to its previous height, "do you allow people to stay at the Female Mission who aren't employed by the Mission?"

"Mr. Steele, we're enjoined by Christian charity to assist those who fall on misfortune. I find that everyone who comes to me can contribute something." Miss Pigot gives us all a winning smile.

"So, you employ them?" I ask, somewhat surprised by this practice.

"Yes, Mr. Hastie. I've just added two *zenana* teachers, for example."

Miss Pigot prattles on about our duty to the unfortunate, effectively silencing Mr. Steele until he slaps his hand on the table.

"Miss Pigot," he thunders, "you have no standing with the Corresponding Board and aren't entitled to offer any opinion on any subject. I don't know why we allow you to attend the meetings. Why is that, Dr. Charles?"

Miss Pigot's draw drops in surprise. Before Dr. Charles can answer, Mr. Wilson breaks into the discussion.

"Mr. Steele. Miss Pigot. Please, can we return to the issue of whether we choose to accept Mr. Robson's offer to teach at the College for two months? As it happens, we've covered his classes on English Literature and have no need for his services."

"That being the case," I chime in, "I suggest we proceed to the issue of evicting Mr. Robson from the College."

For a few moments, no one speaks. Miss Pigot appears shocked. Dr. Charles polishes his glasses. The others gaze at various points of the cracked wall plaster as if measuring it for repairs.

"This situation with Mr. Robson is unprecedented," Mr. Steele comments in a civil tone. "Have we heard from the Foreign Mission Committee at home? If not, I'm inclined to proceed with the eviction."

"They haven't acted," Dr. Charles responds. "I thought we'd at least have a telegram by now."

"They don't act as quickly as one might hope," I say. "I suggest we forward Dr. Robson's letter and our response to the Committee, and also inquire if they accept his resignation. If so, I'll evict him immediately. Mr. Gillan, please send our request at the soonest possible moment." I wait until Mr. Gillan's pen stops scratching before I continue. "In the meantime, I'll speak to Mr. Robson and inform him I don't allow people without a connection to the College to live there. Will that be satisfactory to everyone?"

Miss Pigot raises her hand to speak but Dr. Charles ignores her and closes the meeting. Miss Pigot's face is expressionless as she looks at each one of us in turn. She stands, puts on her *topi*, and wishes us a good day. Miss Pigot stands at the door a minute, then closes it softly. I've never seen a woman behave this way.

On my way back to Scottish College I consider how best to remove Miss Pigot from meetings of the Corresponding Board. I intend to exert my authority as head of the Church of Scotland mission in Calcutta.

The drive to Scottish College takes about half an hour. The College sits on the outskirts of Calcutta in the northern sector. I share my quarters with Mr. and Mrs. Edwards. He's on the faculty, and his wife is some sort of housekeeper. The house is for my sole use, but I can't throw them out until we have a proper housing option for them.

The school itself is in very good repair with housing for teaching staff and students. The curriculum is appropriate, and I think with some encouragement the students are ripe for conversion to Christianity. I'm pleased with my choice to take this position. Europeans and Hindus both respect the College and preparatory school, and my experience here will enhance my application for a university position in Scotland.

Mr. Wilson arranges my induction to the College, and a significant number of Europeans and educated Indians attend, as do reporters from the local newspapers. Most gratifying. I speak about my background and explain I didn't seek this position. Rather, members of our church's General Assembly urged me to take it. My remarks go over well, of course. It's a lovely occasion and a good introduction to Calcutta society. Unlike Mr. Wilson, I'm prepared to lead the school into new directions, one of which will be to stop observing local holidays.

This month the College will close during the last week in January for a Hindu festival. Such rubbish. But Mr. Wilson and Mr. Edwards argue there's no point holding classes when most students won't attend. I hope to remain on good terms with Mr. Wilson until he goes on furlough, so I agree to closing the College for the day. But once Mr. Wilson is gone, I shall end the practice. If students enroll in a Scottish school, they must adhere to Scottish standards.

On the festival day in question, Mr. Wilson and his cousin fund an outing at Barrackpore Park for the orphans and teachers at the Female

Mission. A useless extravagance if you ask me, but I agree to attend. The picnic is completely lacking in decorum and illustrates the extent of reforms I must make as soon as possible.

Mary Pigot

Barrackpore Park, about twenty miles north of Calcutta, is a wonderful spot for an outing. It has lawns and towering trees. English flowers and proper pathways. And we take the train, which is always such an adventure. I love to watch the scenery pass and look out at the people along the way as the train wobbles to its destination. The children and teachers are beside themselves with excitement, and who can blame them? The only worm in the gourd, as Job might say, is Mr. Hastie's presence. I don't think he approves of any type of enjoyment.

"Mr. Wilson," I say as we approach the station, "I can never thank you enough for this marvelous gift. A picnic. It will be heaven."

Mr. Wilson clears his throat. "Perhaps not that marvelous. My cousin Mr. Douglas and I just want you and your charges to enjoy yourselves. We'll complete the arrangements while you get everyone off the train."

Mr. Wilson signals his cousin, a taller version of himself. Both men adjust their *topis* and head for the exit.

"Mrs. Tremearne, Miss Leslie. Please line the children up on the platform. The senior girls will help you," I say.

I wave my hand and wait while teachers and matrons usher the children out of the compartment. I nod for the remaining teachers to precede me. I like to take my time, but just as I reach the exit door, Mr. Hastie leaves his seat to open it. I can't decline his manners, so I pass before him without comment. He makes himself my walking partner. What shall we talk about? I say the first thing that pops into my mind.

"I love this station." I gesture towards plants at the station entrance and the small lawn. "Barrackpore is so orderly compared to Calcutta. Probably because there are troops deployed here. And, of course, the Viceroy and his associates often come out on the weekends."

"Is that why we came midweek?" Mr. Hastie asks.

"I believe that's one of the reasons. That, and the school holiday. Mr. Wilson, we're just coming," I call. "Hurry up, Mr. Hastie. The children are in the wagons."

"Miss Pigot," Mr. Wilson directs, "you and Mr. Hastie take this carriage. My cousin and I will go in the wagon with the supplies. Mr. and Mrs. Thomson went ahead. We'll meet at the banyan tree in the park."

"How will we know where the tree is?" Mr. Hastie asks.

I laugh. "Don't worry. It's enormous." I gesture with open arms. "The Viceroy gives dinner parties under the branches. Just look around, Mr. Hastie. It's a glorious day."

It takes almost an hour for our cavalcade to reach its destination. In tandem with the other women, I follow the children across the grass as Mr. Wilson and his cousin direct servants to set up the table for *tiffin*. The senior girls carry mats to lay in the shade.

"Make a thick surface so the roots don't poke through," I say. "Once you've done that, go look after the younger children."

"Girls, wait." Mr. Douglas trots up with an ungainly bundle. "I brought kites for you. Share them out."

"That's uncommonly generous of you, Mr. Douglas," I smile. "Just being here is enough."

"Our girls know other children fly kites to celebrate the festival, and the breeze is perfect. The orphans deserve a bit of fun as well," Mr. Douglas replies.

I tilt my head so I can see his face. "Thank you again," I say. "Where're you setting up for *tiffin*?"

"Just on the other side. I think everyone's here now," Mr. Douglas says.

"Indeed, we are," Mrs. Edwards comments. "I have an idea. Instead of standing on these mats, we should sit."

Mrs. Tremearne plops herself on the ground under the tree and sits with her legs straight out.

"Oomph. We should've brought more pillows," she laughs. "We need something to lean against."

"I know," a feminine voice calls out. "We can lean against each other's backs. That way we'll support each other."

"Let's sit in a circle and tell stories," Mrs. Tremearne says. "Miss Pigot, you know lots of stories. Tell us about today's festival."

I've never sat back-to-back before. It seems so personal, especially since Mr. Wilson is closest to me. Such proximity could be considered intimate. I see Mr. and Mrs. Thomson support each other. Of course, they're married. Miss Barnham leans against Mrs. Tremearne. Mrs. Edwards and Mr. Douglas. I'm being silly. This is a party after all, and we've known each other for years. Mr. Wilson has a good back, a trustworthy back. Not that I know much about backs.

"Miss Pigot, tell the story," Mrs. Tremearne insists.

"It's not an important festival," I say. "The Hindus call it *Vasant Panchami* for their Goddess Sarasvati. The festival welcomes spring."

"You know quite a bit about Hindu religion," Mr. Thomson comments.

"Not really. I forget how I heard about this one," I say. "Oh, look. Mr. Hastie's back from his walk. Mr. Hastie, do join Mr. Wilson and I."

I pat the mat beside me.

"This is quite the most unusual seating arrangement." Mr. Hastie purses his lips.

"Just for the moment, until *tiffin* is ready," Mr. Wilson says.

Mr. Hastie lowers himself onto the ground. He looks uncomfortable, so I encourage him to rest against my shoulder. I'm surprised he accepts my invitation. I daren't move. He might misinterpret it.

"Miss Pigot, do you know any stories about the goddess?" Mrs. Tremearne asks.

"Here's one. A foolish man married a beautiful princess. One day she realized how silly her husband was and threw him out of the house. The man didn't know what to do and was going to kill himself. Sarasvati told him to bathe in the river. He did, and when he came out, he was wise."

"Did he get his wife back?" Mrs. Tremearne asks.

"I don't know," I smile. "Maybe. What do you think Mr. Wilson?"

"I think it's time for *tiffin*." Mr. Wilson stands up and gives me his hand. "May I escort you?"

With Mr. Wilson on one side and his cousin on the other, I lead the way across the grassy ground to the *tiffin* tables. The children sit on benches at a separate table.

Mr. Hastie walks with Mr. and Mrs. Thomson.

"Mr. Wilson, you and Mr. Douglas have outdone yourselves," I clap my hands. "And look at all the cakes and biscuits."

"And fruit, Miss Pigot," Mr. Douglas says. "You and Mr. Wilson sit here. And you also, Mr. Hastie. I'll find a place on the other side of the table."

I swing my legs over the bench, making room for Mr. Hastie on my left and Mr. Wilson on my right. The pineapple is sliced and ready to eat. I spy pomegranates, my favorite fruit.

"We also have lentil dhal and rice," Mr. Douglas continues, "though that's more for the children, some lovely bread, cold potatoes, and a light curry. Shall we start passing dishes?"

Mr. Wilson scoops out curry to go on his potatoes. "Mr. Hastie? Try some."

Mr. Hastie takes bread and potatoes but waves away the curry. He slaps at the mosquitos snacking on his wrists.

Eat your fill, I think, because Mr. Hastie's demeanor is so stiff. Then I admonish myself for being uncharitable.

A few days later, I stretch out on my bed, musing on the gardens at Barrackpore. My room is still shadowed, so I've a few more minutes before bed tea. Outside, crows begin calling. I hear rustling on the floor. How many teachers came in last night? Too many. For some reason they feel safer in my room. How can I turn them away?

Light seeps through the shutters. Mrs. Tremearne comes in, stepping lightly around the still sleeping bodies. Mrs. Tremearne is a widow. She came to me as a *zenana* teacher, and she's very good at it, very popular with the ladies. But within a few months she took on a role as my personal attendant, and I let her do it because it makes me feel as if someone cares about me.

"Good morning, Miss Pigot," she says. "You're supposed to go to Kidderpore today. I woke Miss Bartlett. She'll meet you downstairs."

"There's something else I'm supposed to do," I say.

"Yes, Mem. You have Mr. Steele's party this evening."

"How can I be out all day and prepare for one of Mr. Steele's dinners?" I ask. "It's too much."

"Yes, Mem," Mrs. Tremearne quickly claps her hands. "Get up, everyone. Mem has to dress. Up! Out!"

Shapes unroll. Women with disheveled hair gather their bundles and scurry out.

"You shouldn't allow everyone in your bedroom, Mem," Mrs. Tremearne advises. "It sets a bad example."

"For whom?" I ask.

"It's not the English way, Mem. You must be like them," Mrs. Tremearne says.

"Like the Scots, you mean." I wrinkle my nose. "They're worse than the English, if that's possible. So long as my companions are female, it's no one's business who sleeps in the room."

"Yes, Mem. I give you looser dress so you don't need corset. It's too hot," Mrs. Tremearne says.

I walk into the bathroom just as the sweeper closes the outer door. Mrs. Tremearne pours cool morning water around my neck and shoulders while I hold up my hair.

"Do my hair first," I say. "And make it secure. I won't have time to do it again this evening."

The driver secures the prize boxes. "You did them in order?" I ask.

"Yes, Mem," he says. "Two for the ladies and top one for school."

Miss Bartlett appears, her brown hair already coming out of its bun. She starts to climb into the carriage.

"Miss Bartlett, where's your *topi*?" I ask.

"I thought since we have umbrellas, I could wear a normal hat," Miss Bartlett says. She bites her lip.

"Miss Bartlett, in the Female Mission all teachers wear the *topi* outside," I say. "Go get it and be quick. I'd like to arrive before the heat rises."

"Yes, Miss Pigot," Miss Bartlett goes back inside.

She returns several minutes later. I'm annoyed. I don't have time for stupidity.

"Do you have everything now?" I ask. "You can be comfortable inside the carriage, but never be in the sun without your *topi*. I won't remind you again. Understood? Driver, go down the Strand."

The streets are clear except for servants heading for the bazars. I love this time of day. Quiet. Interesting. The Maidan appears, and the carriage turns onto the Strand. I gaze at the Hugli River, its waters changing color as the sun rises. Shipping crowds close to shore. The Kidderpore Church spire appears in the distance. Miss Bartlett's head lolls backwards.

"Miss Bartlett, are you asleep?" I ask.

"No, um, perhaps a little," Miss Bartlett mumbles.

"Well, wake up. We'll be at the school in a minute. You'll need strong tea to get you through the day."

Mrs. Henderson is my person at Kidderpore. She came with her husband to convert Indians and remained after his death to educate them. She shares my view to "educate first, convert later—if ever."

"Miss Pigot. Miss Bartlett. Welcome to Kidderpore. I arranged a light breakfast for you. Not all the students are here yet."

Mrs. Henderson leads us onto the veranda, her posture ramrod straight. It gives her a formidable look she counters with a ready smile that shows her discolored teeth. The veranda itself is narrow with mats on a wood planked floor. I squint as the sun slants onto the surface.

"Will you lead morning prayers?" Mrs. Henderson asks.

"Yes, and then to the prize distribution," I say. "We brought dolls. It's a pity we can't make more of an event of it this time, but I'm sure the students will be pleased. We also have dolls for the *zenana* girls."

Mrs. Henderson gives me a questioning look. "I thought the dolls were our inducement for girls to leave the *zenana*."

"They are, but it's not as if the children have a choice. And if they find out other girls get prizes for learning the same thing, they'll have no reason to learn."

"Girls," Mrs. Henderson calls in Bengali, "look who's here today. Miss Pigot will teach you herself, and she has a special surprise for those who passed their exams."

Forty-six pairs of eyes focus on me. I sit on a mat on the dais so everyone can see me. The children spread out in a semicircle with the sun on their backs. The younger ones sit closest to me.

"Today we'll talk about the farmer and the seed," I say. "Have any of you heard that one?"

"No, Mem. Well, maybe," a child says. The little girl flashes a smile showing dazzling white teeth against her dark skin.

I beckon her forward. "Then you must sit by me and correct me if I'm wrong. What's your name?"

"Lalita," she says softly.

"Very well, Lalita. Begin the story and speak loudly so everyone can hear."

Lalita puts he hand over her mouth as she giggles. "Oh, Mem. I can never do that."

"I'm sure you can. Try."

Lalita pulls a face and stands up. Mrs. Henderson nods encouragingly. The *pundit* who teaches Bengali and Sanskrit puts his hands together. Lalita takes a deep breath to compose herself and begins.

"There was a farmer," she says in a light singsong voice, "and his field was all mixed up. It had rocks and thorns. But some of it was good for growing. When he spread the seeds, only the ones on good earth grew. Mem, a farmer knows the land. Why would he waste his seeds?"

"It is a good question, Lalita. I don't know the answer."

There's a small gasp from the students.

"This is what I know," I say. "The story isn't about farming. It's about Jesus and how his teaching is for everyone. But only those who listen with their hearts understand. They can't be thinking about something else. It's a good story don't you think?"

As we drive away from the compound to move on to our first *zenana*, I ask Miss Bartlett about her Bengali lessons. The *pundit* I hire to teach the language told me he seldom sees Miss Bartlett.

I gaze directly into her pinched face. "Miss Bartlett, why do you think you have so much trouble learning Bengali? You grew up here. It should be easy for you to speak the local language."

We sit in silence as the *gharry* sways towards our destination.

"Miss Bartlett?"

"It's too confusing. And the girls I teach know English."

"Do you think students should speak your language, but you don't need to know theirs?"

"That's not what I meant. I just meant it's difficult for me. I always spoke English at home and school. My father didn't allow us to speak Bengali or mingle with local people."

"That's no excuse," I say. "I hired you to work as a *zenana* teacher. If you can't learn proper Bengali, you're of no use to me, and I'll have to let you go."

"The Bible women can translate for me," Miss Bartlett says, smugly.

I want to box her ears. "Bible women assist, but they can't speak for you. You'll be entering these ladies' homes and it will be the height of rudeness if you're unable to show progress in their language. How can you share God's word if you can't ask for a drink of water? Do you even know the word for water?"

"*Pāni?*" Miss Bartlett gives me a hesitant look.

"Very good. See, you understand more than you think," I nod. "Our first stop is the house of Babu Biswas. He's a civil servant with a wife, three daughters, and a sister. His mother runs the household. Miss Graham, a Scotswoman who speaks fluent Bengali, will meet us there." I give Miss Bartlett a pointed look. "Miss Graham has been working with the family. We want to encourage them to send their girls to school. Come, you'll see how important it is to speak Bengali."

The carriage stops in front of a narrow lane.

"We walk the rest of the way," I say. "Wear your *topi.*"

I engage a bearer to follow with the box and lead the way through a maze of narrow lanes. Men stand at courtyard entrances and watch the us pick our way through manure and other assorted rubbish. Babu Biswas has a modest house—only one courtyard and two stories. The courtyard is freshly swept. The *durwan* gestures for us to go around to the back. The exterior stairs are steep.

"Leave the box here, please," I say to the bearer.

I knock soundly on the door to the *zenana.* A maidservant lets us into the room. I see Miss Graham sitting near the high window that provides natural light. The room itself is gloomy. The light catches Miss Graham's fair hair. A small child sits next to her on the floor. The child's legs are crossed and she holds an embroidery circle.

"See how well you do, Giri. Let's show our visitors. Hello, Miss Pigot," Miss Graham says.

Giri holds her embroidery out to me so I can exclaim about her progress. The fabric looks a bit worse for wear.

"They've sent for chairs and refreshments. How was your journey?"

I nod my head. "Miss Graham, this is Miss Bartlett. She has little Bengali, so you'll have to translate." Miss Bartlett looks slightly embarrassed.

"That's alright." Miss Graham holds out her hand to my protégé. "Oh, here are the chairs. We must arrange them."

"What do they normally sit upon?" Miss Bartlett asks, glancing toward the women.

"Floor mats and cushions, Miss Bartlett," Miss Graham says. "The chairs are from the men's side of the house, a sign of honor. You take the central one so everyone can see you. Ladies, this is Miss Bartlett, a special friend."

"*Nômoshkar,*" the women say, before they start patting Miss Bartlett's clothing. I hear them ask about her home, family, and if she brought them any bangles.

A look of panic crosses Miss Bartlett's face.

"Don't be alarmed," Miss Graham says. "They love meeting new people and want to know everything about you. Why you aren't married, why your skin is pale, why your family lets you wander around. Shall I translate?"

Miss Graham returns to the school with us for *tiffin*. I enjoy the curried rice, but notice Miss Bartlett moves the food around on her plate without eating.

"Miss Bartlett, is there a problem with the food?" Mrs. Henderson asks.

"No. It's just so hot today," Miss Bartlett replies.

"It's only February. Wait until the Hot Weather arrives in March," Mrs. Henderson smiles.

"That's what everyone says." Miss Bartlett frowns. "I'm not someone fresh from Scotland. I've lived here all my life. I know about the Hot Weather. It's hot in the Cold Weather when you're forced to be outside or in dark, closed-in spaces. At home we kept the doors and windows open to the breeze, and we had trees near the veranda."

Miss Graham shakes her head and goes to wash her hands. I move to a chair on the veranda so I can listen to Miss Bartlett complain without having to answer her. She isn't suited to the work. If she doesn't change her attitude, I'll have to let her go. I sigh. Mrs. Henderson probes to find the cause of Miss Bartlett's distress.

"If you're feeling ill, I'm sure Miss Pigot would leave you here while she visits another *zenana*. You could help me record marks."

"That won't do." Miss Bartlett shakes her head. "Miss Pigot wants me to be a *zenana* teacher. If I don't go, I could lose my job."

Mrs. Henderson gives her a sympathetic look. "Perhaps you could find another way to earn your living."

Miss Bartlett shakes her head and brushes crumbs off her dark skirt. Miss Graham comes back from the convenience and picks up her *topi*. I stand up.

"Miss Bartlett. Miss Graham. Are you ready?" I ask. "We have one more house. Mrs. Henderson, what can you tell us about the Dutta family?"

"Babu Dutta wants his daughters to learn English and needlework. He sends his younger girls to our school. I think if his wife is pleased with her *zenana* lessons, the girls may be allowed to stay," Mrs. Henderson says.

We mount the *gharry* and drive back into the village. The Dutta house is larger than our first house, its gate facing a wider street. No one seems at home. Green shutters close against the sun.

"Miss Graham, I don't see anyone," I say. "We can't spend the day standing here."

As we reach the courtyard veranda, the *durwan* runs out.

"Ladies, please excuse, we didn't expect you so early," he says panting slightly. "Everyone resting. But Mata said, bring you to her."

The *durwan* leads us through the public areas to the back of the house and then up a curved staircase. There's a lattice screen on the landing. The ladies probably like to watch from here. Especially, the children.

The *durwan* knocks at the door, then stands respectfully to the side. It opens slightly. A brown eye looks me up and down.

"If eyes are the mirror of the mind, then your eyes tell me you are both beautiful and clever," I say in Bengali. "Admit us, and you can look all you wish."

A chorus of giggles breaks out behind the door.

I ask the girl to bring Mata.

"She doesn't like to be disturbed when she's resting," the girl replies.

"If you don't let us in, you won't receive the dolls we brought," I say.

The door opens a little wider. Miss Graham holds up a porcelain doll with flaxen curls.

"She's beautiful." A small hand reaches out.

"No. You must let us in first. Please get Mata."

A pair of bare feet trots over mats. Soon after, a more pronounced step makes its way to the door. A woman of medium height with disheveled hair stands on the threshold.

She holds out her hand. "Give me the doll."

I put my hands together. "Mata, your husband invited us to see you. He wants you and your daughters to learn English and needlework. My name is Miss Pigot. Tell me your name."

The woman turns back inside but leaves the door open. We follow her to the *tuktaposh,* a broad bench with cushions, pillows and bright fabrics.

"Shall I comb your hair?" I ask.

The woman nods. I loosen her thick braid and begin combing through it.

"So, what's your name?"

"Padmini."

"Lovely. Padmini, do you want me to put decorations in your hair?"

The woman smiles while I weave a net through her hair.

Getting *zenana* women to trust you is time consuming. I keep my entire focus on Padmini, pointing out the games Miss Graham and Miss Bartlett play with her children. Exclaiming over the doll's perfection.

"Let Miss Graham teach you and your daughters," I say. "You'll earn more dolls and other good things. And we'll tell you stories about Jesus."

I hold a mirror so Padmini can see her hair.

"Yes, come back tomorrow," she says.

"Miss Graham will come back tomorrow. I'll visit again soon."

I'm surprised how low the sun is when we climb back into our carriage.

"Miss Graham, we'll take you back, but then we must head directly home. I have a dinner engagement." I turn to Miss Graham. "Do you have everything you need to visit the Duttas tomorrow?"

"Yes, and I'll take a senior student with me to work with the children."

"See if you can persuade Padmini to send the girls to school," I say. "That may mean you'll have to visit frequently at first. See if she has other relatives who might like to join her. That sort of thing. You're doing very good work here."

Slipping into the west, the sun glints off the Hugli River. I feel my tensions slipping too. Miss Bartlett sleeps, her head bouncing from side to side. The young woman is useless. Miss Graham takes everything in stride. I could use a dozen like her.

As the carriage moves further north, traffic increases. Just my luck: everyone's starting their evening drive early. And, of course, they all have to stop and speak to one another.

I let the breeze take my mind off things. It's not like I can move traffic.

An hour later, we still aren't home. I know I'll be late. Why did the party have to be today? I couldn't postpone the school visit again. I was supposed to go when I was nursing Mr. Hastie.

The road winds around Eden Gardens as it leaves the Maidan.

I tap the driver with the end of my umbrella. "Why are you slowing down?"

"Traffic building, Mem." His melodic voice slides back to me. "Have to take our turn."

"Well, go as fast as you can then."

The driver bobs his head.

When we finally enter 125 Bow Bazaar, I hardly wait for the horse to stop.

"You wait right here," I say to the driver. "Don't move. I'll be back directly."

"Yes, Mem." He dismounts and leads the horse under the tamarind tree

Upstairs I shoo everyone out of my room.

"Mrs. Tremearne, where are my evening clothes? I told you to lay them on the bed."

"I'll get them while you wash, Mem."

Wash. I almost forgot. I kick off my shoes, peel off my sweaty stockings and begin unbuttoning my bodice. How can it be this warm in the Cold Weather? Stripped of my chemise, I go into the washroom with its cup, tub, and pitcher of water. Warm. I wish just once it would be cold. I splash off as much sweat as I can, then walk back to the bedroom to let what breeze there is dry me off. Mrs. Tremearne holds out my best chemise. Delicate silk. Such an extravagance. I reach for the corset.

"Don't tie it too tight," I say. "Just enough for the dress."

"Yes, Mem."

The brown silk fits very well. A low neckline with cap sleeves.

I pull a few tendrils of hair around my face. "Do I look presentable?"

Mrs. Tremearne shrugs and hands me fresh stockings.

"I'm so *late*. It's half past seven already." I grab my evening shoes and run out the door.

As the carriage turns onto Mr. Steele's street, the evening air holds a hint of jasmine. "The school and two *zenanas*. Too much for one day," I muse.

"Mem. Mem. We're here," the driver says with a big smile.

"I'll drive myself home," I say. "Go to your family."

My driver smiles, bows, and trots off into the darkness. Mr. Steele's groom leads the horse towards the stables. I pinch my cheeks and allow Mr. Steele's *durwan* to escort me inside.

"Miss Pigot," Mr. Steele calls, "we're just in the drawing room. We were beginning to worry about you."

I walk through the double doors. Mr. Steele is standing in evening clothes with a peg in his hand. Mr. Wilson and Mr. Hastie also have on evening attire. I smooth my skirt and hold out my hand to Mr. Steele.

"I hope I'm not too late. I've been at Kidderpore all day. I'm so sorry." I smile so my dimples show.

"The party couldn't begin before your arrival," Mr. Steele says, his eyes twinkling. *Thank goodness he's forgiven me for our disagreement over Mr. Robson.*

"Will you have a peg with us before dinner?" he asks. "I hope you don't mind my substitution of whiskey instead of brandy. I'm an old Scotsman and favor the home brew."

"I'm honored." I glance at the hunting prints on the whitewashed walls, putting off my greeting to Mr. Hastie. I compose my face.

"Mr. Hastie. Mr. Wilson. I haven't seen you since the picnic. I trust all goes well at the College."

"Indeed." Mr. Wilson shows his teeth in a gentle smile. "With Mr. Hastie officially installed as Principal, I've no concerns at all."

"A toast, I think," Mr. Steele says. "To your very good health, Mr. Hastie. May it continue along with your tenure at the College."

"Dinner is ready, sir," the *durwan* says.

"Miss Pigot, will you take my arm?" Mr. Steele asks. "I'm sure you gentlemen can find your own way."

Mr. Steele has impeccable manners. I'm glad he's recovered from our disagreement about Mr. Robson. I hate being at odds with him, and I think he feels the same about me. As we move into the dining room, I see Mr. Steele has put out his best china and his silver candle sticks. It was porcelain and gas lighting from the wall sconces when Mr. Hastie was ill.

"You set a fine table, Mr. Steele," Mr. Hastie says.

The *durwan* holds out my chair.

"Thank you, Mr. Hastie," Mr. Steele replies. "I'm afraid it's just a simple menu tonight. The *khansama* has managed to perfect his rendition of clear gravy soup. I have a few specialty items that recently arrived, and turkey for main course. Please, sit."

I place my napkin. This is so much nicer than anything we can do at the orphanage. When we entertain, it's all buffets. I sigh.

"Are you unwell, Miss Pigot?" Mr. Wilson asks.

"Oh no, Mr. Wilson. I'm perfectly fine," I smile brightly. "Just a long, hot day in Kidderpore. Very dusty, and no breeze on the Strand."

The *durwan* serves the soup. I lift the cap off my glass so Mr. Wilson can pour me some Madeira wine.

"I do like Madeira," I say. "We seldom see it at the mission."

The *durwan* clears the soup plates.

"Shall I play hostess?" I ask. "Mr. Hastie, will you start the salmon and pass it round? Mr. Steele, you've served it with cucumber. How clever."

"I must give credit to the new *khansama*." Mr. Steele looks at me for approval. He likes to have compliments. "When I learned one of the Anglo-Indian households was dissolving, I made him an offer before anyone else could scoop him up. A slight increase in pay and a decrease in formal meals. My biggest concern is keeping him interested. I hope he stays a few months at least. He's much better than the cook I had when you first arrived, Mr. Hastie."

"Indeed. Forgive me if my memory is less than clear on that point," Mr. Hastie looks in my direction.

What a rude comment. I focus on my food. After a moment, Mr. Steele takes up the conversation.

"Well, I think my new *khansama* is excellent, don't you Mr. Wilson?"

"Yes." Mr. Wilson answers immediately. "Turkey?"

I take a slice even though I've lost my appetite. The *punkah* fan meant to cool the air sounds like thunder as it swings over the now silent room. The *durwan* removes the main course and brings out the fruit and cheese. Mr. Hastie reaches for the blue-veined Stilton and begins to slice it.

"How do you find the College, Mr. Hastie?" I ask.

"Adequate, Miss Pigot," Mr. Hastie says, shutting down further conversation.

"Mr. Hastie will offer classes in Philosophy," Mr. Wilson offers.

"As is his purview, Mr. Wilson," Mr. Steele says. "I believe you're something of an expert on the metaphysical, Mr. Hastie."

"It's reasonable to say I'm by far the most qualified person on the subject. I've met most of the German philosophers and read the ancient sages in their original languages," Mr. Hastie replies.

I nibble my cheese. I don't care for Stilton. It's too strong. Mr. Wilson munches resolutely and puts the napkin to his lips. I put my hands in my lap and try to think of something to say. Mr. Steele folds his napkin.

"Gentlemen, it appears we've finished our meal. Let us retire to the drawing room. Miss Pigot, before you settle yourself, have a look on the veranda. I've gathered some tables and other furnishings that might be useful for the prize distribution. If you agree, I'll send them over."

Mr. Steele pulls out my chair, escorts me to the veranda and goes back inside. I linger over the bazar furniture, inspecting the cane weave. Mr. Steele keeps a supply of this simple furniture and lends it to anyone who needs it. I slowly tag the pieces I want to use. The party isn't going well. Mr. Hastie never enters into the conversation, and then everyone sits in silence. I want to liven things up, but I don't know how. I've only been outside ten minutes when the *durwan* slides open the door.

"Mem, the gentlemen ask for you."

I follow him into the drawing room. The men look up at my entry with expressions of anticipation.

"Ah, Miss Pigot, you've returned." Mr. Hastie arranges his lips in what could be a smile. "Do you play whist?"

"The card game?"

"The very same. I'll partner you, and Mr. Steele can partner Mr. Wilson. Come. You'll need to shuffle the cards, then pass the deck to Mr. Wilson," Mr. Hastie says.

The servants place a round table in the center of the room, cover it with a green *baize* cloth, and set four straight backed chairs around it. Mr. Steele pulls out my chair so I can arrange my skirts. The men take their places. The playing cards are stiff. I'm surprised Mr. Steele even has a deck. I don't know how I can shuffle the cards without spilling them all over the table.

"Mr. Hastie, could you shuffle the cards? I fear my hands are too small."

I pass the deck across the table. Mr. Hastie shuffles, then passes the deck to his left to Mr. Steele. Our host reluctantly deals the cards out. Mr. Hastie is the only one who really knows how to play. He and I take the most tricks, but only because he knows the game. After several cycles, Mr. Steele places his cards face down on the small table. "Mr. Hastie, you put us all to shame. I'm not much of a card player. Shall we sit on more comfortable chairs?"

Mr. Wilson is the first to stand. He pulls out my chair.

"Mr. Steele, may I recline on your sofa?" I ask. "I'm simply exhausted."

"Of course. I'll send for coffee."

I can hardly bear to sit upright. Too much Madeira perhaps, after such a long day—though I'd never say anything to that effect. I sit on the reclining sofa and swing my legs around so that my back is against the reclining arm and my skirt drapes over the side. Mr. Hastie's eyes nearly pop out of his head. I remember when I went to Scotland on furlough two years ago, the women sat ramrod straight at all times. But we aren't so strict in Calcutta, and I'm too tired to meet his expectation. Mr. Steele and Mr. Wilson don't notice Mr. Hastie's reaction, so I let it pass.

"Whiskey, gentlemen?" Mr. Steele asks turning from the sideboard. "I import it from the Auchentoshan Distillery near Glasgow."

"A bit light for evening, don't you think?" Mr. Hastie asks.

"Given the climate, I think lighter whiskey is better suited," Mr. Steele replies. "And it's from home. What do you think, Mr. Wilson?"

"I think it's a rare treat to indulge. To your health, sir," Mr. Wilson toasts.

I wait until the men finish their whiskey before I swing my feet to the floor. If I stay longer, I'll fall asleep. "Mr. Steele, this has been a delightful evening. But I see the *durwan* collecting the glasses and turning down the gas. So, I'll take my leave." I reach for my shawl.

"Miss Pigot, are you well enough for the drive home?" Mr. Wilson asks.

"Of course, Mr. Wilson. The horse does all the work," I smile a tired smile.

"I think since you dismissed your driver, it would be best if I accompany you," Mr. Wilson says. He's always so considerate.

"Mr. Wilson, you're not making sense," Mr. Hastie says. "Mr. Steele provided our transportation. Miss Pigot has her own carriage. The College is nowhere near the Female Mission."

"On the contrary, I think Mr. Wilson has a good point," Mr. Steele says. "By the time he and Miss Pigot reach the College, the evening air will have revived her spirits, and she'll be in fine fettle for the journey home. What say you, Miss Pigot? Will you accept Mr. Wilson's offer?"

"With gratitude," I nod.

"This really is most irregular," Mr. Hastie says shaking his head, no doubt still shocked, because I reclined on the couch.

"You're in India now Reverend Hastie. Very little is as it first appears," Mr. Steele says.

Mr. Wilson hands me into the carriage and walks around to the other side. He leaves next month. I'll have to deal with Mr. Hastie on my own. Mr. Wilson takes up the reins, slaps them on the horse and makes chirruping sounds. We move out the driveway and turn towards the College. I take a breath of the jasmine scented air. It's a perfect evening after the heat of the day. I lean back in my seat.

"So, Mr. Wilson, soon you'll be home. Such a comforting word, home, don't you think?"

"I'm eager to see Mrs. Wilson and my sons," he says, "but the Scottish climate doesn't agree with me."

"No warm scented evenings as I recall from the last time I was there. Such a shame you can't send your sons to school here. Are Scottish schools that much better than our European schools in Calcutta?"

"It's a matter of perspective, Miss Pigot. If I educate my boys in Calcutta, their future will be limited. They'd have to stay here."

"And that would be bad?" I ask as the *gharry* bounces through a rut. If he sent his sons to school here, he wouldn't be going back to Scotland.

"No. But they might not want to stay in Calcutta. This way, they may go wherever God sends them."

"And they'll have a home," I inhale deeply, thinking of Mr. Wilson's departure.

We fall silent for a few minutes.

"The moon's bright tonight," I say aimlessly. "Is the moon this bright at home?"

"It can be. But we often have cloud cover during the summer months, as I'm sure you remember."

Of course, I remember. I'm sitting next to Mr. Wilson and already he feels distant. It's depressing. How can he go when I'll have nowhere to turn for advice or friendship?

"Oh, Mr. Wilson. Must you go?" I blurt. "I'm so uncomfortable with Mr. Hastie. Ever since I returned his book, I feel his constant displeasure, as if he's waiting for me to make a mistake so he can take his revenge."

"Miss Pigot, surely you exaggerate. Your decision stung his pride, but he's quite recovered. There's no reason for you to cross paths very often. And he has no authority over the Female Mission."

"But he wants it."

Mr. Wilson shrugs. "What he wants and what he can have are two different things. He'll be busy making a name for himself. I do have one suggestion. Withdraw your objections about Mr. Robson's situation."

"But they aren't being fair to him."

"Actually, they are," Mr. Wilson cautions. "Our missions are sponsored by the Church of Scotland. It isn't too much to expect those employed by the church to attend the church. Mr. Robson knew what he was doing when he chose the Free Church. Your advocacy won't help him, but it will hurt you. Mr. Steele is still upset about it," Mr. Wilson says.

"He seemed fine tonight," I recall.

"Tonight, was a social occasion," Mr. Wilson reminds me. "And Mr. Steele prides himself on being a perfect host."

"It's such a pleasant evening." Determined to enjoy my friend's company, I put my fears behind me and take off my hat. Mr. Wilson responds with a small smile.

Chapter 3
"I Don't Interfere"

William Hastie

I take rather a long time trimming my beard this morning. Snippets of dark brown hair fall onto the dresser. The mirror is too small to see my face properly, but I do the best I can, and brush the hair onto the floor. The houseman misses the dresser top, but he sweeps the floor daily.

Just as I begin affixing my collar, a student appears with a note. I dismiss him and open the envelope.

Reverend Hastie, if you find it convenient, you may call at 10:00.
Yours sincerely, M. Pigot.

No, it isn't convenient, and I don't wish to speak to you. I wouldn't consider it, except for my duty.

I complete my preparations, read through some correspondence, and begin the journey from Cornwallis Square to Bow Bazar—which is to say from the European center of town to the native district. As the carriage turns onto Amherst Street, sweat trickles down my back. The Hot Season begins soon. No doubt the Fishing Fleet of unsuccessful spinsters looking for husbands is pulling up anchor for another year.

Everything looks calm in the orphanage courtyard. Students are going about their lessons. A servant sprinkles water to keep down the dust. I walk into the entryway and take the stairs to the left.

Sajiva sees me and puts his hands together. "Reverend Hastie, welcome."

"Tell Miss Pigot I'm here." I hand him my *topi* and enter the drawing room. Every surface is covered with something. Books and papers are scattered everywhere, and someone left a sewing basket. It's as if Miss Pigot isn't expecting visitors, yet she invited me to call at ten o'clock. Two men are wrestling a *punkah* fan into position.

"Be careful, sir," Sajiva says before he leaves, "we're putting up the *punkah* for the Hot Weather."

I keep myself away from the workers, pick up local newspapers and put them down. Miss Pigot has a pianoforte that looks a bit like one in my brother's house. I run my fingers over the dusty keys.

"Do you play, Reverend Hastie?" Miss Pigot asks. She's standing in the doorway of another room, wearing a dark dress with a white collar. Her hair is pulled back. She might have been a pretty woman once. Now she has creases around her eyes and mouth.

"Miss Pigot."

"The piano?" Miss Pigot asks again.

"No, I don't play. I haven't time for such frivolities."

"Of course not. There's a small breeze on the veranda. I suggest we talk there and leave the workmen to their task. Refreshments?"

"This isn't a social call."

"Of course not," she repeats. "Well, I didn't have breakfast. One of the girls is ill, and matron needed my assistance. Come through please."

A round table stands a little to the left of the outside door. Miss Pigot pulls up a cane chair, gesturing for me to do the same.

"I hope you don't mind," Miss Pigot says. "The servants are putting up *punkahs*."

"Not at all." I tap my fingers on the table top. A young woman with her hair in a long braid down her back brings a pitcher, two glasses, and two bowls—one with some kind of soup and the other filled with rice.

"This is Bidu Grace," Miss Pigot gestures. "She's training to be a teacher."

"How do you..." I begin. The girl disappears, practically running out of the room.

"My apologies. Bidu is still quite shy around new people. It's a difficult habit for her to break."

"What are you eating?" I ask.

"*Sambar*. It's a lentil soup with vegetables. Would you like some?"

It looks revolting. "I ate earlier."

"Very well," Miss Pigot says as she continues to enjoy her food. "Now. Tell me what I can do for you?"

"It's what we can do together," I say.

"Yes?" Miss Pigot nods her head.

"Miss Pigot, the Foreign Mission Committee in Scotland has concerns about the friction between our two missions."

"Friction? I think we're in perfect harmony," Miss Pigot protests mildly. "We're one mission with two structures. The Ladies' Association works independently and is so authorized."

"But we must cooperate."

"Of course, and we do," Miss Pigot insists. She dabs her mouth with her napkin. "You take care of Scottish College, and I take care of the Female Mission. Your faculty members are generous in assisting me. I couldn't do my work without them. Is there some issue I'm not aware of, Mr. Hastie?"

"It's your behavior." There, I said it. It's refreshing to finally be honest with Miss Pigot.

"My what?" Miss Pigot raises her voice slightly. I may have gotten under her skin.

"Sajiva," Miss Pigot calls. "Bring *chai* at once." Miss Pigot busies herself moving her used dishes to the side. Sajiva appears with a full tea service, pours two cups of steaming liquid with a flourish and clears the table. Miss Pigot blows on her cup and takes a large swallow. I'm quite surprised by her behavior. I take a small taste of the liquid and wish I hadn't.

"Miss Pigot," I sputter, "What are we drinking?"

"*Chai.*"

The strange taste diverts me from our business. "You called it that when you requested it. What is in it?"

Miss Pigot gives me a tight smile. "This is how we drink tea in Calcutta. We take strong black tea, dilute it with milk and add sugar and spices. It's excellent for the digestion. Please, allow me to pour more for you."

I watch Miss Pigot refill my cup. When she finishes, I move the cup away. "To return to our conversation, I must tell you that your behavior is neither professional nor collegial. For example, your insistence in taking Mr. Robson's part at the Corresponding Board meeting upset the other gentlemen. I don't think Mr. Steele is yet recovered."

"Mr. Steele?" Miss Pigot drinks more *chai*. "We were on excellent terms at his recent dinner party. He's most supportive of the Female Mission."

I refuse to be deflected "You were rude at last month's meeting of the Corresponding Board. You didn't respect Mr. Steele's fiscal concerns."

"Pfft. I've attended those meetings for ten years. They never change."

"Why do you attend?" I ask. "The meetings don't concern you."

"The members can't understand my work, especially with *zenana* women. They don't understand the culture or the issues women face."

"Miss Pigot, every member of the Board is highly qualified. They've been in Calcutta their entire careers."

"Reverend Gillan isn't a gentleman," Miss Pigot says matter-of-factly, her face flushing slightly.

I'm shocked she could say such a thing about a minister. "That's a very serious charge. It's also false." Miss Pigot moves her cup to the side, and stares at me intently. It's most disconcerting.

"You haven't been in Calcutta very long, Mr. Hastie. You don't know these men you uphold. They live in the tiny European community and the even smaller Scottish circle. They don't comprehend the local culture they want to improve."

"How am I to take that comment, Miss Pigot?"

"Any way you wish." Miss Pigot returns to her *chai*.

Remembering my position, I hold on to my temper and change the topic. "Miss Pigot. Please. Listen to me. The Corresponding Board respects your work, but you can't continue in this manner. You take a false step when you interfere with their decisions."

"I don't interfere," Miss Pigot says with a slight frown. "I simply express my views."

"This business with Mr. Robson, for example. Miss Pigot, you know how the Board, particularly Mr. Steele, sees his behavior. Yet you gave him a prominent role in the last public Student Prize Distribution. If this sort of flaunting doesn't stop, you'll lose the Board's support. Don't you see the effect this would have on the Female Mission?"

Miss Pigot stands. "Mr. Hastie, the Female Mission is none of your concern. Neither is the way I conduct myself. You're the one causing trouble between myself and Mr. Steele. Prior to your arrival, we were the best of colleagues."

"Hello, hello," Mr. Robson strides onto the veranda all smiles. He's taken to wearing local dress with a long outer coat over loose trousers. *How dare Miss Pigot invite him to join us.*

Mr. Robson stops as soon as he sees me. "Mr. Hastie. I wasn't aware you'd be here."

"I'm sure you weren't." I don't extend my hand.

"Please sit down, Mr. Robson," Miss Pigot looks flustered but keeps her composure and turns toward me. "Mr. Hastie and I have just finished our conversation. Bidu, please get Mr. Hastie's *topi* and escort him outside. Thank you so much for calling, Mr. Hastie."

I catch a hint of sarcasm in her voice as she holds out her hand straight out like an arrow. The woman has no manners whatsoever. I must steer Miss Pigot onto the right path. She's throwing away her position. Perhaps I should write my concerns to her and give her time to reconsider. Yes, this is exactly what I will do as soon as I return to the College. I'll write a conciliatory note expressing my disappointment that Mr. Robson interrupted our discussion. I will warn her to end her friendship with him and ask to meet with her again.

A week later I receive a note from Dr. Charles, chair of the Corresponding Board, informing me that Miss Pigot has submitted her resignation. What possessed her? We can't accept it, because the Board didn't engage her. The Ladies' Association took her on. Now, a week after the first note, Dr. Charles writes that the Ladies have induced Miss Pigot to stay by separating the Female Mission from the Corresponding Board. What a blunder! I have no choice but to wash my hands of Miss Pigot until she comes to her senses.

Mary Pigot

I must be honest. I don't like The Reverend Gillan. He opposed my appointment, because I'm not from the home country. Our animosity is entirely mutual, so I don't know why he asked me to call at St. Andrew's. I'm supposed to attend Sunday service here, but I don't. I go to the Reverend Chuckerbutty's church. It's closer, and the people there are genuine. They don't judge me because I grew up in Calcutta. Well, I'm here now. May as well enter.

"Miss Pigot, how gracious of you to call on me," Mr. Gillan says with what I'm sure is a sneer instead of a smile. He gestures for me to sit as he remains seated behind his mahogany desk, his bald head gleaming in the glare from the window. He wears his white suit with the black tie. I sit down without extending my hand.

"Are you pleased with the present state of affairs between the Female Mission and the College?" he asks.

"There's no change."

"But you no longer attend meetings with the Corresponding Board."

"You and Mr. Hastie won your point. The Board's business is no concern of mine, and certainly has nothing to do with the Female Mission. In fact, there's no reason for Mr. Steele to continue handling our funds. They can come directly to me as Superintendent."

"That won't be necessary. Mr. Steele resigned at our last meeting."

I bite my lip to avoid smiling. Surely the funds will come to me directly now.

"I will transmit your funds. Your accounts and requests will now go through me." Mr. Gillan gives me a tight smile.

"I see. Then there's nothing further to discuss." I reach for my *topi.*

"Before you go, there are one or two other matters. Your position makes you a leader in our community, yet you persist in attending the native church. It causes us to question where your true loyalties lie, Miss Pigot."

"They lie with God," I say, looking him straight in the eye. Mr. Gillan moves his gaze to the wall behind me.

"Nevertheless, all leaders in the Scottish community attend St. Andrew's. By virtue of your position as Lady Superintendent you should worship here, not at the native church."

I continue looking directly at Mr. Gillan. "Reverend Thomson never suggested it."

"Reverend Thomson was... "Mr. Gillan pauses for emphasis... "lax in some areas. The situation is different now."

I sit silently, sure he has more to say in his condescending voice.

"Your refusal to attend St. Andrew's exacerbates the divisions in our community."

"Divisions?" I feign ignorance.

"Surely, you can't be unaware that relations between Scottish College and your Female Mission are under great strain," he continues.

"Well, I'm certainly not the cause of any strain."

"Mr. Hastie informs me that you practically pushed him out the door when Mr. Robson called on you at the Female Mission. To be truthful, I could hardly believe you capable of such a thing. You were present at the Board meeting when we discussed Mr. Robson's dishonorable behavior. Mr. Hastie was shocked and, frankly, so was I."

I look at Mr. Gillan's pale unhappy face. It's clear he avoids the Indian sun as much as possible and he never calls at the Female Mission. He has no interest in our orphans or our schools. His dislike for me is palpable. Why should I accommodate him? I consider my next words carefully.

"Mr. Hastie and I had simply concluded our business. Mr. Robson's presence happened to coincide with Mr. Hastie's departure." I shrug. "I'm courteous to everyone who calls."

Mr. Gillan's jaw tightens as if he's gritting his teeth. "Miss Pigot, I insist this alienation between you and Mr. Hastie stop immediately. I expect your full cooperation in this matter."

I keep eye contact as I consider Mr. Gillan's new control of our purse strings at the Female Mission. "What makes you think Mr. Hastie would accept any overtures from me?" I say calmly

"Someone must make the first move, Miss Pigot."

"Very well. I'll invite Reverend Hastie to our next Student Prize Assembly," I say.

I keep my word. As soon as I reach 125 Bow Bazar, I write out the invitation. Mr. Hastie declines. Twice. First, he writes to say my invitation isn't sincere. That he knows I don't really want him to attend. Very perceptive. He writes a second time, to say he has no ill will toward me, but as long as our missions are separate there is no reason for him to attend.

The next day, still smarting from Mr. Hastie's refusal of my invitation, I prepare for the three *zenana* visits Mrs. Tremearne and I have today. Try as I might, I can't think of a way to present the scope of my work to men like Mr. Hastie and Mr. Gillan. I doubt even Mr. Wilson fully grasps the requirements of my position, even though his wife was Lady Superintendent before me.

Most superintendents leave external work to subordinates, but I still visit the *zenanas*. I don't want to be a distant *memsahib*. I can't visit every week, but I want each woman in the *zenana* to know I care about them.

Mrs. Tremearne and I have three *zenana* visits today. All in the native district of North Calcutta so we won't have to travel far.

At the Sanyal residence we visit the third flat of the second court. The house has four courts with wrought iron fencing along the edges. The Sanyals are a large family. Each son has his own apartment, with separate women's quarters. During the day, the women like staying together in the largest apartment. Aside from size, the quarters are all dark with a few high windows and kerosene lamps for light. Outside the flat, I rap the door. One of the children opens it.

"Come in, come in, Mems. We've been waiting for you patiently," Mrs. Sanyal calls.

We go forward to shake hands in greeting, and then sit on chairs while the two women make themselves comfortable on the cushioned *tuktaposh*. I prefer cushions, but we all have our roles to play. I look at the chubby woman, her fingers encased in rings, golden bangles on her wrists.

"Mrs. Sanyal, is it just you and your daughter-in-law today?"

"Yes, Mem. The others are busy cooking a special meal for my husband, but I refused to miss your visit. What shall we talk about?"

"I have a special story for you today," I say. "It's about when the devil tempted Jesus."

"Oh, yes. Jesus is always good. He never plays tricks. You said he doesn't want anything from us. What could he be tempted to do?" Mrs. Sanyal pushes back a strand of grey hair as she prepares to listen.

"Not everyone understands so well as you," says Mrs. Tremearne. "The devil knew Jesus hadn't eaten for forty days and thought he could turn Jesus from God. Shall we read it together?"

Mrs. Tremearne opens her Bible to the story in Matthew. I prefer the stories in Luke, because he's more sympathetic to women. However, there's not much difference between the two versions of this story, and Mrs. Tremearne likes the book of Matthew.

"Mrs. Sanyal, can you read this verse?" I ask.

The woman puts her finger on the page. "*If thou be the Son of God, command that these stones be made of bread.*"

"Why did the devil ask Jesus to do that?" I ask her.

Mrs. Sanyal keeps her finger on the page and mumbles to herself. Then she puts her hands in her lap and looks at me. "Perhaps Jesus didn't think it was time to eat yet."

"Why not?" Mrs. Tremearne asks.

"He knows the devil plays tricks, so it's better not to eat with him," Mrs. Sanyal says.

Mrs. Sanyal makes a good point. We move to the second temptation. The devil takes Jesus to the top of the temple and urges him to jump. The devil says angels will catch Jesus. Mrs. Sanyal's daughter-in-law reads the verse. Mrs. Sanyal sits for several minutes.

"I don't think Jesus was worried about falling. He wouldn't jump just because the devil wanted him to."

"Exactly," I say. I'm pleased with her wisdom and engagement. We're making real progress here. "Allow me to read the third temptation." The devil shows Jesus all the kingdoms in the world, and says he'll give them to Jesus if Jesus will worship him. "What do you think, Mrs. Sanyal? Do you sometimes feel you'd like to serve God and yet retain the world at the same time?"

"I do this daily," Mrs. Sanyal says. "I acknowledge idols every day while I worship the true God. My husband requires this. I take the Bible, and my husband is a devoted Brahmin."

This is exactly why we have so few baptisms here in Calcutta. If this woman and her daughter-in-law publicly accept Jesus, they will be tossed onto the street. It is a simple fact of life here. The Reverends Gillan and Hastie don't care to understand this reality, and Mr. Gillan has been here long enough to know better.

We continue to the next *zenana* taking the same lesson to a widow who knows the story of the temptations yet finds it hard to accept. She's a small woman with a crooked back. Her sons give her just enough to live on so she doesn't beg. She likes to read Bible stories, but has trouble believing them. We talk about each temptation of Jesus. After we talk for about an hour, she throws her spectacles at the Bible.

"I simply cannot believe the devil's arrogance. How could he tempt God?"

"The devil's temptation is my strongest support," I say, "because I believe God as Christ understands how I am assailed every day. And I can go to Him for grace."

She shakes her head. "It's hard to accept."

"Then take heart," I say. "One of our Brahmin converts told me the parts of Scripture he understood the least became his strongest supports."

"I feel like I'm under a fog, but if you continue to teach me, the fog will lift. You're the rain that cuts the fog," the widow says.

I squeeze her hand. "Mrs. Tremearne also brings rain. In time, you'll understand. God will guide you."

We say a prayer for her heart to open and continue to our last *zenana* of the day. This one is a challenge. We've visited the Misra house for several years, but recently the father told Mrs. Tremearne not to teach from the Bible anymore.

Babu Misra has a modest house befitting a civil servant, but he still keeps the women of the household in *zenana* quarters. The *durwan* takes us through the public rooms with western furniture, then upstairs and to the back of the house where we enter a specious *zenana* featuring both western and traditional furnishings. We knock at the door and walk in.

The house has a grandmother, mother, and two daughters-in-law. Their little girls attend our school. The ladies have on their jewelry to reflect their status. We have refreshments. Everything seems as usual.

After discussing embroidery patterns, we talk about Jesus and the temptations, though the women don't answer my question about whether we can serve God and the world.

"What a disappointment it will be if our lessons stop," Mrs. Misra sighs. She looks at me with sorrowful eyes, her round red marriage *bindi* standing out in the center of her pale forehead. "We're learning in a systematic way now, and it's become a true pleasure. My sons think reading from the Bible will turn their wives against them, and my husband agrees with them. Young women can be foolish." Mrs. Misra shakes her head as she speaks. "There must be other books to read. If only you could yield on this point, we can continue our visits."

I sigh and shake my head. "I'm sorry, Mrs. Misra, but you know we can't do that. We teach from the Bible or we don't teach. Every time I come, we read the stories and talk about what they mean. Do you want to stop reading the stories?"

"No, but we would rather read other books than stop reading," Mrs. Misra says.

"Why do you think Mrs. Tremearne and I visit you?" I ask. "Would you do for me what I do for you? Would Hindus open schools for Christians?"

"We know you're good women. That you care for us," Mrs. Misra says. Her eyes fill with tears.

"We aren't the only ones who love you. Christians you've never met send money so we can come to you," I say, wiping away my own tears. I reach to hold Mrs. Misra's hand. "We visit you because we love you. We teach because Christ creates that desire within us. Do you doubt what I do and teach?"

"We're not the ones who need convincing," Mrs. Misra nods. "Speak to my husband."

Mrs. Tremearne and I take our leave and wait for Babu Misra in the outer court. His women keep such strict *purdah* he doesn't enter the *zenana* if his daughters-in-law are there. The ladies sit in there all day with nothing to do. And he would take away their Bible. It breaks my heart.

Babu Misra is a man of medium height dressed in a white *dhoti*. Many civil servants dress traditionally at home. I put my hands together to greet him and wait for him to begin the discussion.

"You wish to see me?" Babu Misra asks, his face expressionless.

"I received a message that you wanted to see me." *How I dislike playing these games.*

"I'm concerned this Bible-reading will affect the ladies," Babu Misra says.

"Surely an enlightened man like yourself doesn't take this view."

He shrugs as if the issue isn't important. "They cannot judge for themselves, and we hear rumors of women being kidnapped."

"You know Mrs. Tremearne and I are missionary teachers," I remind him. "Would you consider me an honest woman if I didn't use the Bible to give lessons? And if I don't teach your women, who will?"

"The question is whether such teaching is necessary at all. I'll consider the matter and speak with my sons. Please excuse us until we decide."

As we walk through the graveled courtyard, tears drip down Mrs. Tremearne's cheeks.

"Don't worry," I say. "Often these things blow over after a few weeks. Better an occasional Bible lesson than unhappy women."

I write the Ladies' Association to report the sad news that Miss Anne Barham, music teacher in our Upper School, has died after a short illness. Probably cholera. She was a lovely young woman, and we all feel the loss. Worse news, Mrs. Tremearne suffered a breakdown when Miss Barham passed, and had to return to her home village twenty miles away. I rub my head. I am tired. I miss Mrs. Tremearne. She did so many small things to make my life less complicated.

I accept the Ladies' Association's suggestion to send me an assistant from Scotland. There's so much work to be done, and I can't keep doing it alone. I need someone who knows what to do without coming to me for every instruction.

With Mr. Wilson on furlough and Mrs. Tremearne ill, I've no one to help me, except a young man I've known since before I started working for the Female Mission. Kali Churn Banerjee is not really that young any more, but he's a good ten years younger than I am. I met him after he began working as a barrister at the High Court. He has five children in our school, and since Bow Bazar is between his home and the court, he stops in to pick up his children and often stays to assist me with correspondence and other school matters. Kali Churn seems too quiet to be an effective barrister, but perhaps he's more strident in court.

Sometimes I sit and talk with him if he eats his dinner in the drawing room.

Kali Churn is a member of the Free Church, so perhaps I shouldn't allow him to contribute so much. As the Corresponding Board often reminds me, the Free Church broke away from the Church of Scotland in 1843. Something to do with church politics. At home the two churches never cooperate, but there are so few Christians with Scottish affiliations here in Calcutta that many of us work together. Of course, this cooperation upsets Mr. Hastie and Mr. Gillan greatly.

I look upon Kali Churn as a mother interacts with her son, watching him make his way in the *babu* community of educated Indians. He's well thought of in the Free Church and invited Mr. Hastie to preach at their church service. Mr. Hastie probably thought his preaching would end the rift in Calcutta and bring everyone back to St. Andrew's. I chuckle to myself imagining his disappointment. Despite Mr. Hastie's eloquence, no one in the Free Church set foot in the Church of Scotland.

Chapter 4
"My First Convert"

1880

William Hastie

I stride into the classroom with a spring in my step. What better way to start the day than with a discussion of William Wordsworth? The students stand when I enter.

"Good day, gentlemen. Be seated."

I wish they could sit without scraping their chairs on the floor. Such a grating clatter. "Today we'll discuss *Excursion* and contemplate Wordsworth's point on using inner dialogue to achieve the sublime connection. Wordsworth draws on nature's beauty to guide us. He writes about the Lake District in northwest England, but his poetry reminds me of my own home in Wanlockhead in Scotland. The two areas are much the same. February here is warmer than a Scottish summer. Does anyone know what the weather is like in Scotland this time of year?"

Mr. Bhaduri, a bright student with hair down to his shoulders, raises his hand. "Excuse me, sir. I think perhaps it is snowing."

"Correct," I say. "It's also damp and cold. But to be there in summer is bliss. Long days. Gentle sun. I ask you to close your eyes and let your imagination take you away from the heat and chaos of Calcutta to a place of peace."

Everyone dutifully closes their eyes.

"Now listen as I bring you into Wordsworth's world," I say. "We're going to meet The Boy. He experiences a sublime moment as he transitions into the state of Youth such as you enjoy.

I speak clearly and slowly so the words roll off my tongue.

> *"Such was the Boy, but for the growing Youth*
> *What soul was his, when, from the naked top*
> *Of some bold headland, he beheld the sun*
> *Rise upland bathe the world in light! He looked—*

"Gentlemen, can you see it in your mind?" I'm hoping my enthusiasm is contagious. "The Youth is at the top of the world. Everything is bathed in the mystical light of the sun and when he looks down, he sees...

> *Ocean and earth, the solid frame of earth*
> *And the ocean's liquid mass, in gladness lay*
> *Beneath him —Far and wide the clouds were touched,*
> *And in their silent faces could he read*
> *Unutterable love.*

Unutterable love. What powerful words. Do you feel it, lads?" I ask, excitedly. "The Youth is beyond himself. He and God are one. Nothing else exists. Here is perfection. You can open your eyes now."

The students blink as their eyes adjust to the light. They don't seem interested in Wordsworth. "When I was your age, my brothers and I climbed the hills near Wanlockhead. Those excursions taught me to melt into the sublime." For a moment, I'm lost in the beauty of Wordsworth's words. I remember my own transcendent moment when I reached beyond the Self. I inhale deeply.

"Gentlemen, what does Wordsworth say to you?" I ask.

Blank faces.

I focus on one of the more insightful students. "Mr. Dutta, what do you think?"

"Perhaps the Youth isn't in his correct mind?" Mr. Dutta suggests.

"He's not in his mind at all. Where is he?" I ask.

"Perhaps, sir, the Youth is in a trance? Although I don't believe such a state can exist," Mr. Dutta responds.

The students nod in agreement.

I take another approach. "Do you know of a man called Sri Ramakrishna? If you want to see a man taken up in a trance in which 'his mind is a thanksgiving to the power that made him,' visit his ashram. But don't be taken in by his teaching."

Mr. Dutta makes a note.

"To help you consider the possibility of transcendence," I continue, "I set you an essay due at our next meeting. Using Wordsworth's poem as your guide, explain why we need to cultivate inner dialogue as a way to reach the sublime. If you visit the ashram, you may incorporate your observations. Questions?"

No one asks anything, so I dismiss them. The essays should enlighten our next discussion. Most of the students scramble out of the room, but Mr. Mukherjee remains. He's a quiet lad, slender with intense brown eyes.

"Do you have a question, Mr. Mukherjee?" I ask.

"I didn't like to say it in front of the others, but I know the transcendence of God. I meet regularly with Mr. Edwards. We discuss the Bible, and I realize I must be baptized," the young man says.

My first convert! I can hardly speak for my emotion.

"I thank God! Mr. Mukherjee, let me shake your hand. Welcome into the true church." I pump his arm in my enthusiasm.

"Yes, sir. Thank you, sir. But my family will be angry. We're Kulin Brahmins, and my brothers are lawyers. I'm afraid of what they may do."

"Don't worry, son. You're under our protection. Let us pray together."

I place my hand on Nitya Gopal Mukherjee's head, and pray in thanksgiving and for his growth in understanding. I feel God's spirit stir within me. Surely others will follow his example.

Over the next month, I work with Mr. Mukherjee to be sure he understands the requirements. I arrange the ceremony at St. Andrew's Church on the seventeenth of May. When the day arrives, the entire Scottish mission community as well as native converts attend. Even Miss Pigot makes a rare appearance at St. Andrew's. The Free Church appoints Kali Churn Banerjee to witness the grand occasion. I think it's inappropriate to invite dissenters from the Church of Scotland, but no one here thinks anything of it. The weather is wretchedly hot. I stand at the baptismal font with The Reverend Gillan and Mr. Mukherjee. The lad professes his new faith and bows his head. Mr. Gillan dips a shell into the water three times for the Father, Son, and Holy Ghost. I am transformed by the enormity of this ceremony and blink a tear from my eye. Scottish and Indian, we unite in our profession of faith.

Mr. Mukherjee is so concerned about his family's reaction that I arrange for him to stay at Mr. Steele's house on his first night as a Christian. I don't tell anyone what I'm doing, because such a secret couldn't be kept. When we arrive, the *durwan* takes Mr. Mukherjee to his room, and I return to the College where everything is in chaos.

Mr. Edwards rushes into my rooms demanding to know where Mr. Mukherjee is. "Why disguise his location?" he demands. "I'm the one responsible for his conversion. Tell me where he is."

The man is out of control, flailing his arms and shouting. I try to placate him and speak in a low voice. "Mr. Edwards, calm yourself. You said you didn't want to know Mr. Mukherjee's whereabouts, so that if his family and friends come to the College, you can deny knowledge."

"A brother was here already. The danger is over. Tell me where Nitya Gopal is," Mr. Edwards says again.

"The crisis isn't over, Mr. Edwards. Mr. MacDonald told me one of their converts was seized after his baptism. And he was staying in the European quarter. I'll keep the arrangements I made."

"You don't have the right to hide my convert," Mr. Edwards shouts. "I want him here."

I don't know what's come over Mr. Edwards. I draw myself up. "I'm head of this mission and my decision stands," I thunder to get his attention. "Get out of my rooms, go downstairs, and return to your senses."

Mr. Edwards looks like he might lay hands on me, but he goes downstairs. I'll deal with his behavior later. He can't be allowed to question my decisions.

I visit Mr. Mukherjee's father the next day, because I don't want any difficulties at the College. The family has a large compound with several courtyards. I feel some trepidation when I enter the men's part of the house. Mr. Mukherjee's father is an elderly gentleman with a shock of white hair. Several relatives are with him, possibly his other sons. One rises with a belligerent gesture, but the senior Mukherjee waves him aside and motions me to sit on the *tuktaposh*. Refreshments are on the table, but I don't take any. This isn't a social call.

"Where is my son? Is he with you?" Mr. Mukherjee's father asks in a firm voice.

"Nitya Gopal is safe," I say.

"But, where is he? His brother went to the College for him. He wasn't there. You've stolen my son," Mr. Mukherjee's father accuses.

The young men move closer to me. I don't know how to respond. "You sent him to the College," I remind the father.

"To learn...not to betray his family. He's dead to us now. You killed him!" His voice rises. The young men take on a menacing aspect. I need to diffuse the situation. I look at Mr. Mukherjee's father.

"We would never hurt Nitya Gopal," I say gently. "We gave him the key to Eternal Life. He's part of God's family now. You must let him go." I offer a silent prayer for protection.

The father shakes his head, suddenly subdued. "Then keep him. My son is lost to me. He's lost to his brothers. He's your responsibility now." Tears slip down the old man's cheeks. He grasps my hand firmly. "Promise me you will take care of him."

"I'll treat him as my own son," I vow. "He'll sit at my table, and sleep near my rooms. Your son is in good hands."

"That is well, for he is dead to us," the father repeats.

The young men open a pathway so I can depart. Their father may have forgiven me, but they haven't. I remove myself as quickly as possible.

Mr. Edwards's outburst over Mr. Mukherjee's location isn't the only time my staff has questioned my authority. He and Mr. Thomson fight every innovation. Mr. Wilson didn't keep these two men in good discipline, and they reject my leadership. They and some members of the Corresponding Board oppose my proposal to open new mission fields among the Santhal hill people at Govindpore. The people are so innocent, so open to the word of God. I press forward with support from the Board treasurer Mr. Wetherill and Mr. Gillan, but my detractors complain to the Mission Committee at home.

Those same enemies allow vicious falsehoods to circulate without a word of protest. When dissenters split from the Church of Scotland and founded their Free Church, there was also a split in the Calcutta Mission. Dr. Duff founded Scottish College in 1830, but he left it to join the Free Church. Eventually, he founded another college for them. Now the Free Church College wants to celebrate their Fiftieth Anniversary by claiming their college was founded in 1830, which it wasn't since they didn't exist then. And the Church of Scotland was going to let them get away with it.

I found out what was going on when Kali Churn Banerjee had the effrontery to invite me to address their celebration. I spoke out immediately and wrote the newspapers to bring out the truth. It became quite a public debate, which I relish. Christian converts from leading Bengali families worship at the Free Church. My qualifications far exceed anything their preacher spouts. By exposing the lack of integrity in the Free Church, I hope they'll visit our native church led by Reverend Chuckerbutty and send their sons to Scottish College.

But instead of applauding my efforts to bring respect to the Church of Scotland, the Corresponding Board and the Mission Committee tell me to desist. They claim our community is too small for such public division. It's the Robson case all over again. Don't they realize we must teach the true Gospel? Surely if I'm willing to exert myself during this season of sweltering monsoons, the least they can do is support my efforts.

I've no doubt the climate here is but a foretaste of the misery sinners will find in Hell. First God sends the Hot Weather with nothing but merciless sun. Everyone who can afford it decamps to the Himalayas, including the Viceroy and most of the government. The desire to escape the heat and glare of the sun is so strong, we actually rejoice when the relentless monsoon rains arrives, despite the months of overcast skies we know are ahead. And when it isn't raining, steam rises from the ground. Mosquitos surround everything. I break out in boils, which I remember as one of the seven plagues God rained on Pharaoh. And I cannot imagine why Dr. Duff founded our College in July. We can't even conduct classes.

The Free Church has their little party. And an anonymous article called "One Against Two Thousand" appears in the *Indian Christian Herald*. The minute I see it, I know the writer is Kali Churn Banerjee. He means I am the "One," and the "Two Thousand" is the audience in attendance at the Free Church celebration. To attack me without attaching his name is very low indeed. And to pretend he understands the issues surrounding the schism of the Church of Scotland is ridiculous.

He refuses to acknowledge his authorship on the basis of journalistic propriety. Our notes fly back and forth, which is a wonder when paper wilts and ink runs from the damp.

Sir, the proprieties of journalism are not at stake in this question.

I shall assume you are the writer of these most insolent articles and deal with you accordingly unless you disclaim them.

Very truly yours, W. Hastie

*

Sir–I'm in receipt of your notes.

I write this only to say that I won't receive any more of your most impertinent and impudent letters.

As for your assuming or threatening this, that, or the other thing. I know how to rate them at their real worth.

Your last letter shall be dealt with as it deserves.

Yours truly, K. C. Banerjee

The man is insufferable. And my colleagues on the Corresponding Board are no better. Again, I ask for support. They say they have no control over the *Indian Christian Herald*. What rot! I put it to them directly:

Apart from you, the men as well as the articles are beneath my notice.

Any reply deserved by these insolent Babus would have to be delivered from the tip of my boot.

It's possible I may have over-spoken my case. But such insolence and falsehood must be exposed.

In the midst of this animosity, I hear a rumor about improper relations between Babu Banerjee and Miss Pigot. He spends a great deal of time at the Female Mission where he has a daughter and a niece enrolled. Surely, he could send them to the Free Church School. Why lurk about the Female Mission unless there's some basis for the rumor?

Under the circumstances, I ban Kali Churn Banerjee from the Female Mission.

Mary Pigot

Reverend Hastie is beyond belief. He has no right to ban a parent from the Female Mission. This feud between he and Kali Churn is out of control. I blame the heat. Kali Churn should know better than to engage in public correspondence during the monsoons when everyone's temper is short. There must be some way I can smooth things out. Kali Churn refuses to listen to me, so I've sent for Mr. Fish. He's a poor substitute for Mr. Wilson's assistance, but I've no one else to consult.

Mr. Fish arrived in Calcutta just after the new year and I don't think he's adjusting well. He doesn't eat any of the local food and follows Mr. Hastie around like a lapdog. His brogue is so thick, I'm sure his students can't understand a word. Mr. Fish agrees to help me on occasion, but often seems to resent being asked. I'm hoping he'll agree to persuade Mr. Hastie to take a more reasonable course. There's no one else I can consult. I invite him for *tiffin*, and here we are, under the *punkah* in the drawing room.

"More sweetmeats, Mr. Fish?" I smile.

"These are quite tasty." Mr. Fish nibbles delicately. "We don't have sweetmeats at the College." He dabs his lips with his napkin as if we're at a formal dinner. "You mentioned you're in some difficulty. What service can I do for you today?"

"I need your help to stop this feud between Mr. Hastie and Babu Banerjee. Kali Churn told me he's written another article," I say.

Mr. Fish raises his eyebrows. "I see. What's it about?"

"I've no idea, but it will escalate matters. I'm sure he wrote it because Mr. Hastie banned him from the Female Mission. Mr. Hastie has no authority to do that."

"That's not for me to say." Mr. Fish reaches for the last sweetmeat.

"I doubt the Corresponding Board approves of his public discourse. What do you think?" I make my eyes big and give him an appealing look.

"What do you think I can do, Miss Pigot? I'm Mr. Hastie's assistant, not his superior. Babu Banerjee is impertinent and deserves censure. Mr. Hastie won't desist because of anything I say. Besides, your disobedience doesn't help matters."

My what! Let it pass. I inhale to calm myself. "But if you could just speak to him?" I say. "I'm sure if Mr. Hastie lets matters lie, I can persuade Babu Banerjee to withhold the article. The situation will die a natural death."

"I'll do what I can, but don't expect success." Mr. Fish stands and extends his hand.

I rise and touch his sticky fingers. "I hope you'll attend our social gatherings when the weather cools." I walk Mr. Fish to the lower veranda and watch him put on his galoshes.

"At least I don't have to wear my *topi* this time of year," Mr. Fish says.

I laugh. "That's one good thing."

The rains recede in September and October. Not enough to be pleasant, but life resumes its normal pace. It's safe to plan social events and one of my pleasures is the regular monthly social gathering at the Female Mission. I keep an open house in any event, but the social gatherings are a chance for European and native Christians to join members of the Hindu community on an informal basis. This November our event follows a weeklong meeting of native pastors from all over Calcutta. I invite everyone for a meal and magic lantern show.

The orphans and students decorate the courtyard with hanging lanterns, transforming the space into a multi-colored fairyland. For a moment, you might believe it's heaven. Brahmin cooks prepare curries. There are at least six hundred people here. We have musicians so everyone can sing hymns. A magic lantern and twelve slides depicting the story of *The Prodigal Son* from the book of Luke caps a perfect evening.

I chose this story to fit the theme of family. Respect for parents is important in Hindu culture, so the story resonates with everyone. As soon as it's dark, Mrs. Tremearne, who returned last week, and the other teachers bring women and children into the drawing room. Men watch from the veranda and side rooms. We push the furniture against the walls and place mats on the floor so we can fit more people in. Everyone points at the large sheet hanging from the rafters.

"Welcome," I say. "Have you had enough to eat?"

Everyone laughs.

"We're turning down the gaslights so the magic lantern show can begin."

Mr. Edwards nods and the first slide appears. The colors are so clear it's like being in the father's house with entry stairs and columns, not unlike some palaces in Calcutta. The slide where the younger son takes leave of his father is heartrending. He goes off without a single look behind him.

I read the story from Luke as the slides come up. Some women cry when the boy sits near the pigs with nothing to keep him warm. And then the family reunion. Everyone laughs and applauds.

When the program finishes, teachers bring in sweetmeats for everyone. I sit at the piano, and we sing. Mr. Edwards closes the evening with prayer. It's nearly midnight before the courtyard clears.

One of my most successful projects is a program I started for "parlor boarders," local women married to European men. Their husbands send them to Bow Bazar to learn proper manners and etiquette. I assign one of our senior girls to each woman. Some arrive with more education than others, but all need tutoring.

Mrs. Mullick comes to me in tears one morning. "They're gone, Miss Pigot. My husband will be angry. I've looked everywhere."

"Please sit, Mrs. Mullick. What's missing?" I ask.

"My *bangri*. The gold bracelets my husband gave me when we married." Mrs. Mullick dabs her eyes.

I call for my assistant Mrs. Ellis and tell her to go with Mrs. Mullick to search her room. "If you don't find the bracelets, bring Bidu Grace to me." Mrs. Ellis puts her arm around Mrs. Mullick's shoulders and guides her out of the drawing room. Next to Mrs. Tremearne, I depend on Mrs. Ellis to keep things in order in the orphanage.

Mrs. Tremearne gives me a long look. "You think Bidu stole the jewelry."

"I don't know, but she's Mrs. Mullick's tutor, and we've been having a rash of thefts. We know Bidu took another girl's dress and cut out the name tag. But we had no proof."

"But, Bidu has been here most of her life," Mrs. Tremearne says. "You've given her everything. There's no reason for Bidu to steal."

"Young girls. Pretty things. She sees Mrs. Mullick's bangles and new saris. She probably thought Mrs. Mullick too timid to complain."

About an hour later, Mrs. Ellis returns.

"Miss Pigot? I have Bidu Grace with me," Mrs. Ellis says.

"Bring her into the anteroom, Mrs. Ellis. I want you and Mrs. Tremearne present while I talk to Bidu Grace." We move to the small room between the drawing room and my bedroom. "Bidu, are you aware Mrs. Mullick is missing some gold bracelets?"

"No, Mem," Bidu replies with her eyes on the floor.

"I heard you have a new ring. Is that true?"

"The girl Eleanor, she gave me the ring," Bidu answers.

"Why?" I ask.

"I bought it."

"Did Eleanor give you the ring or sell it to you?"

Bidu's dark eyes begin darting around. "I don't remember."

"Where's the ring now?" I ask.

"I pawned it," Bidu replies.

"Is that what you did with Mrs. Mullick's bracelets?"

"No, Mem," Bidu shakes her head.

"Where are they?"

"I don't know."

"Did you help Mrs. Mullick look for them?"

"Yes, Mem. But we didn't find them. We looked everywhere." Bidu nods her head up and down.

"I see. Bidu, how long have you been with me?"

"A long time, Mem. Since I was a small girl."

"Have I ever been unfair to you?"

"No, Mem," Bidu whispers.

"Then tell me the truth. Did you take the bracelets?"

"No."

"I'll have to punish you if you lie to me. Did you take the bracelets?"

"Yes," Bidu replies.

"Where are they now?"

Bidu shakes her head.

We take Bidu into my bedroom. "Take off your blouse, please," I say.

"No, Mem. Don't hit me," Bidu cries. "Please! I am sorry. I won't do it again."

"Miss Pigot, are you sure?" Mrs. Tremearne asks.

"This isn't just about Bidu. I have to make her an example or we'll keep having thefts. Mrs. Tremearne, Mrs. Ellis, hold Bidu. I don't want to cause her unnecessary harm."

I strike Bidu across the back with the broadside of a cane. I strike her three times. The girl screams blue murder, then hangs onto Mrs. Ellis, sobbing.

"Get dressed please," I say. "Bidu, you're going to spend the next two days in isolation in the attic above this room. Please climb up the ladder."

"Please don't make me stay up there," Bidu sobs.

"You'll be perfectly safe. Mrs. Tremearne will check on you, and you can leave the hatch open."

We don't find the bracelets. I redeem the ring from the pawnshop and return it to the rightful owner. After the first two days, Bidu stays in my room, and later in one of the rooms downstairs. Sometimes love requires strong measures. At the end of her punishment period, I tell Mrs. Oliver, one of our matrons, to return Bidu to her usual duties.

The thefts stop, but other discipline problems remain. The girls constantly complain about the food. We serve lentil dahl, rice, and curry, the same food eaten by nearly everyone in Calcutta. Do they expect to eat like the

Viceroy? Mrs. Oliver, a strong-willed woman, takes their side and brings me a plate of the food. It's fine. I remind Mrs. Oliver the girls are fortunate to have regular meals of decent quality. I order her to bring me the next girl wasting food or refusing to eat it. Mrs. Oliver brings Joboni, a headstrong girl who encourages others to disobey the rules.

"Joboni, Mrs. Oliver tells me you won't eat your food. Why not?"

"I don't like it," Joboni says.

"I see. Hold out your hand."

Joboni steps away, shakes her head, and pulls her hands behind her back. I reach for her left hand and strike her open palm.

Smack. The child screams.

"Miss Pigot!" Mrs. Oliver hugs the shrieking girl to her. "If I realized you meant to strike Joboni, I wouldn't have brought her."

"Mrs. Oliver, our orphanage will fall into chaos without discipline. If children can't be persuaded by other means, I must use physical deterrents. The girls cannot waste food." I pull the child away from Mrs. Oliver and look into her face. "Joboni, the next time you think about wasting food, remember what happens to bad little girls."

There's a reason so few matrons become superintendents. They don't take responsibility. Mrs. Oliver and her mousy colleague Miss Gordon disapprove of my methods. They don't see it's the nature of children to be naughty and the job of those who love them to keep them in check.

If my only duties involved the children, life would be very smooth. But I write constant reports home as well as articles for missionary papers. I write applications for government grants, and I have to get along with missionaries, government officials, and anyone else who thinks they know my tasks better than I. Most mornings I sit in the anteroom between my bedroom and the drawing room writing until I can't see straight, which is what I'm doing when Sajiva brings me a calling card. Mrs. Monomohini Wheeler, Inspectress of Schools, has come to call. No doubt to remind me of her position. Many years ago, Mrs. Wheeler and I were at school together, her father a native clergyman, and mine a lowly hotelier. She married a missionary and was left a widow with two children. Now she has a government post while I toil at mission minutiae. I adjust my skirt and order refreshments while Sajiva seats Mrs. Wheeler at the small table on my veranda and takes a position near the door.

"Mrs. Wheeler, how good of you to call." I pour out tea and wait. She's wearing a small hat that's slightly crushed from being under her *topi*.

"Do you have a head matron for the orphanage?" she asks.

That's a bit abrupt. "Why do you ask?" I counter.

"The lower veranda is filthy with food refuse and bits of clothing. I'm surprised to see such disarray at the Female Mission," Mrs. Wheeler says.

"I'm short-handed at the moment." I look around. "Sajiva?"

"Yes, Mem," Sajiva glides forward.

"Mrs. Wheeler tells me the lower veranda needs attention. See to it immediately."

"Yes, Mem," Sajiva says. He bows and rushes out calling to the housemaid on duty.

I turn my attention back to Mrs. Wheeler. "What brings you here? Not to inspect the lower veranda, surely?" I ask.

"No." Mrs. Wheeler puts down her cup. "In the course of my duties, I visit your *zenanas*."

My stomach lurches. Mrs. Wheeler looks for breaches of conduct. "I trust all is in order. I visit as frequently as I'm able to be sure the lessons are going well. Are you concerned about the lessons?"

"You appear to be meeting the standards," Mrs. Wheeler says. "However, I've encountered several instances that show a lack of concern for teacher behavior and qualifications."

"I assure you every teacher is fully qualified."

Mrs. Wheeler shakes her head. "Miss Pigot, you employ *zenana* teachers who've been turned out of other missions for gross misconduct."

I stir my porcelain cup with its small blue flowers around the rim. "Mrs. Wheeler, you have good connections and a fine education. When you fell upon hard times, you obtained a respected government position. Such is not the same for most women. They turn to the missionary community for employment. If they lose their position, they're penniless."

"You avoid my question."

"These women need help. We frequently have vacancies for matrons or *zenana* teachers. I've employed Mrs. Oliver as a matron, for example. I believe in second chances. Didn't our Savior say the same?" I smile.

"Nevertheless, the *zenana* ladies shouldn't be exposed to such women," Mrs. Wheeler says.

"Everyone in my employ knows any irregularity results in immediate dismissal."

"Then you must be unaware of what goes on. When I inspected your school at Kidderpore, I observed the Christian woman in charge sitting with an utter disregard to modesty. Here at Bow Bazar there are native Christian teachers wearing saris with a certain border, the type of sari favored by women of disreputable character.

And on one of my visits," she continues, "a *box-wallah* appeared. As the peddler set out his wares, a Christian teacher came forward. When she bent over, the upper part of her body was so poorly covered it was as if she were naked from the waist up." Mrs. Wheeler touches her bodice. "I was deeply shocked. No respectable lady would appear as this woman did. I'm sure the Scottish ladies would be appalled if they knew how their teachers dress."

The woman is so harsh. I can't think why she's so uncharitable. "Mrs. Wheeler, you're not in much contact with the average Indian woman, and you wear European clothing. You may have forgotten that native women aren't as particular about their dress as educated women would like them to be."

Mrs. Wheeler purses her lips. "Christian women, especially teachers, must set an example of modesty. As Superintendent you're responsible for the appearance and behavior of everyone on your staff."

"How kind of you to bring these matters to my attention," I say with a straight face. "As it happens, the Ladies' Association is pleased with my work, as are the parents of our students. I'm sure you're aware we have fifty-six fee-paying students in our Upper School. You mention three occasions you deem inappropriate. I regret your discomfort. But I can't police everyone and still do my job, which is to insure our students place well on government examinations. I'll have a word with our matrons and teachers."

Mrs. Wheeler finally leaves, probably running to The Reverend Hastie with her observations.

I'm lonely without Mr. Wilson's company and encouragement. My only solace is Kali Churn Banerjee's frequent visits. We've known each other almost twenty years. I know his wife and children. Six of his children attend our school. He lives about half a mile away; close enough to stop at the school as he goes to work at the High Court.

Kali Churn picks up his children about five o'clock. One girl has a later class, so he sends the others home in one carriage and waits to leave with her an hour later. Sometimes he comes up to my veranda and we talk. Nothing much. Just about his day and mine.

Kali Churn helps with tasks for the Upper School. He draws up the program of studies and assists me with my reports. He arranges our monthly social gatherings. When he has meetings in the evening, I invite him to dine with the teachers. Kali Churn sometimes eats in the drawing room. Perhaps to get a break from the women.

Kali Churn and Mr. James do public preaching on Sundays. Mr. James is a Baptist. I often invite them to rest at my house during the heat of the day. Once, Kali Churn came in his stocking feet carrying his boots and grimacing.

"Nothing to worry about," Mr. James says. "His boots are too tight, and he had to remove them. I don't know why you wore them in the Hot Weather."

"They're a gift from my wife," Kali Churn replies. "But they aren't meant for standing. And I haven't worn them for some time. Now my feet are too swollen to put them back on. And we have another preaching engagement. This is a dreadful situation." He shakes his head with dismay.

I look at his stiff shoes. I don't know how he even put them on in the first place. The leather is cracked, and the sole of one shoe is peeling. I don't know why men want to wear leather in our climate. It has to be constantly polished or it rots with mildew. "I may have a pair of slippers you can use. Help yourselves to *tiffin*. It's a bit sparse now. The teachers ate earlier. I'll be right back."

I select a pair of slippers from the collection I keep for gifts. They're a soft felt, not suitable for outside wear, but it's the only pair I have that will fit Kali Churn. At least the slippers are black, so they won't stand out too much from Kali Churn's trousers.

"Here, try these on. Not so sturdy as leather, but decent enough for the purpose," I say.

"Miss Pigot, you're truly a mother to me. Making sure I'm not in my stocking feet," Kali Churn nods.

"Now," I say, "tell me how your preaching went this morning."

"We had a very good crowd," Kali Churn says. "We stood in the bazar under the shadow of some houses and started reading from a tract on Jesus's life."

"And people stopped to listen," Mr. James continues.

"Did they stay for the entire session?" I ask.

Kali Churn wipes his mouth. "There was a small boy with a parcel. He stood a few minutes. And a man carrying a bundle of straw put down his burden to listen."

"Possibly he wanted an excuse to rest," Mr. James laughs. "I'm most touched by the little girls we see. I thought about bringing them here, but they may have families. They stand there with their bright eyes, sometimes carrying a younger child with its little feet clinging around the older one's waist."

I gaze at the two stalwart young men in my drawing room. Kali Churn with his dark eyes, smooth skin, and enthusiasm for life. Mr. James, English to the core and committed to sharing God's word in every possible way. Kali Churn's slight build looks smaller next to stocky Mr. James. I try to imagine Mr. Hastie preaching in a bazar. Impossible. I return to the present conversation.

"Did you see any women?" I ask.

"No," says Kali Churn. "Most of our hearers are men. Mr. James and I are more taken with the children. Perhaps because we wish them a good future."

"How I wish I could go with you one time, but it wouldn't be appropriate for me to go out into the crowds," I say.

"Which is where we must return." Mr. James wipes his hands on a napkin and stands.

"Not now, during the heat of the day," I say. "Everyone will be resting and so should you. If you've finished eating, please wash your hands and rest in my bedroom."

"We couldn't inconvenience you," Mr. James says.

"Nonsense. I'll be here in the drawing room. Stay until it's cooler."

When the gentlemen leave the room, I continue with my endless reports until I hear a commotion outside. Sajiva rushes into the room with a distraught expression.

"Mem, there's a crowd in the courtyard. They demand to see Caroline Swaries."

My pen nib breaks. That girl is a constant source of trouble. She sneaks out, disrespects the staff. And now we have ruffians at the gate. "Tell them to leave."

"They refuse." Sajiva holds out a slate with a crude message suggesting illicit activities with Caroline and my orphans. I consider whether I should wake the men but decide to handle things myself. I go downstairs and find a mob of ten or twenty young men. Sajiva and the groundskeeper stand on either side of me and shout at the crowd. I notice the men waving sticks. My breathing becomes shallow. I shout out in Bengali, ordering them off the property. The crowd presses closer.

A rock passes by my head. More follow, and I duck behind the railing. Sajiva leaves me to rouse the household. Mr. James and Kali Churn rush onto the lower veranda. The *khansama* runs out with a cleaver. The struggle raises clouds of dust until I can hardly breathe. The men detach the railing to make clubs of their own. Kali Churn tells me to go inside, but I refuse.

Mr. James and the men jump to the courtyard, presenting a united front and swirling their clubs. The mob begins to back away. I don't know whether it's the presence of an Englishman or the fury of my defenders. They push the mob out the gate and lock it. I can still hear them shouting. Mr. James and Kali Churn carry me back inside and lay me on the cane lounge on the verandah. Mrs. Tremearne comes out with a cool cloth to wipe my face. I notice she's crying. Sajiva brings strong tea.

Mrs. Ellis comes to me, her hair flying around her face. "The matrons and I have looked everywhere for Caroline Swaries. She's nowhere on the property."

I nod. "Notify her family. Tell them that if she comes back, she won't be admitted."

Kali Churn hovers next to the lounge. "Are you feeling better, Miss Pigot? Would you like us to stay longer?"

I notice Kali Churn hasn't managed to pull on both sleeves of his coat. Strange to see him so disheveled. "I'm quite recovered now. You and Mr. James can continue your preaching."

"I don't like to leave you in this state," Kali Churn says.

I pat his hand. "All is well now. And Mrs. Tremearne is here if I need anything."

Mr. James stands at the door holding his *topi*. "Come, Babu Banerjee. The crisis is over. Put your coat on properly, and we'll return to our work.

Chapter 5
"They Should Go Elsewhere"

1881

William Hastie

Mr. Wilson is back from furlough. I hoped he'd retire from the field, but here he is again. I invite him and his cousin to chum with Mr. Fish and me, so we can reduce expenses. And what does he do in return? Mr. Wilson objects to sharing the dinner table with a native convert who's still a student. Not only that, he insists on having his old rooms at the top of the house across the courtyard, which means I have to relocate Nitya Gopal. I concede on the rooms but make it clear Nitya Gopal dines with us.

While Mr. Fish, Mr. Wilson, and I are at breakfast, the post arrives. Mixed in with mail for Scottish College is an envelope addressed to Nitya Gopal at the Free Church on Duff Street. Clearly the postman mixed the letters, but that isn't the point.

I wave the letter. "Mr. Fish, Mr. Wilson, see what I have here—a letter addressed to the Free College."

"Typical mistake," Mr. Wilson says.

"The letter is from Reverend Thomson to Nitya Gopal. Why would a letter to Mr. Mukherjee be addressed to the Free College?" I ask.

"The answer's obvious," Mr. Wilson says. "You decided to censor Reverend Thomson because he didn't support your plans for a new mission and forbade any correspondence between Mr. Thomson and our students. You didn't accept Mr. Edwards' advice that Mr. Thomson and Nitya Gopal had a close relationship."

How dare Mr. Wilson question my decisions? Mr. Thomson blocked all my reforms, and now he's interfering from his new post in Pune. I feel my temper rising. "That doesn't explain this letter."

"It does," Mr. Wilson says. "You just don't want to admit it. Nitya Gopal and Mr. Thomson have been writing letters behind your back, and Nitya Gopal picks them up at the Free College." Mr. Wilson gives me a cynical smile. "What will you do with the letter?"

"I'll have Nitya Gopal open it and read it to me. Falak," I call, "take this letter to Mr. Mukherjee. Tell him to bring it with him and come to my study."

"Are you sure that's wise?" Mr. Wilson asks, "opening another man's mail?" Mr. Wilson chuckles.

I throw my napkin on the table and retire to my study. A few minutes later Falak returns with the letter. Mr. Mukherjee isn't in his room. I take the letter back, wave Falak away, and open it. Nothing much to it. I'll send it to the Mission Committee so the members can see for themselves the kind of insubordination I encounter.

My so-called superiors at home don't support me as they should. They reinstate Mr. Thomson after I suspend him and send him to Pune, completely undercutting my authority. When I respond with an honest application for a university position as a lecturer in the Hebrew language, they fall all over themselves justifying their behavior. Mr. MacLagan, a member of the Mission Committee, confesses he disapproves of my stance with the Free Church and censure of Mr. Thomson. The truth at last. Further, he admits my work as Principal and missionary is exemplary. Wants me to continue here for many years. Unlikely, but satisfying to know

Mr. Herdman, another member, also praises my work and commends my self-denial on behalf of my students. He thinks I'm too forceful with my colleagues. As far as I'm concerned, if they can't obey my leadership, they should go elsewhere. I doubt he'll come to their defense again. Now that I've made my point, I'll continue in Calcutta a bit longer.

Despite our occasional disagreements, it's surprisingly pleasant to have Mr. Wilson back among us. The rest has done him a great deal of good. And he's an excellent assistant. Mr. Fish is jealous, of course. He's accustomed to being the only man I trust. He still is, if only because he's too timid to go against me. I tell Mr. Wilson to watch his back.

Mary Pigot

I'm listening to the rain and watching Sajiva lay out the breakfast things. He's so precise. It's really the *khitmutgar's* job to serve as the table attendant, but Sajiva argues that since I'm on the veranda, it's not worth the *khitmutgar's* time when he could be supervising staff meals. I like Sajiva. He's unobtrusive.

"Shall I drop the *chick*, Mem?" he asks. "The rain's coming in."

I nod. He lowers the bamboo screen, instantly plunging the veranda into gloom while increasing the ambient humidity. Like most people, I dislike the monsoons. I watch a brown gecko crawl over the veranda ledge. At least he'll reduce the mosquito population.

Mrs. Tremearne comes in. "Good Morning, Miss Pigot. Will you be coming to the *zenanas* with me today?"

"No. I have to supervise a staff change."

"Oh?" Mrs. Tremearne looks at me curiously.

"I'm terminating Mrs. Oliver's employment," I explain.

"Are you sure that's wise?" Mrs. Tremearne asks. "She's got a temper. You know how she was when you disciplined Joboni. If you dismiss Mrs. Oliver, she'll look for ways to damage your reputation."

"All the more reason to be rid of her." I begin counting off my fingers. "She questions my decisions. On her recommendation, which I foolishly took at face value, I engaged Mrs. Pigott as a matron, only to find out she's Roman Catholic."

"I didn't think you cared for such things," Mrs. Tremearne says.

"I don't, and I needed a matron. But the Scottish church opposes Catholics, and I could be censured for knowingly hiring one."

"But you didn't know," Mrs. Tremearne says.

"Not when I hired Mrs. Pigott. But I kept her on after I found out."

"I'm sure you had a good reason," Mrs. Tremearne says.

"If Mrs. Oliver or Mrs. Pigott revealed she was Catholic, I wouldn't have hired her. But I'm not going to dismiss her for that. The point is Mrs. Oliver knows this is the Scottish Orphanage, and she shouldn't have recommended someone unsuitable."

"You don't usually dismiss people on such simple grounds," Mrs. Tremearne says. "Mrs. Oliver hasn't broken any rules."

"Why are you arguing with me?" My voice is exasperated. "Mrs. Oliver is disrespectful. Three days ago, she offered to resign. I would have accepted there and then, but I can't let her leave with nothing," I say.

"So, you're dismissing her?" Mrs. Tremearne asks.

"If I dismiss Mrs. Oliver without notice, I have to give her a month's salary, and that's what I shall do."

William Hastie

I hear Mr. Wilson clumping downstairs and humming under his breath. He takes his seat at the breakfast table. I rattle my newspaper. There's a basket of papayas and guavas on the table and another with bread. The *khitmutgar* pours out coffee.

"You seem in a good mood this morning," I say.

"It's a fine morning, and I've just written a letter to my wife," Mr. Wilson says. "Writing Katy always lifts my mood. For a few minutes, it's as if there aren't so many miles between us. Anything of interest in the newspaper, Mr. Hastie?"

"The usual nonsense. That fellow who assassinated the American President Garfield is on trial," I say.

"Who's that?" Mr. Wilson asks.

"A madman named Charles Guiteau," I say. "Testified a few days ago, trying to say he wasn't in his right mind. So, Mr. Wilson, will you have eggs this morning?"

"Just some bread and oily butter," Mr. Wilson replies. "I do miss proper butter."

Mr. Fish enters the room smelling of strong soap. "Good morning, gentlemen."

"You're looking somewhat dapper," I say.

"Yes, sir. Thought it was time to trim my mustache," Mr. Fish replies. "Mr. Wilson, when shall we leave for the Female Mission?"

"About half past ten should get us there in plenty of time," Mr. Wilson answers.

"I don't know why you gentlemen persist in doing that woman's job for her. Miss Pigot claims to run the Female Mission without assistance, when in fact she couldn't do anything if you two weren't always going over to teach or do accounts. What is it you're doing today?" I ask.

"Assisting with the oral examinations for the Upper School. They're the fee-paying students." Mr. Wilson explains as if I don't know. "The students are individually examined, and Miss Pigot doesn't have enough teaching staff to complete the process. Surely you don't begrudge our participation?"

"Mr. Wilson, you're free to do as you wish on your own time. I merely point out that Miss Pigot can't run the Female Mission without using our staff, yet she refuses to unite our two efforts for the greater good. I don't see how our Mission Committee at home can allow this situation to continue. And you, Mr. Fish? You're going with Mr. Wilson?"

Mr. Fish's pale grey eyes dart around the room. "Well, sir, I thought it would be better if both of us went, rather than just one. Unless you have a need for me here."

I raise my eyebrows. "Not at all, Mr. Fish. By all means, accompany Mr. Wilson. Do make a note in your diary. I may need an accounting of how many occasions the College staff are called upon to provide services to the Female Mission." I return to reading *The Statesman*.

Mary Pigot

"Mr. Wilson. Mr. Fish. Thank you so much for coming," I say. "The girls are waiting for you upstairs, Mr. Fish. Mr. Wilson, I hope you don't mind, but could you possibly help me make sense of the accounts? I can't get the figures to match up, and the Ladies' Association is fussy about that sort of thing."

"Of course, Miss Pigot. I'll do what I can," Mr. Wilson says.

"Thank you so much," I say. "Mr. Fish, come with me. I'll escort you to the examination room. The girls will wait their turn outside the door, and you'll have the room to yourself." I chatter as we leave the room. Otherwise the only sound will be our shoes on the wooden stairs.

I return to the drawing room to find Mr. Wilson looking at the newspaper.

"Don't you have newspapers at the College?" I ask.

"Mr. Hastie only orders *The Statesman*. I much prefer the *Indian Daily News*. I'm just looking at the cricket scores."

"Dear Mr. Wilson, please come into the anteroom," I invite. "I've got everything laid out. All the bills of sale, and daily accounts. I just can't seem to get the figures to come out correctly. You see my worksheet here. It's all a muddle."

"That's fine, Miss Pigot. I'll just start the sequence again, and we'll see what happens. Go about your other tasks." Mr. Wilson takes off his jacket and rolls up his sleeves.

The anteroom is a small area between the drawing room and my bedroom. I use it as an office, but it's too small for the task. Everyone throws papers on the desk and they get shoved into drawers. By the time I'm ready to make the account report, the chits are crumpled and sometimes lost. Mr. Wilson tells me to keep them in order as they arrive, but it's too much trouble. Mr. Wilson sorts them out for me. I like to stop in while he works to see if things are going smoothly. I enjoy talking with him. But today Mr. Wilson tells me to stay away until *tiffin*. I don't know why he gets so put out just because I'm not good with paperwork.

"Mr. Wilson, it's time for *tiffin*." I stand before him, my arms akimbo. "Everything's laid out in the drawing room. Do put aside your work and come."

Mr. Wilson stands, stretches and puts his jacket back on.

"Your hair is coming out of its bun," Mr. Wilson says. "Katy's hair does that sometimes."

I don't know how to respond. I pat my hair self-consciously. "It's Bengali food," I chatter. "Biryani with vegetables and chapatti. I told the *khansama* not to add many spices. Will that be all right for Mr. Fish? I don't have any English food."

"If this is what you have, it will do. He gets plenty of English food at the College. It smells lovely," Mr. Wilson says.

"Have some beer while we wait for Mr. Fish," I offer. "I thought he'd be down by now."

"He's probably double checking his marks. Ah, here he is now."

Mr. Fish hands me his notes on the oral examinations and wipes his brow with a slightly dingy handkerchief.

"Have some beer," Mr. Wilson hands him a glass. "You must be thirsty after a morning of oral examinations."

"Yes, I am. Thank you."

Mr. Fish takes the glass but doesn't quench his thirst. He puts the glass on a low table. "What do we have for *tiffin*?" he asks.

"Vegetable biryani. Have you had it before?" I ask.

Mr. Fish makes a face of distaste. "I don't recognize it. What's in it?"

"Well," I say. "In addition to the rice, there are carrots, cauliflower, and some tomatoes. There's cardamom, turmeric and coriander, for a light spice."

Mr. Fish decides it's safe to try the food, though he eats mostly rice. He and Mr. Wilson sit at the *tiffin* table. Mr. Wilson takes two large portions.

"I hope you don't mind, Miss Pigot," Mr. Wilson says. "Mr. Hastie keeps to the Scottish diet as much as he can, so our food is very bland." Sweat from the spices runs down the side of Mr. Wilson's face.

Mr. Fish makes a small mound of uneaten food in the center of his plate. "Miss Pigot, aren't you going to eat?"

Even though he didn't take very much biryani, I think he's wasteful to leave it. I shake my head. "I seldom eat when others are present. I'll eat later in the evening." Thank goodness my *khitmutgar* comes in to clear the table. "Now that *tiffin* is finished, will you take some whiskey, Mr. Wilson?" I ask. "I won't ask you, Mr. Fish. You haven't finished your beer."

Mr. Fish clears his throat. "I don't drink beer during the day. And I must get back to the examinations. I could use your help, Mr. Wilson," Mr. Fish rises.

"I'm sorry, Mr. Fish. I haven't completed the accounts for Miss Pigot yet," Mr. Wilson says.

"I thought we were both doing the examinations."

"That was the original plan," I interrupt. "But I'm late with the account report, and I can't make any sense of it. Do forgive me for taking Mr. Wilson from you." I try to look humble.

"There's nothing to forgive, Miss Pigot. As always, we're both at your disposal," Mr. Fish says in his thick brogue.

December 1881

My Christmas comes early this year. The Ladies' Association engaged Miss Georgiana Smail to serve as my assistant. Mrs. Ellis and I stand on the quay to meet her and arrange for her baggage. We nod to the Walkers. Colonel Walker is an Elder in St. Andrew's and close friends with Mr. Hastie. They and Mr. Gillan never stop trying to get the Female Mission back under their thumbs. Mrs. Walker is Miss Smail's sister. I'm nervous she may try to influence her sister to question my methods of organization.

I don't know who told Miss Smail about the vacancy. She could've read about it in the newspaper—or her sister might've written her. Miss Smail didn't agree to a specific term of service, and she paid her own passage. She has no commitment to the Female Mission beyond her own inclination. I wonder if Miss Smail will come back with us or go to her sister's home first.

A small woman with a parasol is on the gangway. That's probably her. Colonel Walker and his wife step forward. I'm not going to push in front of them. The two women embrace each other and walk towards me arm-in-arm. Miss Smail is a slender version of Mrs. Walker. Both have blue eyes, pale skin, and dark hair. Mrs. Walker's skin is a bit blistered. I think she forgets to wear her *topi* in the garden.

"My dear Miss Pigot, allow me to introduce my sister and your assistant, Miss Smail," Mrs. Walker gives me a longsuffering smile. "She's decided her place is with you this evening."

"It's a great pleasure to meet you." I extend my hand. "This is Mrs. Ellis, our senior staff member. Will you ride with us to Bow Bazar?"

Miss Smail inclines her head and starts to follow Mrs. Ellis.

"Surely not," Mrs. Walker interrupts. "Georgiana, at least allow us to drive you to the mission. It's so long since we've seen each other." She pouts.

"Would you mind awfully, Miss Pigot?" Miss Smail finally says.

Yes, I would, but it would be rude to protest. "Of course not," I say. "Dinner is at eight o'clock. We're punctual at the mission."

"We'll just show Georgiana a few of the sights and have tea. I'll have her to you in plenty of time for dinner. Come along, Georgiana."

Since it's Miss Smail's first evening with us, I make a dinner party of it for the teachers as well. I order the *khansama* to prepare a simple meal of mulligatawny soup, roasted chicken with peas and potatoes, and caramel custard for dessert, which is the best we can afford.

The clock chimes eight o'clock. At quarter past eight, Miss Smail still isn't here. The teachers sit in their places around the long table on the veranda, conversing quietly as I fume.

"Sajiva, you may begin serving," I say. Ten minutes later Miss Smail arrives.

"Miss Pigot," Miss Smail says from the doorway. "I'm sorry to be late, but I haven't seen my sister in so long, and we had so much to talk about."

"Come take your seat," I say. "We're halfway through our soup. In future, please remember we're punctual about meals. Miss Smail, this is Sajiva. He'll explain the household to you tomorrow."

Sajiva puts his hands together. "Welcome, Mem."

"Thank you," Miss Smail says with barely a glance. "May I have some soup?"

Sajiva fills Miss Smail's bowl.

"What is it?" she asks.

"Soup, obviously," I reply dryly. "We don't have mulligatawny soup very often, but I'm sure you'll enjoy it when you visit your sister."

It's difficult orienting a new arrival from Scotland. No matter how much they read about Calcutta, they remain unprepared. Some take to it with alacrity, embracing the people, customs and even the dust. Others constantly compare Calcutta with Scotland. Within the week, I know Miss Smail is in the latter group. Each morning we meet for breakfast on the veranda. I with my sambar and rice. She has what we call *rumble tumble,* and she calls scrambled eggs and bread.

"How are you this morning, Miss Smail? Are you finding the bed more comfortable?"

"The mattress is hard," Miss Smail complains. "And I keep getting tangled up in the netting. Is it really necessary?"

"A feather mattress such as you're used to would attract vermin. I'm sure your sister's mattresses are stuffed with horsehair. We can't afford horsehair, so we use nut husks. As to the netting...you're welcome to provide needy mosquitos with a meal, but I don't recommend it."

"Yes, yes. You're right, of course." Miss Smail picks at her meal. "It's just that everything is so strange."

"Take this," I say, placing a large key in Miss Smail's soft, small hand. "This is the key to the storeroom. Each morning you will issue the *khansama* foodstuffs for the day. Mrs. Ellis will explain the process to you."

"Why are you giving this to me?" Miss Smail asks.

"Mrs. Ellis is my senior staff person. You're my assistant—you must do it. And you're also in charge of giving the *khansama* and Sajiva funds for expenses and keeping the household accounts. Mrs. Ellis will show you."

"But why can't Mrs. Ellis keep doing it?" Miss Smail pouts. "I didn't come to do domestic things. I came to work in the mission."

"And so you do. You came to be my assistant. And your first lesson is that there is a strict hierarchy of staff and servants. Mrs. Ellis functioned as my second. Now, you're my second. Whoever is my second handles the storeroom and all purchases. So that's what you'll learn first."

Miss Smail looks overwhelmed. "But I can't speak to the servants. I don't understand what they're saying."

"Mrs. Ellis will shadow you while you learn. And your Bengali lessons begin this morning. You can't achieve anything until you speak the language. I hope you're a quick learner."

"But I..." Miss Smail begins.

I wave my hand. "Sajiva is here to introduce you to the *pundit*. I wish you good morning."

I wonder how many months it will be before Miss Smail is of any actual use?

When I was a child, before my father died, we celebrated Christmas. We went to St. John's Church and decorated our gateposts with poinsettias and marigold garlands, and we strolled by the posh shops in the European side of town. Some of them had mechanical toys. And there were beautiful dolls. Not for me, of course—those were for the English. But it was fun to see it. My father used to tell stories about when he grew up in Scotland. I couldn't imagine a country so cold.

Since I started working for the Ladies' Association, I've had to stop celebrating Christmas. The Church of Scotland doesn't approve. I do have the groundskeeper decorate our gates. Miss Smail asks about that. I tell her anything that draws attention to the Female Mission is good for our work. I don't mention how much I enjoy it.

On Christmas Day, Miss Smail and I will attend St. Andrew's. Then she'll stay with her sister through the New Year. They can celebrate *Hogmanay* to their heart's content, and we'll be glad of a break. Miss Smail's arrival, which I'd thought of as an early Christmas gift, turns out to be coal in my stocking. Nothing suits her. She has a notebook she carries everywhere. She says it's to write down words and take notes so she remembers everything. Perhaps.

Chapter 6
"The Ladies Sent Me A Viper"

January – March 1882
William Hastie

It appears 1882 is off to a quiet start; at least it is at Sealdah Railway Station. Not nearly as busy as a normal day. The platform is deserted with no other passengers for the first-class cars. Even the porters are dozing.

The Reverend Gillan joins me on the platform for the train to Dum Dum. We're invited to celebrate *Hogmanay* with the Walkers. I don't often see Mr. Gillan looking so relaxed. Perhaps it's the whiskey we shared after church last night. He extends his hand with an impish smile. "Good morning and happy New Year, Reverend Hastie."

"The same to you. That was a stirring service you preached last night. It gave me much to think about."

"Really? What sins do you repent?" Mr. Gillan chuckles. "You're the most punctilious man I know."

"I wasn't thinking of my sins so much. I'm more concerned about my failure to restore harmony between the College and the Female Mission," I say. "It's the one thing the Foreign Mission Committee specifically charged me to do, and so far, I've failed at every turn. Miss Pigot won't listen to reason, and I can't think of any way to persuade her of the benefits of placing the Female Mission directly under the Corresponding Board."

"I've never found Miss Pigot to be a reasonable woman. She only has a local education, after all." Mr. Gillan looks down the track and takes out his watch. "The train's a bit late, I think. I'm sure you share my hope that Miss Smail's arrival blows winds of change. She's staying with her family for the holidays, so we'll see her today."

The train pulls up to the platform belching steam. People near the second-class cars push forward to board. Mr. Gillan and I show our tickets to the conductor who tips his cap. We find our compartment and settle in for the short journey.

While Mr. Gillan reads his newspaper, my thoughts wander to Miss Smail. I wonder how much younger she is than her sister. Mrs. Walker has a few streaks of grey in her hair and is somewhat stout. After meeting Miss Smail, I see what attracted Colonel Walker to his wife. Miss Smail is small-boned with luminous blue eyes and lustrous dark hair. And she's not afraid of me. Not that she should be, but a man of my standing often intimidates young women.

Colonel Walker sent a *gharry* to meet us and soon we drive up the circular drive to the Walker bungalow. It's a substantial structure, befitting Colonel Walker's rank, with deep verandas on all sides. Our host stands on the steps.

"No regimentals today, Colonel?" Mr. Gillan asks.

"Just an intimate gathering to celebrate *Hogmanay.* Mrs. Walker and her sister prepared a day of delights," Colonel Walker says. "Come inside. The ladies are in the drawing room."

The room is as lovely as the climate allows. The walls are whitewashed since the damp precludes wallpaper, but Mrs. Walker has put up attractive stenciling and local fabrics provide splashes of color. There's a large mat on the floor, cane sofas and chairs with cushions.

Mr. Gillan and I give our *topis* to the servant.

"My dear, our guests have arrived," Colonel Walker announces. "Gentlemen, it's time to start the festivities. Will you have a dram of whiskey?"

"Isn't it a bit early?" Mr. Gillan asks.

"Nonsense. Normal rules suspend for *Hogmanay*. Ladies, will you join us?" the Colonel asks as he pours.

"Alexander, you're embarrassing our guests. Welcome Mr. Hastie, Mr. Gillan. You must forgive my husband. It's the military influence, I'm afraid," Mrs. Walker says. "And *Hogmanay* is his favorite holiday. Georgiana, would you ask the *durwan* to bring tea."

In due course, the servants bring a tea table and appropriate dishes. Mrs. Walker serves out the tea.

"Miss Smail," I say, "how are you getting along with Miss Pigot?"

"Would anyone like a piece of shortbread?" Mrs. Walker asks. "Georgiana and I baked them especially for the holiday."

"You must excuse the poor quality of the butter," Miss Smail says in her light Scottish accent. For a moment I think I'm at home.

The conversation turns to the impossibility of getting ingredients to make proper food. After the servant clears the tea things, I try to return the conversation to Miss Pigot.

"Anyone care for a game of whist?" Colonel Walker asks.

"I don't care for card games," Miss Smail says.

"Good. That makes our numbers exactly even. Mr. Hastie, what say you and I play against my wife and Mr. Gillan?" Colonel Walker picks up the deck of cards.

We play until the servants begin lighting the kerosene lamps. Colonel Walker and I take most of the tricks. Mr. Gillan is a poor player, and Mrs. Walker's attention wanders, but they keep the game lively.

"I think I'll stroll in your gardens to stretch my legs," I say. "Mrs. Walker, will you join me?"

I am pleased when she says yes. As we walk, Mrs. Walker points out her English flowerbeds, explaining each plant. She points out multi-colored carnations and sweet peas, all nicely in bloom for the Cold Season. I compliment her and ask about a citrus fragrance I detect.

"That's just wax flowers," she says dismissively. "Come and see my camellias."

She leads me further into the garden. It's a pleasant evening. We gaze at the stars a few minutes and turn to go back.

"It must be nice for you to have your sister nearby," I say, hoping to find out how Miss Smail and Miss Pigot get along.

"I'm afraid I've enjoyed it more than she. Georgiana itches to get to work. When she isn't drawing up lists, she's putting together reports to send home," Mrs. Walker says.

"Reports?" I ask.

"Yes. Apparently, the ladies don't think Miss Pigot gives them enough information and asked Georgiana to send particulars about everything she sees," Mrs. Walker says.

"And what has she seen?" I ask.

"She won't say. Just that nothing is as she expected. I told her that's what India's like. Nothing is ever what you think it should be," Mrs. Walker sighs. "But she says it's more than that."

The *durwan* draws near us holding up a lantern.

Mrs. Walker's tone changes. "What is it?" she snaps.

"Excuse me, Memsahib, the Sahib asks you to come in now. The darkness," the *durwan* says.

"Give me your lamp." Mrs. Walker reaches for the light. "We were having such a nice conversation, but Alexander's probably tired of entertaining Mr. Gillan."

We return in time to change for dinner and enjoy the pre-dinner peg at leisure. This time Mr. Gillan and the ladies join us. At precisely eight o'clock, the *durwan* throws open the dining room doors and announces dinner. Colonel Walker escorts his sister-in-law, so Mr. Gillan and I walk on either side of Mrs. Walker. The table sparkles with a snowy tablecloth, ivy greens running down the center, and two silver candelabras. The place settings are perfectly aligned. Colonel and Mrs. Walker take their seats at either end of the table. Mr. Gillan sits to the right of Colonel Walker, and I to the left of his wife. Miss Smail's place is centered across from us. I'm surprised Mrs. Walker has an uneven number of guests, but perhaps there was no one else suitable available. As we take our places, the *khitmutgar* and his assistants pour Madeira wine and begin bringing out the food. To my surprise, the starter looks like Cock-a-Leekie soup.

"Do my eyes deceive me, Mrs. Walker?" Mr. Gillan asks. "Is this Cock-a-Leekie soup?"

"A modified version." Mrs. Walker dimples becomingly. "We had to substitute round onions for the leeks. We wanted to serve a traditional meal, but everything is somewhat adapted."

"Damn shame." Colonel Walker's voice booms down the table. "Excuse me Reverends, but the issue of food always frustrates me," he says in a normal voice. "I don't see why the quartermaster doesn't grow proper leeks, or turnips for that matter. When I retire, what I'm most looking forward to at home is the food."

"Colonel Walker," I say. "The opportunity to eat food from home, however modified, is a rare privilege."

After the soup plates clear, we sit for several minutes. Suddenly bagpipes are heard producing their unique sound, excessively loud in a small space. The *durwan* holds open the door to the drawing room. A piper enters and walks around the table playing *Scotland the Brave*.

I haven't felt so joyous since I arrived in Calcutta. "Colonel Walker," I shout, "this is wonderful."

Behind the piper, the *khitmutgar* carries a large platter above his head. When the piper departs, the *khitmutgar* places the platter between Miss Smail and Colonel Walker. The *khitmutgar* and his assistant begin serving our plates.

I look at the brown minced meat on my plate, hardly daring to define it. "Can it be haggis?"

"Depends," Miss Smail says quietly. "Sheep can't be had here, so I substituted turkey. And there's no turnips, but we do have mashed potatoes."

"Mrs. Walker, you have hidden talents, indeed," Mr. Gillan says.

"Not I. Georgiana figured everything out. And she personally prepared Tipsy Laird Trifle for dessert."

"My compliments to you, Miss Smail," I say. "You've given two old missionaries a taste of home."

"Not so old, I think," she says softly.

The dessert comes in individual cups and is the stuff of dreams.

"Miss Smail," I say, "if you hadn't portioned our servings into glassware, I would consume the entire trifle bowl. The custard is so light, the whipped cream so thick. I don't know how you managed it."

Miss Smail smiles at me showing very even white teeth and a small dimple. "I'm delighted you like it. It was difficult getting it to set, and I had to substitute papaya for the fruit which completely threw things off."

"Don't be so modest, Georgiana," Mrs. Walker says. "My sister is far too humble. In fact, she never takes credit for her accomplishments."

Miss Smail presses me to take a second portion. How can I refuse? Colonel Walker joins me, but Mr. Gillan demurs. After dessert, we move back into the drawing room for coffee and whiskey. We sit in sated comfort until the table clock chimes ten times.

"Oh dear," Mr. Gillan says. "We'll have to hurry, Mr. Hastie, or we'll miss our train."

I speak to Miss Smail on my way out. "May I make a small recommendation regarding your work at the Female Mission?"

"Of course."

"Speak to Mrs. Wheeler, the Government Inspectress of Schools," I advise. "She has information I think you'll find interesting. Good evening."

Mary Pigot

The woman I expected to take on the day-to-day management of the mission complex comes to me every morning with a new list of problems. She complains about the accommodation, the food, the way our teachers dress, how I discipline the children, the cleanliness of the house, and our entertainments. Nothing satisfies her.

"Miss Pigot, we must speak," she says. "Things can't continue as they are. I came here with the purest of motives to assist in every way I can. But the household is poorly managed. There's no order to anything. The Ladies' Association will be appalled to learn of conditions here."

I look at her pale, narrow face. The lace collar at her throat. She would have the servants spend the day sweeping out the dust and whitewashing the walls. We don't have a military household like her sister.

"I'm grateful to have you," I say. "As you point out, there's much to be done. What do you suggest?"

"We need a thorough housecleaning," Miss Small says. "The walls are filthy. Everyone here needs better hygiene."

"Why don't you supervise the household?" I suggest. "You can work with Sajiva."

"Tell him to obey me," Miss Smail demands. "I take him through the house and show what needs to be done. He nods, but nothing happens."

I allow myself a small smile. "Servants are more responsive to Bengali than English direction. Perhaps you could begin learning Bengali. The teachers are here in the mornings."

On another day, probably a Monday, Miss Smail opens the conversation with the same question as Mr. Gillan.

"Miss Pigot, why don't you attend St. Andrews?"

"I think it better to attend the native church with our teachers and orphans." I don't say it's better for me. "It's wonderful that you represent the Female Mission at St. Andrew's."

Then I excuse myself before she asks me to recite the catechism. I know she runs to her sister's house to elaborate on our business. I suspect she writes home with her misunderstandings.

I expect Mr. Wilson to eat *tiffin* before he starts helping me with my correspondence. Any number of guests may stop in. The table is ready in the drawing room, and the boy waves a fan to keep the flies away. But no one's here yet. Miss Smail gets overly upset about these things. She bursts into my anteroom.

"Miss Pigot, there's a table full of food out there and no one to eat it," Miss Smail complains.

"I always set a *tiffin* table for anyone who stops by. We're known for our hospitality."

"We're known for waste. And flies," Miss Smail retorts.

"The boy does his best."

Miss Smail turns into the drawing room. I hear voices. One of them sounds like Mr. Wilson introducing himself. I go to the doorway.

"Mr. Wilson, I'm glad you're here," I say. "Miss Smail worried there wouldn't be anyone to share *tiffin*."

"And I came specifically to partake," Mr. Wilson says tilting his head to one side.

"Really? Don't they serve *tiffin* at the College?" Miss Smail asks.

Mr. Wilson smiles. "It's not as generous. I'm here to help Miss Pigot, but I came early to help myself, so to speak. Join me. You can tell me your impressions of Calcutta."

Mr. Wilson motions Miss Smail to take a seat at the table. He pours out fruit juice for Miss Smail and makes himself a plate of cheese and naan bread.

"Do you like that bread?" Miss Smail asks.

"It holds the cheese," Mr. Wilson says without expression.

"Mr. Wilson," I say. "When you finish *tiffin*, help me with these letters. The churches at home all want the same information, and it takes so long to write it out for everyone. Besides which, my handwriting is poor."

"I won't be able to stay past six o'clock. I have an engagement this evening," Mr. Wilson says.

"I don't think you'll finish so early."

"I'll do the best I can, but I do have other responsibilities."

"Oh," I say. "I didn't mean... I just thought you'd stay until dinner. Wait, I have an idea. I can send someone for your evening clothes and you can change here. That will save you some time."

"Excuse me," Miss Smail sends me a disapproving glance and retires to the other side of the drawing room where she remains the rest of the evening.

After Mr. Wilson writes out the letters for me, I tell him to change in my bedroom since he has to go through it to reach the washroom. When he emerges, he looks elegant in evening dress. I walk him as far as the downstairs veranda and watch him get into his carriage. It's a clear night. Gazing at the stars I make a wish that can never be granted. Mr. Wilson will never be Principal of Scottish College.

"Miss Pigot, I'm very upset," Miss Smail says.

She sits before me, her shoulders hunched into her ears. I look at her, then glance over the veranda rail before returning my attention. "I'm sorry," I say. "What seems to be the matter?"

"This mission is sponsored by the Ladies' Association of the Church of Scotland. Yet with only one exception, none of the staff are members of our church," Miss Smail says. "I find this deeply distressing."

"If I required church membership, there would be no staff," I say. "The home church sends very few teachers. Matrons and servants have to be recruited locally. What would you have me do?"

"And you, yourself," she begins.

"I?" I ask.

"I spoke with Reverend Gillan. He tells me you aren't a member of St. Andrew's," Miss Smail charges. "It's unacceptable to have our mission led by a woman who isn't part of the Church of Scotland. Reverend Gillan said you belong to the Church of England."

"I haven't attended since I took this position fourteen years ago, nor have I made any secret of my affiliation," I say. "Reverend Thomson and the Ladies knew I was baptized into the Church of England when they engaged me. Have the rules changed?" It takes all my effort to maintain a civil voice. Who does she think she is?

"Reverend Hastie mentioned the Female Mission hasn't had any converts, and I believe it," Miss Smail says aggressively.

"Ask him how many converts he's had since his arrival. The number is very low. In fact, I can only think of one."

"But why aren't we actively evangelizing? The parlor boarders, for example. We could easily teach them the Bible," Miss Smail suggests.

"We could," I admit. "And we do if they express any interest. It's a slow process demonstrating the benefits of Christianity. Their husbands have no charity for the Church of Scotland. They want their wives to learn deportment. Sometimes the women want to learn more, and we're pleased to assist. We take small steps of change. When you speak Bengali, you're welcome to work with them." I smile. "Miss Smail, you don't seem happy here. Am I correct?"

"I'm not happy with how things are done at this mission. I came to spread the Gospel, not administer the house."

"And yet, you can't speak Bengali. Nor did you come as a missionary. You came as Assistant Superintendent. The two positions are quite different."

"You don't want me here," Miss Smail blurts out. "You don't want me to know what's going on and how the Ladies' funds are wasted. But you're too late. I've written my reports."

I sit dumbstruck at her betrayal. I know she's writing letters, but reports? She should have told me. I can't stop her. But to be so underhanded about it. So dishonest. I'm rigid with anger. "I think, under the circumstances, you should find accommodation elsewhere." I stand.

"You can't dismiss me. I'm assigned to the mission," Miss Smail says.

"I'm not dismissing you. I'm ordering you off the premises. You may work or not as you please, but you will no longer live under my roof."

Miss Smail stands with her hands stiffly at her sides. "You'll regret this. I'm not the only one aware of your mismanagement."

"Sajiva," I call. "Miss Smail is moving out. Please have her things packed."

Miss Smail turns her back on me, takes a breath so large I see her ribs expand, and follows Sajiva out of the room.

I sink back into my chair, my head pounding. I feel tears behind my eyes. It's just frustration. I work so hard to bring light and charity to everyone around me. I look after orphans and teach in *zenanas* and supervise schools. I asked for help, and the Ladies sent me a viper. Dear God, what's to become of me?

"My Issues With Miss Pigot Are Purely Constitutional"

April – May, 1882
William Hastie

When I first met Miss Smail, I thought her a breath of fresh air—her piety as unquestionable as her devotion to duty. Her task is more daunting than mine, because as an assistant she can only suggest changes. Miss Pigot thwarts every attempt at reform, even those relating to basic cleanliness. Miss Smail tells me Miss Pigot engages Brahmin cooks at her so-called social gatherings, so unbelievers can maintain their ritual eating. I didn't realize the situation was so dire.

After less than three months, Miss Smail accepts Miss Pigot's demand and moves outside the mission. The Ladies' Association severs Miss Smail's employment. I often see her when I visit the Walker household. She becomes less reticent in my presence and asks Colonel Walker to read a letter she's about to send to Edinburgh to justify her actions. The *durwan* serves out pegs of whiskey as Colonel Walker starts to read in a sotto voice that sounds like gravel hitting the pavement. Miss Smail sits in a cane chair with her hands folded in her lap. She doesn't look at me while her brother-in-law reads.

I quickly understand why Miss Smail didn't read the letter aloud herself. She writes of Miss Pigot's gross mismanagement of funds, the lack of supporting financial vouchers, and the poor condition of the orphans with their frequent illnesses.

I have to put my glass down to prevent spilling it. It's all I can do to sit still. Mrs. Wheeler told me of the immoral lack of deportment she observed, but Miss Smail goes further. It turns out the bulk of the teachers aren't members of the Church of Scotland. Mrs. Tremearne keeps a picture of the Sacred Heart of Jesus and paid for masses to be said for pains in her leg. One matron, another Pigott, is an avowed Roman Catholic. Miss Pigot and many of her teachers identify with the Church of England. How can a mission sponsored by the Church of Scotland be staffed by our enemies?

As if these conditions weren't sufficiently shocking, Miss Smail moves on to Miss Pigot's deportment. Mr. Wilson is often at the mission. Miss Smail writes she saw him enter Miss Pigot's bedroom one late afternoon and come out dressed for the evening. She observed what she calls a long-standing flirtation between Miss Pigot and Mr. Wilson.

I finish my whiskey and nod to the *durwan* to refill it. I recall the picnic at Barrackpore Park. Miss Pigot and Mr. Wilson sitting back-to-back. And the evening of Mr. Steele's dinner party when Mr. Wilson drove home with Miss Pigot because she'd had too much Madeira. I know Miss Smail's observation to be true. But to write it? For a moment, I'm speechless. I must persuade her to destroy the letter.

"You bring up serious matters," I say. "I advise you not to send this letter. You should omit this business with Mr. Wilson."

"Why? Because Mr. Wilson teaches at the College?" Miss Smail looks up, her blue eyes boring into my forehead. "The Ladies' Association asked me to send reports of conditions in the Female Mission. I did so. They took no action and blamed me for telling the truth. I won't be discounted. This is my final effort to do my duty. Perhaps my observations of Mr. Wilson and Miss Pigot will get their attention at last."

"I urge you not to report this alleged flirtation," I say. "Mr. Wilson has a stellar reputation. He has a wife, children. This a serious allegation, one the Ladies' Association won't accept."

"I saw it with my own eyes," Miss Smail says firmly.

"Nevertheless, I question the wisdom of sharing the information. You'll ruin the reputations of two people who've been with our mission many years," I say.

"Perhaps that's the problem. If I were Mrs. Wilson, I'd want to know the truth of my husband's fidelity. I understand she recommended Miss Pigot for the position. It's nothing short of wicked for her kindness to be repaid this way."

I'm stunned. "Mrs. Wilson recommended her?"

"How else could a woman like Miss Pigot be employed in such a high position?" Colonel Walker says.

"What do you mean?"

"Dear Reverend Hastie," Colonel Walker shakes his head. "Are you unaware that Miss Pigot's always lived in Calcutta? To have her in a position of authority over a true Scotswoman is unacceptable."

"I hadn't thought of the situation from that perspective," I say. "I thought her parents were Scottish."

"We know her father was, but it's mothers who bring up children," Colonel Walker says. "I've been in this country twenty-five years. Since the 1857 rebellion. I know how these people are. Miss Pigot's behavior is typical. They seem honest and self-effacing. But they only want to take advantage of our good will."

"Nevertheless, the charge involves a member of my faculty." There's a pounding in my head. The embarrassment that a member of my staff... it's too much to contemplate.

"Do you doubt its truth?" Miss Smail asks.

"I think you should leave Mr. Wilson out of this," I say.

But nothing dissuades Miss Smail's determination to bring matters to a head. Indeed, the fresh air Miss Smail brought with her is now quite stale.

James Wilson

Once again, Mr. Fish and I are on our way to the Female Mission to help Miss Pigot put together the prize lists. When Miss Smail came, I thought she'd take it over. Pity she and Miss Pigot couldn't work together. It's a warm ride in the *gharry*. At home, March comes in like a lion and out like a lamb. Here, March comes on like a slow fire. Another week, and we'll have the humidity. Mr. Fish and I don't have much to say to each other. His increasing collegiality with Mr. Hastie makes me uncomfortable. I get the feeling he reports our conversations.

"So, Mr. Wilson, what do you think about this business with Miss Smail?" Mr. Fish suddenly asks.

"I don't think anything," I reply. "Matters at the Female Mission aren't our concern."

"If that were true, we wouldn't be on our way to provide assistance. I agree with Mr. Hastie. We should let Miss Pigot get on with things without our participation. She shouldn't have dismissed Miss Smail," Mr. Fish says.

I shrug. "No one forces you to assist. Return to the College, if you like." Of course, Mr. Fish can't report back to Mr. Hastie unless he joins me. I watch Mr. Fish out of the corner of my eye.

"I put our good reputation first. It's better if the public remains ignorant of our, ahem, difficulties," Mr. Fish says.

"Well said, Mr. Fish." I clap him on the back.

We climb the outside stairs to the second level and enter the drawing room from the veranda. Nitya Gopal Mukherjee and Mr. Wetherill, a member of our Board, arrived before us. Mr. Wetherill is the only Board member who assists Miss Pigot. The others ignore the Female Mission.

"Good afternoon," Mr. Wetherill says. "Miss Pigot's just gone to get the student lists."

Miss Pigot comes through from the anteroom. She looks her usual disorganized self, speaking a little too quickly, but with a certain charm.

"Wonderful, we're all here now." She beams. "Thank you also much for coming. I could never get through everything without you. What we need to do is arrange the pupils' names in order of merit. The student at the top of the list holds the highest honor. So, first you have to add up each pupil's marks and then list them in proper order. I asked Babu Mukherjee to help us with the students using Bengali names, and of course, if you have any questions about student names or can't read my writing, you've only to ask."

"Where would you like us to set up?" Mr. Wetherill asks.

"We usually use the table on the veranda," I suggest.

"Yes, I think that would be perfect. I'll put the lists in the center of the table," Miss Pigot says.

Mr. Fish and I pull out the telescopic table to accommodate everyone.

"Oh dear," Miss Pigot says, "we only have three chairs. Mr. Wilson, would you mind pulling that bench over? We can share it, though I don't expect to be sitting much."

I smile. "You never do."

We spend the next two hours sorting through names and marks. I do think Miss Pigot could have the teachers do this, but she wants what she calls "fresh eyes." Miss Pigot looks over everyone's shoulder, spelling names and providing more paper. Babu Mukherjee has little to say. Not surprisingly, his list is the longest. At about six o'clock, Mr. Wetherill stands up. "That's my lot done. Sajiva, fetch my *topi*. How are you getting on, Mr. Wilson?"

"Just a bit more. Going out this evening?" I ask.

"I have an appointment with a new book by Bankim Chandra Chatterjee. I like to keep up with Bengali literature," Mr. Wetherill says.

"Better you than me," Mr. Fish mutters.

Mr. Wetherill looks like he's about to respond but adjusts his *topi* instead. "Just so. Well, I'm off."

"Would you like refreshments?" Miss Pigot asks. "Sajiva, bring tea while I escort Mr. Wetherill downstairs."

Mr. Fish and I finish shortly after Mr. Wetherill leaves, but Babu Mukherjee keeps working.

"Babu Mukherjee, surely you can finish tomorrow," Mr. Fish says.

"No, sir. I promised to finish this evening," Babu Mukherjee says, impatiently.

"It's seven o'clock. We need to get back for dinner. Why not finish at home and send the results to Miss Pigot in the morning?" I say. "Is that agreeable to you, Miss Pigot?"

"Yes. The teachers will be coming for their dinner soon," she says. "Thank you so much for doing the lists. I hope you'll all be present for the Prize Distribution."

Prize Distributions are a staple community event. Regardless of the school, *babus* and Europeans come to see, be seen, and applaud student accomplishments. Miss Pigot invites the entire Scottish community, though I don't suppose she included Miss Smail on this year's invitation list. She did invite Mr. Hastie who, as usual, respectfully declined.

Mr. Fish and I are somewhat early as Miss Pigot wants us in the annual orphanage photograph. We take our positions flanking students in front of the orphanage. The girls are nervous about the program they have to present. The photographer keeps fiddling with his equipment.

"It's hot in the sun," I complain. "Perhaps you'd like us to come back later, after you sort out your settings."

"No, sir, I'm just ready now," the photographer says.

"Where's Miss Pigot?" I ask. "Mr. Fish, go fetch her."

Mr. Fish leaves for about ten minutes and comes back wiping his face. "She's just coming. She stopped to speak to Mr. Thomson."

I see the two strolling in our direction. "Miss Pigot," I shout. "We're standing in the sun waiting for you."

Finally, she arrives and the photographer immortalizes our image for countless missionary publications at home.

"Miss Pigot," I say, as the students move into the shade, "I know it wasn't intentional, but it was inconsiderate of you to keep everyone standing in the sun."

Miss Pigot looks flustered. "I'm so sorry, but I couldn't wait for the picture when there are so many details. Forgive me?"

Miss Pigot has a way about her. An artless lack of awareness. She didn't leave us in the sun; she went to make Mr. Thomson welcome. "Nevermind, Miss Pigot. I'm going to the refreshment table."

I get myself a glass of iced tea and watch the growing crowd. *Oh dear!* Mr. Gillan is at the gate with Miss Smail and Mrs. Walker. I drop my glass and rush to the entry gate. *Too late.*

Miss Pigot, her face twisted into an ugly expression, points her finger at Miss Smail. "Mr. Gillan, remove that woman immediately," she shrieks. "There will be no Prize Distribution while that woman is here."

I've never seen Miss Pigot look this way, with a red face and sheer fury in her expression. I didn't think her capable of such anger. Miss Smail shrinks against the gatepost.

Mr. Gillan stands bewildered. "Whatever's the matter?"

"Mr. Gillan," I say, "you shouldn't have brought Miss Smail."

"I see that, but why not?" Mr. Gillan asks. "Prize Distribution is a public event."

"The rift between Miss Smail and Miss Pigot," I say. "Please escort Miss Smail away."

"Get her out of here!" Miss Pigot shouts.

The courtyard falls deeply silent. Guests look from the corners of their eyes as they sip their drinks. Newspaper reporters watch, their pads of paper ready.

"Mr. Gillan, if you don't take Miss Smail away, this will be in the newspapers tomorrow," I say.

"I can't bear public scenes," Mr. Gillan sighs. "Come, Miss Smail, it's better for us to go."

"I have every right to be here," insists Miss Smail.

For a moment I think she won't leave. It's like I'm watching a play. Miss Pigot with her pointing finger. Miss Smail's erect posture and defiant stance.

Mr. Gillan takes Miss Smail's arm.

Miss Smail pulls away. "Let go of me."

"Please, Miss Smail, for the good of the mission, we need to go."

"I think Miss Pigot's behavior should be reported," Miss Smail says.

"Not now, Miss Smail, not now." Mr. Gillan touches Miss Smail's elbow. She sweeps out the gate ahead of him. Around me, conversations resume in hushed tones.

Despite the sun, I feel a distinct chill.

Fortunately, Easter holidays follow the Prize Distribution. Miss Smail and the Walkers come in from Dum Dum for Easter services at St. Andrew's.

Miss Pigot attends the native church. The following week, the College *khansama* goes back to his village, leaving us to our own devices. Mr. Hastie expects to dine with Mr. Steele. Mr. Fish and I leave Mr. Hastie to his own devices and take up Miss Pigot's standing dinner invitation. I do, anyway. I suspect Mr. Fish just likes to shadow me.

"Good evening, Sajiva," I say, handing over my *topi*.

"Welcome, Mr. Wilson, Mr. Fish. Miss Pigot and Dr. Valentine are in the drawing room. I will prepare a special table for you, away from the teachers."

Sajiva escorts us upstairs, scolds the young *punkah wallah* for not keeping a steady flow of air, and brings us inside the drawing room. Dr. Valentine, a medical missionary stationed in Agra, greets us. It's always pleasant to see him. His affable nature brings him through every social situation. I see he hasn't taken his own advice to stay out of the sun. His face and wrists are dull red.

"Mr. Wilson, what brings you here?" Dr. Valentine extends his hand.

"We're here for the hospitality of the house. How long will you be in Calcutta?"

"Just the week. Miss Pigot kindly offered me a room." Dr. Valentine returns to his seat under the *punkah* fan.

Mr. Fish purses his lips. "You could've stayed at the College. We've plenty of room."

"Allow me to introduce Mr. Fish," I say. "I think he joined our faculty after your last visit."

Dr. Valentine stands again to extend his hand. "Miss Pigot and I are old friends."

Miss Pigot comes in from the veranda. She's wearing a white dress with her hair coiled above her head. Quite a change from her usual black missionary garb. Miss Pigot flashes a happy smile.

"Mr. Wilson, Mr. Fish, how lovely to see you. Dr. Valentine, you must be delighted to have fresh dinner companions. I'm a poor conversationalist. Sajiva tells me the teachers will stay outside. He'll set a table in here for us."

"Miss Pigot, are you keeping well?" Mr. Fish asks perfunctorily.

"Dr. Valentine assures me I'm in the best of health." Miss Pigot laughs. "May I offer you a peg before dinner? Or we have hill beer."

After an eclectic meal that begins with clear soup and ends with fruit, Sajiva removes the table and brings coffee.

"Miss Pigot," I say, "I have a bit of news you might not have heard. Mr. Gillan's going home for his health. He says he doesn't dare stay through the monsoons."

"Is he coming back?" Dr. Valentine asks.

I shrug. "I presume so."

"When does he leave?" Miss Pigot asks.

"In about two weeks. I think he sails the first week in May."

Miss Pigot drums her fingers on the arm of her chair. "I suppose he'll stop in with the Foreign Mission Committee in Edinburgh."

"No doubt," Mr. Fish says.

Miss Pigot bites her lip so hard she draws blood, and quickly covers her mouth with a handkerchief.

Mary Pigot

The earth has swallowed me. I feel myself falling down a dark, bottomless pit. I try to stop myself, but there's nothing to hang on to. I swirl into an endless void.

"Miss Pigot, Miss Pigot, wake up." Someone's shaking my shoulder. I take a sudden breath and feel myself jolted back to the surface.

"Let me wipe your face." Gentle hands move hair off my forehead. Coolness and a soft cloth cover my eyes.

"Who is it?" I ask.

"Mrs. Tremearne, of course."

"Thank you. What time is it?"

"Time for you to rest," Mrs. Tremearne says. "After the gentlemen left, you came in here and swooned. I shooed everyone out and sat with you all night."

I move the cloth and squint into the morning sun.

"I don't know what happened," Mrs. Tremearne says, "but you had quite a shock. Kept crying out in your sleep. Do you want to talk about it?"

I shake my head, trying to remember. And there it is. Mr. Gillan leaves for Scotland in two weeks. Miss Smail sends reports to the Ladies' Association. The Committee will want to see him, ask him about Miss Smail's charges, whatever they are. How can I fight what I can't see?

"Mrs. Tremearne, help me up. I have to write a note to Mr. Wilson."

Mr. Wilson arrives about eleven o'clock. I lie on the wicker lounge on the veranda trying to control my headache.

"Miss Pigot, what's the emergency?" Mr. Wilson asks.

"I leave for Scotland as soon as I can make arrangements."

"What?" Mr. Wilson looks startled. "Why?"

I move my feet so Mr. Wilson can sit at the end of the lounge.

"My enemies conspire against me. First, Miss Smail's reports. Now, Mr. Gillan leaves for Edinburgh. The Committee will interview him. He'll make false charges against me."

"Miss Pigot, calm yourself. You're creating problems where none exist. Mr. Gillan is going for his health, not to speak against you." Mr. Wilson pats my hand. "You've nothing to worry about."

"You're the one who doesn't understand. Neither did I, at first. I must be in Edinburgh when Mr. Gillan meets the Missionary Committee. He won't lay false charges if he has to look me in the eye. But if I'm not there, I shudder to think what he might say. And I need to speak to the Ladies' Association in person, assure them that whatever complaints Miss Smail made are mistaken."

Mr. Wilson shakes his head. "You're determined to do this?"

"I must defend myself. And I need your help. Mrs. Ellis can run the orphanage on a daily basis, but the schools need oversight, and the *zenana* visits have to be properly organized. And then there's the classes I teach in the Upper School. I need you to stand in my place."

"Me?"

"Who knows more about the Female Mission than you do? Your wife ran it before I came. You're my most trusted colleague. You must do this for me."

"I'll have to discuss it with Mr. Hastie and the Corresponding Board," Mr. Wilson says.

"And if they refuse?"

"With you away, I'm sure they won't. But I implore you," Mr. Wilson says in a soothing voice. "to think this through carefully. Your enemies are here, not in Scotland. Everyone at home applauds your work. If they believed there was anything amiss, you'd know it. But if you go, you'll give any complaints credence. Trust me. Keep doing your job. Everything will blow over. Besides, you'll have to get permission from the Ladies' Association. You can't just show up."

"I'll write today, but I'm going either way. I won't let my future be decided in my absence."

James Wilson

After dinner I start a letter to my wife to let her know Miss Pigot's plans and ask her to offer our hospitality. I think Miss Pigot is making a mistake, but she won't be deterred. By the time she returns, the Corresponding Board will be running the Female Mission. Out of sight is out of mind. Mr. Hastie will certainly take advantage of the vacancy. I write out my concerns, hoping Katy sends back sensible ideas.

A shadow falls over my desk. "Mr. Wilson, sir," the houseman says. "The Memsahib waits for you. Will you come?"

I nod, put on my jacket and go downstairs to the outside steps. I'm not surprised to see Miss Pigot sitting in the mission *gharry* with one of her teachers. She likes to stop by when she's out for fresh air. I try to dissuade her, without result. She got in the habit when Katy was still here.

"Miss Pigot, you should send a note," I say. "I can easily come to the orphanage."

"Nonsense, I have several stops to make after this." She thrusts a book at me. It looks water damaged. "I brought something you can use for the Entrance Class."

"You should have sent it," I say.

"It was no trouble to bring it."

"Please send a note next time. I'll have someone pick up anything you care to send. You can't just stop by whenever the mood strikes you." I know neither of us is talking about the book.

Miss Pigot bites her lip. "I thought you'd like to know, I booked my passage for the thirteenth of May. I'm going by way of Bombay."

I shrug. Nothing I say will change her mind. "Thank you for the book, and for dropping by. Mr. Hastie takes a dim view of unaccompanied women visiting his faculty."

Miss Pigot pays no attention to my request and returns two days later. This time she doesn't wait outside in her *gharry*. She comes up to my room with the houseman.

"The Memsahib is here, sir."

The room seems to shrink as Miss Pigot grabs my hands. "Mr. Wilson, I want to see your room so I can give Mrs. Wilson an accurate description when I see her." She beams and looks around.

My papers are messy. The houseman starts to close the door. "Wait, please stay."

"Yes, sir." The man stands with his back to the door and looks across the room to the opposite wall. Regardless, I know he observes everything

"Miss Pigot," I remonstrate, "you shouldn't be here. I'm not dressed properly." I roll my sleeves down and put on my jacket. "Really, Miss Pigot, this is most inappropriate. Let me escort you downstairs." It's as if I haven't spoken of this problem before.

"This isn't a very nice room. There's no comfortable chair. Everything is stark. Mrs. Wilson will be most upset when I tell her," Miss Pigot turns her gaze back to me. "Shall I send some cushions and draperies from the orphanage?"

"No. Absolutely not. Miss Pigot, you must leave immediately. Don't you realize I can be dismissed over this?"

"I don't see why. We're just two friends. Are you sorry I came?" Miss Pigot pouts.

"Yes, Miss Pigot." I gesture towards the door which the houseman opens. "I am sorry you came. Now turn around and go."

"Oh, very well. I'm sure Mrs. Wilson will agree with me when I tell her how silly you're being."

Finally, I get Miss Pigot pointed down the stairs and into her gharry. I begin to look forward to her departure.

Two days before Miss Pigot leaves, my cousin and I arrange a farewell party for her at the Female Mission. We think it only right since who knows when or if we'll meet again. We supply sweetmeats and tokens for the orphans and matrons. The teachers attend, as do several of the College staff, including Mr. Fish. On the thirteenth, I go to Howrah Station after dinner. Miss Pigot is organizing the porter for her luggage. Mrs. Ellis stands nearby with several teachers.

"Miss Pigot, why on earth do you have so much baggage?" I ask.

"Oh, Mr. Wilson, I'm so glad you came. I was just thinking how nice it would be to say good-bye to you in person again. And here you are," Miss Pigot beams.

"What are you taking with you?" I ask again.

"Mostly fabrics. The ladies like to sell them at the church fetes. Mrs. Ellis, can you check what carriage I'm in?" She turns to look at me. I'm not a tall man, but Miss Pigot barely reaches my shoulder. I feel a sudden urge to protect her.

"Do you have any last advice for me, Mr. Wilson?"

"You generally ignore my advice, so I'll just say this. Get some rest on the journey and bundle up. You know how cold Edinburgh can be in the summer."

The conductors blow their whistles. "You're in the third car, Miss Pigot," Mrs. Ellis says. "Hurry."

"Well, this is it, then." Miss Pigot holds out her hand. I shake it and hold her elbow as she mounts the train carriage.

"Will you be coming to the mission tomorrow, Mr. Wilson?" Mrs. Ellis asks.

"Mr. Edwards and I will be up in the afternoon to see what needs doing," I reply.

I go outside and motion to my driver. As I travel back to the College I feel a great sense of unease, as if the tenuous web that holds our mission together is fraying to a point of no return. The pungent fragrance of wood smoke assails me. Groups of people surround the cooking fires by the side of the road. I blink the smoke away.

When I arrive at the College, my melancholy has turned to despair. Whatever happens in Scotland, Miss Pigot and I can never resume our easy friendship. The rift between our missions can only grow wider, and she will stand alone. Miss Pigot is too innocent and undisciplined to understand that goodwill isn't enough.

I go to the drawing room in search of whiskey. Mr. Hastie and Mr. Fish sit playing some sort of card game. Cinch, I think they call it.

"Is she gone?" Mr. Hastie asks.

"So it would seem," I reply. I swallow the whiskey, relishing the burn.

"I assume our two institutions will finally be able to cooperate. Am I correct?" Mr. Hastie asks.

"I see no reason we shouldn't," I reply. I pour another whiskey.

"Don't drink it all," Mr. Fish says.

I take a handful of coins from my pocket. "Buy another bottle."

William Hastie

I don't know what got into Mr. Wilson last night unless Miss Smail's suspicions have merit. Nevertheless, the woman is gone now. With any luck, she won't be back.

"Coffee, Sahib?" Falak pours.

I savor the brew with my moment of triumph. For two years, I begged God to return harmony to the Church of Scotland mission. At last, He has removed the obstacle. The Lady Superintendent is on her way to Scotland where her mismanagement will be proven.

All this time, I watched and held my tongue. Now is the moment to shape the future before the Ladies lose their way again. Now is the time to write the Mission Committee my views on the best way forward so our two missions can become one in structure and purpose.

Contemplating the blank page before me, I conclude I'm not Miss Pigot's enemy. She's her own enemy. I haven't even spoken to her for two years. I merely witness her inability to perform her duty. The blame falls to the Ladies' Association, which never sent anyone to investigate the situation and disregarded Miss Smail's observations. They neither sought advice, nor accepted it. This point needs to be made plainly and clearly.

My issues with Miss Pigot are purely constitutional. We're one mission with two hands. And the primary consideration for any Lady Superintendent must be genuine and public loyalty to the Church of Scotland. There must be no confusion.

I can hear Dr. Scott's inevitable inquiry, asking what I recommend. The Female Mission must be under firm management by a standing committee of the Corresponding Board, which will handle financial affairs and have the power to discharge any agent suspected of immoral activity. Mrs. Wheeler's observations about inappropriate clothing come into play here. There must be no question, no suspicion about our local employees. The Lady Superintendent may speak on any issue, but the standing committee will make the decision.

The Mission Committee should reinstate Miss Smail. She was without guidance in an impossible situation. She deserves another chance to prove herself.

I spend the morning wording things properly and making a clean copy for the Mission Committee.

"Sahib, Colonel Walker is here," Falak says.

Excellent. I want Colonel Walker's opinion. I enter the drawing room genuinely pleased to see the man. "Colonel Walker, I didn't know you'd be in town today."

"Had to file some papers, so thought I'd stop by for *tiffin*," Colonel Walker says.

"Of course. Would you care for a peg first?"

"Capital idea," Colonel Walker reaches out his hand.

I pour out our beverages. "Colonel Walker, I'm writing a memorandum for the Mission Committee. With both Mr. Gillan and Miss Pigot in Edinburgh, I think it prudent to offer our views."

"Miss Pigot is off then?" Colonel Walker asks.

"Mr. Wilson saw her onto the train himself."

"Good, good. My wife and sister-in-law will be pleased, though difficult to say how things will turn out. Miss Pigot's too clever by half."

"Which is why I've put together this memorandum. I suggest a standing committee under the Corresponding Board to oversee the Female Mission. As an Elder at St. Andrews, I propose you as a member."

"I accept." Colonel Walker makes a saluting gesture. "Who else do you suggest?"

"Mr. Wilson, of course. He knows more about the Female Mission than anyone else here. I think we should give Reverend Chuckerbutty a seat. He does religious instruction for the orphans. I thought perhaps Mr. Steele as well."

"All good, solid men," Colonel Walker says. "Look here. What's to become of Miss Pigot? She's done a lot of good work over the years. We can't just turn her out. I caution you that's not my wife's opinion, so please don't bring it up with her."

I chuckle. "If Miss Pigot agrees to work under the standing committee and the Corresponding Board, I see no difficulty with her return. But with her temper and alienation from St. Andrew's Church, I think she should relinquish the leadership position and return to her educational endeavors."

"Don't recommend my sister-in-law as Lady Superintendent. She came out to be a *zenana* teacher. That's where her heart is. She's engaged a *pundit* to teach her Bengali—that's how serious she is. Do you have anyone in mind for the position?" Colonel Walker asks.

"Don't mention it to Mr. Wilson," I say, "but I'm going to suggest his wife. The Female Mission ran very well when the two of them supervised things."

"Thought she went home for her health."

"No, it was family concerns. I think it had something to do with their sons."

"Should send the children to boarding school, like everyone else does," Colonel Walker says. "Where's she living?"

"Crieff, I think," I say. "Shall we go in to *tiffin*?"

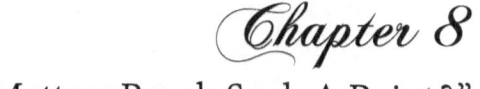

Chapter 8
"How Did Matters Reach Such A Point?"

May – June, 1882
SCOTLAND
Mary Pigot

I almost didn't get on the train. I could've turned back as Mr. Wilson advised. But I must go home and defend myself. If it were just Miss Smail's letters, I could let it go, but the Mission Committee will interview Reverend Gillan, and he dissented when Reverend Thomson recommended my employment. He's never done more than tolerate my presence, and since Reverend Hastie arrived, he's found an ally against me. I must be there.

The train clacks down the track. My determination echoes the sound like a mantra in my head. *I-must-be-there. I-must-be-there. I-must-be-there.* My body sways from side to side. I suddenly remember how sick I get on trains. Everyone thinks they're such a marvel, and they are. But I do get sick. And it takes a day and a half to get to Bombay.

It's three o'clock in the morning when the car stops swaying. We're on the platform at Bori Bunder Station. I lean my head against the window. No need to get off until daylight. A few hours later, I wake up with a headache. I smooth my hair, put on my *topi* and join several passengers heading for the same meeting point inside the station. The representative from the Anchor Steamship Line collects our luggage tickets and directs us to meet our transportation to Apollo Bunder Pier. I'm assigned to a large coach that seats six people. There's an older couple, who look like missionaries, and a youngish woman with her arms around two children: a boy who looks to be about eight years old and a girl who looks a bit younger.

After half an hour, we arrive at the fog-swathed pier. A ship's steward in a white uniform with a square cap escorts us to the gangplank. The woman falls to her knees, hugging her children close and smoothing their hair.

"She's sending them home," the older woman says to me. "We're to look after them on the journey. I'm Mrs. Martin." She holds out her hand.

"Miss Pigot," I say.

"This is my husband, Reverend Martin. We're going home for good after thirty years in Madras. We're with the Church Missionary Society. And you?"

"I'm Lady Superintendent at the Scottish Ladies' Association Female Mission in Calcutta. I'm going home on furlough."

"Will you go back?" Mrs. Martin asks.

"Most certainly. Are the children from your mission family?" I ask more to change the subject than because I care. I think sending children away from their parents is barbaric. At least Mrs. Wilson returned with her sons. But it's a great sacrifice for Mr. Wilson.

At last the ship's officer stands at the bottom of the gangplank. I walk up and hand him my papers.

"Welcome aboard, Miss Pigot. We have your cabin on the starboard side," he says.

I stand at the rail and feel wet, moist air waft across the deck. The first time I went home I was beside myself with excitement. Now I'm just weary. I don't know what kind of reception I'll get in Edinburgh. I watch as Mr. and Mrs. Martin finally separate the children from their mother. She stands bereft as they walk up the gangplank. The little boy turns to wave when he gets to the top.

The voyage will take five or six weeks. For someone accustomed to being busy all day long, the prospect is daunting. There isn't much to do at sea. First class passengers have shuffle board courts and a billiards table in the saloon. But even they must get bored. I walk briskly around the deck every morning and afternoon, chat with other passengers, and read books from the library. Some of the passengers play cards or checkers, but I don't enjoy games. The sea air is wonderful, though the sun can be harsh. Reverend Martin conducts Sunday services on the forward deck. If he didn't I might lose all track of time.

Our vessel, S. S. *Britannia,* is only a few years old, so the cabins are still in good shape, though the carpet in the saloon is a bit worn. I think the worst part of the voyage is crossing the Arabian Sea. I don't like being so far from land. What if we get lost? A week out of Bombay we turn into the Red Sea. Arabia on one side, and Africa on the other. The empty landscape of sand contrasted against the blue water makes me long for dusty Calcutta.

It takes a few days to reach the Suez Canal, and then we have to reduce our speed to five knots. The *Britannia* seems to be standing still as we slowly make our way through the bleak waterway with nothing but desert on either side. It's such a narrow canal. I hope we don't meet any ships going the opposite way.

At last we reach Port Said, an unattractive town that's really just a coaling station. Every steamship going through the canal picks up coal here. Gangs of Arabs load the coal into the bunkers at the side of the ship. I'm not going to disembark. There's nothing to see, and I don't fancy riding a camel.

As soon as the coal is loaded, we steam into the Mediterranean Sea on our way to Marseilles to pick up mail and cargo. I stand by the rail as we coast up the side of Italy. I'd like to go there someday. See the Roman ruins Mr. Hastie talks about.

"There it is," Reverend Martin says two days after we leave Marseilles, "the Rock of Gibraltar. Will you be going ashore?"

"I can't decide," I answer.

"I'm just going down the gangway so I can set my foot on European soil. It's a little ritual I have. Will you join me?" Reverend Martin asks.

"What about your wife?"

"Mrs. Martin's taken up with those children. I told her they would make her voyage a misery, and they have. One or the other is generally sick. And when they aren't sick, they play up."

I smile. "They do seem energetic when they're on deck, but it's hard for children to be cooped up."

"I fear I'm an old curmudgeon now. Anyway, may I escort you down the gangway and back up again?" Mr. Martin asks.

"I would be honored." I raise my parasol and lay my hand on his arm. "You're right," I say, "it's good to be in Europe again."

After three more weeks at sea, we arrive at Liverpool. I stand at the rail with the other passengers, all of us reviewing our plans for after we disembark. Excitement is high, and with everyone by the rail I expect the ship to tip at any instant, but it stays upright. It seems like years since I left Calcutta. Mrs. Martin stands with a child on either side. I hope someone meets them, so they don't have to drag the children somewhere else. My eyes move to the dock where stevedores wait to unload our cargo.

Once the gangway is down I adjust my hat and make my way ashore. After so many weeks at sea, I can hardly stand on the dock's solid surface. I hand my luggage tickets to the purser who arranges transportation for me and my boxes to the Lime Street Train Station. Before I know it, I'm sitting in a second-class carriage on my way to Waverley Station in Edinburgh. Everything looks different here. The greens seem pale, the air wet. As I watch the scenery, I go over what I'll say to whoever greets me at 22 Princes Street, the headquarters of the Ladies' Association. I sent a telegram from Liverpool, so they'll know when to expect me.

I arrive at Waverley Station about six o'clock in the evening, leave my luggage for pickup later, and walk out of the station to the modest house on Princes Street. It has a bay window on the second level. I climb the outside steps to the first level and pull the bell. *Clang!* Nothing happens, so I pull it again. I hear clattering. The door swings inward. A pale, thin girl with a fierce expression appears.

"Yes?" she asks.

"I am Miss Pigot. I am expected,"

"Come in, then," says the unsmiling girl.

I follow her upstairs and into the drawing room.

"Please sit. I'll tell Mrs. Williamson, you're here." The girl closes the door on her way out.

The room is plain, the furniture serviceable, and the fireplace swept. I sit on a horsehair sofa. The mantel clock makes a very loud tick. Suddenly I'm nervous. My only plan was to get here. I don't know what to do now.

The girl comes in with a tea tray.

"I thought you might want something to eat after your journey," she says. "Mrs. Williamson says she canna come down tonight, but she'll see you at breakfast. I'll come back in a bit and take you upstairs."

"Thank you." I'm surprised this Mrs. Williamson doesn't greet me. Perhaps she's angry with me for showing up without an invitation. Despite my queasy stomach, I nibble a piece of shortbread, enjoying the buttery sweetness. In contrast, the tea is scalding.

The girl who tells me her name is Fiona returns twenty minutes later and takes me to a cold room. "We don't light the fires in spring," she says. She gives me an extra blanket for the bed, but I still wrap my shawl around my nightdress. I don't sleep well. I'm too worried about what tomorrow will bring. I don't know if I'll be snubbed or welcomed. I don't know what the ladies have been told. I bounce around the bed, and doze just as the dawn's light seeps into the room.

When I come down for breakfast, Mrs. Williamson sits eating her porridge while glancing at the newspaper. She looks middle aged with fine lines around her eyes and lips. Mrs. Williamson smiles and gestures to the chair beside her.

"Welcome, Miss Pigot. I didn't come down to greet you last night because I wasn't well."

"I understand. I hope you're better this morning," I say, wondering if that's the real reason she didn't come down.

Fiona puts a plate eggs in front of me.

"Much. Thank you," Mrs. Williamson says. "So, how was the journey? Did you take the opportunity to rest?"

"There isn't much else to do," I say with a tired smile.

"I suppose not. Why are you here?"

Why, indeed? I clear my throat. "I realize my decision is unusual," I begin.

"To say the least." Mrs. Williamson interrupts me, her voice stern. "You've put the Ladies' Association to great expense, paying for a journey we didn't initiate. What possessed you?"

I blink a tear and shake my head. I thought once I arrived I'd know what to do. Now I realize the ladies may believe Miss Smail's accusations, whatever they are. I shouldn't be so apprehensive, but I can't help it. Maybe it's just lack of sleep last night. Mrs. Williamson watches me, waiting for an answer. "I'm afraid," I finally reply.

"Of the Ladies' Association?" Mrs. Williamson asks in surprise.

"I know there's a terrible misunderstanding," I say. "And I must be here to clear things up. To answer questions and explain, well, why there may be confusion."

"Have you finished?" Mrs. Williamson asks, eyeing my congealed eggs.

I nod.

"Then, come into the drawing room. The ladies will join us at ten o'clock."

The room looks different. The furniture has been rearranged with the sofa facing several chairs arranged in front of the widow. There's a chair at a right angle to the sofa so the occupant can face both ways. The bell downstairs starts clanging as women arrive in bunches of twos and threes. Their favorite color seems to be black. They wear black bonnets that tie under their chins. Some ladies remove their bonnets which makes them less intimidating.

I stand in front of the sofa with Mrs. Williamson who introduces me to each unsmiling woman. Some of the ladies pour themselves a cup of coffee from the service on a small table at the far side of the room before taking their seats. When all the ladies arrive, the room can hold no more. The ladies speak softly until Mrs. Stevenson, as chair of the Ladies' Association, takes the seat at the right angle to the sofa. She's a tall, thin woman in a black dress with small black buttons on the front of her bodice. She nods to me but doesn't extend her hand. I feel her disapproval. Her attention is taken by documents in front of her.

"Miss Pigot," Mrs. Stevenson says in a piercing voice, "I see no reason why we should postpone this unpleasant discussion. Matters could have been handled without your presence, but as you're here, we shall be direct. We're very disappointed that you and Miss Smail couldn't pull together for the good of the mission. You requested assistance. Miss Smail is eminently qualified and served at her own expense. What was the difficulty?"

I begin cautiously and try to be diplomatic, so they don't think I disapprove of Miss Smail—even though I do. "Unfortunately, Miss Smail arrived with an unrealistic set of expectations. I believe India was a great surprise to her, as it is to many new arrivals. I think perhaps Miss Smail thought an orphanage in Calcutta would be like an orphanage here. And it can't be. India isn't like Scotland."

"You'll have to do better than that, Miss Pigot," Mrs. Stevenson says. "Every teacher we've sent before has done very well. Miss Smail is the first to move out of the mission. Why did she move?"

I inhale deeply and tell the truth. "I told her to leave."

The room flutters with a collective intake of breath.

"You told her to leave?" Mrs. Stevenson looks shocked. "How did matters reach such a point?"

How did they? "I can't say exactly. From the moment she arrived, Miss Smail was unhappy. She didn't like her bed or the food. She wanted to go to the *zenanas* before she could speak Bengali. She demanded the servants obey her, but they couldn't understand her."

I stop. I feel so vulnerable my eyes tear up. I inhale and will myself to remain strong. No one in the room says anything, so I continue.

"Miss Smail also thought our teachers weren't under proper discipline. She felt offended that most of us, including myself, aren't baptized members of the Church of Scotland. I explained that we need matrons and teachers and can't always be choosy."

"But none of this explains why she moved out, or the letters she wrote," Mrs. Stevenson says. "Your comments don't explain how matters could reach such a point that we had to direct Miss Smail not to work at the mission at all. Tell us what happened."

"What did Miss Smail write in her letters?" I ask.

Mrs. Williamson interjects. "Mrs. Stevenson, I think you should explain about the procedure."

"Forgive me, Miss Pigot. I should've done that in the first place," Mrs. Stevenson says. "When we sent Miss Smail to the Female Mission, we asked her to send us information about the daily activities at the orphanage and schools. You're most diligent in your reports to us and the parish churches. We know from your statistics you're overworked, and we didn't want to ask you to do more, so, we asked Miss Smail to send us details."

I'm bewildered. "But I would have been only too pleased to send you more descriptions."

"Well, that's neither here nor there. Miss Smail inferred serious problems in the Female Mission, and the issues are of such a nature that we consulted with the Foreign Mission Committee. Our combined Investigating Committee will meet with you tomorrow to sort things out,"

Mrs. Stevenson says. "Our difficulty is understanding the discrepancy between what we've always understood to be true and Miss Smail's observations. We need to know what happened between you and Miss Smail."

I sit speechless. *What did she write in those letters?* "Can you tell me her charges?"

"That discussion is out of our hands now," Mrs. Stevenson says.

"Miss Pigot," Mrs. Williamson says, "most of our members met you ten years ago on your first trip home. And all of us are impressed with the quality of your work. The best way for us to help you, and for you to help yourself, is if you can explain to us what happened between you and Miss Smail."

"Truly, if I knew I would tell you," I say. "There are those who disagree with my methods. Several, including Miss Smail's brother-in-law, sit on the Corresponding Board. And it's no secret that The Reverend Hastie tried to bring the Female Mission under his direct control, an effort I strenuously opposed. I think perhaps Miss Smail fell under their influence, especially since she must have felt overwhelmed by Indian culture."

"What about church attendance?" asks Mrs. Bruce, a young woman with dark hair and a strident voice who is sitting by the window in the last row of chairs. "Miss Smail intimated you don't attend St. Andrew's because you belong to the Church of England."

It's as if I'm back in Calcutta arguing with Miss. Smail. Remembering those conversations, I fix my gaze on the window so no one can say I looked away while I answered questions. "I attend the native church with our teachers and orphans. I do so to support Reverend Chuckerbutty, to set an example for the children, and to encourage native Christians attending the Free Church to consider our services." My voice hits a higher pitch. "If I were a member of the Church of England, I would attend St. John's. Reverend Gillan takes my absence from St. Andrew's as a personal affront, and undoubtedly shared his views with Miss Smail. I haven't attended St. John's since you engaged my services thirteen years ago."

I move my eyes to each woman's face. No one engages with me. Have they already made their decision? I decide to be even more forthright. What difference can it make now? "And while we're on this subject, Miss Smail also objects to what she calls my lack of evangelism. I don't believe in dosing people with religion. I think our faith speaks for itself, and we can't share the Gospel until a woman or girl is ready. In the meantime, we share Bible stories and use the Bible as our reading text in the *zenana*.

"And don't forget, if a woman openly requests baptism, her family will disown her. So how shall we count conversions? By the number of believers, or the total of public professors? What do you ladies expect from your mission?"

The room becomes thunderously quiet. *I've nothing else to argue.* I keep my posture erect.

Mrs. Stevenson smooths some non-existent wrinkles on her skirt. "It appears you and Miss Smail were unevenly yoked. I think your decision to send her out of the mission unwise, but I understand your frustration. For the moment, let us leave things as they are until after you meet with the Investigating Committee." A smile cracks her face. "Have you had the opportunity to walk in the Princes Street Gardens? They're quite lovely this time of year."

"No, I just arrived last night," I say.

"Then we'll excuse you. A breath of fresh air in the gardens will do you a world of good," Mrs. Stevenson says. "Try not to worry about tomorrow. I'm sure everything will work out."

I put on my coat and walk to the other side of the train station where the gardens begin. The medieval Old Town sits above verdant lawns and trees in the East Garden. I walk for about ten minutes in the brisk air, before I sit on a bench facing a Gothic monument to Sir Walter Scott. Thinking of Scott reminds me of Mr. Hastie reciting his poetry *ad infinitum.* The monument's over-decorated sandstone columns plunge into the sky. Scott's statue shows a man bundled up against the elements and wearing sturdy shoes, but no hat or gloves to guard against the chill. I curl my fingers into a fist and resolve to hold my ground tomorrow.

About mid-morning the next day, Mrs. Williamson and I stand outside the door to Number 24 Princes Street. How convenient that the Foreign Mission Committee's office is so close to the Ladies' Association. Plan or happenstance?

"Are you ready?" Mrs. Williamson asks.

I nod.

She squeezes my arm, then lifts the brass knocker and bangs it on the door which opens immediately.

"Mr. Macrae," Mrs. Williamson gasps. "Were you standing behind the door?"

"I happened to see you through the window." Mr. Macrae gives what could pass as a smile. "Come in, Mrs. Williamson. And you must be Miss Pigot." He extends his hand.

"I am. Thank you."

Mr. Macrae seems a nice man. He wears spectacles and a high collar above his jacket. I wonder if it's detachable. His gray sideburns cover half his face. If he had a hat on, you wouldn't be able to see it at all.

"Come upstairs," he says leading the way. "With only six members, the Investigating Committee fits nicely into the drawing room." When we arrive at the drawing room, Mr. Macrae opens the door and gestures for me to go inside. Mrs. Williamson stands aside.

"Aren't you coming in?" I ask.

"I'm sorry, Miss Pigot. The Investigating Committee is in closed session, so I'll leave you here."

I'm surprisingly bereft as I watch Mrs. Williamson go back downstairs.

The drawing room is like Mrs. Williamson's house, though instead chairs and a sofa it has a large round table. Mr. Macrae takes me to an empty seat at the table and seats himself at a small desk to the side just behind me. Six men sit around the table, three on either side of me. The man on my right stands and extends his hand.

"Miss Pigot, I'm Dr. Scott, convener of both the Foreign Mission Committee and this Investigating Committee. To my right are Mr. Phin and Mr. Murray. To your left are Mr. Stevenson, Mr. Muir, and Dr. Herdman," Dr. Scott says, gesturing to each of the men as he states their names.

I look at this man that I've heard so much about. He's tall with a demanding presence and a deep voice. His hair and beard are steel gray as are his bushy eyebrows.

"How do you do?" I say. Though I'm standing at attention, I say this as if we're about to have tea. What a silly phrase.

"Please be seated. I hope the journey from Calcutta wasn't too arduous?" Dr. Scott says pleasantly, as if I'm on a social visit.

"We didn't encounter any major storms," I say as I sit carefully on the chair that has been designated for me, "so the journey was quite pleasant, thank you."

"What ship were you on?" Dr. Phin looks at me intently, though he sits with a slight stoop.

"The S. S. *Britannia* from the Anchor Line," I answer politely, though these pleasantries are making me nervous. Surely, they are avoiding the topic and have something terrible to say. "Excuse me for asking," I blurt out, "but yesterday Mrs. Stevenson said you wanted to ask me questions about some letters Miss Smail wrote."

"Ah, yes, Miss Pigot." Dr. Scott responds calmly. "Did you discuss them with Mrs. Stevenson or any of the Ladies?"

"No. I don't know what's in the letters. Mrs. Stevenson expressed concern about my relationship with Miss Smail, which I assure you was purely professional." I wait for Dr. Scott to solve the mystery and relieve my anxiety.

"Miss Smail made several observations which, under normal circumstances, appear baseless," Dr. Scott says. "However, Reverend Gillan recently arrived and, as a matter of course, the Mission Committee interviewed him. He also brought up various incidents regarding the Female Mission. Consequently, the Ladies concluded it prudent to investigate the entire matter so we can put it behind us."

I sit up straight and fold my hands on the table. "How can I help you?"

"Is it true that most of your staff isn't affiliated with the Church of Scotland?" Dr. Scott asks.

"Yes. Our teachers are Christian, but there aren't a sufficient number of Church of Scotland members to fill out our staff."

"Where do their loyalties lie, Miss Pigot?" Dr. Phin asks before I have a moment to think.

"I'm sorry?" I ask. What does he mean?

"There are indications that some of your staff are Roman Catholic. Is that true?" Dr. Phin asks.

"I accidentally employed a woman as matron who I later learned is Catholic," I explain. "But since she did her duties without spreading her ideas, and since there wasn't anyone else available, I kept her on. If I'd known she was Catholic, I wouldn't have hired her, but it didn't seem fair to dismiss her when there was nothing wrong with her work. She has two or three children to look after."

"Do you have a convent education?" Mr. Muir asks, his pale face almost luminous.

"No. I attended Calcutta Normal School, a school for European children."

"Tell us about your program for Parlor Boarders," Dr. Scott says.

"As the records show, it's a successful program. These are women of limited or no education married to European men who want them to learn European customs. We teach them English, using the Bible as our text. We also teach them proper etiquette, how to wear western clothing, hygiene, and anything else they need to run their homes and teach their children. The women board with us so they can see how a western household works. We charge tuition, which has been a great blessing in funding the Female Mission."

"Do you make any effort to convert these women?" Dr. Scott asks.

"Only by example." I clear my throat as I organize my thoughts. "I believe conversion comes through experience, not fear. That it must grow slowly through positive relationships. That as the women learn through the Bible, their hearts will be touched. I use the same method in the *zenanas*. I'm always aware that husbands don't give us access to their wives for religious instruction. They want their wives to learn western ways. Forgive me, but I think the desire for public conversion is detrimental to the mission enterprise."

"You're very bold, Miss Pigot," Dr. Scott says with some disapproval.

My stomach begins to quiver. I think of the orphans I care for and the women who depend on me for their livelihood. The ladies trying to understand why the devil tempted Jesus. Those women and girls depend on my strength, not my nerves. Dr. Scott is right. I am bold. I came all this way to state my case, and that's what I'm going to do.

"I sit before you, a lone woman without a defender. I supervise a large female mission. If I'm not strong, I can't educate my children, protect my staff, and keep my servants employed. It all depends on me, and through me, it all depends on you." I slowly glance around the table, making sure to stop and look each man in the eye.

The questions continue for at least another hour, but with declining enthusiasm. I stand my ground. At last Dr. Scott knocks the table with his knuckle.

"Gentlemen, I think matters sufficiently clarified for our investigation to move forward. Miss Pigot, thank you for coming in today and for answering our questions so forthrightly. We'll make our conclusions in due course," Dr. Scott says as he motions me to stand. He escorts me to the door.

Mrs. Williamson waits outside. "Come, my dear, let's get you home. You must be exhausted. I have good news. Mrs. Wilson invites you to stay with her at Crieff so you can have a proper rest."

At midmorning the next day, I wave to Mrs. Williamson and settle into my seat. It was nice of her to come with me to the Caledonian Railway Station on Princes Street when I'm sure she has better things to do. Since my meeting with the Ladies' Association, Mrs. Williamson seems almost protective. It's nice to have someone looking after me.

Crieff is further from Edinburgh than I expected. It takes five hours to reach the station. I gather my things while the train slows and stops in front of a long wooden building with two chimneys. The conductor puts my carpetbag on the platform. No one else gets off.

I pick up my bag and walk through the station. Now what? There seems to be no one here to meet me.

"Miss Pigot," a voice calls across the station. I turn to see Mrs. Wilson walking rapidly through the station's main entrance. "Dreadful train's never on time. This time it's early. My sincere apologies. You must have thought no one was coming for you."

I close the distance between us and we embrace. I feel tears running down my face. I'm so happy to be with someone I know and love, and know she cares about me as well. I don't have to put on my brave face. Mrs. Wilson holds me a moment, then stands back to look at me. She smiles and takes both my hands.

"Whatever's the matter, Miss Pigot? You've nothing to worry about here." Mrs. Wilson releases my hands. "Come, we'll have a lovely visit before you have to go back to Calcutta."

"I don't know why I'm crying. It's just so wonderful to see you again." I smile broadly through my tears. "I've missed you. I can't believe we're together again." I sniffle slightly.

Mrs. Wilson passes me her handkerchief and pats my shoulder. "There, there. You're here now for a good long rest." She's changed since she left Calcutta. Her expression is less harried and her blue eyes sparkle. In fact, she radiates good health.

"I'm so glad to be here," I say through wet eyes. "I didn't know if we'd ever meet again."

"God has mysterious ways." Mrs. Wilson's eyes twinkle. "This is Catriona. Say hello to Miss Pigot."

A young girl with dark hair curtseys to me. She can't be more than twelve. Catriona looks up and smiles. "How do you do?"

"Very well, thank you." The child shakes hands solemnly and looks back to Mrs. Wilson. She has an air of self-assurance, as if she knows her place in the world.

"Give Catriona your bag. She and her sister Flora stay with me to learn household skills so they can get a position in service." Mrs. Wilson motions towards the station entrance. "Come, we've a bit of a walk. I have a cottage just outside the village. Come along, everyone."

Mrs. Wilson sets a brisk pace and we walk steadily for some time. The cold air hurts my lungs. I'm gasping for breath when Mrs. Wilson finally stops and says, "Here we are. This is my wee cottage."

The stone cottage has two windows in the front and a chimney at either end. Stone steps lead to a central door covered by a small extension of the roof. Inside, one hearth is in use for cooking. There's only one room.

"Ah. I know what you're thinking," Mrs. Wilson says. "Ye want to know how we all fit. The lasses have pallets for sleeping. You and I will share the bed."

"Your sons aren't here then?" I ask.

"Not at the moment. They both work at farms in the area and sleep there. They visit every few weeks."

I take my hat off. I'm perplexed. "I thought you came back so your sons could attend school."

"Aye. But when classes end for the summer, they work to earn money for the following year. We canna pay their tuition if they dinna work,"

Mrs. Wilson says in her thick Scottish brogue. "Now then, get settled while I prepare our tea. I sent Catriona to the bakery this morning to get shortbread. Ah, Catriona, lay the table for tea, as I showed you. And make a tray for yourself and Flora."

"Where should I...?" I begin as I look around for a place to put my bag.

"I cleared a few hooks on the wall over there, and there's a shelf for you," Mrs. Wilson motions. "I thought after tea we'd have a wee stroll through the gorse."

On the long table facing the window, Catriona puts down a tablecloth, napkins and two place settings with soup bowls, small plates, and rounded spoons. There's a slab of butter and sliced soda bread in a basket.

"Flora, serve the soup, please," Mrs. Wilson says.

I watch Flora swing out the pot crane from the fire and ladle soup from the iron pot into a tureen which she places at the end of the table. She then positions a large teapot in the center beside the bread basket. Catriona opens the door with her foot and takes a tray with plates and bowls outside.

"Is there anything else?" Flora asks with a quiet smile that shows her dimples.

"Is there anything else, Madam?" Mrs. Wilson corrects. "No. Join us for grace, and then serve yourselves."

Mrs. Wilson and I take our places. The girls stand at the end of the table with their hands folded.

"Would you like to say the blessing, Miss Pigot?" Mrs. Wilson asks.

"Some have meat and cannot eat. Some no meat but want it. We have meat and we can eat and so the Lord be thanked. Amen."

"Fancy you remembering that old blessing," Mrs. Wilson says, her eyes twinkling.

"I learned it last time I was home. I think it applies to so much more than food." I smile back. It is so very good to be here with Mrs. Wilson. For a moment, I feel a million miles away from my difficulties.

"Mrs. Wilson, please slow down," I call as we walk through the tall gorse. "I can't keep up."

"We're almost there," Mrs. Wilson calls back to me. "I want you to see the view from this hillock. Come on."

I hitch my skirt up and climb the last few yards. Mrs. Wilson spreads her tartan on the ground.

"Isn't this glorious?" Mrs. Wilson does not seem the least bit winded by our jaunt to the top. "We can see for miles." She pats her tartan. "Come, sit, and take everything in."

I catch my breath and look towards Glen Turrett. Green valleys stretch out before us and into the hills beyond. Clouds hide the sky, but not the light. This gives the grass and trees an emerald hue. What strikes me most is the emptiness of the space and the chill in the air. We sit in silence for some time.

"Tell me," Mrs. Wilson say finally.

"Tell you what?"

"Everything," she replies in her matter-of-fact voice.

I start with news I think might cheer her. "Just before I left, I visited Mr. Wilson in his room, so I could tell you about it. It's such a plain room, and he wouldn't let me send any fabrics to cheer the walls. And I don't think the ventilation is good. But he told me not to bother."

Mrs. Wilson looks at me with a shocked and concerned expression. "Miss Pigot, that was a silly thing to do. You put my husband in a compromising position."

"But we are old friends." I am surprised at her reaction.

Mrs. Wilson sighs. "I hoped you might have gotten a bit more sense working for the Church of Scotland. An unmarried woman unaccompanied in a man's room. It isn't done. I'm disappointed you misused our trust in such a way. You need to be more careful, more aware, Miss Pigot. Now, tell me the rest."

And since I can't disappoint her any more than I already have, I tell her everything. I describe how Mr. Hastie and Miss Smail and the others want to take the Female Mission away from me. I tell her about Miss Smail's betrayal and the letters and the Investigating Committee. I explain my staffing issues. And as my story goes on, I begin to cry. Mrs. Wilson puts my head in her lap and strokes my back as if I'm her child. Finally, I stop crying and just lay there, sad but comforted to be with such a dear friend.

"If you don't sit up, Miss Pigot, you'll miss the sunset which would be a shame, because that's what I most want you to see."

I push myself into a seated position. The cool air has soothed my red eyes and the sky explodes into a thousand hues of gold.

"I never tire of the sunset in summer," Mrs. Wilson says, her expression pure serenity. "The sun's rays transform the clouds into golden threads that light up the land. When I see it, I know God is ever-present. It gives me great comfort." I nod in agreement without taking my eyes from the sky.

The days take on a comforting regularity. If the day's fine, I sit outside to drink my morning tea. Flora calls me when the porridge is ready. Then I wash and dress. Mrs. Wilson won't let me assist in the housekeeping. She says it upsets her training program for Catriona and Flora, so I gather flowers for the table. There's a field of Scottish blue bells near the cottage that I visit nearly every day. I also walk to the village several times a week. When I first arrived, the walks were too long, and I had to turn back. But after a week or so, I could go the village, stop in the post office, and peer in the shop windows. On one trip, I buy a tartan shawl to take back. Every evening, if it doesn't rain, Mrs. Wilson and I walk up the hillock to celebrate the sun's departure. My headaches go away for the first time in years. Then, in an instant, my idyll ends.

"Mrs. Wilson, I picked up your letters," I announce one afternoon after my trip to the village. "There's one from the Ladies' Association."

"Put them on the little desk," Mrs. Wilson directs. "I'll open them after tea. I've a special treat for you. The butcher had lamb shanks yesterday, and Catriona made a lovely stew for our tea."

"But what if the letter's about my report? It's been two weeks. There must be a verdict."

"I'm sure there is, but it can wait another two hours. Go gather flowers for the table," Mrs. Wilson scoots me out the front door.

As predicted, the meal is exceptional. Mrs. Wilson leaves the clearing up to the girls and takes me outside for our evening walk. I ask my most pressing question. "Mrs. Wilson, will you return to Calcutta after your sons finish school?"

"Nay. My life in Calcutta is over."

"But Mr. Wilson is lonely without you."

"And I'm lonely without him, but at the moment, we can't be together. He must continue to serve God and the Church of Scotland while I have my life here. Crieff is my home," Mrs. Wilson says. "Mr. Wilson came here as the school teacher, and I thought we'd always be here with our children and grandchildren."

"Why did he apply as a missionary?"

"It was his health, you see. Mr. Wilson has a terrible time with his lungs. Every year it got worse, until the doctor said he must leave for a warmer climate where perhaps his lungs would clear. And we saw the advertisement in the newspaper. They needed teachers at Scottish College. So Mr. Wilson applied and we went. It near broke my heart," Mrs. Wilson says. "His lungs improved, but he couldn't bring himself to leave Calcutta. I stayed until our sons needed to come home."

"And you won't return?"

"Nay," she says and lifts her eyebrow with a quizzical smile. "Have you any more questions for me?"

"No, only gratitude," I squeeze her arm as we walk side by side.

When we return to the cottage. Mrs. Wilson opens the envelope from the Ladies' Association and hands me the sealed letter inside. My hands start to shake as I slip open the flap. Mrs. Wilson takes the letter from me.

"Sit down, dear."

"What does it say?" I whisper. "Am I dismissed?"

Mrs. Wilson puts on her spectacles, reads the letter, and shakes her head. "Ugh. How inconsiderate. Mr. Macrae wrote it."

I realize I'm holding my breath, and exhale. Whatever the letter says, I've done everything possible to defend myself. I offer a quick prayer for strength. "Mrs. Wilson, please, what does the letter say?"

"Nothing useful, as is typical for churchmen. They want you back in Edinburgh as soon as possible." Mrs. Wilson gives me a short hug. "I'm sorry for your trouble."

I feel elated and distraught at the same time. Elated that I'm not dismissed. Distraught because I haven't prevailed. I put the letter in my pocket and walk outside. Flora and Catriona sit sewing in the sun. They wave at me. I burst into tears.

Chapter 9
"I Have Long Been Suspicious"

June - November 1882
Edinburgh
Mary Pigot

From the moment I received the letter, my mind has been a jumble. I'm glad Mrs. Wilson didn't give it to me right away, because now I don't know what to think. My fate is decided, yet I remain ignorant of the decision. Two days after the letter arrived, I'm back at Number 22 Princes Street. Mrs. Williamson leaves me alone in the drawing room to wait for Mrs. Stevenson. I pace in front of the bay window like a bird flapping its wings. I see movement on the pavement. A woman turns at the house. She's here. I pick up the *Missionary Journal* and sit on the sofa, as if nothing is on my mind.

Mrs. Williamson comes in with Mrs. Stevenson who is taking off her gloves. I stand.

"Mrs. Stevenson, how nice to see you again," I say. I almost curtsey but catch myself in time.

"Miss Pigot," she smiles and extends her hand.

Fiona comes in balancing a tray with a coffee service. I watch her place the cups and coffee pot. I must tell Mrs. Williamson about Mrs. Wilson's pupils.

Mrs. Williamson pours the coffee.

"Could you put my cup on the table, Mrs. Williamson?" I ask. "I'm a bit unsteady this morning." I pick up my cup with both hands. The ladies watch me from the corners of their eyes but don't say anything.

"Miss Pigot, the Investigating Committee has issued its report. The Ladies' Association agrees with their findings. And now it is only for you to concur with their recommendations," Mrs. Stevenson says.

"Yes?" I whisper, feeling as if I might faint.

"We hope you will continue as Lady Superintendent," Mrs. Stevenson says.

Oh, Dear God, thank you! "Most assuredly," I say enthusiastically, shaking both of Mrs. Stevenson's hands. "Thank you! Thank you for your continued confidence."

Mrs. Stevenson extricates her hands. "Your work has always surpassed our expectations," she says warmly. "There was never any doubt in my mind as to the outcome of the investigation. But the misunderstandings had to be sorted out. Before you decide whether or not to continue in our service, let me outline the new terms."

"I'm sure they'll be agreeable," I say confidently. After all, I've been running the mission for more than ten years.

Mrs. Stevenson shifts in her seat. "Hear me out before you agree."

I adopt an interested expression.

"The reports from Miss Smail, Reverend Gillan, and Reverend Hastie pointed to mismanagement and a lack of harmony between Scottish College and the Female Mission." Mrs. Stevenson makes a dismissive gesture with her hand. "Miss Smail's charges are without merit, however Mr. Hastie made several suggestions for the restoration of harmony."

I try to adopt the humble expression Mrs. Stevenson seems to expect, but I'm confused. "Excuse me, but why would you accept Mr. Hastie's suggestions when he wants to usurp my authority?"

"Yes, the entire situation is a muddle." Mrs. Stevenson looks exasperated. "The Investigating Committee includes the Ladies' Association in its deliberations, but the Foreign Mission Committee has a stronger influence. The long and the short of it is that if you continue as Lady Superintendent, you must comply with new rules." She stands up and walks to the window, her hands clenched by her side.

I allow her to collect herself before I speak. It occurs to me that the bigger issue is about who controls the Ladies' Association. The missions sponsored by the Ladies' Association are incidental to church politics. How can I turn this to my advantage? I turn to Mrs. Williamson.

"Will I be subordinate to Reverend Hastie? That is the only thing I can't bear."

"Assuredly not," Mrs. Williamson speaks emphatically. "The Female Mission remains under the sole supervision of the Ladies' Association." She nods her head for emphasis. "Isn't that correct Elsie?" she asks in a raised voice.

Mrs. Stevenson turns back from the window. "Yes, insofar as communications between the Female Mission and the Ladies' Association, but in order to return you to your post, Miss Pigot, we've accepted a significant compromise that affects the local lines of authority."

Mrs. Stevenson returns to the window. I join her and place my hand on her arm. She's even more distraught than I am. "What do I need to do?" I ask her.

Mrs. Stevenson faces me and shakes her head. "Miss Pigot, I'm sorry we couldn't come to a more satisfactory arrangement. There's no easy way to say this. The Corresponding Board in Calcutta will name from its members a Consulting Committee to oversee the Female Mission."

No doubt one filled with my enemies.

"The Lady Superintendent, that is to say you, will have a seat on this new committee and an equal voice on all matters." Mrs. Stevenson returns to her chair leaving me at the window. I dimly hear a train whistle and observe the soot on the sandstone buildings. Equal voice indeed. One among how many? I collect myself and return to my place. Everyone's coffee is cold. Mrs. Williamson rings for a fresh pot as we all sit silently. When it arrives, she pours it out. Steam circles over the table.

"What exactly is my relationship to this Consulting Committee?" I ask.

"I think it's important for you to understand that you remain the sole supervisor of the Female Mission," Mrs. Stevenson says. "You'll simply have to bring business matters to the Consulting Committee."

"I'm not sure I understand." My heart begins to pound inside my chest. "Will I report to this Consulting Committee?"

"You'll continue to supervise the Female Mission." Mrs. Stevenson reiterates. "The Investigating Committee believes, and we concur, that this new structure is the best way to restore proper communication and harmony between the two missions in Calcutta."

"It's just a formality," Mrs. Williamson adds. "You'll still be Lady Superintendent, and the Ladies' Association will still be your superior body."

Do they really believe that? I sip my coffee, trying to digest the news. I keep my position but without my former independence. Alternatively, I lose everything. The room is silent. Mrs. Stevenson and Mrs. Williamson gaze everywhere except in my direction. It is clear I have no options.

"Very well," I say, placing my coffee cup and saucer on the table. "I accept the new rules. Do I need to sign something?"

Mrs. Stevenson smiles with relief. "Yes. I have two copies of the agreement. We each sign both copies, and then you have a copy to take away with you."

We go to a small writing table in the corner of the room. A few inky strokes later, all is changed. I accept my copy and we return to our coffee.

"Good, that's settled," Mrs. Williamson beams, as if something wonderful has happened.

"May I make arrangements for my return to Calcutta now?"

"I admire your enthusiasm," Mrs. Stevenson says. "You can extend your stay if you like."

"Thank you. No. I need to return to my duties."

"I'll make arrangements for your medical clearance," Mrs. Williamson says. "It would be good if you could stay another fortnight and speak to the ladies and local parishes about our work. Also, we can gather bazar goods for you to take back."

I agree to stay. The ladies sip their coffee enthusiastically and the conversation drifts into items that might be welcome in Calcutta. All the while, I wonder how this new arrangement will work, and question whether it's a ruse to push me out.

A Telegram to O. Steele, Calcutta
Will arrive Calcutta in six weeks.
M. Pigot

Calcutta
William Hastie

Great Scott! That woman's bamboozled Dr. Scott as well as the Ladies' Association. Miss Smail's letters, Mr. Gillan's testimony—all for naught. I read through Mr. Macrae's letter again. Miss Pigot agreed to the new arrangement. Of course, she did. It's exactly the same as the old arrangement, with the added bonus of humiliating the Corresponding Board. Is there no end to their blindness and stupidity?

"Mr. Hastie, sir?" Falak stands at the door. "The gentlemen are in the conferring room."

"Very well," I say.

The conference room is a bit small for the entire Board, but I want our discussion to be without restraint. There's a round green *baize*-covered table with seven chairs. Two windows lighten the otherwise dim room. My colleagues look up when I enter. Colonel Walker with his stiff posture; Mr. Gregory, our new chairman; Mr. Edwards from my faculty; Mr. Broughton and Mr. Steele from the business community, and Mr. Wilson who now spends more time at the Female Mission than the College. My mind separates friend from enemy. Colonel Walker must be as appalled as I am. Mr. Steele and Mr. Wilson are sympathetic to Miss Pigot. I'm not sure where the others place their loyalty. I drop the report and my response in front of my place.

"Gentlemen," I say, "I wish it didn't fall to me as Officiating Secretary to bring this matter to your attention. Mr. Macrae requests a prompt answer to the Ladies' Association proposal creating a so-called Consulting Committee to oversee the Female Mission with the Lady Superintendent as an equal member. Mr. Wilson, you've been overseeing the mission. What do you think?"

"It appears the Investigating Committee altered our proposal, in favor of their own. It's entirely appropriate," Mr. Wilson says in his deferential way.

"Appears?" I question. "Appears? No sir, they have altered it beyond recognition and completely separated any connection between the Female

Mission and the Corresponding Board." I bang my hand on the table for emphasis. "The entire document is an embarrassment to the Church of Scotland. It's expressed in English that would shame our Bengali school-boys. It is careless, equivocal, one-sided, and feeble. It treats our recommendations with contempt. And it exonerates Miss Pigot from misdeeds which no amount of falsehood or imbecility can conceal."

"Steady on," Colonel Walker says. "I, too, am gravely disappointed in the result. Miss Smail is particularly slighted. It's clear she won't be invited to return to the Female Mission."

"Indeed," I reply. "If Miss Pigot is willing to let the past be forgotten, as the report states, Miss Smail should have been immediately recalled."

"Gentlemen," Mr. Steele says, "there's no point in going over this. The decision is made. We have only to implement it by appointing the proposed Consulting Committee."

"Not so, Mr. Steele. I protest everything in this so-called report. I can't believe Dr. Scott condones it, and there are no names attached to it. The report abounds in falsehoods. For example, it claims that if we placed the Female Mission under the Corresponding Board's supervision, Scottish ladies would lose interest and funds fall off. I put it to you, when the Female Mission was under the Board in 1877, funding was at £4,212. In 1881, funding fell to £3,459. The decline is nothing to do with the Female Mission being attached to the Board."

"Mr. Hastie," Mr. Gregory admonishes me, "we can go round and round with this and it won't change the outcome. The Mission Committee wants a Consulting Committee with Miss Pigot a full member. As Chair of the Corresponding Board I advise we acquiesce to the compromise. If the scheme fails, we have a point to argue. Nothing is permanent, after all."

Are these men blind to the truth? "Don't you see the scheme is a complete humiliation for our Board? That it's a dreadful kicking downstairs?"

"It's really our Consulting Committee," Mr. Gregory observes. "We nominate the members from among ourselves."

"Yes, it's a sweet little sugar ball they've given us meant to make us stop boo-hooing. But once the sugar comes off, it's a bitter pill. I've already heard rumors of who we should or shouldn't nominate. This is a travesty!" I say.

Mr. Wilson stands. "I haven't time to listen to your rants, Mr. Hastie. The Board's approval isn't required. It's expected. Have a little trust in God. It's His mission, after all. We're just wind and fury."

I stop and take a breath, composing myself for this audience of fools. "Of course, but it's an opportunity lost to put the Female Mission on a sound footing. For myself, I've no objection to any of it. Miss Pigot is welcome to return. I shall observe rigid neutrality in all matters relating to the Female Mission and let matters run their course." I'm confident the plan will fail in the end.

Edinburgh
Mary Pigot

As it turns out, my nemesis Reverend Hastie isn't suggested as a member of the Consulting Committee. At least that proposal is in the open. I hold it in my hand with my copy of the Investigating Committee Report and my signed acquiescence to the new rules.

My true enemy is anonymous and slips into Scotland with a leaflet signed by *"A Member of St. Andrew's Kirk."* It is distributed to parishes across the country. The writer reveals Roman Catholics in a Scottish orphanage. It doesn't name me directly but speaks of a Eurasian superintendent who laughs at the Church of Scotland. It charges that the orphans live in filth and that mission funds are squandered and used to entertain unbelievers. Worst of all, the writer claims the Female Mission lacks all morality. Every word is a lie. The writer says the superintendent was recalled to Scotland to meet these charges but was exonerated. He or she urges good Scots to withdraw their support from foreign missions. Puzzled pastors forward this vile document to the Foreign Mission Committee, and I find myself testifying a second time in the small drawing room at Number 24 Princes Street. I once again look at my interrogators with their craggy brows and gray hair and I ask God, *how can this be happening?*

This time the gentlemen dispense with pleasantries. I sit in the same spot with my hands folded on the table. Mr. Macrae's pen scratches behind me. The clergymen stare at me almost blankly as if hoping I will disappear. My stomach roils as I try to arrange my face and keep my courage.

"Have you seen this leaflet, Miss Pigot?" Dr. Scott pushes the pamphlet towards me.

"Yes. Mrs. Stevenson showed me a copy. It's nothing but lies."

"Do you have any idea who wrote it?" Mr. Phin asks in his thin voice. I shake my head.

"Could it be Miss Smail?" Dr. Scott asks.

"It could be anyone," I reply. "But if Miss Smail authored such a leaflet, she would sign her name. Of that I have no doubt."

"I think the contents are more important than the author," Mr. Muir, a parish minister, says. "We have a serious situation. Parishes are holding back their donations until we issue a response to these allegations."

Dr. Scott drums his fingers on the table while his colleagues wait for him to speak. "The public nature of this document means our response must be equally public. We're obliged to announce our findings in the *Missionary Journal*. Miss Pigot, I regret your name will be associated with our deliberations."

I take a deep breath and look across at these men, who hold my fate in their hands. What can I say? I feel myself shrinking even as I straighten my back.

Dr. Scott's voice penetrates my thoughts. "We began our deliberations as soon as the leaflet came to our attention. We've been in contact with Mr. Wilson who made further inquiries into the allegations."

It's interesting that they didn't come to me first. Perhaps they don't expect me to tell the truth. Maybe this is all just a formality before my dismissal. I imagine a headline: 'Mary Pigot, the Eurasian Who Thought She Was Scottish.'

Someone is speaking to me, but my head is throbbing with thoughts. "I'm sorry. What did you say?"

It's Dr. Scott enunciating his words. "We've just a few questions before we come to an official conclusion. Are you up to it, Miss Pigot?"

"I'm ready to answer any questions," I say mechanically.

"I'm concerned about the sanitary conditions at the orphanage," a male voice says. I look around and see Mr. Muir's lips moving. "The allegations that the children are sick and suffer from lice are very troublesome."

I feel myself back in Normal School and almost raise my hand to recite my answer.

"I presume you refer to head lice. It's a constant problem." I deliver this news matter-of-factly. "The matrons and staff wash bedding and clothing as frequently as possible. If we find a child with lice, we isolate her. Sometimes we shave her head, but we don't like to do that because of the stigma. I assure you, we are quite diligent. The problem is worse with the younger children. We train the girls to comb each other's hair close to the scalp with a fine-tooth comb. I assure you we do all we can."

"Miss Smail also commented on the cleanliness of the orphanage," Mr. Muir says.

"I can only say we do our best." I nod my head. "Calcutta is a tropical area. We fight mosquitoes to prevent malaria as well."

"There's an inference...in the leaflet. I don't like to think of it, Miss Pigot, but it must be said," Dr. Scott offers, pausing between each phrase. "There is an inference that... moral behavior is not upheld at the Female Mission. Do you know the girl Rhoda who's mentioned in the leaflet? It states she's ruined for life."

Rhoda? Who could that be? There are so many orphans.

"I don't know anyone called Rhoda. The entire reference is a vicious lie. There's no proof offered. Surely you can't take any of this seriously."

"And these entertainments?" Dr. Scott asks.

"One of the reasons Reverend Thomson employed me was because I have many connections in the local community. The Ladies' Association encourages me to hold events where missionaries can mingle with local people, so we can build trust and a good reputation. This has borne fruit as the number of parents who send their girls to the tuition-paying Upper School has grown."

The questions continue for more than an hour until I feel squeezed dry. Finally, I am dismissed. I don't remember walking back to Number 22. Perhaps I didn't. I feel completely numb, entirely disoriented.

"Do you know where you are?" a woman's voice asks. "Can you open your eyes?"

I try. Slowly, the room comes into focus. I'm in my bedroom at Number 22. A man stands in the doorway.

"Remember me?" he says with a concerned look on his face. "I'm Dr. McEwen. Three weeks ago, I gave you a clear medical certificate."

"Oh," I whisper. Mrs. Williamson stands next to the bed.

Dr. McEwen looks me over and shakes his head. "Miss Pigot, you've had a complete collapse. You must give yourself over to rest. It's the best cure for you. I'm writing a certificate to keep you home for a year."

"A year!" I sit straight up in bed; my head is pounding. "No! I have to..." I must lay back down immediately.

Mrs. Williamson interrupts. "Miss Pigot, you must recover your health. That's all there is to it. We're sending Mrs. Fergusson to take over the Female Mission and sort everything out."

I begin to tremble and sob.

"Don't fret, Miss Pigot," Mrs. Williamson says. "Mrs. Wilson wrote she's happy to have you. You looked so well when you came back. I'm sure Crieff is the best place for you. Don't you agree?"

I nod weakly. Where else can I go?

"She's sending her girl to take you back, so you've nothing to worry about," Mrs. Williamson says.

Nothing at all, I think. Just my entire life.

It's cold, the leaves have changed color, and I don't have proper clothes. I huddle over my spinning wheel at the hearth, next to the cauldron where dinner boils. Mrs. Wilson has a tall spinning wheel. I sit in a straight-backed chair in front of it and turn the wheel with my right hand while I pull the wool fiber towards me as it winds onto the bobbin. Pulling and turning. Turning and pulling. Spinning doesn't take much attention and my mind wanders. I don't think of Calcutta. I wonder how Catriona is doing at her new position at Crieff Hydropathical Establishment. I hope the Wilson lads do well at school. Mrs. Wilson and I don't climb the hillock because it rains most afternoons. Some days it's all I can do to get out of bed, but most days I spin.

One day, perhaps a month later, Mrs. Wilson interrupts my spinning to tell me I have a letter.

"Shall I open it?" Mrs. Wilson looks concerned.

"If you like," I say. I don't really care.

"It's the report from the Investigating Committee. Oh, Miss Pigot, let me read it to you."

I nod, because I can tell she wants to read the letter.

"The letter says, '*We come again to the unanimous conclusion that with the exception of certain statements affecting the cleanliness of the orphanage, the most important charges in this anonymous leaflet are either unsupported by evidence or they are directly contradicted by the information we have obtained.*" Mrs. Wilson grabs my hand off the spinning wheel. "Miss Pigot! You're exonerated! You'll be able to go back. This is very good news." She leans over to embrace me.

I manage a weak smile, put my hand back on the spinning wheel and resume my task. I'm exhausted trying to meet everyone's approval. "Why is everyone obsessed about cleanliness? You know it's impossible to meet Scottish standards. What will they do about it anyway?"

"They'll ask Mrs. Fergusson to pay particular attention to housekeeping and hygiene. She'll make recommendations. It's nothing." Mrs. Wilson laughs. "They have to say something's amiss to prove their diligence. By this time next year, you'll be going back. You dinna look pleased."

I stop the wheel and consider whether I'm pleased. "As you say, this is very good news."

"But?" Mrs. Wilson asks.

"It's just that they declared me fit once before and look what happened."

"Oh, Miss Pigot, the situation's entirely different now. The first report was a private matter. The leaflet made everything public, so they had to go through things more formally. In fact, their findings will be in next month's *Missionary Journal*. Once that comes out in October, this will all be behind you. I'm so certain, that if there's more questions, I'll go to Edinburgh with you myself and tell those men what's what."

"You'd do that for me? Go to Edinburgh?" I ask, my smile a bit brighter.

"I promise," Mrs. Wilson says enthusiastically. "Now don't you worry. You're going to recover your spirits, and I willna be leaving Crieff."

Calcutta
William Hastie

I attach my *topi* to the hook inside the door and stand a moment until my eyes adjust to the dim interior.

"Falak," I call. "Bring cider to my study."

I hang my jacket on a chair and roll my sleeves up. It's been a long morning with a meeting at St. Andrew's and several calls on the way back to the College. I prefer to lump my calls together, but it sets a grueling pace in the heat.

Falak nudges the door with his foot and brings in a tray. He sets the cider on my desk corner and places letters in the center.

"The post, sir." Falak bows.

"I've quite a bit of work, so no calls before *tiffin*," I say.

"Yes, sir." Falak closes the door behind him.

The top envelope looks a bit thick. It's from Colonel Walker. I open it first.

> *"My wife requested I forward these letters to you*
> *With Compliments, A. Walker."*

That's odd. I saw Colonel Walker last week. He didn't mention any letters.

"For Mr. Hastie and Mr. Gregory's perusal, but afterwards to be sent on to Dr. Jardine, Brokville, Ontario, Canada."—Mrs. A. Walker

Why would Mrs. Walker send anything to Dr. Jardine? He's been gone from Calcutta these past four years.

I pick up the first letter addressed to Mrs. Walker from a Mrs. Ella Augier. My God, it's about the Female Mission. She writes about a Burmese lady parlor boarder, beaten. Children suffering from fits and other ill health. Hearsay that the orphanage is little better than a brothel.

Beatings? I'd no idea things were at such a state. Miss Pigot always struck me as a woman who avoided corporeal punishment. I feel my neck curl into my skull. How can this be? But a refined lady like Mrs. Walker wouldn't spread scurrilous gossip. I sit dumbfounded while sweat trickles down my face. I force myself to pick up the next letter.

This one's from a Miss Gordon who worked as a matron. Children beaten for refusing food.

Oh, Dear Lord, forgive us! The Gordon woman saw Miss Pigot and Babu Banerjee in the drawing room with their arms around each other. Another time she saw Babu Banerjee going down the outside stairs while putting on his coat.

I feel as if someone struck the air out of me. This cannot be true. It mustn't be! What am I to do? I sweep a pile of documents off my desk. There's another letter. I inhale deeply, unfold it, and skim quickly through it.

Nothing about indiscretions, thank God. Just comments about food and clothing given to the orphans. A more detailed account of a child caned as punishment.

I hear tapping at the door.

"Go away," I shout. "I'm not at home to anyone."

I pace the room until, exhausted, I fall on my knees before God.

"Dear Lord," I pray. "I'm not equipped to deal with such scandal. I've done everything in my power to remove the Lady Superintendent, yet she comes back again. And now I have this information, what shall I do with it? Who will believe me? What would you have me do?"

I stay on my knees, lost in time and space. I remember the prophets and how God called Jeremiah. The prophet said he couldn't speak, because he was a child. I too am a child in these affairs.

I rise and pick up my Bible. Turning to a page in Jeremiah I read:

"But the Lord said unto me, Say not, I am a child; for thou shalt go to all that I shall send thee, and whatsoever I command thee thou shalt speak. Be not afraid of their faces: for I am with thee to deliver thee."

I sit on the hardback chair facing my desk, mulling what I must do. I'll consult with others to be sure the letters ring true. If so, I'll do my duty. Before my resolve fails, I write a cover note: *This communication has just been received by me and read. I wish it had not been sent to me. It has certainly taken me by surprise. I feel bound by my sense of duty to forward it. I shall accordingly post it without further comment.*

The next morning, I take the first train to Dum Dum and make my way to Colonel Walker's house. I arrive while the servant still sweeps the porch, hand my *topi* to Colonel Walker's *durwan* and go to the breakfast room. The *durwan* rushes to open the doors for me.

"Sahib, you have a visitor."

Colonel Walker glances up from his newspaper. "Mr. Hastie, I didn't expect to see you. I'm just back from putting the ladies on the train for Darjeeling. Sit down."

The *durwan* pours out a cup of coffee for me. I nod towards him.

"Leave us," Colonel Walker says. "What brings you here? It must be a serious matter."

"I find it so," I reply. "Yesterday I received a packet of letters from you."

"Yes, Mrs. Walker wanted me to send them as soon as possible, but I hardly expected a visit from you." Colonel Walker looks puzzled.

"Have you read them?" I ask.

"Yes."

"Do you think the accusations are true?"

"If I didn't, I wouldn't have sent them," Colonel Walker says.

"You believe them?" I ask, incredulous.

"Yes," Colonel Walker nods. "I do."

I'm aghast. "You believe Miss Pigot was indiscreet with Babu Banerjee? It's a most serious charge, one that could ruin us all."

"I find it completely in keeping with information I have from Miss Smail," Colonel Walker says.

There's an insect on the wall behind Colonel Walker. I watch it weave itself through the stenciling. "I have my differences with the Lady Superintendent, but I can't besmirch her reputation without cause. This Miss Gordon, who is referenced, can her word be trusted?"

"I had Mrs. Walker make inquiries. She consulted with the Leslies whom we know well, and they vouched for Miss Gordon's reliability. You can forward the letters to Dr. Scott with every confidence," Colonel Walker says.

"Mrs. Walker requested they be sent to Dr. Jardine. Why would she do that?" I ask.

"Mrs. Walker thinks highly of him, but he isn't the right man for the purpose," Colonel Walker says. "Dr. Jardine was one of your predecessors at the College. He opposed Miss Pigot's appointment. But he can't do anything from Canada. Dr. Scott is head of the Foreign Mission Committee. He'll mount a full investigation, and we'll put a stop to Miss Pigot once and for all."

I ponder the situation. It's my duty as head of the mission to send the letters on, but once unleashed, who knows where the accusations will go?

"Mr. Hastie, if you don't send the letters to Dr. Scott, then I will. This is the proof we need to remove Miss Pigot and restore harmony among the greater mission."

I stand and put out my hand. "Colonel Walker, I truly wish I'd never seen these letters."

I travel back to Calcutta and take a carriage to St. Andrew's Kirk, hoping to catch Reverend Gillan in his office. I tap on the door and hear his voice telling me to enter. Mr. Gillan sits in his shirtsleeves. He motions me in. "Just going over tomorrow's sermon. What brings you here on a Saturday?"

"I've something to show you." I reach in my pocket for the letters. "I received these from Mrs. Walker. I can hardly believe what they say, but I've just been at Dum Dum, and Colonel Walker vouches for their contents. I think you should read them." I sit across the room at the conference table so Mr. Gillan can read them in some privacy. Out of the corner of my eye I see Mr. Gillan reading the letters. He polishes his spectacles and begins reading them again.

"Well," he says. He walks over to the table and hands the letters back to me. "Well," Mr. Gillan says again and sits down so heavily I think the cane chair may give way. "I am shocked." He bows his head and then looks up. "Mr. Hastie I can only say that after reading these documents, I feel ashamed to go to the pulpit and preach the Gospel of the Lord Jesus Christ on Sunday."

"Mr. Gillan, no shame attaches to you, surely."

"I testified against Miss Pigot before the Investigating Committee. Clearly, I was a poor witness since the Committee dismissed all charges. I've failed the church to which I've dedicated my life." Mr. Gillan passes a hand over his bald head. "I thought Miss Pigot misguided and inept. I never recognized how evil she is. When she comes back, I must raise the question with the Elders about whether I should admit her to the communion table if she decides to worship here." Mr. Gillan steeples his hands. "What do you think? Should the woman be admitted to the communion table? She's sure to kick up a fuss if we deny her."

"Mr. Gillan," I interrupt. "I need to know whether you think I should forward the letters to Dr. Scott. Colonel Walkers says if I don't, he will. But the charges may be baseless."

"Yes, I see we need to decide." Mr. Gillan strokes his chin. "You can't ignore them. You have to send them somewhere, but Jardine can't do anything useful with them. Under the circumstances, I suggest you send them to Dr. Scott. Perhaps he'll see sense at last."

I rise to depart and rest my hand on Mr. Gillan's shoulder. He looks at me. "May God forgive us all for our ignorance," he says as I step outside, unconvinced we have been ignorant. I'd heard rumors about Miss Pigot and Banerjee, but until now there was no actual evidence. Inspectress Wheeler complained about cleanliness at the orphanage but said nothing about children being beaten. Now the situation has utterly changed. I have irrefutable proof of Miss Pigot's behavior and must send it forward.

I consider my options until I arrive back at the College a shattered man. I conclude the allegations are true but I am reluctant to do my duty. The scandal will overwhelm us all, and the blame will fall upon me as head of the mission. I would rather wait until Miss Pigot returns, and then force her resignation.

Mr. Gregory, chair of our Corresponding Board, is kind enough to call on me in the early evening. We meet in the conference room. He looks tired from whatever exertions he had during the day.

"May I pour you a peg?" I ask him. "I think after reading these letters I received, you'll have need of it." I also pour myself a generous portion.

Mr. Gregory reads through the letters quickly, as if the paper burns his fingers. "I mentioned when we contemplated the change in mission structure that nothing is permanent," Mr. Gregory says. "You received this information at a propitious time."

"I prefer not to be involved," I say. "The woman is arrogant and obstructive, but I don't like to think the charges are true."

Mr. Gregory shakes his head. "You're too upright to see what's before us. Everything we've observed can be interpreted in two ways, except this. Given options, the Ladies' Association and the Foreign Mission Committee chose to overlook issues of hygiene and employees. But this. There can be no doubt of inappropriate behavior between Miss Pigot and Babu Banerjee. Either they stood with their arms around each other or they didn't. Send the letters to Dr. Scott and get on with your work."

"And if the charge is false?" I ask.

"You miss the point, Mr. Hastie. We have no authority to investigate the charges. It's your duty to forward the letters to someone who can."

Mr. Gregory shakes my hand and leaves without finishing his peg. I sit staring at the green *baize* on the table. Miss Pigot is irascible and unreasonable, but I have no wish to destroy anyone's life. Could she possibly behave in such a fashion? I search my memory.

Yes, her manner with men is indelicate. There was her behavior at Mr. Steele's dinner party when she threw her legs on the sofa, and the way she fawned on Mr. Wilson at the Barrackpore picnic. Others have commented on Miss Pigot's loose conversation and behavior. Numerous people came to me as a minister in the Church of Scotland, and I chose not to pursue their information. I can't turn my back again, not in light of these latest accusations.

I read over my cover note and begin writing a postscript.

I shall only add that I have long been more than suspicious of such things as are stated here and have myself observed that every external propriety was more than disregarded. I have, however, not had such documentary and authenticated evidence put into my hands until now.

I bundle the documents and address the envelope to Dr. Scott. I have one more person to speak to before I send them.

Reverend Chuckerbutty is pastor of the native church that Miss Pigot attends with her students and teachers. He has direct knowledge about the orphanage. I invite him visit me at the College.

"Reverend Hastie, how very nice to see you again," Mr. Chuckerbutty says eyeing the refreshments I have ordered for his visit. I offer him a plate.

"I wonder if you could advise me on a very delicate matter, Mr. Chuckerbutty," I lean forward. "Nothing we speak of can leave this room."

Mr. Chuckerbutty fills his plate and smiles pleasantly. "Of course. It is between us, then."

"I have received unsettling information about Miss Pigot and Babu Banerjee. You spend a lot of time at the orphanage. Have you noticed any familiarity between them?"

Mr. Chuckerbutty strokes his white beard as he contemplates my question. "Well, there was one time a couple years ago. I climbed the stairs to the veranda, and when I got there, I could hear them speaking in the room next to the staircase. And about an hour later Kali Babu came out of that room and went downstairs."

"When was this?"

"Maybe two years ago. Just after you arrived. I often see Kali Babu go into Miss Pigot's room without knocking. And I see them come out together."

Mr. Chuckerbutty continues after taking another bite of his refreshment. "And one Sunday morning after service Miss Pigot asked me to call. I went about four o'clock that afternoon and went upstairs. I looked into the drawing room..." He pauses as if deciding whether to continue.

"Go on, Mr. Chuckerbutty."

"Well, Kali Babu was sitting on a mat on the floor wearing just his trousers and shirt. I was shocked, I can tell you, Mr. Hastie. And Miss Pigot was lying on the sofa."

I can scarcely believe what I am hearing. "What did you think when you saw them?"

"I thought they might be committing adultery," Mr. Chuckerbutty says as if it was a common occurrence.

"And why didn't you say anything?"

"Who would believe me? And I didn't want to cause any trouble. You understand," Mr. Chuckerbutty spreads his hands. "Should I have come to you?"

I assure Mr. Chuckerbutty that he has done the right thing in telling me about these events. He leaves me to take *tiffin* elsewhere, and I go to the washroom to vomit. I clean up, return to my desk, and call for Falak.

"Put this in the next post." I hand over the envelope.

I pull out a blank postcard: *My dear Mrs. Walker, the letters you sent me surprised me very much. I feel it my duty to send them to Dr. Scott convener of the Foreign Mission Committee, which employs Miss Pigot and not to Dr. Jardine to whom they are of no consequence. Need I say how sorry I am they ever fell into my hands.*

I underline the last sentence twice to emphasize the seriousness of her actions and mine.

Edinburgh
Mary Pigot

It's November, and so cold. I don't know how I'll last the Scottish winter. Mrs. Wilson believes walking solves most things, so she lends me her coat and sends me to the village to pick up any letters. Today there's one for me from Dr. Scott. I want to tear into it, but I'm afraid. I don't want to open it alone. I head back to the cottage and Mrs. Wilson and I open the letter together. The note is very short. Dr. Scott requests that I come to his office at my earliest convenience. I'm speechless as I am sure this is not a good sign.

"We'll go on Tuesday," Mrs. Wilson says, squeezing my hand. "Be strong, my friend."

While we sit in the drawing room at 24 Princes Street and wait for Dr. Scott, I feel the nightmare beginning again. Mrs. Wilson pats my hand over and over. There's a hot tea service on the table. Neither of us partakes despite the cold.

Dr. Scott comes into the room alone.

"Mrs. Wilson," he says raising his eyebrows. "I didn't expect to see you."

"I'm sure you didn't," Mrs. Wilson say assertively. "Every time you summon Miss Pigot, the poor lass is shattered. I haven't brought her back to health again for you to undo all my efforts. Anything you have to say, can be said to me as well. After all, I've not only lived in Calcutta but served as Lady Superintendent. I know exactly what the conditions are."

"Are you in agreement, Miss Pigot?"

I nod. I can hardly bear to look at the man. I feel my body begin to shake.

"Miss Pigot, Mrs. Wilson, what I'm about to say is between us," Dr. Scott begins. "Under the circumstances, it's the least I can do. Mr. Hastie forwarded a packet of letters that Mrs. Walker sent him. Mrs. Walker's husband is an Elder at St. Andrews and a member of the Corresponding Board."

"I know who she is," I say quietly. "She is also Miss Smail's sister-in-law."

"Yes, well it appears she solicited letters from three ladies regarding conditions at the Female Mission."

Mrs. Wilson interrupts. "Isn't that something for Mrs. Fergusson to deal with?"

"When you read the letters, you'll understand why matters can't be left to Mrs. Fergusson," Dr. Scott continues. "Also, Mr. Hastie wrote a note and postscript verifying the contents of these letters. I'll leave you to read the letters without interruption. I think you'll agree it would be better if they aren't shared with anyone else." Dr. Scott leaves the room before I can respond.

I stare at the envelope. Why is this happening again? How many times will I have to prove myself? Mrs. Wilson and I sit in silence for what seems like an eternity but is probably only a minute or two.

"Would you like to read the letters alone?" she asks.

My eyes fill with tears. I look at her kind, familiar face. "They must be very bad, Mrs. Wilson, if Dr. Scott has left for me to read the letters by myself. Will you think less of me, if we read them together?"

"You've stayed at my wee cottage for these six months, Miss Pigot. I know who you are inside. Nothing in these letters will change my regard for you. Now then, I find it's best to meet enemies head on. Shall we begin?"

An hour later, Dr. Scott returns. It takes all my strength to look him in the eye, but I do.

"None of this is true."

"I believe you," Dr. Scott says. I sense he means it and wants to be my ally. "But Mr. Hastie, a respected man both here and in Calcutta, validates the letters. We cannot dismiss his authority."

Mrs. Wilson looks Dr. Scott directly in the eye. "You've investigated Miss Pigot twice now. Ye know the truth of the matter."

"We looked at the charges regarding the Female Mission," Dr. Scott says. "This new allegation regarding inappropriate behavior is something else entirely."

"Stuff and nonsense," says Mrs. Wilson. "Miss Pigot is a good Christian. She'd never commit such an indiscretion."

"Miss Pigot, if the allegation appears publicly, you will lose your position regardless of the truth. I suggest you persuade Mr. Hastie to withdraw his validation. Without the weight of his authority to carry these charges, they come to nothing."

"And how am I to do that?" Surely, Dr. Scott understands that this is an impossible situation. Mr. Hastie hates me.

"I'll tell you how," Mrs. Wilson says. "You'll square your shoulders, go back to Calcutta, and meet the devil head-on."

Dr. Scott gives me a copy of the letters and advises me to clear matters up as soon as possible.

I'm numb as I retrace my journey. On board the ship, I see young giggling girls on their way to find husbands during the Cold Season. I stand by the rail, praying God will hear my prayer. Psalm 130 is my hourly mantra.

Out of the depths, I have cried to thee, O Lord.
Lord, hear my voice: let thine ears be attentive to the voice of my
supplications.
If thou, Lord, shouldest mark iniquities, O Lord, who shall stand?
But there is forgiveness with thee, that thou mayest be feared.
I wait for the Lord, my soul doth wait,
And in his word do I hope.

195

Chapter 10
"Truth Shall Be My Shield And Buckler"

February 1883
Serampore, India
Mary Pigot

I don't live in Calcutta any more. My home is now a boarding house in Serampore. It's cheaper, and few people know me. I don't have to answer questions here. To make ends meet, I might have to get a position at the Girls' School, though I'm not sure they'd employ me. How do I explain what happened at the Female Mission?

Serampore is a thirteen-mile journey from Howrah Station. Too far for visitors. Besides, who wants to call on a disgraced lady missionary?

I've been here two months with no progress on my vindication. The mission shuns me. Reverend Hastie doesn't reply to my notes. And, really, there's no reason he should. He has complete control of the Female Mission. It's as if the last thirteen years of my life never happened. If I don't do something soon, it will be too late. But what options do I have?

I contact Mr. Steele about taking legal advice. I tell him the truth—matters regarding my employment need clarification. Mr. Steele recommends a solicitor with the impressive name of Arthur St. John Carruthers. I don't know anything about him, but I have an interview with him this morning.

I peer into the cracked mirror checking myself one final time. Pointless really. By the time I take the train and then a *gharry* to Dalhousie Square, I'll be a dusty mess. What does it matter anyway; I pick up my *topi* and walk to the station.

At the High Court, I ask for directions to Mr. Carruthers's office When I enter, a clerk greets me and inquires as to my business.

"I have an appointment with Mr. Carruthers."

"I see." The clerk consults a book. "You must be Miss Pigot. Come with me."

We go down a short, narrow hallway to a room with a large partner's desk. A stooped, gray-haired man stands by the window.

"Miss Pigot, sir," the clerk says to the gray-haired man.

"Yes, yes." The man waves the clerk away. "Bring tea."

I'm not sure where I should sit. The man looks at me. His eyes are a pale blue and look large behind his spectacles.

"Miss Pigot?" he says.

"Yes, I am Miss Pigot."

"Please sit." Mr. Carruthers gestures at a hard-backed chair in front of the desk. "What can I do for you?"

"I need advice. Are you familiar with the Church of Scotland's Female Mission?" I ask. "Until recently, I was the Lady Superintendent."

"Yes?" Mr. Carruthers nods.

"I'm presently suspended, because of false rumors."

The door opens. The clerk sets a tea tray down on the desk and leaves.

"Continue," Mr. Carruthers says without changing expression.

"These rumors forced me to go to Scotland to defend myself."

"Were you successful?"

"Yes. But after the initial investigation, an anonymous pamphlet appeared, and I had to defend myself a second time." I begin narrating my depressing story. "This time the Ladies' Association..."

"Ladies' Association?"

"Yes, my employers," I explain. "The second time, they sent Mrs. Fergusson to take over while I was on medical leave. But then, these letters appeared..." I stop again.

"Excuse me," Mr. Carruthers interrupts. "I must pour the tea now, or it will be too strong."

I watch steamy liquid flow into the porcelain cups.

"You were saying something about some letters?" Mr. Carruthers encourages me on.

"Yes. These letters appeared with Reverend Hastie's cover of authorization. And I was suspended. Dr. Scott—he's head of the Foreign Mission Committee—told me I have to solve the matter myself. But I haven't been able to, and I don't know what to do." I hear my voice start to tremble.

"Do you have the letters with you?" Mr. Carruthers asks.

I reach into my reticule and hand them across the desk. Mr. Carruthers adjusts his spectacles and begins reading. Sweat dribbles down my back. He makes a note. At last he folds the letters up.

"There's no doubt the letters damage your reputation. And you're suspended from the Female Mission?"

"Yes. I'm staying in Serampore at the moment."

"Loss of livelihood," Mr. Carruthers mumbles as he makes another note. "What do you want me to do for you?"

"The Ladies' Association hasn't seen the letters. If Mr. Hastie retracts his endorsement, the letters may be overlooked."

"That's a possibility, I suppose," Mr. Carruthers leans back in his chair. "However, Mr. Hastie isn't the source of the letters. A Mrs. Walker initiated these responses. Whether the letters will go further is impossible to say. Do you have any idea why Mrs. Walker solicited these letters?"

"Her sister, Miss Smail, was my assistant for a short while. We...um...didn't get on well. I understand Miss Smail sent her own version of events back to Scotland, but the Investigating Committee exonerated me from any wrongdoing."

"Do you think Miss Smail bears a grudge? Or this Mrs. Walker?" Mr. Carruthers asks, but continues without waiting for my response. "Why not demand a retraction from them?"

"They don't matter. If Reverend Hastie takes back his endorsement, things will return to normal. But if he doesn't, matters might escalate and I could lose my position permanently," I say. "You must help me."

The clerk comes in with a note. "I'll answer it later," Mr. Carruthers says. "You can take the tea." After gathering the dishes, the clerk opens the door with his foot to exit. The cups rattle. Mr. Carruthers turns his attention back to me. "Have you tried approaching Mr. Hastie through mutual colleagues? Often these matters can be settled informally."

That's all I've done since my return. Despite our friendship, even Mr. Wilson barely keeps in contact. I don't understand this and wonder if it's because he and Mr. Hastie chum together to share expenses at meals. "None of my former colleagues want anything to do with me. And Mr. Hastie doesn't answer my notes."

Mr. Carruthers stares at me as if my hat is crooked.

"Miss Pigot, shall I tell you the truth?" he asks.

I nod vigorously.

"Miss Pigot, if you engage me to do anything, these letters will become a matter of public record. Once that happens, their contents can never be removed from people's memory." Mr. Carruthers puts the letters back in the envelope. "Though it's a difficult pill to swallow, I think your best course would be to find other employment."

"But that isn't right!" I clench my fists. "There's not a shred of truth in any of these letters. They are all lies!"

"Nevertheless, Miss Pigot. I often find truth is of little consequence in these sorts of matters."

How can that be? The truth doesn't matter?

Once I took my father' pen without permission. I wanted to draw something, but I broke the nib. I was horrified. I carefully put the pen in its place. When my father asked me about the pen, I said I hadn't seen it. "Is that the truth, my girl?" he asked. "Think carefully, for without truth we have no way to stand before God." I confessed to him immediately. He smacked my wrist with a ruler and told me I was a good girl for speaking up. I must speak up. I want Mr. Hastie to admit the truth.

"Mr. Carruthers, there must be some action we can take. Some way Mr. Hastie will admit his error and withdraw his endorsement."

"What do you suggest?"

"What if *you* approach Mr. Hastie and ask him to withdraw his statements?"

"Why should he do that? He's not the injured party here. You are. I only know of Mr. Hastie from his reputation. From what I've heard, he's not a man who wants to look foolish, which he will, if he withdraws his endorsement. You'll have to bring stronger pressure to bear if you want a result."

"What sort of pressure?" I ask.

"I suggest we draw up a lawsuit against Reverend Hastie and accuse him of malicious libel. Which is surely the case if these letters are false."

"A lawsuit?" I whisper.

"If we threaten Mr. Hastie with a public action, he may acquiesce and withdraw his endorsement," Mr. Carruthers replies calmly.

"That seems extreme." I imagine my name in the newspaper in the section on court proceedings. How humiliating that would be.

"You're in a serious situation," Mr. Carruthers reminds me as if there's a chance I've forgotten my dire circumstances, "one that can destroy your reputation. With nothing to lose, there's no reason for Mr. Hastie to withdraw his statement."

"But a lawsuit? Won't that make everything public?"

"It will, which is why you must consider the possibility from all sides. The fact that we draw up the suit doesn't mean we'll file it. But if Reverend Hastie refuses to recant, it will be your only alternative if you wish to restore your reputation. To the extent such a remedy is viable. Do you understand?"

Sweat pours down my face as I gather my thoughts. "But, Mr. Carruthers, the letters are private now. No one knows their contents. Won't I be in a worse situation if they become public?"

"That's for you to decide. From what you said, I understand you have neither position nor references. I don't know what your future plans are, but rumors can be just as damaging as facts."

"Will I have to appear in Court?"

"Of course, if the lawsuit goes to Court. The only defense against libel is to prove the allegations are true. Reverend Hastie will find witnesses to corroborate his statements. We'll prove his witnesses are not accurate or reliable—that they didn't see what they saw. You know, that sort of thing."

"I see," I say, though—in truth—I see nothing at all except public humiliation.

"Think it over. Take advice from your friends. Let me know how you wish to proceed. But don't leave it too long." Mr. Carruthers hands me back my letters and walks me to the door.

"Sometimes, Miss Pigot, the hardest path is also the most direct."

William Hastie

I tap a visiting card on my desk. A Mr. A. St. John Carruthers awaits me in the drawing room. There is a matter he wishes to discuss in regard to Miss Pigot. What can she want now? I'm certainly not giving her a reference.

"Falak," I call.

"Yes, sir."

"Please escort Mr. Carruthers in and bring refreshments."

I hear Falak speaking to my guest and stand as they reach the door.

"Come in, Mr. Carruthers." I extend my hand. "I don't think we've met."

"A pleasure, Mr. Hastie," Mr. Carruthers says. "I've come on a matter of some delicacy regarding Miss Pigot."

"Please sit down." I gesture to an easy chair and sit down on wingback chair next to it. "Rest assured, I'll keep anything we discuss in complete confidence."

"May I be direct?" Mr. Carruthers asks.

"I generally find it the best way of doing business," I reply, but I wonder what he's getting at.

"I'm preparing a civil suit against you on behalf of my client."

My chin drops. "Miss Pigot is mounting a lawsuit against me? I'm astonished. On what grounds?"

"Malicious libel," he replies without emotion.

I can't keep myself from laughing. The very idea that I libeled that woman is ridiculous. Mr. Carruthers looks taken aback. Surely he sees the absurdity of the situation. A disgraced lady missionary suing the Principal of Scottish College. Who could believe such a thing could happen?

"Mr. Carruthers," I say at last, "you're mistaken. I don't know what Miss Pigot told you, but my interactions with her have been entirely professional. Nothing that could be remotely construed as libel."

"As it happens," Mr. Carruthers says smugly, "your postscript on a packet of letters delivered to Scotland last November falls under the legal definition of libel. Specifically, your comment that you had long been suspicious of the allegations contained in those three letters, and that Miss Pigot lacked external propriety."

"I merely meant for the Foreign Missionary Committee to investigate the situation. I made no charges against Miss Pigot." I sit back in my chair and consider whether to take Mr. Carruthers seriously.

"You endorsed the letters as documentary and authenticated evidence. We view this alleged libel as the final step in a systematic persecution of Miss Pigot."

"Persecution?" I lean forward to make my point. "I merely expressed an informed opinion of the woman."

Mr. Carruthers continues as if I haven't spoken. "My client informs me the charges made against her in those letters are untrue and unfounded. Your concurrence with those allegations can only be seen as the product of a deep-seated malice."

"Poppycock!" I explode. "Her behavior has caught up with her, and she wants someone to blame. Well, she's looking in the wrong place. I've done nothing more than my duty." I stand. "If that's all you came for…" I gesture towards the door.

Mr. Carruthers waves me back into my chair. "May I continue?"

I grudgingly resume my seat.

"Miss Pigot prefers not to move forward with the suit, provided you publicly retract your statements in the postscript dated 11 November 1882. She also requires a public apology. If we don't hear from you in three days, we'll file suit without further notification."

I grab hold of my temper. "Mr. Carruthers, let me be clear. I made those comments in my official capacity as head of the Scottish Mission. I've nothing to apologize for or retract."

"I urge you to reconsider. You have three days, Mr. Hastie. Good day." Mr. Carruthers stands up and sees himself out.

Despite the heat, I feel frozen in my chair. The idea of a public lawsuit makes my blood run cold. The entire tawdry mess will catch the eye of every newspaper reporter in Calcutta, and the Mission Committee will blame me. I never wanted the responsibility of forwarding those letters. But Colonel Walker insisted I do my duty, and Mr. Gregory concurred. How did Miss Pigot find out about the letters when I sent them to Dr. Scott? Could this lawsuit be Dr. Scott's doing? The only way Miss Pigot could have the letters is if he gave them to her. Why would he do that? Am I the target of his actions and Miss Pigot a pawn in his strategy? I shake my head. Miss Pigot is a determined woman, but she won't follow through with this suit. She isn't that headstrong.

I am wrong. I receive a copy of Miss Pigot's official Complaint on the thirty-first of March. The next day is April Fool's Day—which would have been a more fitting delivery date. Her Complaint is a complete joke. The woman is delusional. She describes the Calcutta mission as an idyllic Eden before my arrival. Yet the Mission Committee specifically requested me to restore harmony. She paints me as her enemy when all I've done is my duty. She alleges I, Miss Smail, and Reverend Gillan slandered her. And as proof, she points out that the Ladies' Association exonerated her of any wrongdoing. The charges weren't false, and the Investigating Committee made a bad mistake.

Miss Pigot blames her present circumstance not on her own amoral behavior, but on Mrs. Walker's letters and my endorsement. She ought to blame the Committee for absolving her in the first place and giving her a false hope of redemption. Dr. Scott and the ladies hushed things up, but the truth always reveals itself.

Dr. Scott shouldn't have given Miss Pigot the letters. I sent them to him as a privileged communication, which establishes my desire to do my duty without spreading further discord. Miss Pigot will be sorry she brought these charges into the light of day. I have no concerns about this case. As it says in Psalm 91, *Truth shall be my shield and buckler.*

I return my attention to the text of Miss Pigot's Complaint, so I can compose my response. It reads like a checklist, making my task more efficient. Yes, the first three items are true. Then, we come to the fourth paragraph. Miss Pigot states conditions between our two missions were harmonious until I arrived. No, no, dear lady. They certainly were not. The Mission Committee had serious concerns, which I can prove.

The Complaint is all falsehoods from there, especially this idea of systematic persecution. Clearly Miss Pigot suffers from what French pathologists call "delusions of persecution." Poor Miss Pigot. I hold her in compassion, but I shall defend myself and the mission.

Any intelligent judge will dismiss this suit as a waste of the Court's time.

What I can't discern is how Miss Pigot can afford to mount a lawsuit. Rumor has it she's short of funds. I heard that Sajiva, her former *durwan*, called on her asking for work. She said she couldn't retain him. So how will she pay Mr. Carruthers? And then she'll need a barrister and there will be court costs.

Perhaps Miss Pigot appealed to Mr. Steele for assistance. He often takes her side against the Corresponding Board. But would a confirmed bachelor risk his reputation over such a woman? I put on my jacket and grab my *topi*. Time for a call.

For a man of his stature, Mr. Steele keeps a gloomy place of business. Keeping the sun out doesn't cool the room as much as one might hope, and the filtered light gives everything a dingy appearance. Mr. Steele's office is at the back of his mercantile establishment. I walk through the storage area and knock on the open door. Mr. Steele sits in his shirtsleeves going over a book of accounts.

"Reverend Hastie," Mr. Steele says, shrugging into his coat. "What brings you here?"

"I'm here to discuss the lawsuit Miss Pigot is bringing against me. I presume you've heard of it?"

"I daresay everyone in Calcutta knows about it. The publicity will be bad for us."

"So you know the contents of the suit."

"Not precisely. Miss Pigot asked my advice in a roundabout way. I gather you made some statements that she claims are false. Are you sure you can't accommodate her request?" Mr. Steele waves me into a chair and sits down again.

"I'm a man of my word, Mr. Steele."

"So I've noticed. Are you certain your words are always correct?"

Mr. Steele seems to doubt my veracity. "Yes, I am." I withdraw a notebook from my pocket. "I'm here because I want to confirm my memory of events that occurred at your home shortly after I arrived when I was ill with cholera. At that time, did you observe Miss Pigot being free with Mr. Wilson in your drawing room?"

"I beg your pardon?" Mr. Steele looks at me with a startled expression.

"Were they free with each other? Did they behave in an intimate manner? My nurse at the time threatened to leave because of their behavior."

"I don't know anything about that, and I don't believe a word of it!"

Mr. Steele's face flushes. I wonder why he's so quick to defend Miss Pigot. "I also remember a dinner party," I continue. "Mr. Wilson and Mr. Clarke were there. Miss Pigot had her arm around your necks, and said, 'What a picture, Reverend Hastie. I wish I had a photograph of it.' Do remember that incident?"

"No, Mr. Hastie, I do not." Mr. Steele's face reddens. "I've never had a woman's arm around my neck in all my life. I'm shocked you would even suggest such a thing. You may leave now and take your notebook with you."

I put my notebook away and take a more assertive approach. "Before I leave, answer me this. Miss Pigot hasn't the funds to mount a lawsuit. Are you using your influence to support this whore and provide her with funds?"

Mr. Steel's face turns nearly purple. "Get out," he shouts and points to the door. "I won't stand for you defaming Miss Pigot! But to answer your question, no, I haven't given her any money."

"I see," I say calmly "Then it must be your brother John."

"That's a lie. Please leave immediately."

"Mr. Steele, I need your support in this lawsuit. This entire matter could have been avoided if you'd counseled Miss Pigot against it."

"Get. Out. Of. My. Office." Mr. Steele grabs my right arm to push me out the door.

I can't believe it. I fall back a couple steps, then take his arms firmly.

"No, Mr. Steele. We mustn't part this way. You've been kind to me in the past, and I have an affection for you. I value your friendship, but I must defend myself." I drop his arm, but Mr. Steele is glowering at me as if he wants to strike me.

I can't leave things this way with a man of his standing in our missionary community. He could turn others against me. "Please, Mr.

Steele." I hold out my hand. "We can't part this way. Let us at least shake hands like gentlemen."

Mr. Steele turns away in disgust. His servants stand in the doorway. One of them brandishes a club. It can't be said that Mr. Steele and I parted on bad terms. I walk in front of Mr. Steele, grab his hand and shake it twice. He looks at me in surprise. I hurry out the door before the situation deteriorates further.

With Mr. Fish now by my side to take notes, I continue to interview other potential witnesses. I search out all the people I can find who had any interactions with Miss Pigot from her earliest employment. Mrs. Wheeler promises to testify about Miss Pigot's staff. I find that infernal nurse. I look for the students referred to in the letters. And, when Mrs. Fergusson is off the premises, I go to the Female Mission to interview staff members about Miss Pigot's relationship with Babu Kali Churn Banerjee. Miss Smail inferred it was more than a flirtation. If I can find someone to testify directly, the case will be over.

I ask Mrs. Ellis if she saw Babu Banerjee in Miss Pigot's bedroom or bathroom.

"No, sir," she says, "but I know he used the washroom."

Mrs. Tremearne says the same.

I also ask if they know anything about relations between Miss Pigot and Mr. Wilson. But no one admits anything. I start looking for the students named in the letters, and anyone who has ever worked for Miss Pigot. A pattern of behavior begins to emerge.

Mary Pigot

It's only ten o'clock in the morning, and already the sun is burning. I see a few resting pariah dogs in the courtyard shade. Last night I heard a jackal howl. I wanted to howl with it. What shall become of me?

Someone knocks. I pull my wrapper around me and open the door an inch.

"Mem, please come. Someone came for you. I put him in the drawing room," the servant says.

"Who is it?" I ask.

The man shrugs and leaves.

I dress quickly, put up my hair, and go downstairs. In the drawing room, my dear friend Mr. Wilson turns around. Praise God! It is so good to see him.

"Mr. Wilson, I'm so pleased to see you. Sit here." I smile and gesture to the cane lounge. "Let me call for refreshments." I extend my hands, but Mr. Wilson holds his *topi* with both hands.

"No, Miss Pigot. This isn't a social call. I'm here about your lawsuit."

"Has Reverend Hastie agreed to retract?" For a moment, I am hopeful.

"Far from it. He'll never withdraw. You've ruined us," Mr. Wilson says without any expression in his voice.

"How? How could I have ruined us? The Court will unmask Reverend Hastie as the vicious man he is."

"You don't know, do you?" Mr. Wilson asks incredulously.

"Know what?"

"Reverend Hastie is interviewing everyone you've ever known, as far back as your first employment. Perhaps even further. He's looking for any mistake or misunderstanding that ever occurred in your life." Mr. Wilson drops his head. "I'm sorry to be the one telling you this."

I can't breathe. The room is completely silent. The sun beats on the shade, revealing dust particles swirling in the light. I sink onto the horsehair sofa. I feel a pain in my head like a knife cutting through it.

Mr. Wilson remains standing. "There's more. Reverend Hastie's determined to prove an inappropriate flirtation between you and Babu Banerjee. That way he can punish you both."

"But, I don't understand. Kali Churn is a son to me. There's nothing inappropriate about our relationship." What is Mr. Wilson talking about? And why does he have such a look of disappointment on his face?

"And now," Mr. Wilson continues, "Mr. Fish informs me Reverend Hastie plans to drag me into this mess. Your hasty actions will ruin two reputations besides your own. Not to mention the shame my wife and children will suffer." Mr. Wilson begins pacing. "Filing this suit is the most foolish thing you've ever done. None of us will come through this intact."

I stand and reach out my hand towards him. He steps away with a distraught expression.

"Don't touch me," he snaps. "My wife and I have been your friends. We recommended you as Lady Superintendent. And you repay us by dragging us into your difficulties."

"Mr. Wilson, I never meant to cause you or your wife any harm. You are both my dear friends." How can I repair the damage I've caused? I wrap my arms around each other.

"But you did cause us harm. If this suit goes to court and I'm called as a witness... Don't you understand? Calcutta gossips will be riveted by the testimony. It will be in all the newspapers. None of us will live this down.

You did this out of pride, Miss Pigot, without any consideration of how it would impact others."

Pride? My head is spinning. Why does Mr. Wilson not understand my position? How can he say such a thing? The mat on the floor is loose. It shifts every time Mr. Wilson puts his foot down. I wait until his pacing slows, so I can think.

"You know I would never do anything out of pride. Dr. Scott told me to defend myself. He said I have to make Mr. Hastie retract his statements. He said to do whatever is necessary."

"I very much doubt that. To drag the entire mission through the muck because you can't get along with one man? Dr. Scott never told you to do that."

"He did. He told me to defend myself."

"So you conclude the best plan is to attack a powerful man and embarrass the mission?"

"No, it isn't like that at all. Please listen to me. Mr. Carruthers thought if we threatened to sue Reverend Hastie, he would recant."

"Did he now? Well, he was wrong. Reverend Hastie won't let this go until he destroys us all," Mr. Wilson is pacing madly now.

"I'm so sorry. Please forgive me," I sob. "I'll withdraw the suit."

Mr. Wilson stands in front of me, his arms at his sides. His anger is gone, leaving only sadness in his eyes.

"It's gone too far, Miss Pigot. The suit is filed in the public court. The news seeps all over town. My colleagues look at me in alarm. This is the last time we will speak."

He can't mean that. "Please forgive me," I whisper.

"Of all the mistakes in your foolish life, this is the most thoughtless, Miss Pigot. My forgiveness won't change the facts, but I give it to you and wish us all well." Mr. Wilson still holding his *topi,* leaves the room. The door jangles as it closes.

I sink back onto the sofa. What will I do without Mr. Wilson's friendship, his sense of humor, and useful advice? I never meant to harm anyone. I can't destroy everyone who matters to me. I decide to stop the lawsuit. I grab my *topi* and head for the train station.

It's after *tiffin* when I arrive at Mr. Carruthers's office.

"Miss Pigot, I'm so sorry," the clerk stammers when I come through the door. "Mr. Carruthers is out. Was he expecting you?"

"No, but I must see him today. I'll wait for his return." I take a seat on the bench and rest my back against the wall. The clock chimes the hour. Three o'clock. Four o'clock. Five o'clock. The clerk looks up at me over his work. He offers me tea. At last the door opens, and Mr. Carruthers arrives in a rush.

"Miss Pigot," he says on the way to his office. "I've been in court all day. Whatever brings you here?"

"I must speak with you," I say. "I want to withdraw the lawsuit."

"Surely not. Come inside." Mr. Carruthers opens his office door.

The clerk motions me in, and then follows with a sheaf of documents. "I finished the filings, sir," he says.

"Good, good." Mr. Carruthers puts on his spectacles and glances through the papers while he talks to his clerk. I clear my throat. "Mr. Carruthers, please. I need to speak to you."

"And I need to approve these documents before the end of the day. Perhaps you'd like an appointment tomorrow?" Mr. Carruthers says with slight annoyance.

"No. I'll wait."

"Very well."

I feel lightheaded, probably because I didn't eat *tiffin*. Thunder sounds in the distance. The monsoons will arrive soon, and the thick air they bring. Finally, the clerk leaves with his papers.

"Miss Pigot, what is so urgent?" Mr. Carruthers asks impatiently. "I have an engagement this evening."

"I want to withdraw my lawsuit," I stammer

"Why? Are your allegations false?"

"No, but..."

"Then..."

"Reverend Hastie is looking for people to testify against me," I explain. "And he's trying to..." I feel as if I might faint. "He is... It's unspeakable."

"I did try to warn you, Miss Pigot."

"But Mr. Hastie isn't behaving as a gentleman should."

"Well, that won't get you very far in court. He has the right to defend himself from your charges. If he proves any of the allegations are true, he will win the case," Mr. Carruthers says flatly.

"Mr. Carruthers, you must tell me what to do!" The room feels like it is closing in around me. I try to calm my shallow breathing.

He leans back and steeples his fingers. "There is a possible alternative."

"What? I'll do anything!"

"We could stay the suit against Mr. Hastie, and file against the woman responsible for the letters. What was her name?"

"Mrs. Walker."

"Yes," he says. "We could amend the suit to focus on her as the source of the allegations. The case will be weaker, and Reverend Hastie would have to testify on your behalf stating that Mrs. Walker sent him the letters and gave him a false impression or something along those lines. Is this what you want to do?"

I don't like the suggestion. It seems cruel to save myself by dragging another woman into public scrutiny, but she never gave a thought for me. "Yes."

"There's nothing to say Mrs. Walker won't take the same line of defense and justify the allegations," Mr. Carruthers says.

"But no one will believe her, surely. She has a grudge against me because of her sister."

"Miss Pigot, as I've explained, going to court is a very serious business. There is no guarantee of a favorable outcome." Mr. Carruthers speaks to me seriously as if he's scolding a child. "Suits cannot be frivolously filed. If Reverend Hastie isn't willing to support a suit against Mrs. Walker, there's no point in going forward."

"But what about my reputation?"

"I shall follow your directions and approach Reverend Hastie," Mr. Carruthers says. "But, if he doesn't cooperate, I advise you to reinstate the suit. Events have moved forward, Miss Pigot. If you withdraw your lawsuit completely, you risk assumption by the public that the allegations against you are true."

"I understand." I stand up slowly. Mr. Carruthers comes around his desk to open the door for me and instructs his clerk to take me downstairs and summon a *gharry* to take me to the train station. As the *gharry* pulls into traffic, I realize events are rapidly taking on a life of their own.

William Hastie

Falak hands me a card. Well, well, well. Miss Pigot's solicitor returns.

"Show him in," I say and put on my jacket as Mr. Carruthers enters. I shake his hand, gesture to the hardback chair in front of my desk and resume my seat. I wipe my hands with my handkerchief.

"Mr. Carruthers, what brings you here again?" I point at the document in front of me. "I'm just finalizing the written statement for my defense."

"In that case, my arrival is timely," Mr. Carruthers sits and takes out a notepad and pencil.

I'm intrigued. "How so?"

"Reverend Hastie, my client proposes to stay her suit against you and replace it with a suit against Mrs. Walker."

I imagine the scandal such a suit would bring. A lady missionary and a colonel's wife? I can't imagine Miss Pigot being so crass, but the woman continually surprises me. "Why would she sue Mrs. Walker?" I ask. "I'm perplexed at this change of direction."

"Upon reflection, Miss Pigot reached the conclusion that Mrs. Walker is the true source of the malicious libel and you were merely an unwitting messenger."

True, of course, though I don't like his inference to me as "unwitting." I ask the man what he means.

"We propose to associate Mrs. Walker with the suit rather than yourself."

"To clarify, you want to postpone action against me until you raise it against Mrs. Walker?"

"We don't propose to take any action against you, Mr. Hastie. We only request your testimony about Mrs. Walker's involvement, specifically that Mrs. Walker is the source of the letters."

Hallelujah! I can put this whole sordid mess behind me. But is it right to watch Miss Pigot drag Mrs. Walker through the public courts?

"Mr. Carruthers, nothing would give me more pleasure than to move past this unfortunate business. Prior to my arrival, Miss Pigot accomplished many good things as Lady Superintendent. However, I'm not privy to anything Mrs. Walker said or did."

"We don't ask you to testify against Mrs. Walker, merely to the way in which you received the letters."

I presume he means that Mrs. Walker forwarded the letters to me. "Any answer I give would be in consequence of the specific question asked. I can't comment on my answer until I hear the question."

I thank Mr. Carruthers for his visit and let him see himself out. It's ridiculous to think Miss Pigot will file suit against a colonel's wife. I'm just glad to be out of it. I must write Mr. Wilson immediately to reinstate our chumming agreement. No sense paying unnecessary costs when we can share expenses for our food.

Mary Pigot

Someone left yesterday's *Indian Daily News* in the drawing room of my residence. The print is hard to read. I suppose I need to get spectacles. I look at the advertisements. A drawing room suite at C. Lazarus and Company. Fashionable footwear with buckles and straps at Cuthbertson and Harper. Yardley's Lavender Soap. There's a small notice in the bottom corner. Do my eyes deceive me? It's about the Scottish mission. I bring the newspaper closer to my face. I can't believe it. I'm dismissed. Well, not precisely. But the notice announces Mr. Mason, Mr. Wilson and

Mr. Clarke now oversee the Female Mission. Clearly they want everyone to know I won't be back.

To see Mr. Wilson's name as one of the Female Mission supervisors is too much. It was on his account I withdrew the lawsuit against Mr. Hastie. Pure sentiment on my part. And now his name is given as one of those responsible for the Female Mission. The only way to get back my position is to reinstate the lawsuit. If Mr. Wilson and Babu Banerjee are harmed in the process, so be it.

Chapter 11
"How Shall I Phrase My Anguish?"

Mary Pigot

I'm late. Again. I used to rush everywhere doing God's work. At least I think it was His work. But if that's true, I wouldn't be on my way to meet my barrister. I can't believe I'm doing this. Mr. Carruthers finds my case distasteful. I can tell by the way he shuffles his documents and looks at me over his spectacles. We've been going over my Complaint for days. Am I absolutely sure? And do I know how the witnesses will testify? He interviewed them. None of them want to come to court. Not Kali Churn Banerjee, who is like a son to me. Not Mr. Wilson. Not even Mr. Robson, the man I defended in his hour of need.

Mr. Carruthers told me I could withdraw, but I can't. If I don't vindicate myself, I'll never have another position. I'll have to be a governess, or worse. No, I can't think about that right now.

The roads are muddy from the monsoons. My dress will be ruined before I even meet this barrister. What will he think of me? Mr. Carruthers said he didn't want the case—that we have to engage his associate as well. If I don't win the case and receive monetary damages, I'll be penniless.

"Driver," I say, "Get as close to the building as you can."

"Yes, Mem."

I pull my skirts up and step out of the *gharry*. *Squish*. My boots sink into the mud. I stamp up the steps and drop my skirts. Inside, I climb to the second level. I'm out of breath, hot, and sweaty.

There's a brass plaque next to the door: *"Premises of Mr. E. J. Trevelyan, Q. C."* I turn the oversized brass knob and go through.

A clerk jumps up. "You must be Miss Pigot," he says. "Mr. Trevelyan expects you. Your solicitor is with him. If you'll follow me please."

We walk down a musty corridor and stop at an open door. The *punkah wallah* glances at me. Instead of sitting properly to pull the cord that moves the fan inside the next room, he's tied it to his foot and moves it up and down against the floor mat. I never allowed my staff to be so lazy. The clerk gestures for me to enter. Three men in their shirtsleeves stand, their clothing damp from the humid air. They don't put their jackets on as they should with a lady present. Perhaps this is how barristers behave. I wish I could remove my own jacket.

Mr. Carruthers comes forward and escorts me to a large cane chair. "Beastly weather, Miss Pigot," he says. "Allow me to introduce Mr. Trevelyan, our lead barrister, and his associate Mr. O'Kinealy, recently arrived from England."

Mr. Trevelyan is a handsome man, his face in perfect proportion. He has dark hair and eyebrows and deep-set brown eyes which presently look at me as if I have three heads. I return his stare. "Forgive me," he says, "I like to assess my clients. Mr. Carruthers tells me you're determined to go forward with this suit. Why?"

I get out my handkerchief and blot the sweat from my face. How shall I phrase my anguish? How much does he already know? "May I have a glass of water?" I ask.

Mr. Trevelyan motions to his clerk who leaves to fetch one. It's difficult to talk to Mr. Trevelyan. He has no facial expression.

"Shortly after he arrived," I begin, "Reverend Hastie made it clear he thought the Female Mission should be subordinate to him. When I refused, he sought alliances with like-minded people on the Corresponding Board of the Scottish Mission. He became intimate friends with Colonel and Mrs. Walker and with Reverend Gillan who opposed my initial appointment. It became increasingly difficult for me to operate as Lady Superintendent."

Mr. Trevelyan interrupts. "I understand the crisis began after..." He looks at his notes. "After a Miss Smail arrived."

"Yes. She was an impossible woman. I threw her out of the Female Mission, which may not have been my best decision."

Mr. Carruthers raises his eyebrows.

"What happened then?" Mr. Trevelyan asks. I notice Mr. Trevelyan has a mole on his jaw. Somehow it makes him seem more human. I relax slightly.

"Miss Smail and her sister Mrs. Walker began soliciting people who had a grudge against me to write false accusations. I had to go to Scotland to clear my name. But just as things resolved, Mr. Hastie forwarded the letters Mrs. Walker solicited. How could I prevail if a man of his standing accused me? Dr. Scott told me I must clear my name. So here I am."

Mr. Trevelyan leans forward across his desk. "I ask you again. Are you sure you want to go forward?" His dark eyes bore into me. "I understand Mr. Hastie has been busy gathering witnesses. He'll present his case first, and it will be in his interest to prove the allegations are true."

"No! They're not true." I start to jump up but force myself back into the chair.

Mr. Trevelyan doesn't change position. He continues to observe me. It's unnerving. "Nevertheless, Mr. Hastie will press his case," he continues as I regain my composure. "You may end up worse off than you are now. The very fact that you'll appear in court will cause comment. And you'll have to testify. There will be journalists present. Are you sure you can withstand this type of pressure?" Mr. Trevelyan leans back in his chair and watches me.

"I can do whatever is required," I say softly.

"Are you sure?" Mr. Trevelyan turns to his associate. "Mr. O'Kinealy, do we have a judge?"

"Yes, sir. We have Mr. Justice John Freeman Norris."

Mr. Carruthers groans.

"Is that bad?" I ask.

"It isn't the best news," Mr. O'Kinealy comments. He's a reedy sort of man and still has a London accent. "Justice Norris came out last year and is known to be impatient. He dislikes Indians, which is bad for us in view of the allegations about you and Babu Banerjee. We will, of course, argue that such a relationship wouldn't be possible for a woman of your standing."

"What do you conclude?" Mr. Carruthers asks his colleagues. "Is this a winnable case?"

"Though we don't have the most sympathetic judge, the fact that this case is about two members of the mission community should mitigate any of the judge's social concerns," Mr. O'Kinealy says.

Mr. Trevelyan turns his attention back to me. "I ask you a final time, Miss Pigot. Do you wish to continue?"

"Yes." I say firmly. I've gone too far to stop.

"Very well. I have my instructions. Mr. Carruthers will be in touch when we have a court date," Mr. Trevelyan says.

Mr. Carruthers gathers his papers and escorts me out of the office. When we reach the entry to the building, he puts me in a *gharry* to the train station. "I'll be in touch, Miss Pigot. If you think of anything else I should be aware of, notify me immediately."

The rain falls in sheets making it as wet inside the *gharry* as out. No one can see my tears.

William Hastie

"Mr. Hastie, you've put together an excellent case. You hardly need my services." Mr. Geddes chuckles.

Annoying man. I'm not paying him. The mission will have to absorb the cost. I did nothing but my duty. In fact, I did more. I put together the entire case. I could have done the filings if the High Court allowed laymen to do their own work. Mr. Geddes is short, stout, and has a runny nose. The less time spent with him, the better.

"I engaged Mr. Gasper as your barrister." Mr. Geddes wipes his nose. "He's an excellent man."

"I shall represent myself."

Mr. Geddes stops wiping his nose and turns to look me straight in the eye. "Surely not."

"I've read the law on libel. This is an open and shut case. Once the judge rules anything relating to Mrs. Walker's letters and my endorsements are privileged communications, the woman has no case. I see no reason for the mission to pay for unnecessary services."

Mr. Geddes stops looking through my written statement. "You know it's highly irregular for an individual to represent himself."

"Yes, but that's because the average layperson hasn't got the mental capacity to understand the law. I do. In fact, you don't need to come to court either."

"With respect, Mr. Hastie. High Court rules require my presence. And whether you can represent yourself is at the judge's discretion. We've drawn Justice Norris, and he's a stickler for procedure. If you allow me, I'll engage Mr. Gasper for the first day, and ask him to keep his calendar open."

"I assure you his services won't be necessary."

"There's no way to know how Justice Norris will respond. Perhaps you'll allow me to have him available?" Mr. Geddes asks with a touch of deference.

Geddes is so exasperating. But it's too hot to continue this meeting. It'll all be over the first day anyway.

"Very well," I say. "Make arrangements for him to be available, but make it clear I shall manage my own case. I fully expect the matter to be settled during the pre-trial motions."

"I'll follow your instructions. Thank you for taking my advice," Mr. Geddes says. "The documents are in order, so I'll take my leave."

He picks up his umbrella and heads out into the rain. I remain in my stifling study trying to figure out how this suit ever made it onto the High Court calendar. Mr. Carruthers assured me the woman would withdraw, and then she changed her mind. To what purpose? The Ladies' Association dismissed her on grounds of mismanagement, so she has no position to regain unless she thinks they'll reinstate her. The newspapers will have a field day sharing her misdeeds. Clearly, the woman is mentally unstable. For her own sake, I wish her friends had persuaded her to withdraw. Then again, perhaps she has no friends left.

It makes no difference. The letters are privileged, which means no libel occurred. That'll stop everyone in their tracks. No need to go further into this scurrilous affair.

Chapter 12
"I Think There's Evidence Of Malice"

Tuesday, 28 August 1883
Mary Pigot

With its red brick façade, the High Court may be the most majestic building in all of Calcutta, but I've no time to look at it today. I had an urgent note from Mr. Carruthers this morning: Justice Norris has moved the case up. I climb the stairs to the second level. The case is in one of the smaller courtrooms. The Gothic windows face east, which might make the afternoon more comfortable, but at eleven o'clock, it's stifling. The *punkah wallahs* keep the air moving with various degrees of enthusiasm.

I have dressed carefully for my appearance in court. I am wearing a new fitted black dress with a white fichu, and a modest hat. My outfit is already drenched, of course. My boots squeak as I walk to the plaintiff's table. Reverend Hastie, wearing his academic robes, sits at the defendant's table writing furiously. I look away. Mr. Carruthers stands to greet me. I notice he's wearing a short black robe with a stiff collar that has bands coming down and a white wig that doesn't entirely cover his head. A smiling middle-aged man stands beside him in a court robe with gathered sleeves and a wig with tight curls above his ears on either side of his head and a small sort of tail coming onto his collar. I've never seen anyone dressed for court before. Both men are sweating profusely.

"Mr. Carruthers," I say. "Who's this? Where's Mr. Trevelyan?"

"Allow me to introduce you to Mr. Philips," Mr. Carruthers says. "We weren't expecting the case to be called today, and Mr. Trevelyan isn't available. Mr. Philips will make the opening statements."

Mr. Philips puts out one hand while clutching a handkerchief to his nose with the other.

"Are you unwell?" I ask.

"Just a summer cold," he says.

"Order. Order. All rise," the clerk calls out. "Court is in session. His Lordship, the Honorable Justice Norris presiding."

I watch the man who will decide my fate come through a door behind the dais and take his seat above us. Justice Norris wears a scarlet robe and a white horsehair wig that falls on either side of his chin. His face is thin with a beaked nose. He adjusts his wig to allow for slight side ventilation which makes it off-center.

"Sit, sit," he says, waving his hands impatiently. "Now then, what have we before us? Who speaks for the plaintiff?"

Mr. Philips wipes his nose and rises. "My Lord," he says," there's an unfortunate case on Your Lordship's board of *Pigot vs. Hastie*. It's a suit for defamation by Miss Pigot against a clergyman of the Church of Scotland. My Lord, we didn't expect the change in your calendar. Mr. Trevelyan isn't available. I ask Your Lordship to let the case stand over until Thursday. The defendant, Mr. Hastie appears in person." Mr. Philips sniffs.

Justice Norris polishes his glasses. "I'm disappointed in your lack of preparation, Mr. Philips."

I cringe. Behind me, Mr. Carruthers clears his throat.

"Mr. Hastie, where's your counsel?" Justice Norris asks.

Mr. Hastie stands. "My Lord, I represent myself in this painful case. The announcement the case would come on today took me by surprise, but in the interests of the mission, I'm ready to argue the case and bring the matter before Your Lordship in fair form." Mr. Hastie rocks back on his heels.

"The interests of the mission," Justice Norris says sternly, "won't influence me in the least. I'm sitting here as judge, and at present I'm only interested in your individual capacity as a defendant." Justice Norris looks towards our table. "Will you be ready after lunch, Mr. Philips? I want the case to begin as soon as possible so it doesn't go over vacation. Will there be a preliminary point of privilege?"

"Yes, My Lord," Mr. Philips says. "But even if the question is decided in Mr. Hastie's favor, it won't affect our case."

"Very well," Judge Norris says, "we stand adjourned until after *tiffin*." Justice Norris bangs his gavel and departs.

"What just happened?" I ask Mr. Philips.

"Justice Norris extended our opening until this afternoon. Please excuse me." Mr. Philips disappears out the main door as Mr. Carruthers takes my arm.

"Don't fret, Miss Pigot. Mr. Philips is a very good man."

I fret anyway. We've only just started, and I've already made a bad impression on the judge.

William Hastie

The morning session was a complete waste of time. Let us hope the afternoon will be more worthwhile. Mr. Trevelyan is here now and will state the case for Miss Pigot. That shouldn't take long. She looks calmer than she did this morning. I look at my watch. The judge is three minutes late. So much for his reputation for punctuality. Justice Norris emerges in a flurry of red. We stand and sit as ordered. Justice Norris looks at the plaintiff's table.

"Ah, Mr. Trevelyan," Justice Norris smiles grimly, "good of you to join us."

"My Lord," Mr. Trevelyan bows. "Allow me to get right to the point. This is a suit for damages in the amount of twenty thousand rupees for defamation of character. The plaintiff was employed as Lady Superintendent of the Female Mission, and the defendant as Principal of Scottish College. Both institutions are connected with the Church of Scotland mission in Calcutta." Mr. Trevelyan hits his rhetorical stride. "Mr. Hastie's view, rightly or wrongly, was that the Female Mission ought to be subordinate to the Scottish College, and he seems to have done his best to cause that to be done."

And I would have succeeded if the Mission Committee hadn't interfered.

"Miss Pigot," Mr. Trevelyan continues, "resisted this attempt, and Mr. Hastie made charges against her. She was found free of all blame. Mr. Hastie then adopted another course of action, which can't be characterized in words strong enough or bad enough. He seems not to have kept his tongue from lying and slandering." Mr. Trevelyan rocks back on his heels as he finishes speaking.

I start to rise. Mr. Geddes distracts me by putting his hand on my arm. He shakes his head. Surely I should object to this vilification. Mr. Geddes glares at me and shakes his head again. The judge takes notes and nods as Mr. Trevelyan continues his falsehoods.

"Mr. Hastie," he asserts, "published a vulgar libel against Miss Pigot—a libel charging her with the grossest possible immorality. He alleged she entertained a native Christian gentleman at night, suggested this person is in the habit of going at night into her rooms, and that he's been seen coming down in the morning with his coat off and his boots in his hands."

I feel my body temperature rising. I never suggesting anything of the sort.

Mr. Trevelyan then admits I based my statements on the letters, which he says I might be justified in forwarding. An odd turn of phrase, "might be." Does that mean he accepts the letters as accurate? Mr. Trevelyan finally reaches his point.

"Your Lordship, we contend that Mr. Hastie had no justification in writing the covering memorandum, which makes the libel worse. When we approached the defendant to withdraw his comments, he declined to apologize in any way. Indeed, he admitted publishing the libelous note. Now he is trying to claim it was a privileged communication. My Lord, the lady lost her employment in consequence of these libels."

Untrue. She lost her employment because she mismanaged the Female Mission. The charges against her behavior have nothing to do with it. Justice Norris completes his notes and looks up.

Mr. Trevelyan then goes through Miss Pigot's Complaint, reads the letters I forwarded for Mrs. Walker as well as my memorandum from last May in which I said Miss Pigot had done good work. Surely the judge could read this for himself without taking up everyone's time. Mr. Trevelyan reads my written statement. Without rebutting it, he claims the libel proven and the only question remaining is the amount of damages.

The judge agrees. "The onus of proving the statements are true rests with the defendant."

Mr. Trevelyan sits down looking very smug.

"Mr. Hastie," Justice Norris asks, "do you have anything to say?"

I stand. "This situation isn't what it appears," I say. "Miss Pigot is suing me for a decision I made as head of the Scottish Mission. It wasn't a personal opinion. If anything, Miss Pigot should sue the Church of Scotland, not me. I merely did my duty as Principal of Scottish College."

Justice Norris interrupts me. "Mr. Hastie, before you proceed further, would you like a recess so you can obtain counsel? It's most irregular for defendants to represent themselves. In fact, no one in my courtroom has ever done so."

Out of the corner of my eye, I see Mr. Geddes's triumphant look.

"Your Lordship, I admit my decision to represent myself places me at a disadvantage. I'm not familiar with court procedures, however I'm highly qualified to explain matters pertaining to the Church of Scotland and the mission in Calcutta."

"Very well," Justice Norris waves his hand, though whether the gesture is meant for me or an insect I'm not sure.

I continue. "Following Mr. Trevelyan's example, I presume I'm expected to read my written statement which Mr. Trevelyan just read. This strikes me as a waste of Your Lordship's time. I simply plead that the information contained in those letters and my postscript is privileged, and that I acted within the limits of my official duties."

Judge Norris looks down his nose at me. "Mr. Hastie, whether a statement is privileged is a question of law."

"Yes, Your Lordship. I researched the law and discovered a privileged publication is one related to a subject in which the party publishing it has an interest, and the person receiving it, has a similar interest. On that basis, I can prove the communication justified and privileged."

I continue. It's almost enjoyable explaining the relationship of the Ladies' Association and the Church of Scotland, and the governance of both—my point being that the Ladies' Association is subordinate to the General Assembly which governs the Church of Scotland. After which I explain the relationship of the Corresponding Board of which I am a member. Surprisingly, Justice Norris hardly takes a note. He's so motionless, I wonder if he's even listening. Having laid my foundation, I reach my point.

"Now, My Lord," I say, "it's important to note that at the time of these alleged libels, I was a member of the Corresponding Board and Officiating Secretary. This brought me into direct communication with the Foreign Mission Committee. I now must explain Dr. Scott's position." I inhale to begin.

Justice Norris sits upright and raps his knuckle. "Not today, Mr. Hastie," he says. The judge takes out his watch, peers at it and snaps it shut. "We're presently ten minutes past the usual time for the court to rise. We'll reconvene tomorrow at eleven-thirty, at which time I expect you to appear with Counsel."

Justice Norris bangs his gavel and leaves the room, completely destroying the momentum of my discourse. Mr. Geddes whispers in my ear that Mr. Gasper will appear with me tomorrow.

Since I haven't yet met Mr. Gasper, I go to court half an hour early. According to my research, Mr. Geddes engaged the most expensive barrister available. Mr. Gasper is young, a member of the Armenian community, and lead barrister of the High Court. I resent Justice Norris's implication that I can't manage my own case, but it's gratifying to have such an accomplished colleague.

"Mr. Hastie." Mr. Gasper extends his hand. "Mr. Geddes briefed me on your case, and I read your testimony in the *Indian Daily News* this morning. Pay no attention when I tell the judge I'm not prepared. I'm always prepared."

The man carries himself as if he's the only person of any importance in the courtroom. I feel the case being lifted from my control. As they confer, I see Mr. Geddes listen raptly to every instruction Mr. Gasper gives him and then leave the courtroom.

"All rise," the clerk says.

We stand and watch the judge take his seat.

"Mr. Gasper," he beams, "what an unexpected pleasure to see you this morning. Your very presence elevates this case."

"My Lord." Mr. Gasper gives a slight bow. "I'll proceed on the supposition that the facts necessary to establish privilege have been indicated. I simply ask Your Lordship to rule that the materials before you demonstrate their privileged status. I submit that the plaintiff's Complaint discloses facts that repel any inference of malice."

He says it with such authority I don't see how anyone could question my innocence. Mr. Gasper then puts my case, in almost the same words I spoke yesterday, though his grasp of previous cases is greater than mine.

"Very well," says Justice Norris, "subject to what Mr. Trevelyan says, I'm bound to think the communication was privileged."

Mr. Trevelyan is on his feet immediately. "Your Lordship, we contend that even if the occasion was privileged, the defendant didn't properly exercise his rights, and his note and postscript take away the question of privilege."

"We have no difficulty there," Mr. Gasper counters. "On the question of malice, there is no evidence to show Mr. Hastie acted out of malice."

"I disagree, Mr. Gasper," Justice Norris begins. "Reviewing the documents, I think there is evidence of malice. The note and postscript are clearly malice. There is a precise regard for punctuality: *'this communication has just been sent to me.'* And why send the letters to Dr. Scott rather than Dr. Jardine? I find this is further evidence of malice. And there's a difference between the note in which Mr. Hastie was taken by surprise, and the postscript in which he had *'long been suspicious of such things.'*"

Justice Norris strokes the sideburn by his left ear. "Furthermore, as I read Mr. Hastie's written statement, I'm of the opinion that if this case were being tried by a jury I would ask them: Do you think when Mr. Hastie sent this letter to Dr. Scott, he was actuated solely by the interests of the Female Mission? Or do you think he jumped at the opportunity these letters presented to remove a person odious to him, and if not odious, at least a thorn in his side? There being no jury, I ask myself the same questions." Justice Norris falls silent.

Mr. Gasper interrupts the judge's reverie. "Your Lordship ought not to rule the note and postscript are evidence of malice."

"I think they are, Mr. Gasper," Justice Norris replies. "When a man writes, *'this has taken me by surprise,'* it's tantamount to saying, 'I hadn't the least suspicion of such things.' And two days afterwards, there's no evidence he made any attempt to discover whether these things were true or false. When he says *'I have long observed that every external propriety was more than disregarded. I have however not had such documentary and authenticated evidence put into my hands till now.'* To treat such communications as these as *'authenticated'* evidence without making any inquiry is evidence of malice."

"My Lord," Mr. Gasper counters, "you've left it to Your Lordship's mind as a judge of fact to decide whether these materials are or aren't sufficient for the purpose of finding malice. Allow me to point out that, as a matter of fact, Your Lordship ought to hold..."

Justice Norris interrupts and looks at my barrister with annoyance. "As a matter of fact, there is enough evidence of malice to go to a jury."

"Your Lordship should hear me before coming to that conclusion," Mr. Gasper tries again. "Mr. Hastie's memorandum..."

Justice Norris stops him. "Mr. Gasper," he thunders. "I emphatically tell you there is ample evidence of malice."

My man doesn't quit. "But, Your Lordship," he insists. "in the memorandum written last May, Mr. Hastie said *I shall be ready as ever to cooperate with Miss Pigot...*"

"Indeed, Mr. Gasper, your client says in effect 'I shall be as ready as ever to cooperate with a woman who has entertained this man in her bedroom,'" Justice Norris sneers. "He's a Christian minister! He, a member of the established Church of Scotland, is willing to cooperate with a woman guilty of gross immorality. The entire supposition is preposterous."

Mr. Gasper steps towards the judge's bench and spreads his hands, and says, "My Lord, such things..."

"Your client writes he will help a woman he observed to have disregarded every propriety!" Spittle flies from Justice Norris's mouth. "And then Mr. Hastie forwards these letters to Scotland. By his own admission, he has no reason to send them other than malice."

Mr. Gasper stands in front of the bench, shakes his head, and quietly speaks. "My Lord, I can't bring myself to believe Mr. Hastie has thrown off all notions of morality."

"Then you are lacking in skills of observation, Mr. Gasper. I judge the case from the facts before me, not from clouded opinions." Justice Norris looks down on my barrister. "It's plain Mr. Hastie was jealous of Miss Pigot and annoyed at the independent position she occupied."

Mr. Gasper bows and returns to our table. He turns for a parting comment. "Mr. Hastie might have been jealous, My Lord," Mr. Gasper says, "but jealousy is a righteous emotion."

The judge's head whips up from consulting his watch. "Well, Mr. Gasper, that is a question for the jury, and I'm the juror in this case." Justice Norris enunciates his words. "I say that on the face of these things, there is ample evidence of malice; and if you do not admit this is so, you must go into the case and endeavor to remove that impression. We adjourn for *tiffin*." The judge bangs his gavel.

My stomach clenches as I watch the judge leave the courtroom. He has already decided against me. What's the point of going forward?

"That went well, don't you think, Mr. Hastie?" Mr. Gasper says as he picks up his papers.

"Not from where I'm sitting. How do you propose to reverse the judge's opinion?"

"This is nothing. Now that Justice Norris thinks he's put the barristers in their place, we can begin our case in earnest." Mr. Gasper chuckles softly and shakes my hand. "I'll see you when court reconvenes."

Mary Pigot

Mr. Carruthers takes me to his office where a modest *tiffin* is set out on the table. He selects curry and a small beer. "Eat, Miss Pigot. There's no way to be sure when court will adjourn this evening."

"I'm too nervous," I say. "Did we win? It sounds like the judge agrees there was malice."

"Justice Norris gets carried away. What he thinks now may change. Don't forget, Mr. Hastie will bring witnesses to show his allegations are true. If he succeeds..." Mr. Carruthers shrugs. "Eat something."

When we return to court, Mr. Gasper and Mr. Trevelyan seem engaged in convivial conversation, quietly laughing at some shared joke. Mr. Hastie looks as annoyed as I am.

"Mr. Carruthers, are Mr. Gasper and Mr. Trevelyan friends?" I ask.

"I don't know. But they've been colleagues for several years, as have Mr. Geddes and myself."

"Oh," I say. "But if Mr. Trevelyan's my advocate, doesn't that make he and Mr. Gasper adversaries?"

"Only when court is in session." Mr. Carruthers gives a slight smile and takes his seat behind me.

Barristers repeat themselves. Mr. Trevelyan speaks again about the relationship of Scottish College and the Female Mission in January 1879, when Mr. Hastie arrived and how it changed in April. "Since the defendant wasn't superintendent of the Female Mission at the time, the question of privilege falls to the ground."

Mr. Trevelyan says Mr. Gasper implied that because Mr. Hastie is a clergyman, he can make statements without any inquiry as to their truth.

"The defendant wants to avoid paying damages," Mr. Trevelyan continues. "So, he pleads both privilege and that the allegations are true. Further, the libel isn't about what happened in 1879. The libel occurred in 1882 when there was no connection between Scottish College and the Female Mission. The only interest Mr. Hastie could have is if it is a duty for one Christian to find out the faults of another Christian and tell them to a third Christian. Mr. Hastie had no duty to act as he did."

"I've heard enough," Justice Norris says. "I'm prepared to rule."

I fist my hands in my lap.

"The defense admits the publication and the libels," Justice Norris says. "There's no doubt the libels are of a gross nature and the plaintiff is entitled to substantial damages. If this case went to a jury, I would ask: 'Do you believe that the same Christian minister who wrote in May that he was willing to cooperate with the lady—that this same man would believe the allegations in those letters to be true?'" Justice Norris looks at both barristers in turn. "Would the person who wrote he'd observed a disregard for propriety be the same person who, five months before, wrote that he was willing to cooperate with her? Did the defendant have any desire to get rid of an element of the Female Mission with whom he wasn't in harmony? Does the jury accept that he believed all the aspersions upon her character, chastity, decency, and all that was womanly in her nature? The jury would have to decide these facts."

Justice Norris sighs. "We have no jury, because there are too few qualified men to serve, which is a great travesty. We have only myself as judge to decide these matters. And I rule the occasion wasn't privileged and there is evidence of actual malice." Justice Norris bangs his gavel. "Mr. Gasper, proceed with your defense tomorrow morning."

I'm breathless, my heart pounding so hard it must be visible through my bodice. I've won. I think. I want to cheer. I also want to crawl under my chair.

"What's happened, Mr. Trevelyan?" I ask.

"The trial begins tomorrow," he replies.

"But we won."

"Not yet. If the judge ruled the communication was privileged, Mr. Hastie would be off the hook. Now he must prove the allegations are true or pay damages. You should direct your concerns to Mr. Carruthers. I merely act on instructions."

Mr. Carruthers escorts me to my hotel near the High Court. We're both drenched in sweat when we arrive. He sees me to the lobby, tells me we've had a successful day, and turns to go.

"Wait, Mr. Carruthers, I don't understand why the trial isn't over. The judge agrees Mr. Hastie defamed me."

"Mr. Hastie has the right to defend himself," Mr. Carruthers says patiently. "I've explained this to you several times. He will testify, and then call witnesses to demonstrate his actions were appropriate."

"But he lied."

"That has yet to be proven," Mr. Carruthers says. "Miss Pigot, I suggest you eat something and get some rest. From what I've seen so far, you'll need fortitude and sustenance to get through Mr. Hastie's testimony."

Chapter 13
"I Didn't Know I'd Be Worse Off Than Before"

Friday, 31 August 1883
Mary Pigot

The next morning, I take a *gharry* to the High Court and climb the stairs to my courtroom. I feel embedded in the furniture and that after the trial is over my ghost will still be here. My head is so full of pressure from the humidity that I can hardly see, but this isn't a day to be absent. I take my place next to Mr. Trevelyan and notice Mr. Hastie and Mr. Gasper in close conversation. Both men look exasperated. Perhaps they'll melt.

"All rise," the clerk calls out.

Justice Norris swiftly strides to his chair and seats himself in a swirl of red. "You may proceed, Mr. Gasper."

The barrister hooks his hands into his lapels. "Thank you, My Lord. I hope to persuade Your Lordship that my client's actions weren't malicious in any sense."

"I didn't say there was malice."

A look of surprise briefly crosses Mr. Gasper's face. "I don't say Your Lordship said there was malice. Your Lordship noted there is sufficient evidence of malice for the case to go forward. This is a long step from holding there's sufficient evidence to prove malice."

Justice Norris appears mollified and leans back in his chair. Mr. Gasper pauses as if a thought just came to his attention.

"But the fact Your Lordship thinks there's enough evidence to go forward makes me think Your Lordship has an opinion, and it's my duty to prove the facts of my client's note, postscript, and memorandum aren't sufficient to prove malice."

Mr. Gasper drones on about how the Church of Scotland organizes missionary work. The judge makes an occasional note.

"My Lord," Mr. Gasper says, "we now come to the Scottish Ladies' Association. This is a society of ladies who promote Christian female education in Calcutta. Members contribute five shillings each so every woman in Scotland may join."

"I suppose they'd have no objection to accepting five shillings from a woman who isn't Scottish," Judge Norris chuckles. "Now then, suppose the Ladies' Association held a meeting and said to the Missionary Committee, *'We're very much obliged to you for your assistance, but we don't want it anymore.'* The Missionary Committee would have to take themselves off. They'd have no control of any sort."

Mr. Gasper smiles at the judge's joke. "Giving all the credit I can to the business capacities of women, I hold old-fashioned ideas. I think however much women may be capable of managing their own affairs, they benefit by having men of business assist them."

The judge's expression shifts and his amiable mood passes. "That is a matter of opinion, Mr. Gasper," Justice Norris says. "It may be the low opinion held of women in this country which brings you to that conclusion. I don't agree with you. In respect to business capacity and intelligence, a woman is in all respects the equal of a man."

"But as a matter of history and common opinion," Mr. Gasper says, "there is a large body of people who don't think so."

Justice Norris lifts his eyebrows. "There are a few fossils who don't think so."

The court erupts in laughter, though I can't tell whether it's directed at the judge's joke or Mr. Gasper. Mr. Trevelyan seems especially amused.

"Your Lordship," Mr. Gasper says, "my point is that at the time this alleged libel took place, the Ladies' Association appointed the agents and teachers of the Female Mission, subject to Missionary Committee approval. And regarding these letters, I ask Your Lordship to consider whether there may be any truth in the charges. Mr. Hastie wasn't trying to broadcast their contents, but what was he to do? He didn't have Miss Pigot's address in Scotland, so he sent the information to Dr. Scott knowing he would be able to contact her."

"He could've sent the documents in a letter to Miss Pigot, care of the Ladies' Association," Justice Norris observes.

"Quite so, Your Lordship," Mr. Gasper says, "but he sent the documents to Dr. Scott with whom Miss Pigot was in direct communication. Mr. Hastie did the only thing he could do if he believed credible persons wrote the letters."

I write a note to Mr. Trevelyan. *Mr. Hastie didn't ask Dr. Scott to forward the letters. He sent the letters to Dr. Scott directly.* Mr. Trevelyan shakes his head.

Justice Norris seems to be questioning Mr. Gasper on my behalf. Or perhaps he just likes to argue. "Explain to me, Mr. Gasper, how Mr. Hastie could write a note in May in which he praises Miss Pigot, and six months later believe the contents of those letters."

"My Lord, it's clear Mr. Hastie doesn't approve of Miss Pigot's character and manner," Mr. Gasper says. "Isn't it likely Mr. Hastie thought Miss Pigot could be allowed to continue, subject to external control? If that's true, then my client could've written this memorandum in May and yet believe what he wrote in November. If he wrote truthfully, there's no malice. In fact, my client doesn't have to prove the statements are true, only that he believed them to be true."

"I agree," Justice Norris nods and strokes his sideburns. "The grounds of Mr. Hastie's belief are relevant as to whether he acted with integrity."

I'm shocked. Is the judge saying it's acceptable to spread lies as long the perpetrator believes them?

"I shall prove that Mr. Hastie believed the contents of the letters," Mr. Gasper says. "Here is the case in a nutshell, My Lord. He received the letters from Mrs. Walker, a woman he knew quite well, whose husband is an Elder in St. Andrew's Kirk. He consulted with a native minister. Whether every native who is a Christian is a person to be believed or not is a point I don't care about. The point is what Mr. Hastie thought. Mr. Hastie went to that witness and asked him about things he'd seen.

"This isn't a man actuated by malice. Mr. Hastie's object was the good of the mission. Miss Pigot was a matter of perfect indifference to him. Your Lordship, I shall present the evidence, and when it comes, it will be nauseous enough. I shan't allude to it now."

Mr. Gasper returns to his table and looks to the judge expectantly. The judge nods.

"May it please the Court, the defense calls Reverend William Hastie."

William Hastie

I proceed to the witness box, raise my hand, and swear to tell the truth. Perhaps this time the judge will pay attention. Mr. Gasper goes through everything in the Complaint and my rebuttal. Who I am, where I come from, who I work for. I begin explain the role of the Foreign Mission Committee and move to the Ladies' Association. "It's a voluntary group with branches throughout Scotland," I say. "Local ladies form committees to gather funds. This is why the Ladies' Association has to be part of the Church of Scotland. Otherwise, they can't raise the necessary funds."

The judge scratches his ear. He obviously has no concept of structural organization.

"Nothing could prevent those ladies from continuing their collections," Justice Norris says. "I believe Mr. Gasper said it was five shillings per member."

"But they couldn't be part of the Ladies' Association."

"They could change the name," Justice Norris comments.

"People donate to the Association," I repeat.

"Mr. Hastie," Mr. Gasper changes the subject. "Is there a presbyterial body in Calcutta?"

"Yes," I reply.

"Can you say whether the agents, teachers and Lady Superintendent of the Female Mission attend any place of worship?" Mr. Gasper asks.

Why does he keep changing topics? "They attend the native church," I answer. I pause and think. Yes, that's correct. "The native church is for them." I nod for emphasis. "That is their church."

Mr. Gasper gives me an odd look. "What church did Miss Pigot attend?"

"She attended the native church with the children in the mornings," I say, "as well as St. Andrew's."

Justice Norris raps his gavel. "I think this is as good a place as any to stop proceedings for the day. We'll reconvene Monday at eleven o'clock."

I walk back to the defendant's table and sit down. I'm exhausted from standing in the witness box and talking all afternoon. Mr. Gasper looks energized. "Mr. Hastie," he says. "I urge you to pay close attention to my questions. You must give precise answers."

"What do you mean? I provided all the information you required."

"When I asked where members of the Female Mission attend church, you should have answered the question properly without a follow-up question." Mr. Gasper shakes my hand and leaves the courtroom.

Monday, 3 August 1883

I'm back in the witness box. Mr. Gasper takes his place and continues his questions. He asks about my education and my contributions to mission funds. I find these questions irrelevant to the issue of libel, but I go along the path Mr. Gasper marks out. I won't have him chastise me a second time.

"Remind me again, Mr. Hastie," Mr. Gasper says. "What is the relationship between the Female Mission and St. Andrew's Church?"

"Members of the Female Mission attend St. Andrews."

"Which members, specifically?" Mr. Gasper asks.

I pause, trying to figure out what Mr. Gasper wants to hear. I go with the obvious.

"The Lady Superintendent and other lady teachers attend," I say. "I've never been to a service without seeing some of them there."

Mr. Gasper walks back to the table and turns towards me. "Do you exercise any oversight of these parishioners?"

"I'm a member of the Kirk Sessions which gives me ecclesiastical control over all worshipers regarded as members of St. Andrew's." I pull at my collar to make more space around my neck. The room is stifling. Mr. Gasper looks as crisp as when we began the court session.

"By ecclesiastical control," Mr. Gasper continues, "do you mean anything connected to the church?"

"It could be construed that way."

"And how does this relate to your role as a member of the Corresponding Board?"

"Missionaries and other members from St. Andrew's serve on the Board," I explain. "I'm an *ex officio* member and have attended every meeting since I came to this country. Except the first when I was ill."

"So you were a member in 1882 when the alleged libels took place," Mr. Gasper says.

"I was an *ex officio* member until Mr. Gillan left in May when I became Acting Secretary. He returned in November, in poor health."

"Were you a member when you wrote the note accompanying the letters?" Mr. Gasper enunciates his question.

"When I wrote the note, Mr. Gillan was official secretary, but I relieved him of his duties."

"Do you know a Mr. Robson?" Mr. Gasper asks.

Robson? Why is he bringing up his name? "He was a professor at Scottish College. When I arrived, he'd resigned, but still lived at the College."

"Was Miss Pigot acquainted with Mr. Robson?" Mr. Gasper asks.

"Yes. I met him at Miss Pigot's on several occasions. I heard them speak of each other as friends. I advised Miss Pigot to end the friendship."

"Was there any friction between Mr. Robson and the Corresponding Board?"

"The Board thought Mr. Robson treated them unfairly with his early resignation," I say.

"So," Justice Norris says. "The Board thought Mr. Robson dealt unfairly with them."

I crane my neck to look up at the judge. "Yes, Your Lordship."

"Mr. Gasper," Justice Norris says, "is it necessary to go into these events preceding the alleged libel?"

I'm wondering this myself.

"Your Lordship," Mr. Gasper says. "I bring these matters before the court because they relate to whether the defendant behaved in a malicious manner. Our evidence will show my client never behaved with malice."

"Very well." Justice Norris waves his hand and Mr. Gasper resumes.

"Is Miss Pigot a member of St. Andrew's Kirk?"

"You raise an interesting point," I say. "Miss Pigot's attendance is infrequent, however, when I discussed the letters with Mr. Gillan, he worried whether he should continue to admit her to the communion table which indicates she is a member."

"Did you consult with anyone else about the letters?"

"I consulted Mr. Gregory, chair of the Corresponding Board; Reverend Chuckerbutty of the native church, and Mrs. Walker's husband."

"Why did you send the letters to Dr. Scott?" Mr. Gasper asks.

"I consider Miss Pigot an employee of the Mission Committee. They have the power to dismiss her."

"Why forward the letters at all?" Mr. Gasper asks. "You could've returned them."

I wish that I had, but I can't share my regret now.

"I forwarded them for the sake of the mission. My mission as well as hers. If the allegations are true, they bring a deep stain and slur upon the mission and myself. There had to be a formal investigation."

"And, in sending the letters from Mrs. Walker, were you actuated by malice?" Mr. Gasper looks me straight in the eyes.

"Mr. Gasper," Justice Norris interrupts peevishly. "You may not ask that question. It is for the court to decide."

It's easier giving a lecture than standing in the witness box. We've been at it since eleven o'clock with the heat rising every second. The *punkah wallahs* don't do their job properly. There isn't a breath of air in the room. That's probably why the judge is so exasperated. He keeps mopping his face with a yellow handkerchief.

When I lecture, I build to moments of climax. I walk around, and gesture. But here, everyone conspires to interrupt my flow of thought and my knees lock.

"Mr. Hastie," Mr. Gasper says, "when you wrote the cover memorandum to the letters you received from Mrs. Walker, were you carried away in the moment? Did you write anything that might be inaccurate?"

"The letters shocked me," I say. "I'd heard complaints about the Female Mission and rumors of improprieties, but nothing like the contents of those letters."

"You said you were taken by surprise," Mr. Gasper says. "How so?"

"Mrs. Walker is a lady of delicacy and propriety," I say. "To receive such letters through her was dreadful." My feelings from the first time I read the letters return. "To read such statements about Miss Pigot from different writers, all signed and attested as correct. I scarcely knew what to think. There were addresses and dates about which I knew nothing."

"When exactly did you write your note?" Mr. Gasper asks.

"Before *tiffin*. I came home weary, read my mail, and wrote the note," I say. I wish the judge would bang his gavel and adjourn court, but the questions continue.

"Did you discuss matters with anyone before you wrote the postscript?" Mr. Gasper asks. *Again.*

"I saw Mr. Gregory, Mr. Gillan, and Colonel Walker before I wrote the postscript; and Mr. Chuckerbutty before I sent it on."

"What did you discuss with Colonel Walker?"

"I... I asked if these writers could be believed." My voice chokes.

"What did he say?" Mr. Gasper asks.

I inhale. "He said he thought them truthful accounts. I asked about Miss Gordon's statement and whether she might be Eurasian, like Miss Pigot."

"And?" Mr. Gasper asks.

"Colonel Walker said that though she was born in this country, her parents are Scotch."

Mr. Gasper approaches the witness box. "In your memorandum you wrote that you'd had suspicions about Miss Pigot for some time. Yet in May, you wrote you would cooperate with her. What changed?"

"Because all I had in May were suspicions. I couldn't form a moral judgment that caused me to think cooperation impossible," I say. The *punkah* fan falters. The boy must have fallen asleep. The courtroom falls into humid silence.

Justice Norris leans over the dais. "You wrote not only *suspected*, but *long more than suspected.*"

"Yes, My Lord," I say slowly. "The phrase is consistent with my state of mind. I had some objective evidence, but I wasn't carried away by it."

"Describe this objective evidence," Justice Norris says.

"One of my Christian agents hinted that relations between Miss Pigot and Babu Banerjee weren't satisfactory," I say. "There were also immoral agents of a lower class employed by Miss Pigot."

"Immoral in what way?" Mr. Gasper resumes.

"I was told they were little better than common prostitutes. These were women who accompanied the children to school. Miss Pigot exposed innocent children to these women." My sense of outrage returns.

"Objection," Mr. Trevelyan says. "Surely we can't listen to everything this gentleman may have been told."

"Your Lordship," Mr. Gasper says, "Miss Pigot was responsible for her agents. We must show complaints were made against them. The children were under Miss Pigot's charge. Much depended on the moral character of persons she engaged. We argue she should've reported her agents' conduct before it became a scandal."

The *punkah* fan starts again, showering the room with dust.

Justice Norris wipes his face. "Very well."

Mr. Trevelyan sits down. Miss Pigot's hands on the table pull so tightly around each other they look as though they might break. I close my eyes a moment. When I open them, Mr. Gasper is inches from my face.

"Now, Mr. Hastie," Mr. Gasper says, "when you said *frequently observed*, what did you mean?"

"Miss Pigot drove into the College compound to visit one of my colleagues." I say the first incident I think of. "I don't consider this external propriety. Sometimes she came alone, and sometimes she left a girl in the *gharry*."

"Who was this colleague?" Mr. Gasper asks.

"Mr. Wilson, our senior lay missionary." I didn't mean to drag him into this, but Mr. Gasper grabs the opening to discuss my colleague.

"Is Mr. Wilson still employed by the mission?" Mr. Gasper asks.

"He is at the moment," I reply. "Look here, I made no complaint about him."

"And you found it inappropriate for Miss Pigot to visit him," Mr. Gasper says.

"I don't say she went to him for an immoral purpose," I say. "Far be it from me to say so. Merely that she should not have called on him."

"What was the duration of her visits?" Mr. Gasper asks.

"I can't say exactly. I observed the *gharry* waiting for a considerable time."

Justice Norris interrupts. "A lady of her age visiting a person—you wish to know the duration of the visit?" Justice Norris asks. "Where's the impropriety?"

"My Lord," I answer, "I find it unseemly for a lady of any age to visit a gentleman without a chaperone."

Mr. Gasper asks if I observed any other improprieties. I describe the dinner party at Mr. Steele's home and the behavior of Miss Pigot and Mr. Wilson at the Barrackpore picnic.

"The closeness of their position impressed me," I say. "He reclined with his head slightly on her shoulder."

"Do you know the ages of Miss Pigot and Mr. Wilson?" Mr. Gasper asks.

"Miss Pigot is slightly over forty," I say. "Mr. Wilson is a bit older."

"Are there other instances when you observed Mr. Wilson and Miss Pigot?" Mr. Gasper asks.

"Whenever I've been at the orphanage, I've been dissatisfied with what I observed. I once called on Miss Pigot, and Mr. Wilson came out from what I thought was her bedroom," I say. "I'm not suggesting anything, but I know the drawing room, and he didn't come from there."

"Did you ever hear anything about Miss Pigot and Babu Kali Churn Banerjee?" Mr. Gasper asks.

"I heard rumors there was an improper relationship between them," I say. "When I say improper relationship, I mean an improper intimacy." Perhaps I can draw Mr. Gasper's attention away from Mr. Wilson.

When Justice Norris adjourns the court for *tiffin,* I'm humiliated by the testimony I presented. It's not my nature to slur a woman's reputation, even if the facts are true. To do so under such circumstances is most uncomfortable. Miss Pigot didn't react to anything I said. Kept her eyes on the judge and her hands folded on the table.

Friday, 31 August 1883, Evening
Mary Pigot

I pace around the conference table stamping the outrage I've felt all day through my feet. I wanted to call out Mr. Hastie for the liar he is, but all I could do was stare straight ahead. I asked for an interview with Mr. Trevelyan. I demand to know why he doesn't stop Mr. Hastie's lies and innuendos. I want Mr. Trevelyan to wipe the smirk off Mr. Hastie's face every time he doesn't "suggest" anything. It's as if I'm the one on trial.

But Mr. Trevelyan just sits there. Occasionally he makes a note. Meanwhile, Mr. Hastie accuses me of being a trollop or worse, though I don't know what could be worse than that. Dear God, how can this be happening?

The side door opens, and Mr. Carruthers walks in. I don't want to talk to him. I want Mr. Trevelyan.

"Do sit down, Miss Pigot," Mr. Carruthers says. "It can't be good for your health to pace in this heat." He wipes his face.

"If I sit, I'll collapse. How could Mr. Trevelyan sit there while Mr. Hastie and his henchmen broadcast those lies?" I ask. "Mr. Wilson and I never did anything inappropriate. His wife is my dearest friend. And Babu Banerjee is like a son to me. Mr. Hastie and his lies disgrace the church. Why doesn't Mr. Trevelyan object?"

"There's no reason to do so," Mr. Carruthers says. "The defense hasn't brought out anything new."

"But to say such things in public. I'm ruined." I sit and hold my pounding head.

"Miss Pigot, I'm sorry for your discomfort," Mr. Carruthers says, "but there's nothing to be done."

"I have the right to object," I say.

"We'll have a chance to cross-examine the witness," Mr. Carruthers says.

"Where's Mr. Trevelyan?" I demand.

"He has another engagement," Mr. Carruthers says. "Don't worry. We'll respond at the appropriate time, but until then you'll have to soldier on."

"Even though he's lying?" I ask, my indignation dissolving into exhaustion.

Mr. Carruthers shrugs and pats my hand. "May I engage a *gharry* to take you back to the hotel?"

I sit in the *gharry* going by the Maidan, and all I see is black. I trusted Dr. Scott when he told me to defend myself. I thought it was a simple matter of truth. I didn't know I'd be worse off than before.

Tuesday Morning, 4 September 1883
Mary Pigot

"Miss Pigot, you look pale," Mr. Carruthers says. "Are you ill?"

"I'm fine," I reply grimly.

Mr. Trevelyan turns to me. "Mr. Carruthers told me of your distress," he says. "Rest assured, we'll go after Mr. Hastie when it's our turn."

"And when will that be?" I'm a bit snappish today.

"Perhaps today."

"All rise," the clerk calls.

Mr. Hastie resumes his place in the witness box with Mr. Gasper planted in front of him. "Reverend Hastie," Mr. Gasper says, "does Miss Pigot have a bad temper?"

Why don't you object to that, Mr. Trevelyan?

"Several colleagues mentioned an outburst at a prize-giving event last year," Mr. Hastie says.

"Did the teachers employed by Miss Pigot serve very long?" Mr. Gasper asks.

"For the most part, they didn't."

"And did this frequent turnover and the inference of Miss Pigot's bad temper influence you when you wrote the postscript?" Mr. Gasper asks.

"Did you think there was something at the Female Mission that encouraged staff turnover?"

Mr. Hastie strokes his facial hair. "I believe the moral atmosphere made it undesirable for the young ladies to remain. I don't have specifics."

"Was there a particular matter that influenced you?" Mr. Gasper asks.

"Miss Smail's complaint."

"My Lord," Mr. Gasper says, "I propose to ask what complaints she made."

"Objection. Miss Smail's complaints aren't in evidence." Mr. Trevelyan says.

Finally, an objection.

"Move on, Mr. Gasper," Justice Norris says, swatting at a mosquito.

"Did anything else influence you?" Mr. Gaspers asks.

"Miss Pigot's manner before men was indelicate," Mr. Hastie says. "At Mr. Steele's dinner party, I observed a lack of external propriety."

"That doesn't tell us anything," Justice Norris says. "What did you see?"

"I'm trying to save Miss Pigot unnecessary embarrassment," Mr. Hastie says.

"It's a bit late to be concerned about that now," Justice Norris says. "If the lady was afraid of being embarrassed, she wouldn't have filed this lawsuit."

I'm far beyond embarrassment. I reach both hands to steady my head. Mr. Trevelyan taps my elbow and I put my hands back on the table. What's Mr. Hastie saying now?

"When we retired to the drawing room after dinner, Miss Pigot flung herself upon Mr. Steele's sofa and threw up her legs. I've never seen a lady do that before," Mr. Hastie says.

"Did anything else happen at this dinner party?"

"Miss Pigot behaved frivolously."

What's that supposed to mean?

"My Lord," Mr. Gasper says. "I propose to ask Mr. Hastie if he heard conversations in which Miss Pigot's name was connected with the name of any man."

"My Lord!" Mr. Trevelyan leaps up. "I object most strenuously. Clearly Mr. Gasper's entire case rests on casting unproven aspersions against my client."

I'm amazed. I never thought Mr. Trevelyan would actually defend me. The judge rules in our favor. Mr. Gasper goes on as if nothing important happened.

"Mr. Hastie, do you want to add anything about Barrackpore Park?" Mr. Gasper asks pointedly.

"What struck me most was the open, continuous, and almost exclusive attention Miss Pigot paid to Mr. Wilson."

"There's no fact there," Justice Norris says.

"Thank you, Your Lordship." Mr. Gasper glares at Mr. Hastie and speaks slowly. "What we want to know, Mr. Hastie, is how you reached that conclusion."

"Whenever I saw them, they were together," Mr. Hastie says.

Justice Norris taps his knuckle. "Allow me to interject, Mr. Hastie. What the learned counsel wants to know is if there was any other physical fact you observed? Something besides your impression."

"Your Lordship, I can't forget Miss Pigot's continuous attention to Mr. Wilson. She neglected her duties and set a bad example."

Mr. Trevelyan stands. "My Lord, I object to this way of answering the question."

"Noted, Mr. Trevelyan," Justice Norris says. "Mr. Hastie, I invite you to state any facts connected with Miss Pigot's life you found to be unwomanly."

"My Lord, I'm not referring to Miss Pigot as a woman," Mr. Hastie says. "She was our Lady Superintendent. When I speak of her lack of external propriety, I mean anything inconsistent with the conduct we expect of our Lady Superintendent. I request Your Lordship give some regard to my view."

"You're entitled to your view," Justice Norris says, "and may sometimes express it. But you didn't express it in the postscript. You wrote a bold and naked statement. Move to your next question, Mr. Gasper."

"I have no further questions, My Lord," Mr. Gasper returns to his place.

Our turn at last. I hope Mr. Trevelyan breaks open Mr. Hastie's testimony to expose his deceit and innuendos. Mr. Trevelyan looks at his notes and walks towards the witness box. He has a slight stoop. He looks at Mr. Hastie for several minutes. Eventually, Mr. Hastie looks uncomfortable.

Mr. Trevelyan begins in a conversational tone. "Mr. Wilson is a married man, is he not?"

"Yes," Mr. Hastie replies.

"Has he got children?"

"I believe so," Mr. Hastie says.

"Are you still living in the same house with Mr. Wilson?" Mr. Trevelyan asks.

"We never lived in the same house."

"Oh. Have you ever *chummed* with Mr. Wilson?" Mr. Trevelyan asks.

"I don't use that expression," Mr. Hastie says.

"A bachelor in Calcutta and you've never used the term?"

"I've used it on occasion."

"When don't you use it?"

"I don't use it in the company of English gentlemen who know the English language," Mr. Hastie says.

"Would you ever write that word in a note?" Mr. Trevelyan asks.

"I might, if I were writing to a close friend," Mr. Hastie says.

"So, only to a good friend," Mr. Trevelyan says, "a person with whom you were on terms of intimacy. And you wouldn't be on terms of intimacy with a person who was guilty of any impropriety of conduct."

"I don't say that." Mr. Hastie shifts his feet.

"If you knew a person was guilty of impropriety, would you continue your intimacy with that person?" Mr. Trevelyan asks.

"I would limit my friendship as much as possible."

"When did you cease to chum with Mr. Wilson?" Mr. Trevelyan asks.

"A few months ago, since this suit came up," Mr. Hastie replies.

"We filed suit on the twenty-first of March. I have a letter you sent Mr. Wilson at the end of April saying you won't chum with him anymore. Do you recognize the letter?"

Mr. Trevelyan hands Mr. Hastie the letter. He glances at it, hands it back, and agrees he wrote it.

"Why did you stop chumming with Mr. Wilson?" Mr. Trevelyan asks.

"I didn't like his dinner conversation," Mr. Hastie says. "And I thought he would side with Miss Pigot."

"When you were at Barrackpore Park, did you note any improprieties by Mr. Wilson?"

"It was on both sides," Mr. Hastie says.

"Did you speak to Mr. Wilson about his conduct?"

"No. He left on furlough."

"When Mr. Wilson came back from furlough, did you remember these improprieties?"

"I did," Mr. Hastie says.

"Yet you chummed with him," Mr. Trevelyan says.

"Yes."

"I'm puzzled," Mr. Trevelyan says. "Did you think it proper Mr. Wilson should continue teaching boys if he was guilty of impropriety?"

My draw drops. What a question to ask. Mr. Wilson will be mortified.

"I knew of no improprieties with boys," Mr. Hastie says.

Mr. Trevelyan takes a step back. He looks stunned. I wonder if he expected Mr. Hastie to give that answer. "I'm shocked you say a man is only unfit to teach boys if he's guilty of improprieties with them. I submit that if he's guilty of improprieties with women, he isn't fit to teach boys."

"Mr. Hastie," Justice Norris interjects, "did you think a person guilty of impropriety with a woman in a public manner in Barrackpore Park was fit to teach boys?"

"I haven't charged Mr. Wilson with any offenses, My Lord," Mr. Hastie says, looking bewildered.

"But you charge him with a familiar and indecorous manner with a woman you thought was also accepting embraces from a native of this country?" Justice Norris asks.

"No, My Lord," Mr. Hastie looks around. "The suspicion of impropriety with this other party arose while Mr. Wilson was away." Mr. Hastie looks like a goat on a spit.

"Mr. Hastie," Mr. Trevelyan says. "I have another letter you wrote to Mr. Wilson, in which you state that since this suit was being withdrawn, you hoped the two of you could resume chumming. Did you write this letter?"

"Yes. At the time I thought the cause of our quarrel resolved," Mr. Hastie says.

"Why did you invite Mr. Wilson to return to your table when you thought his dinner conversation improper?"

"I hadn't consulted with our other member Mr. Fish, and I thought Mr. Wilson should have a choice to return." Mr. Hastie is starting to sound desperate.

"You were willing to put up with improper conversation?"

"Yes."

"In order to reduce your domestic expenses," Justice Norris says.

"No, My Lord. I thought Mr. Wilson had changed," Mr. Hastie says.

"Mr. Hastie," Justice Norris says. "You said you wanted to restore the chummery to save expenses. You also said it was on Mr. Fish's account. Did you consider whether or not Mr. Fish was edified by Mr. Wilson's conversation?"

"I didn't restore the chummery to save money," Mr. Hastie says.

"Then why did you write that the chummery was of great advantage to you?" Justice Norris asks. "Didn't you mean it enabled you to live more economically?"

"Yes, My Lord. I'm careless of these matters, but the existence of the chummery saved me expense," Mr. Hastie says.

"Mr. Hastie," Justice Norris says, "why did you want the chummery relationship to resume?"

"I felt we should come together again, and that the discontinuance was a discipline to Mr. Wilson," Mr. Hastie says.

What a strange thing to say. Mr. Hastie is losing his composure at last.

"What!" Justice Norris says. "You thought discontinuing this dinner arrangement was good for Mr. Wilson's soul?"

Mr. Hastie seems stunned by the judge's temper.

Mr. Trevelyan clears his throat. "To return to Barrackpore Park. Why was it Miss Pigot's business to attend to the guests?"

"Because the picnic was given to her and the orphans," Mr. Hastie says regaining his composure.

"You think it improper for a principal guest to devote herself to her host?" Mr. Trevelyan asks.

"It was improper to exclude others."

"Were you neglected?" Mr. Trevelyan asks in a gentle tone.

"No. She neglected her teachers and the orphans."

"Couldn't the orphans run about by themselves?" Justice Norris asks. "There weren't any tigers or bulls, were there?"

"My Lord," Mr. Trevelyan says with a slight smile, "there was a tiger once in Barrackpore Park. In a cage. I think it's been moved to the Calcutta Zoo."

"I disagree, My Lord," Mr. Hastie says before the judge can respond.

"But what could she do for the children?" Justice Norris asks, "except let them enjoy themselves."

"She should've kept her eyes on them," Mr. Hastie says.

"Describe to me exactly the position of Mr. Wilson and Miss Pigot," Mr. Trevelyan says. "Were they lying down or sitting?"

"She reclined," Mr. Hastie says.

I didn't.

"Did Miss Pigot recline full length on her back, or leaning against a tree?"

"Leaning against something."

"What?"

"Perhaps a pillow or a bundle of shawls," Mr. Hastie says.

"What was Mr. Wilson doing?"

"He sat beside her with his body touching hers," Mr. Hastie says.

"As they would sit in church?" Justice Norris asks with arched eyebrows.

"Certainly not! His head was on her shoulder in a way I didn't like," Mr. Hastie says.

"Did anyone remark on it?" Mr. Trevelyan asks.

"I don't remember any comment at the time," Mr. Hastie says.

Justice Norris pulls out his watch. "We'll adjourn for *tiffin* now."

William Hastie

Before I can step out of the witness box, Mr. Gasper has a word with Mr. Geddes and leaves the courtroom. I thought he might stay to shake my hand. I did very well under trying circumstances.

The judge is biased against me. He intervenes to help my enemies at every opportunity. And that barrister—where did she find him? No thought of basic conversational civility. Badgering me, before I complete my thoughts. How does he expect me to remember things from last year? Preposterous! And why didn't my man speak up?

I have a crashing headache and my knees feel like jelly. I hold on to the rail as I step down. Mr. Geddes takes my arm. "Sit down, Mr. Hastie. You've had quite a long morning," Mr. Geddes says.

"No thanks to you," I complain.

Mr. Geddes draws himself up. "I beg your pardon."

"Your barrister never objected to any of the questions. Never told that man to stop badgering me," I snap.

"Opposing counsel is allowed to question you about your testimony," Mr. Geddes says. "So long as he sticks to that, we've nothing to say."

"He should say something to the judge."

"It's Justice Norris' courtroom. He may speak whenever he likes. Now, come with me for *tiffin* and you can put your feet up before we resume."

"Resume?" I ask in disbelief.

"Mr. Trevelyan hasn't finished yet," Mr. Geddes says.

I hobble out of the courtroom. Never has my fortitude been so tested.

Mary Pigot

I'm elated. Mr. Trevelyan tied Mr. Hastie in knots. When he returns to our table, I touch my barrister's arm. "Thank you. You've shown what kind of man Mr. Hastie is."

"We're not done yet, Miss Pigot. Have a little faith."

"You made him look a fool, Mr. Trevelyan."

"I merely let him reveal himself," Mr. Trevelyan says. "Are you ready for the afternoon session?"

I nod. "Will we end today?"

"No, but we have a good start," Mr. Trevelyan says.

"Of course," I say, as Mr. Trevelyan dashes off. I don't know where he goes, but he's always in a hurry to leave.

After a two-hour break, we start the afternoon session. Mr. Hastie looks wobbly as he returns to the witness box. Mr. Trevelyan looks up and pauses. Is he trying to prolong Hastie's discomfort? I hope so.

"Just a few more questions, Mr. Hastie," Mr. Trevelyan finally says, rising to his feet. "This business of Miss Pigot coming alone to visit Mr. Wilson. Were you living in the same house?"

"No," Mr. Hastie says.

"Then, how could you see them?"

"I saw her *gharry* arrive. I saw her in it, and I saw her *gharry* without her in it."

"Please answer my question, Mr. Hastie. Did you see her in the same house?" Mr. Trevelyan asks.

"No." Mr. Hastie shakes his head.

"Where did you live?"

"In another house, about a hundred yards from Mr. Wilson's."

"Did anyone else live in that house?" Mr. Trevelyan asks.

"Yes," Mr. Hastie replies. "His cousin."

"What time of day was it when you saw Miss Pigot's *gharry*?"

"Afternoon."

"In daylight?" Mr. Trevelyan asks.

"Yes."

"Did a lady ever visit you at your house?" Mr. Trevelyan asks.

"I've had several visits from a lady." Mr. Hastie pauses. "Actually, no, very seldom. Perhaps two or three times."

"Well, which is it?" Mr. Trevelyan asks patiently.

Mr. Hastie looks at the ceiling. "In the past four and a half years, I only remember one lady visiting."

"And, when a lady visits you, is it an impropriety?" Mr. Trevelyan asks.

"I've never had a visit I'd call improper," Mr. Hastie says.

"Is it the mode of the visit that makes it improper?"

Mr. Hastie glances in my direction. "It is the mode of the visit, the frequency of the visits, or anything which would cause an unfavorable opinion. I allege nothing about these visits to Mr. Wilson, except that they occurred."

Justice Norris breaks in. "But you allege Miss Pigot disregarded every mark of external propriety."

"Yes, My Lord." Mr. Hastie looks up. "I regarded the visits as improper."

"Why were they improper?" Mr. Trevelyan asks.

"In the first place, they were unnecessary," Mr. Hastie says.

"Confine yourself to improper."

"If any communication was necessary, Mr. Wilson could visit the Female Mission," Mr. Hastie says. "I wouldn't have thought that improper."

Justice Norris restates the question. "Mr. Trevelyan is asking you in what respect you considered these visits to Mr. Wilson improper."

"It wasn't necessary for Miss Pigot to visit him there alone," Mr. Hastie comments. "The visits were frequent and of some duration."

"Mr. Hastie," Mr. Trevelyan asks as if the question just occurred to him, "did it ever pass through your mind that these two persons had sexual intercourse?"

Dear God, how can Mr. Trevelyan put such a question in front of the court!

Mr. Hastie blanches. "No, I never seriously thought sexual relations took place."

Justice Norris looks down on the witness box. "Mr. Hastie, did you think Miss Pigot visited Mr. Wilson for purposes of sexual congress?"

"My Lord," Mr. Hastie hesitates. "I simply thought it improper for the Lady Superintendent to visit any of the male missionaries so frequently."

I am ruined.

"Did you ask Mr. Wilson or Miss Pigot if there was a reason for these visits, or make any inquiries?" Mr. Trevelyan asks.

"No."

"How could you see the *gharry* drive up? Did you stand by the window?" Mr. Trevelyan asks.

"I moved around the compound performing my duties."

"Did you ever consider Miss Pigot was consulting Mr. Wilson about the complaints against her?" Justice Norris asks.

"Well," Mr. Hastie says, "I have no doubt she was consulting him, My Lord."

"You didn't answer my question," Justice Norris says waspishly. "Did you think Miss Pigot was consulting Mr. Wilson?"

"Yes, I did."

"Do you consider that improper?" Justice Norris asks.

"I do."

Mr. Trevelyan stands still a moment before changing the subject. "Let's talk about Miss Pigot putting her legs up on the sofa. After the incident, did you discover that people in this country have easier attitudes than in Scotland?"

"I know that," Mr. Hastie says with annoyance. "I was somewhat aware of it at the time."

"And where did this incident occur?" Mr. Trevelyan asks.

"In the house of Mr. Octavius Steele, a friend of Miss Pigot's."

"The same Mr. Steele who is one of the leading members of the Church of Scotland in Calcutta?"

"Yes," Mr. Hastie affirms.

"Did he tell you then or later than he objected to Miss Pigot putting up her legs?"

Mr. Hastie hesitates. "No."

"Did you mention to him that you thought it improper?" Mr. Trevelyan asks.

"Yes. The next time I saw Mr. Steele I said 'That woman takes great liberties in your house.'"

"And his answer?" Mr. Trevelyan asks.

"I can't remember exactly," Mr. Hastie says. "He winced."

"Do answer Mr. Trevelyan's question," Justice Norris says in an irritated tone. He slaps another mosquito. "Wincing can't be taken as evidence."

"I don't remember his reply," Mr. Hastie says. "It was a sort of mild assent."

"Mr. Hastie," Justice Norris says, "does it strike you that it's neither kind nor decent to refer to Miss Pigot as 'that woman'?"

"I might have said 'that lady,' My Lord," Mr. Hastie responds. "Perhaps I said 'Miss Pigot.'"

"You're under oath," Justice Norris says. "What did you say?"

Mr. Hastie pauses. "I will keep to the phrase 'that woman.'"

"You think it proper or decent to speak of a lady this way?" Justice Norris asks.

"Why not, My Lord?"

"I'm asking you," Justice Norris says.

Mr. Hastie's lips make a flat line. "I didn't use the word 'woman' with any disrespect. In the Bible, the best of all books, we have the word 'woman.'"

"No doubt we have, but the express meaning of 'that woman' depends on the tone, accent, and look that accompanies it." Justice Norris says. "It's a term of contempt. Even without the tone, to speak this way about a lady you'd only known six weeks. Don't you find it an unceremonious way of speaking?"

"It wasn't the first time I spoke of her."

"Did you immediately begin referring to Miss Pigot as 'that woman'?" Justice Norris asks in surprise.

"No," Mr. Hastie replies. "I think it was the first time I used the phrase."

Justice Norris shuffles his papers. "I see it was about that time that Miss Pigot's exertions nursing you saved your life."

"That's incorrect," Mr. Hastie says.

How can he say that after I lost sleep over him?

"Did she nurse you with care and devotion such as a woman shows when nursing a man who is ill?" Justice Norris asks.

Mr. Hastie glances in my direction without looking at me. "Yes, My Lord."

"Carry on, Mr. Trevelyan," Justice Norris waves his hand.

"You got cholera shortly after your arrival?" Mr. Trevelyan asks.

"Yes."

"And Miss Pigot nursed you through the illness?"

"Through part of it," Mr. Hastie replies.

"Which part?" Mr. Trevelyan asks.

The part when you were sick, Mr. Hastie.

"The latter part," Mr. Hastie says.

"Didn't Miss Pigot sit with you four days and four nights?" Mr. Trevelyan asks.

"Oh no." Mr. Hastie shakes his head. "As far as I remember, she only stayed one night."

He knows better than that, Mr. Trevelyan. Make him tell the truth.

"Were you grateful for her devotion?" Mr. Trevelyan asks.

"Yes, of course."

"Do you remember sending a book to Miss Pigot?"

"Yes."

"Did she accept it?" Mr. Trevelyan asks.

"No."

"You autographed the fly leaf of the book, didn't you? Is this it, with your handwriting?" Mr. Trevelyan asks. He picks up the book. I can't think where he got it. Mr. Hastie agrees it's the same book, and Mr. Trevelyan reads the silly poem Mr. Hastie inscribed about woman being uncertain, coy, and hard to please.

"Was it after Miss Pigot returned your gift that you attended the dinner party at Mr. Steele's? The one where she put up her legs on the sofa?" Mr. Trevelyan asks.

"Yes," Mr. Hastie says softly.

"Were you annoyed at her because she didn't accept the book?"

"A little."

"Was your pride mortified?" Justice Norris asks.

"No, My Lord, not in that way," Mr. Hastie responds.

"What annoyed you?" Mr. Trevelyan asks.

"It was the letter she sent with it that annoyed me."

"Were you annoyed because you're her minister and she refused your book?" Justice Norris probes.

"No, My Lord," Mr. Hastie says. "I thought she was capricious to return the book, and the letter she sent with it was most unsatisfactory."

"Did you think Miss Pigot 'hard to please'?" Mr. Trevelyan asks.

"No. She referred to the mission in the letter," Mr. Hastie says, "and said she'd be glad to work with me."

"Tell us what you remember about the letter," Mr. Trevelyan says. "I think that will account for the 'milk in the coconut' as the expression goes."

Mr. Hastie looks perplexed. "If you give me time, I'll try."

Justice Norris bangs his gavel. "Twenty-minute recess so Mr. Hastie can jog his memory." The judge leaves, loosening his collar as he goes through the door nearest the bench.

Mr. Trevelyan returns to our table, sits beside me and asks if I remember the letter more clearly that what I told him before, but I don't—only that I rejected the book as inappropriate. I have no idea what became of the letter. Mr. Trevelyan decides to let the point go.

The break passes swiftly. The judge enters and Mr. Hastie attempts to rise from his chair. He must be in difficulty. His solicitor helps him stand and holds his arm as he returns to the witness box. Justice Norris watches Mr. Hastie grip the rail and pull himself into the box.

"Bailiff," Justice Norris orders, "put a chair in the witness box. It's going to be a long afternoon."

The bailiff takes the closest cane chair from the jury box, drags it across the floor, and pushes it into the witness box. Mr. Hastie has to stand in the furthest corner as the chair is adjusted. He uses the rail to pull himself in front of the chair and collapses with a distinct plop. When he's finally seated he thanks the judge and sinks down into what could be called a slump. I feel no sympathy. Mr. Trevelyan approaches the box and goes after Mr. Hastie like dog worrying a bone. "Did Miss Pigot resign in February 1879?"

"I think it was later than that," Mr. Hastie replies.

"Look at this letter to Miss Pigot dated the nineteenth of March 1879. What is the misunderstanding you refer to?" Mr. Trevelyan asks. "Is it about the book? You say, 'You never made a greater error than in attributing any blame to me.' What did she blame you for?"

"Miss Pigot involved herself in Mr. Robson's resignation and alienated the Corresponding Board. She blamed me for a falling out she had with Mr. Steele," Mr. Hastie says. "They were at daggers drawn over Mr. Robson..."

Mr. Trevelyan throws up his hands. "Do stop, please. We don't want a speech. In this letter to Miss Pigot, why did you write she was misguided?"

"In her support of Mr. Robson and his friends."

"Did you dislike him because he was a member of the Free Church?"

"I don't know that he's a member of any church," Mr. Hastie says in disgust. "He attended the Free Church."

"So what was Miss Pigot's blunder?" Mr. Trevelyan asks.

"She wasn't loyal to the Board."

"Did you convince Miss Pigot she was wrong?"

"No," Mr. Hastie says. "In fact, when I tried to speak to her, she abused the Board."

"And told them to mind their own business?" Justice Norris asks.

Mr. Hastie twists his neck to look at the judge. "My Lord, they were minding their business."

"Is it possible you were a little overbearing?" Mr. Trevelyan asks.

"I spoke a little sharply to her, but I'm never overbearing."

Ask him about his relations with the College faculty.

"Mr. Hastie," Mr. Trevelyan says. "You wrote two letters to Miss Pigot in March 1880. In one letter, you wrote 'I think it will be better for us to keep to our respective spheres.' What did you mean?"

"Our missions weren't connected by a proper constitution. I declined to work in Miss Pigot's sphere."

"Were you asked to interfere with Miss Pigot's work?" Mr. Trevelyan asks.

"In March or April 1882, the Mission Committee at home asked me to restore harmony," Mr. Hastie says. "I was unsuccessful."

"Did Miss Pigot think you meddlesome?" Mr. Trevelyan asks.

"She couldn't, because I never meddled."

"In fact," Justice Norris interrupts, "didn't it amount to this? 'I am much obliged to you, but will you mind your own business'? Wasn't that her response to your concerns?"

"No, My Lord."

"What did she say?" Mr. Trevelyan asks.

"She objected to the Corresponding Board," Mr. Hastie says.

"Did she say, 'as far as you represent the Corresponding Board, I repudiate your right to interfere with me'?" Justice Norris asks.

"No, My Lord, she didn't say that," Mr. Hastie replies.

"Practically speaking, didn't it amount to that?" Justice Norris asks. "And you thought the Corresponding Board should control the Female Mission?"

"I wished to keep the former relationship," Mr. Hastie says.

Judge Norris makes an exasperated sigh. "Go to another topic, Mr. Trevelyan."

Mr. Trevelyan begins asking about the reason Mr. Hastie banned Babu Kali Churn Banerjee from the Female Mission, and their feud over the newspaper articles Kali Churn wrote. I'm too exhausted to listen. I'm amazed at Mr. Trevelyan's energy. He's crushed Mr. Hastie's spirit until the man seems disoriented. Mr. Hastie can't even stand. I feel much better today than yesterday. Perhaps I'll prevail after all.

Chapter 15
"I Never Called Her That In Public"

Wednesday Morning, 5 September 1883
William Hastie

I spent last night on my knees praying the words of Psalm 42: *"I will say unto God, my Rock, Why hast thou forgotten me? Why go I mourning because of the oppression of the enemy? As with a sword in my bones, mine enemies reproach me; while they say daily to me, where is thy God?"* Surely God will answer my prayer and restore me to my rightful place. I don't know how much longer I can bear being questioned about my every thought. I strive to appear strong even though I feel myself collapsing inside. I don't know how much longer I can keep up this external pretense. The Book of Psalms is a great comfort. King David himself cried to the Lord and I'm not nearly the sinner he was.

Falak knocks and lays a tray on my desk. I can't eat with my colleagues. They whisper behind their hands, wondering if I'll lose my position over this travesty of a trial. I deduce God tests my resolve with this farce and fear I may fail. Every part of my body aches, and the infernal heat and rain bring me to despair. I drink my coffee, but the thought of food makes me ill.

I leaf through *The Statesman* to the section covering my trial. The account of my testimony is accurate without any hint of despair on my part. The clock chimes. It's time to leave for court. I check my appearance. If I look anything less than my position, it will be in the newspapers. My beard is trimmed and my suit pressed, though the heat will wilt the fabric.

The driver guides my *gharry* through sheets of rain to the High Court. Mr. Geddes greets me at the steps and offers me his arm. I want to wave it away but have no choice but to take it if I'm going to climb the stairs.

"How much longer will these questions continue?" I ask as we walk inside.

"I don't know, Mr. Hastie," Mr. Geddes says. "Mr. Trevelyan wants to wear you down so you make an ill-advised comment. Keep your wits about you."

Mr. Gasper waits at our table.

"You must stop this travesty," I say after we shake hands.

"The only way to end proceedings is for you to concede," Mr. Gasper says. "Is that what you want?"

I let the temptation hang in the air, then shake my head and offer a silent prayer for strength.

Justice Norris comes in. The man is insufferable, interrupting me all the time. "You may return to the witness box," he says.

I shuffle to my place. The chair is gone.

"Proceed, Mr. Trevelyan," Justice Norris says.

Mr. Trevelyan approaches the witness box holding the front of his robe with both hands. "Good morning, Mr. Hastie," he says. "Let us continue our conversation. I wonder, were you annoyed when Babu Banerjee wrote he wouldn't receive more of your notes? I believe he called them impertinent."

What relevance does this have? "I was."

"Did you think Babu Banerjee impudent?" Mr. Trevelyan asks.

"Yes." I grip the rail.

Mr. Trevelyan looks at me like I'm a mouse and he's the cat. "Is Reverend Mr. Chuckerbutty one of your witnesses?"

"Yes."

"When were you first aware he'd be a witness in this case?"

"More than two months ago—in June or July," I say.

"Are you the author of this circular suggesting donations to honor Reverend Chuckerbutty on the fortieth anniversary of his conversion?" Mr. Trevelyan asks. "And is this your name on the top with a donation of ten rupees?"

He hands me the circular featuring a sketch of Mr. Chuckerbutty. "Yes, I am."

"You saw no impropriety in soliciting donations for your chief witness while this case goes on?"

Although Mr. Trevelyan's face is a complete blank, I detect a sneer in his voice. I've had enough of his innuendos. "Look here, I can't suspend my missionary duties because of this case. Reverend Chuckerbutty's conversion is an example to the community. There's no impropriety in contributing a trifling sum to the celebration."

Mr. Trevelyan walks back to his table leaving my response hanging in the air. He looks down at his notes, then changes the subject. "When did Miss Pigot go to Scotland?"

"In May 1882."

"Did you know she went home to meet accusations made against her?" Mr. Trevelyan asks.

"She didn't confide her plans to me, but I knew there were accusations."

"Yes or no, Mr. Hastie," Mr. Trevelyan says. "Did you know why she went home?"

"I'll say no to that question."

"Did you discover later why she went?" Mr. Trevelyan asks calmly.

"Not until I saw her Complaint in this suit." *Prior to that I could only guess.*

Mr. Trevelyan seems to consider my answer before he continues. "Did you know Miss Smail wrote the Ladies' Association, and Miss Pigot went to Scotland after Miss Smail wrote her letter?"

"I knew Miss Smail wrote a letter, but I didn't connect it with Miss Pigot's departure."

"Did you know the contents of Miss Smail's letter?" Mr. Trevelyan asks.

If I say no, would anyone be the wiser? I can't take the risk. "Colonel Walker read part of it aloud while I was at his home."

"Which part?" Mr. Trevelyan asks.

"The part referring to the filthy state of the house."

"Is that all you remember?"

"It's what I most remember." *Please stop.*

Mr. Trevelyan plants himself in front of the witness box. "Nothing else?" he purrs. "Are you sure? Remember you're under oath."

"I heard another part," I admit. "It seemed to refer to a flirtation between Miss Pigot and Mr. Wilson."

Mr. Trevelyan smiles at me.

Justice Norris breaks in. "How old is Miss Smail?"

"About thirty, My Lord," I respond.

"About thirty," Justice Norris says as he writes a note.

"What exactly did Miss Smail say about this flirtation?" Mr. Trevelyan asks. "Was it a personal grievance?"

"She said it was a grievance with regard to the Mission."

"Did Miss Smail give any dates or times when this flirtation occurred?"

I shake my head. "No."

"Did she use the word 'flirtation'?" Mr. Trevelyan asks. "You do know the meaning of the word."

"I know what the word means," I snap.

"Was that part of your general education as a missionary?" Mr. Trevelyan snipes at me.

Mr. Gasper bounces to his feet. "I object to that question."

Justice Norris looks up in surprise. "Mr. Trevelyan has a perfect right to the question."

"Never mind, Your Lordship," Mr. Trevelyan nods to the judge. "I withdraw it. Tell me, Mr. Hastie, do you remember anything else about the contents of that letter?"

"No," I shake my head.

"Did Miss Smail write the letter before Miss Pigot went to Scotland?" Mr. Trevelyan asks.

"About a month or two."

"Did you know investigations took place while Miss Pigot was in Scotland?" Mr. Trevelyan asks.

"Yes. I became aware of them in July or August 1882."

"And you received a copy of the concluding report from Mr. Macrae."

"I did."

"When did you see the actual report?" Mr. Trevelyan asks.

"Not until December 1882." I suppose now he'll ask why I forwarded the letters in November rather than wait until the final report arrived. I see Mr. Gasper stand up at last.

"My Lord," Mr. Gasper says, "I object to this line of questioning. I don't see it as evidence."

"I agree, Mr. Gasper," Justice Norris says. "Move on, Mr. Trevelyan."

I exhale.

Mr. Trevelyan shrugs. "As you wish, My Lord. Mr. Hastie, did you write a Note Explanatory in August 1882 after receiving news of Miss Pigot's exoneration?"

"Yes, I did."

"To whom did you send this note?"

"I sent a copy to Mr. Gillan and to Colonel Walker."

"Why were you, as you say here, 'ashamed, disappointed and perplexed' with the report?" Mr. Trevelyan continues his line of questioning.

"Mr. Macrae's report insulted our Mission and myself personally," I say.

"Did you think the Church Elders ashamed to sign the report?"

"It wasn't an official communication without the signatures," I say. "We've only Mr. Macrae's word that this was the report."

"You claimed the concoctors of the document couldn't grasp the, I quote, 'evils which make our Female Mission a reproach,'" Mr. Trevelyan says. "What was going on?"

"I referred to the public scandal with Kali Churn Banerjee, the fact that the Mission had no oversight, and Miss Pigot's poor management, habits, character, and manner."

"You say here the Upper School is largely attended by illegitimate half-castes—a class group with which you say Miss Pigot has strong affinities," Mr. Trevelyan says. "Did you mean Miss Pigot is an illegitimate half-caste?"

"It is a known fact."

"Do you think the comment was in good taste?"

"Perhaps not," I say. "But it doesn't change the fact."

Justice Norris raps his knuckle on the bench. "Gentlemen, enlightening as this discussion is, it's time for *tiffin*. This seems as good a place to stop as any."

Mary Pigot

I watch the judge disappear behind his door, already unfastening his robe. What must he think of me now? Mr. Trevelyan returns to our table and loosens his collar. He turns to have a word with Mr. Carruthers. Neither man looks at me.

"Mr. Trevelyan," I say as he's about to leave. "I'm not an illegitimate half-caste. How could you ask such a question? It will be in all the newspapers tomorrow."

"Miss Pigot, you must trust me to handle your case," Mr. Trevelyan tells me. "The more exaggerations and untruths I can get out Mr. Hastie's mouth, the stronger your case will be. Later we'll demonstrate his error. I trust you have legal certificates to prove your legitimacy?"

"Of course I do." I don't bother to hide my irritation.

"We'll introduce them as evidence," Mr. Trevelyan says. "I know what I'm doing, Miss Pigot. Now please allow Mr. Carruthers to take you for *tiffin*."

I stand open-mouthed as my barrister leaves the courtroom. I didn't expect my defender to slander me. My father must be spinning in his grave. I stand frozen until Mr. Carruthers takes my elbow to guide me out.

I can't see where I'm going and realize my eyes are full of tears. Outside we slosh through the mud to Mr. Carruther's office. I go to the washroom and look in the mirror. My hat has melted in the rain. My hair pulls down on either side of my face. I begin to sob. Dear God, why are you putting me through this?

Wednesday Afternoon, 5 September 1883
William Hastie

I return to the courtroom half an hour before we convene. I'm determined not to return to the infernal witness box. The air is putrid and still, because the *punkah wallahs* aren't at their posts. I drum my fingers on the table. After about ten minutes, Mr. Geddes joins me, sodden and cheerful. He whistles through his teeth. How can he be so pleased when I'm in such misery?

"Ready for the afternoon, Mr. Hastie? I'm sorry the judge decided to remove your chair from the witness box. I suppose it was just too irregular for him."

I stare at the man and continue drumming my fingers. The *punkah wallahs* return to their task. A blast of dust fills the room as the fan starts up. Looking up I see a mesh of spider webs in the peaks of the gothic windows. If a courtroom can be this slovenly, perhaps Miss Pigot's housekeeping isn't unusual. The reporters come in, talking softly as they take their seats at the back. I look at my watch. If the judge is punctual, court resumes in about three minutes. Finally, Mr. Gasper comes in, adjusting his collar bands over his black robe.

"Ready for the afternoon?" he inquires perfunctorily.

"Mr. Gasper," I demand, "you must put a stop to this interrogation. It's insulting and it weakens our case."

Mr. Gasper turns his dark eyes on me. "Mr. Hastie, I will tell you this for the last time," he hisses. "We follow the rule of law here. It's Mr. Trevelyan's right to question you on any evidence you've presented. Do not question my strategy again. Do I make myself clear?"

"All rise," the clerk announces.

"As your employer," I whisper, "it's my right to ask what your strategy is."

"My strategy is to win by whatever means the law makes available to me," Mr. Gasper mutters. Justice Norris looks in our direction. "The judge is here. Get back in the witness box and answer Mr. Trevelyan's questions."

Arrogant man! Hand someone a law book and a horsehair wig, and he thinks he's better than anyone else. Why does God test me so harshly? I take Mr. Geddes's arm and hobble back to the witness box. Mr. Trevelyan stands before me like one of the devil's henchmen.

"Mr. Hastie," he says. "To return to our discussion of the Upper School. You wrote there was a Free Church girl in attendance and said her presence was an insult to your church. Who was this girl?"

"She's the so-called niece of Kali Churn Banerjee."

"Why do you say so-called?"

"Her mother lives in Babu Banerjee's house," I reply.

"I see. To return to your Note Explanatory, you wrote you had no objection if Miss Pigot returned to her work. Did anyone care if you did?" Mr. Trevelyan asks.

The judge chuckles.

"A great many people value my opinion." My voice sounds louder than it should.

"I'm sure they do. What was your frame of mind when you wrote the Note Explanatory?"

"I was indignant with the Mission Committee for not setting matters right," I say controlling my temper.

"Were you also indignant with Miss Pigot?" Mr. Trevelyan asks.

"No. I thought her a woman who took advantage of her position and wanted to keep it."

"Much like you, I warrant. How long did your indignation last?"

"After a few days, I was done with the matter," I say. "I had other concerns."

Mr. Trevelyan looks at the judge, then back at me. "Have you ever said you make no serious charges against Miss Pigot?"

"Quite possibly. I've never made any serious charges against her."

"You don't think the phrase you were *'more than suspicious'* serious?"

"That isn't a serious charge," I say. "It's simply a fact."

"So you didn't think the charges serious?"

"No. I certainly didn't believe an action for libel could be based on them."

Mr. Trevelyan pauses a moment. "Are you and Mr. Steele friends?" Mr. Trevelyan suddenly asks.

"We've quarreled, but we were friends before."

Mr. Trevelyan looks at me accusingly. "Didn't Mr. Steele take you by the collar and turn you out of his office?"

No, no. He never did that. We shook hands.

"Speak up, Mr. Hastie. Didn't Mr. Steele throw you out of his office?"

"That's a lie," I shout. The courtroom falls silent.

Justice Norris raps his knuckle on the bench. "Mr. Hastie, you can't behave that way in court. We'll take a few moments for you to compose yourself. Otherwise I'll have to remove you."

The clerk brings me a glass of water. I refuse it. Mr. Trevelyan looks at the judge, who nods. Mr. Trevelyan starts in again.

"Did you ever see a document called a Leaflet?" Mr. Trevelyan asks in a conversational tone.

"Yes, I received a copy."

Mr. Trevelyan speaks more quickly. "Who sent it to you?"

"Mrs. Walker."

"Whom do you think wrote it?" Mr. Trevelyan asks.

"I think Mrs. Walker wrote it."

"Was Mrs. Walker on good terms with Miss Pigot?" Mr. Trevelyan asks.

"I don't think they were friends."

"Did you know Miss Smail wasn't a friend of Miss Pigot?"

"Yes." My pulse races.

Mr. Trevelyan looks at me with his expressionless face. "You stated earlier that Miss Smail was loyal to her church. Who was her minister?"

"Mr. Gillan."

"Is Miss Smail pure European?" Mr. Trevelyan asks.

"Yes," I say.

Mr. Trevelyan pauses before asking "When Miss Smail came to this country and found she would work under a Eurasian, was she distressed?"

"Perhaps," I say. "I don't think she'd make a point of it. She didn't mention it to me."

"Miss Smail left the mission. Was she willing to go back?"

"So far as I'm aware, she wouldn't have gone back under any conditions," I confirm.

"But you wanted to give her an opportunity to go back?"

"Yes. I suggested it in my memorandum of May 1882."

"What business was it of yours?" Mr. Trevelyan asks sharply.

"As a person interested in the mission, it was of great importance. I had no personal interest."

Mr. Trevelyan walks back to his table and turns towards me. "Mrs. Ellis was one of Miss Pigot's senior staff members. Was she a friend of yours?"

"I'm acquainted with her. I wouldn't call her a friend, but I knew her fairly well."

Justice Norris leans over the bench. "Mr. Hastie, you have a habit of avoiding the question at hand. Was this Mrs. Ellis a friend of yours? Do you know what the term 'friend' means?"

"If Your Lordship means she has any preference towards me, I'm not aware of it."

"Have you any preference towards her?" Justice Norris asks.

"No, My Lord." A man of my training consorting with a woman like that. The very idea is absurd.

"Then without speaking of the enthusiasm of humanity and the milk of human kindness, surely you can answer Mr. Trevelyan's question," Justice Norris says sarcastically.

"Mrs. Ellis has always been friendly to me."

Mr. Trevelyan nods and changes the subject. "Mr. Hastie, are you aware Miss Pigot was dismissed?"

"Yes."

"Have you any doubt her dismissal was due to charges contained in the documents you forwarded?" Mr. Trevelyan asks.

"I'm sure that's not true," I say.

Mr. Trevelyan gives me a quizzical look before continuing. "Did you go to the orphanage last March to get information about this case?"

"Yes, I went with Mr. Fish."

"Did you ask whether anyone saw Mr. James and Kali Churn Banerjee in Miss Pigot's bathroom?"

"I asked if anyone saw or knew if Kali Churn Banerjee was in Miss Pigot's bedroom or bathroom."

"You didn't mention Mr. James in connection with the bathroom," Mr. Trevelyan says.

"No."

Justice Norris turns his head towards me. "See what evil results from your meddling," Justice Norris says. "Not only has the linen of your church had to be washed in court, but you've dragged in Mr. James, a member, as I understand it, of another church."

Why accuse me, Justice Norris? I didn't ask the question.

"Did you take Mr. Fish with you to take notes?" Mr. Trevelyan asks.

"He was willing to assist me," I say. "At the time, I wanted to keep the matter as private as possible."

"Who did you ask about Babu Banerjee's whereabouts?" Mr. Trevelyan asks.

"I asked Mrs. Ellis. She said she hadn't seen him in Miss Pigot's bathroom, but she knew he went there."

"Did you ask if Miss Pigot was there at the time?" Mr. Trevelyan asks.

"No."

"But you went there to discover evidence of Miss Pigot's fornication," Justice Norris says matter-of-factly.

I pause. "Yes, My Lord."

"And you didn't ask that question?" Justice Norris shakes his head. "There'd be no harm in his being in the bathroom unless Miss Pigot was there."

"Who else did you ask?" Mr. Trevelyan asks.

"Mrs. Tremearne," I say. "She said no."

"Who was your informant about Mr. James?" Mr. Trevelyan asks.

"Is this necessary, Mr. Trevelyan?" Justice Norris asks impatiently.

"Perhaps not, My Lord," Mr. Trevelyan replies. "My case is that Mr. Hastie has been throwing dirt everywhere."

What is he implying? "I deny I throw dirt *anywhere.*"

"It looks very much like you do," Justice Norris says.

"Did you see Mr. Steele after this suit began?" Mr. Trevelyan asks.

"Yes."

"Did you say to him in reference to Miss Pigot 'You've used all your influence to support this whore'?"

"You called her a whore?" Justice Norris exclaims.

My mouth falls open.

"Don't stand there gaping," Justice Norris says. "Did you or did you not? Answer my question."

"I...did...but I object to the rest of your sentence, My Lord."

"Now look here, Mr. Hastie," Justice Norris says. "Did Mr. Steele say your inference was a lie?"

"He did."

"Did you have a memorandum book in your hand?" Justice Norris asks.

"Yes," I reply, "to note my inquiries."

"You had a book in your hand, and a pencil, and you put long questions to him in the way you did to the mission ladies?" Justice Norris asks.

"Yes, I had questions."

"Was one of your questions whether Miss Pigot went to dinner with one arm around Mr. Steele's neck and one arm around Mr. Wilson's neck?" Mr. Trevelyan asks.

"No."

"Did you say anything of that sort?" Justice Norris demands.

What's happening? Why is the judge so outraged? "My Lord, I put a question that might be exaggerated into that," I try to explain. "I asked if he remembered when Miss Pigot had ahold of him, Mr. Wilson, and Mr. Clark saying she wished she had a photograph of it."

"What statement did you make to Mr. Steele that he called a lie?" Justice Norris asks.

"I thought he was supplying Miss Pigot with funds for her legal fees. He said I was wrong."

"You knew about Miss Pigot before you arrived in India, didn't you?" Mr. Trevelyan asks.

"I'd heard of her, read her name in reports."

"You heard Mr. Thomson praise Miss Pigot."

"Yes."

"You said Mr. Thomson was hostile to your appointment as principal of Scottish College," Mr. Trevelyan continues.

"That's true," I say. "He favored Mr. Wilson's appointment to the post."

"From the time of your arrival, haven't you viewed Miss Pigot as your enemy?" Mr. Trevelyan asks.

"I didn't at first." *But I soon learned otherwise.*

"You say Miss Pigot has claims upon the mission," Mr. Trevelyan says. "Do you mean financial claims?"

"No, I mean her work gave her a moral claim."

"Did you mean you would show her kindness?" Mr. Trevelyan asks.

"If the issue of a pension arose, I would support it," I say. "I wouldn't send her out into the world to starve."

"Would you say to a jury, as a Christian man, that you were prepared to recommend an allowance from mission funds to a woman you stigmatized as a whore?"

"I never called her that in public."

"That may be Mr. Hastie, but you've done so in private," Mr. Trevelyan gives me a triumphant look.

Chapter 16
"My Notions Of Honor Are As Keen As Any Other Man's"

Thursday Morning, 6 September 1883
William Hastie

I nod to Mr. Gasper and Mr. Geddes. Mr. Gasper purses his lips and looks away. I made a grave mistake when I called Miss Pigot a whore. Shouldn't even have thought it. I saw my testimony in the newspaper this morning. What glee it must have given the editors to expose my weakness.

Justice Norris takes his place, already wiping his face.

"Resume the witness box, Mr. Hastie," he motions.

I take my place and prepare myself. Mr. Trevelyan strolls to the witness box, an insincere smile on his face. "Good morning, Mr. Hastie."

I look at his pleasant expression and rub my forehead in despair.

"Yesterday you described Miss Pigot as an illegitimate Eurasian," he begins in his deceptive conversational voice. "Did you know she's the daughter of Mr. Julius Pigot, an indigo planter, and his wife Dorothy?"

"No, I didn't know that. I never heard it."

"Who told you she was an illegitimate Eurasian?" Mr. Trevelyan asks.

"I heard it from Reverend Chuckerbutty." *I should have known better than to believe him.*

Mr. Trevelyan nods. "Now, let me ask you this. Did you intercept correspondence to a man named Nitya Gopal Mukherjee? Yes or no."

"Yes."

"Did you open his letters and read them?" Mr. Trevelyan asks.

"I read one letter."

"Who did you say was the recipient?" Mr. Trevelyan asks as if he hadn't heard me.

"It was addressed to Nitya Gopal Mukherjee from The Reverend James Thomson," I say clearly.

"Did Nitya Gopal Mukherjee give you permission to open letters addressed to him? Yes or no."

"No," I admit.

"Did anyone object when you opened his letter?" Mr. Trevelyan asks.

"He objected when I told him," I say. "No one was present at the time."

Justice Norris gives me a disapproving look.

"Did you send the letter to Dr. Scott?" Mr. Trevelyan asks.

"I sent it several months later."

The judge's head whips around to face me. "What do I hear you say?" Justice Norris interjects. "Did you send Mr. Thomson's letter addressed to Nitya Gopal Mukherjee to someone else?"

"Yes. I sent it to Dr. Scott when I was asked to explain matters."

"Humph." Justice Norris glares at me and leans back in his chair.

Mr. Trevelyan resumes. "Did you, at the time of Nitya Gopal Mukherjee's baptism, say to another missionary 'get out of this house, or I'll kick you downstairs'?"

Who told him that? "I didn't say anything about kicking. I told him to go downstairs."

Mr. Trevelyan walks back to his table. "I have no further questions, Your Lordship."

I thank God my ordeal is over. Justice Norris asks if Mr. Gasper wants to re-examine me. Say no. Please say no. Mr. Gasper rises, thanks the judge, and walks towards the witness box. When we're eye-to-eye, he says, "Tell us more about this baptism."

I presume he wants the entire story. How else can anyone understand about my relationship with young Mukherjee. "Well," I say, "when Mukherjee told me he wanted to be baptized, he was agitated." Justice Norris interrupts before I can explain further.

"Mr. Hastie," Justice Norris says, crossly, "we don't want to hear about someone's agitation."

"Yes, My Lord, but Mukherjee was anxious about his family," I say, "and he begged me to consider how to arrange the baptism. I told him—"

"Mr. Gasper, it's too hot for all this. Tell your witness to shorten his explanation," Justice Norris says fanning himself energetically.

"Yes, My Lord." Mr. Gasper gives me an exasperated look. "Mr. Hastie, please shorten your answer."

"I'll be as brief as possible," I say. *Why are people laughing?* "I consulted Mr. Edwards and Mr. Steele. I arranged the baptism at St. Andrew's. Afterwards I consulted with a member of our faculty—"

"I do beseech you, Mr. Hastie, to save time by shortening your story," Justice Norris snaps.

They're laughing again. There's nothing funny about this situation. I had to protect our convert.

"I arranged for our convert to spend the night at Mr. Steele's house."

"Kindly bring in the missionary, Mr. Hastie," Mr. Gasper says. *He's rushing me.*

"We expected trouble," I say.

"Do come to the point, Mr. Hastie, I pray you," Justice Norris says.

"I am, My Lord. When I returned to our compound, Mr. Edwards rushed upstairs shouting: 'What have you done with him?' I told him our convert was safe. Mr. Edwards wanted to know where Mukherjee was, but I refused to tell him."

"Please come to the point." Mr. Gasper insists.

"I'm just at the point." Everyone's laughing again. "Mr. Edwards demanded I bring Mukherjee to the College. And this is the point. I told him I would hear no more about it and he should go downstairs.'" I fold my arms and look away from my barrister.

"What I want to know, Mr. Hastie, is why you opened another man's letter," Justice Norris interjects.

"This leads up to it, My Lord. I saw the convert's family, and his father put him under my care," I say. "He suggested certain conditions—"

"We don't want to know all that," Justice Norris snaps. "It's a simple question. Why did you open the letter? You're wasting the Court's time."

How does he expect me to answer if he doesn't give me time to explain? "My Lord, it's so important to your question, I can't help relating it." I want Justice Norris to understand I had no malice towards Mukherjee, but I see the judge's impatience growing. He's drumming his fingers and glaring at me. "But if Your Lordship wishes, I'll come at once to the point."

"Oh, do Mr. Hastie," Justice Norris says rolling his eyes.

"I'd suspended Reverend Thomson for insubordination. He moved to Pune and began corresponding with Mukherjee," I say. "I ignored the first letter. I told Mukherjee he had no reason to write to Mr. Thomson. Then, two months later, this letter arrived. I gave the letter to my bearer to take to Mukherjee. My bearer came back, because Mukherjee was out."

"Did the letter come back to you?" Mr. Gasper asks.

"No, I'm coming to that point."

"Well, do come to it," Justice Norris with growing irritation. More laughter in the courtroom. "You've been a long time about it."

"My bearer brought the letter back."

"And you opened it?" Mr. Gasper asks.

"After careful consideration ..." Peals of laughter rain over me. Why won't they let me finish? "... yes. I read the letter."

"Why did you send the letter to Dr. Scott?" Mr. Gasper asks.

"He asked me to explain why I opened the letter, so I sent the letter with my reasons."

"Did you think it was an honorable thing to do?" Justice Norris looks horrified. "To open a letter not addressed to you?"

My temper begins to rise. How dare he question my actions! "As head of the College, I thought it perfectly honorable."

"Is that the standard of morality at the College?" Justice Norris asks incredulously.

"It was a perfectly proper action," I insist. "Mukherjee was my responsibility."

"What?!" Justice Norris says. "Do you say it was an honorable thing to intercept a man's letter and forward it to someone else without his knowledge?"

"Well, I don't know what his knowledge was."

Mr. Gasper steps in to repair the situation. "Mr. Hastie, did you think you acted with full authority according to your notion of what is honorable?"

"I swear I did." I say this slowly and clearly.

"Then all I can say is, it's a remarkably good thing for the universe-at-large that your notions of honor and honesty aren't shared by everybody." Justice Norris gives me a baleful look.

That's enough. I won't allow this meddling judge to insult me any further. "My Lord," I say through gritted teeth, "my notions of honor are as keen as any other man's in the universe, and I'm prepared to discuss that point."

Justice Norris bangs his gavel as if I haven't spoken. "We're adjourned for *tiffin*," he says abruptly and makes a quick exit.

Thursday Afternoon, 6 September 1883

During the break, Mr. Gasper tells me he questioned me about Mukherjee to erase Mr. Trevelyan's insinuations from the judge's mind. That by this evening the judge will forget I used that unfortunate word in reference to Miss Pigot. I'm not convinced. The judge gets upset about the silliest things. What difference does it make if I open a letter addressed to my College? And why can't he let me explain things properly?

When we return to court, and I'm back in that wretched witness box, Mr. Gasper asks me about why I stopped chumming with Mr. Wilson and the confusion about whether this suit would go forward. He asks about the time I almost died from cholera and why Miss Pigot and I drifted apart. It was her fault. Once she said Mr. Gillan wasn't a gentleman, a rift opened between us. Who is she to define who is or isn't a gentleman, especially considering the company she keeps? Mr. Gasper moves on to the business about soliciting donations for Mr. Chuckerbutty's fortieth conversion anniversary.

"Did it ever strike you when you started this testimonial that you were doing it because Mr. Chuckerbutty was a witness in your favor?" Mr. Gasper asks me.

What does the one have to do with the other unless he's implying I was trying to influence Mr. Chuckerbutty's testimony? I don't expect this sort of inference from my own barrister. If I had the energy, I'd be outraged. Then we go back over the quarrel with Mr. Steele to prove he didn't kick me out of his office. Finally, Mr. Gasper finishes.

"Mr. Hastie, you're dismissed," Justice Norris says. Never have I heard sweeter words.

Mary Pigot

Mr. Hastie looks so shaken I'd almost feel sorry for him, if he weren't such a vile man. He's been the center of attention for five days, six if I count the pre-trial motion. He has called me unspeakable names. He has dishonored my parents. He has lied. And now his parade of supporters begins.

The court calls Colonel Walker first. He's in uniform, his red coat matching the judge's scarlet robes. He testifies to his impeccable reputation. An Elder in St. Andrew's. A member of the Corresponding Board. He says his wife gave him the letters to send on to Mr. Hastie.

"Did you read them?" Mr. Gasper asks.

"Yes," Colonel Walker says.

"What did you do then?"

"I handed the letters to Mrs. Walker and said—"

Justice Norris interrupts. "You mustn't tell us what you said, because Miss Pigot wasn't present at the time."

"Colonel Walker, why were the letters sent to Dr. Scott instead of Dr. Jardine, their original recipient?" Mr. Gasper asks.

"My wife has great respect for Dr. Jardine and thought he would be sure the letters went through the proper channels. I requested they go to Dr. Scott, because I knew Dr. Jardine would send the letters to him. Sending them to Dr. Jardine first would just waste time."

Mr. Trevelyan rises to object. "Colonel Walker can't make a judgment on proper channels."

"I submit anything Colonel Walker did in regard to Mr. Hastie is important," Mr. Gasper counters.

"Mr. Hastie already told us he considered Dr. Scott to be the proper channel," Justice Norris says. "Move on."

"Colonel Walker, what conversation did you have with Mr. Hastie?" Mr. Gasper asks.

Mr. Trevelyan stands again. "Objection. Are we to listen to every conversation between these two men?"

Justice Norris makes an exaggerated sigh. "What is the purpose of the question, Mr. Gasper? There's nothing in the Complaint about Mr. Hastie having a conversation with Colonel Walker and we can't spend time on their tête-à-têtes."

"No, My Lord," Mr. Gasper says, "but the Complaint alleges a conversation with Mrs. Walker. I submit the husband is supposed to know all communications made to his wife."

"Certainly not," Justice Norris says. "I never assume such a thing. It would utterly destroy domestic harmony."

Mr. Gasper looks taken aback. "My Lord, I submit civilized domestic happiness couldn't exist without it."

"Well," Justice Norris says, "I make no such presumption."

"In that case, I submit the conversation is relevant for the same reason it was relevant in Mr. Hastie's testimony," Mr. Gasper says.

"It isn't evidence to show honorable intent," Mr. Trevelyan argues. "And if Mr. Gasper wants to know about a conversation between Mr. Hastie and Mrs. Walker, he should ask her."

"Either way," Justice Norris says, "Mr. Gasper still wants to prove these letters are privileged communications, and if they aren't privileged, the information might be relevant for damages to your client."

"My Lord," Mr. Trevelyan says, "two-thirds of Mr. Hastie's answers couldn't be stopped. We couldn't stop him, nor could this own counsel. Is this witness going to testify on all Mr. Hastie's points?"

Mr. Trevelyan lost that argument, I'm sorry to say. The next witness is Mrs. Walker. Her husband escorts her to the box. Despite the mud outside, the hem of her grey dress remains dry. She enters the box and nods to the judge. How she can consider herself a Christian after what she's done, I can't understand. Yet she stands there, every inch a lady.

Mr. Gasper wishes her good day and asks her about the letters she received from Mrs. Augier, Miss Gordon, and Mrs. Oliver. He asks if she gave them to her husband to send while she and her sister went to Darjeeling. To my disappointment, Mr. Trevelyan has no questions.

Justice Norris comes to my rescue. "Mrs. Walker," he says, "were you the author of the anonymous leaflet?"

"Yes," she says clearly.

"And you sent the leaflet to Scotland?"

"Yes."

Mrs. Walker sends me a brief triumphant look before turning her attention back to the judge. She and I both know that the information she sent can never be erased from people's minds, that my reputation is forever tainted. Her admission will never be known by anyone who matters. Justice Norris continues his questions.

"Since you wrote the leaflet, have you learned that the names Pigot and Pigott sound the same, but are spelt differently?" Justice Norris asks.

"I know the name of the Roman Catholic matron at the orphanage has two 't's,'" Mrs. Walker says without a hint of regret.

"I suppose you wanted people to think the two ladies were related," Justice Norris says.

"Yes."

"Did you know the Investigating Committee met in Scotland?"

"Yes, and I heard they exonerated Miss Pigot."

"Did that annoy you?" Justice Norris asks.

"No, it was their prerogative to do so. I was, however, vexed that Scottish ladies continued to support a mission that wasn't to their credit."

"Why did you write the leaflet anonymously?"

"Because I'm Miss Smail's sister." For the first time, Mrs. Walker looks slightly uncomfortable.

"The leaflet would've carried more weight if you put your name to it," Justice Norris comments. "It's evident you were hostile to Miss Pigot and thought your sister dismissed on her account."

Mrs. Walker's face reddens. "My sister wasn't dismissed. She resigned and declined to go back."

The judge does me this service, and then adjourns for the day. Perhaps the worst is behind me.

Chapter 17

"Did You Observe Anything
You Thought Inappropriate?"

Friday, 7 September 1883
Mary Pigot

Mr. Hastie, The Defense as they call it, continues to present witnesses. Mrs. Sharpland starts today's agony. She was Mrs. Briggs when I met her in Mr. Hastie's sickroom. She's grayer than she was then, and beyond stout. I remember she disapproved of me. Her current husband is Chief Officer of Hugli Bridge. Mr. Gasper presses her on whether I attended Mr. Hastie alone or with company. He infers everything without saying anything. Mrs. Sharpland follows along.

"Did Miss Pigot go away alone?" Mr. Gasper asks.

"No. Mr. Wilson came into the room twice, once at midnight and again at four in the morning. And he went away with Miss Pigot in the morning," Mrs. Sharpland claims.

"What was Miss Pigot's behavior like?" Mr. Gasper asks.

"Very unladylike. She lolled on Mr. Wilson and put her hand on his thigh."

She made that up! I never loll, and I wouldn't put my hand any man's thigh.

"How was Mr. Hastie when you quit?" Mr. Gasper asks.

"He was very weak," Mrs. Sharpland says.

"Why did you leave him in such a state?"

"I didn't care to remain in the presence of Miss Pigot's rude behavior," Mrs. Sharpland says in her rough voice.

"Explain what you mean," Mr. Gasper says.

"She acted with the familiarity of a wife towards her husband," Mrs. Sharpland says.

I grab Mr. Trevelyan's wrist as he rises. "It's not true," I whisper. "It wasn't like that."

Mr. Trevelyan goes about his questions as if he's bored by the proceedings. He asks how many times Mrs. Sharpland appealed to Mr. Hastie for favors. She wanted him to help her brother-in-law get a position with the Eastern Bengal Railway. Not much chance Mr. Hastie would do that for someone he knew, let alone a stranger. Mr. Trevelyan works his way to his real question.

"Mrs. Sharpland, on the occasion when you say Miss Pigot put her hand on Mr. Wilson's thigh, were they sitting or standing?" Mr. Trevelyan asks.

"They were both sitting."

"When she put her hand on his thigh, did they say anything?" Mr. Trevelyan asks.

"They were in close conversation. Too close for me to hear."

"Were his lips close to her head?"

"I didn't notice," Mrs. Sharpland says.

"And yet the conversation was too close for you to hear," Mr. Trevelyan comments. "How far away were you?"

Mrs. Sharpland looks up. "About the distance of you from me."

"In the stillness of the night?" Mr. Trevelyan asks.

"Yes."

Mr. Trevelyan lets the answer hang for a moment. "Describe how Miss Pigot lolled." I see the judge pay more attention.

"She lolled with her head upon his shoulder and her right hand on his left thigh," Mrs. Sharpland says.

That's not true.

"What were you doing at the time?"

"Giving medicine to the patient," Mrs. Sharpland says.

"What attracted your attention to Miss Pigot and Mr. Wilson?" Mr. Trevelyan asks.

"Miss Pigot laughed."

Mrs. Sharpland says she left before Mr. Hastie was fit, because of my rude behavior with Mr. Wilson. She says he and I talked and laughed. She says this in a steady voice. The judge tells Mrs. Sharpland to go back to Hugli Bridge.

Mr. Gasper calls Monomohini Wheeler to the witness box. We were at Normal School together. Her father's a minister, and she married a missionary. Now she's Inspectress of Schools, from which perch she passes judgment on those of us without family connections. She stands with perfect posture. Nothing good will come of her testimony. She disapproves of my teachers, my properties, and me. She went to Mr. Hastie with her complaints, and he's kept them up his sleeve until now.

Mr. Gasper greets her politely and gets right to the point. "When you visited the Female Mission, did you observe anything regarding the cleanliness of the place and the clothing of the children?"

Mrs. Wheeler adopts an expression of delicate distain and says she had to pick her way through bits of food and clothing as she passed through the veranda.

Mr. Gasper moves on to discuss my teachers. Mrs. Wheeler doesn't believe in second chances. She knows I do and looks among my teachers for those dismissed from other missions, often for minor offenses. They have nowhere to go and come to me. I put them to work if I can. As long as they follow my rules, there's no difficulty. Mr. Gasper brings up a woman dismissed from the American mission. He asks what she said to me.

"I told Miss Pigot it was kind of her to be friendly with these women," Mrs. Wheeler says, "but it wasn't right to send them to teach in the *zenanas* without supervision. They naturally fall into temptation."

Our Savior said, "Let he who is without sin throw the first stone." I think Mrs. Wheeler missed that passage.

Mrs. Wheeler testifies she saw a native Christian teacher wearing clothing no respectable woman would wear.

"Describe the dress," Justice Norris directs, his gaze intent. "Whether a respectable woman would wear it is another question."

"It was a sari with a border running across the middle," Mrs. Wheeler says.

"Mrs. Wheeler, what sort of women wear the dress you describe?" Mr. Gasper asks.

Mrs. Wheeler says only disreputable women dress that way.

"What did Miss Pigot say when you called it to her attention?" asks Mr. Gasper.

"She said native women aren't particular in their dress," Mrs. Wheeler says. "I told her Christian women, especially teachers, must set an example of modesty and decency."

Mrs. Wheeler says she took her concerns to Mr. Hastie. Frequently, as I understand it.

When it's our turn, Mr. Trevelyan asks what Mrs. Wheeler meant when she said a woman at Kidderpore disregarded modesty.

"The woman had a low-necked thing on, leaving her neck and shoulders bare. And she put red vermillion stuff in the parting of her hair, and black stuff in her teeth," Mrs. Wheeler says.

"Isn't putting a red mark in the parting a sign of marriage?" Mr. Trevelyan asks.

"Among Hindus, not Christians," Mrs. Wheeler sys in her educated voice.

"Would you object to a teacher who became a Christian wearing the red mark?" Mr. Trevelyan asks.

"I would."

Mr. Trevelyan asks what becomes of women dismissed from missions for some sort of misbehavior.

"If they refuse punishment, they're cut adrift," Mrs. Wheeler says. "I don't think another mission has the right to take them in, as Miss Pigot does."

Mrs. Wheeler looks down at me on her way out of the courtroom, as if to say she would never behave as foolishly as I.

Little Bidu Grace comes forward next. I look upon her as a daughter. I know why Mr. Gasper has called her. He wants her to talk about her punishment, which Mrs. Oliver referred to in her letter. I struck Bidu three times across her back and kept her in confinement as a punishment for stealing.

When asked, Bidu denies she took Mrs. Mullick's ornament, but admits she told me she did, hoping to avoid punishment. Mr. Gasper accepts that, but in his cross-examination, Mr. Trevelyan asks where Bidu stayed when she was confined in my bedroom.

"In her own bedroom," Bidu nods. "Miss Pigot slept in the room at the same time."

"Who told you about coming to court?" Mr. Trevelyan asks Bidu.

"The Sahib told me."

"Sahib?"

"Mr. Hastie. He spoke to me the Friday before last," Bidu says.

"Did anyone else speak to you about coming to court?" Mr. Trevelyan asks.

"Reverend Chuckerbutty asked me to come and say I was chastised."

Justice Norris asks Bidu if we treated her kindly at Bow Bazaar. Bidu says we did.

"You were well treated by Miss Pigot and everyone connected with her?" Justice Norris asks.

"Yes."

Justice Norris admonishes Mr. Trevelyan for not bringing this out. "It's very important," Justice Norris says, "because the insinuation in these libels is that Miss Pigot was a harsh and cruel woman."

Mr. Trevelyan bows and returns to our table. I'm disappointed he isn't more contrite.

When Lucinda May Oliver raises her hand and takes the oath, I mentally emphasize she's supposed to tell the truth. She looks like she's had a hard life since she left Bow Bazar. I'm not surprised. She's a difficult woman, always complaining. I had to let her go.

Mrs. Oliver says she doesn't know me very well but worked for me about two years. Of course, she doesn't know me. I don't socialize with matrons.

"Do you remember a girl called Joboni?" Mr. Gasper asks. "Was she punished while you were matron?"

"Are you asking if she was struck?" Mrs. Oliver asks. "Miss Pigot struck her with a cane on the face and shoulders." Mrs. Oliver nods her head for emphasis, making her earrings bounce. "Joboni put up her arms to protect herself."

Mr. Gasper asks why I punished Joboni.

"She refused to eat her food. There were problems with girls wasting food while I was matron," Mrs. Oliver says. "Miss Pigot told me to report the next girl. She wanted to make the girl an example."

"After Miss Pigot beat Joboni, did you say anything about it?" Mr. Gasper asks.

"I told Miss Pigot if I'd known she planned to beat the girl, I wouldn't have spoken about the incident."

Mr. Gasper begins asking Mrs. Oliver about Bidu's condition.

Mr. Trevelyan rises to address the judge. "Why is Mr. Gasper asking this question when Bidu Grace has already testified to Miss Pigot's punishment?"

"Mr. Gasper," Justice Norris asks, "what can Mrs. Oliver add to the testimony of the previous witness?"

"Nothing, My Lord. I simply want to emphasize the statements in Mrs. Oliver's letter are true and there was no libel."

"By contradicting the last witness's testimony that overall she was well-treated?" Justice Norris asks.

"I gave my reason, My Lord," Mr. Gasper says smugly.

Justice Norris looks at his watch and raises his eyebrows. "I give you until court convenes tomorrow to answer my question."

We rise as the judge departs. Mr. Trevelyan chuckles. "The thing about Justice Norris is you never know what will catch his attention. Mr. Gasper made a mistake there."

"Will it help us?" I ask.

"It can't hurt. Have a good evening." Mr. Trevelyan turns to have a word with Mr. Carruthers, who then escorts me to a *gharry*. I go back to the hotel for another sleepless night.

Saturday, 8 September 1883

I think I've aged ten years since the letters appeared and this trial began. I take no joy in anything anymore. My life appears daily in the newspapers. My father told me a lady's name should only appear in print for her birth, marriage, and death. It appears my death is a protracted event.

I arrive just before the judge enters the courtroom. Mr. Gasper looks poised for action, while Mr. Hastie slumps in his chair. My only satisfaction in this affair is its affront to his pride.

Mr. Carruthers tells me I'm bearing up remarkably well. I suppose he expects me to faint. If I do, it'll be from the humidity that sucks all the air out of the courtroom.

Mrs. Oliver makes her way back into the witness box wearing the same drab dress she had on yesterday. It has sweat stains under the arms. She doesn't look as confident as she did yesterday. I expect Mr. Trevelyan to be hard on her today. She wrote one of those beastly letters for Mrs. Walker.

"My Lord," Mr. Trevelyan opens, "I withdraw my objections about what Mrs. Oliver knew about Bidu Grace. I think Mr. Gasper's questions will benefit my case." Mr. Trevelyan bows to Mr. Gasper who inclines his head.

"Very well," Justice Norris says. He tells the clerk to check whether the *punkah wallah* can make the fan move faster and tells Mr. Gasper to commence.

Mr. Gasper asks Mrs. Oliver where she was standing when she heard the Bidu Grace being beaten. She was outside the door and had nothing to say about the event. She never even saw the marks. Sitting next to me at the table, Mr. Trevelyan looks down and smiles.

Mr. Gasper moves on to Kali Churn Banerjee. "How often did you see him at the Female Mission?"

"Frequently."

"When did Babu Banerjee come?"

"He usually came in the evenings between five and six," Mrs. Oliver replies.

"What did you do in the evenings?"

"While I was matron, I looked after the girls in the orphanage on the lower level."

"And what did you do when you were a teacher at the Upper School?" Mr. Gasper asks.

"If I wasn't on duty, I was with the girls on the upper terrace or in the study room."

Mrs. Oliver testifies Kali Churn came nearly every evening and often had his meals at the mission. Initially he ate with the teachers, and then he took his meals in the drawing room. "Twice I saw Miss Pigot with him," she adds.

"Did you see Babu Banerjee in any other room?" Mr. Gasper asks.

"No, but I saw him coming out of the room Miss Pigot uses as an office."

"Did you observe anything you thought inappropriate?" Mr. Gasper asks.

"I saw several things I didn't like," Mrs. Oliver says.

"Tell us," Mr. Gasper says with rapt attention.

Justice Norris leans over to hear better. I hold my breath. Mrs. Oliver recounts some nonsense about me pulling the *punkah* rope outside my bedroom. Mr. Gasper pounces and asks if anyone was in the bedroom at the time. She says she didn't see anyone. I exhale. Mrs. Oliver says I sat on a cane lounge on the veranda in the early evening if I wasn't too tired. And once she saw me reclining on it, and Kali Churn seated near me beside it. "The prayer bell rang twice, and Miss Pigot didn't seem to notice it," Mrs. Oliver says. "I went to call her."

Mrs. Oliver tells how she recommended Catholic Mrs. Pigott as matron, and when I asked why she recommended someone she knew was Roman Catholic, she says she didn't know it at the time. Mr. Gasper asks if I sent her away. How could I send someone away for being Catholic?

Mr. Gasper changes topics. "Do you remember if there was some sort of feast at the orphanage?"

"If you mean the occasion I wrote about, the girls and teachers were at Serampore. I don't remember what the feast was for, but plenty of people came, mostly natives. And there were Brahmin cooks," Mrs. Oliver says with disapproval in her voice.

"You said the orphans weren't fed properly. What did you mean?"

"The food was deficient. The girls brought it to Miss Pigot's attention."

"What happened then?" Mr. Gasper asks.

"She ate it and said it was very nice."

"On the principle, I suppose, that the proof of the pudding was in the eating?"

We laugh at Mr. Gasper's pun. The judge tells him to get on with things. Mr. Gasper asks about the clothing we gave the orphans and whether they had blankets in the winter. Mrs. Oliver indicates she doesn't approve of horse blankets being given to orphans. I suppose she would like them to have virgin wool.

Mr. Gasper returns to Kali Churn's visits. "Did you see Babu Banerjee at other times during the day? Not just the evening?"

"I saw him once about six o'clock in the morning and on two occasions later in the day," Mrs. Oliver says.

"What was he doing in the morning?"

"He entered the drawing room."

"And on the other two occasions, where did you see him?" Mr. Gasper asks.

"He sat writing at a table in the drawing room. Miss Pigot was with him. The doors leading to the veranda were closed. I went in, because I needed to see Miss Pigot."

"No further questions," Mr. Gasper says, and strolls back to his seat with a satisfied expression.

Mr. Trevelyan looks at his notes, stands, and walks towards the witness. "Mrs. Oliver," he says, "when you first came to Miss Pigot, did you have a letter from anyone, or a recommendation?"

"No."

"And, did she take you on?" Mr. Trevelyan asks.

"She said there wasn't a vacancy at present, but there probably would be one soon," Mrs. Oliver says. "I took a position as governess for Mr. Broadway, a Baptist minister at Bankipore."

"When you went to Bankipore, did Miss Pigot supply you with money and clothing for your three children?"

Mrs. Oliver pauses as if she doesn't want to admit the truth.

"Yes, she did," Mrs. Oliver says and starts to become agitated. "It was so long ago, and I've had so many troubles. I can't remember."

"When you first met Miss Pigot, were you a stranger to her?"

"I was."

"At the time you left Mr. Broadway, did you know if she had a situation for you?" Mr. Trevelyan asks.

"No, I took a chance."

"And she took you in?"

"Yes," Mrs. Oliver drops her head.

"Do you think it was a good-natured act on Miss Pigot's part to give you something to do?" Mr. Trevelyan asks.

Mrs. Oliver looks from Mr. Trevelyan to Mr. Hastie and back again. "From what I remember, Miss Pigot made work for me."

Of course, I did. I couldn't let you and the children starve.

"Is it true that one of your children unfortunately died, and Miss Pigot lent you one hundred rupees for funeral expenses?" Mr. Trevelyan asks.

"She didn't lend me money. She advanced my pay," Mrs. Oliver says. "I don't remember the amount."

"And your other children went to the Upper School without paying tuition?"

"Yes."

"When did your connection with the orphanage cease?"

"I think it was July 1881," Mrs. Oliver says.

"Was your leaving somewhat sudden?" Mr. Trevelyan asks. "So that Miss Pigot gave you a month's salary in lieu of notice?"

"That's true," Mrs. Oliver says.

"Why did Miss Pigot want you to leave?"

"She said my manner was too abrupt, and I had a bad temper. I said I could resign," Mrs. Oliver says.

"Was there any foundation for her statement about your temper?"

"It's true. I do have a bad temper."

"If you resigned, why did Miss Pigot give you a month's salary?" Mr. Trevelyan asks.

"She wouldn't accept my resignation. She said 'I dismiss you,' and gave me the money, which I took. I'm tired now. Could I rest?"

Justice Norris looks at his watch. "Since it's now quarter before two, we'll adjourn for *tiffin*. Eat heartily, gentlemen. I've decided to sit until half past seven today and every day until we get to the end of this case or the start of vacation. I do hope it's the former, gentlemen."

When we return, the room is stifling and Mrs. Oliver looks pale. I feel sorry for her but put the feeling aside. She wrote her letter without a thought for me.

Mr. Trevelyan begins asking questions about me. He asks if Mrs. Oliver went to see me last autumn. I don't remember, but she says she visited frequently.

"When you began visiting the orphanage, was Miss Pigot still Lady Superintendent?"

Mrs. Oliver takes a breath. "Well," she says, "let me try and recollect. You seem to think I have nothing in my life to think of but the orphanage." Mrs. Oliver exhales. "I think Mrs. Ellis was there, and Miss Pigot had gone."

"When Kali Churn Banerjee came to the orphanage, did he have children there?" Mr. Trevelyan asks.

"He had children in the Upper School."

"Did he accompany them home in the evening?"

"Generally," Mrs. Oliver says.

"Tell me, did you ever see anything in connection with Miss Pigot that you wish you hadn't seen?"

Why did he ask that? It's bound to bring up some false story.

"I saw Miss Pigot standing at the center window of the drawing room," Mrs. Oliver says.

"Was she alone?"

"I saw Kali Churn Banerjee too."

No, no, no.

"How were they standing?" Mr. Trevelyan asks.

"With their arms around each other."

"What time was this?"

"About dusk," she says.

It's a lie. We never stood that way.

"There's gas in the house. Was it lit?" Mr. Trevelyan asks.

"No," Mrs. Oliver says.

"Why were you there?" Mr. Trevelyan asks.

"I went to get medicine for a sick girl."

"When you saw them, what did you do?"

"I stopped short and called to Miss Pigot."

"Did you see anything else you shouldn't have seen?" Mr. Trevelyan asks.

"I used to see them in close conversation in the drawing room."

"Were they standing or seated?" Mr. Trevelyan asks.

"She reclined on a couch. He sat on a chair beside her with his elbows resting on the couch," Mrs. Oliver says.

You're making this up.

"Anything else you saw?" Mr. Trevelyan asks.

"I saw Miss Pigot laying full length on a lounge on the veranda."

Justice Norris asks where Kali Churn Banerjee was at the time.

"He sat at her feet with his arms across Miss Pigot's feet," Mrs. Oliver says.

I want to sink into nothing. I can't bear to have my feet touched, and this woman says Kali Churn had his arms over them.

"How did you happen to notice this scene?" Mr. Trevelyan asks.

"The children called my attention to it."

Mr. Trevelyan refers to his notes. "Did you ever visit Kali Churn Banerjee and ask him to buy certain articles of furniture from you, because you were badly off?"

"I told him Miss Pigot ruined me, because she sent me away after almost two years without a reference," Mrs. Oliver says.

I gave you a month's pay instead.

Mr. Trevelyan looks pleased with himself as he walks back to the table. Mr. Gasper requests we adjourn. I would like nothing better, but the judge demurs.

"I've already stated the Court will sit until half past seven," Justice Norris says, peevishly.

"My Lord," Mr. Gasper counters, "Mr. Trevelyan would also like to adjourn. Surely since counsel on both sides agree, Your Lordship won't refuse the application?"

"Can you gentlemen guarantee the case will finish by next Friday?" Justice Norris asks. "I want to sum up on Saturday. I won't allow this case to carry into the vacation and then to December. I could die in the interim. The cost for both sides would be enormous. They'd have to start over."

"My Lord," Mr. Gasper says, "I do hope you'll return to us after the vacation. But the weather outside is ghastly, and the testimony has been lengthy. I simply can't continue and beg you to adjourn until Monday."

"Can you guarantee to finish by Friday?" Justice Norris asks.

"It's impossible to say," Mr. Gasper responds.

"Then we'll continue. Call your next witness."

Outside the rain falls in sheets. I hear a clap of thunder in the distance. The room becomes dimmer. Justice Norris looks up in apprehension but doesn't change his decision to continue.

Mr. Gasper calls Grace Gordon, presumably to verify what she wrote to Mrs. Walker. Grace is a Calcutta girl whose aspirations exceeded her abilities. I blame Miss Leslie for that: she told the girl she could qualify as a *zenana* teacher, so Grace never accepted her position as a mere matron. The slight girl makes her way forward and admits she wrote the letter.

"Did you know Kali Churn Banerjee?" Mr. Gasper asks her.

"Yes. I saw him nearly every day at the school." Miss Gordon nods as she speaks. "I always saw him in the drawing room."

"When did he arrive?" Mr. Gasper asks.

"He used to arrive sometime between four and six, and stay until eight o'clock," Miss Gordon says.

"Did he escort his children home?"

"Sometimes the children went home before him and sometimes with him."

"Where was your room, and what could you see from there?"

"My room was upstairs on the orphanage side of the compound," Miss Gordon says. "I could see the front block on the other side. When he came in that way, I saw Babu Banerjee in the drawing room. He took his dinner there."

"Was anyone else there?" Mr. Gasper asks.

"I don't know," Miss Gordon replies. "I just saw dinner placed before him."

"Did you keep in contact with Joboni after you left the orphanage?"

"Yes. I like her."

"You wrote that Miss Pigot beat children for throwing away their food," Mr. Gasper says. "Were the girls in the habit of throwing food away?"

"I don't know."

"You wrote that the mark on Joboni looked like a cane mark. Where was the mark?" Mr. Gasper asks.

"On her cheek somewhere," Miss Gordon says.

"You wrote the mark was blue. What did you mean?"

Grace becomes agitated and begins pulling on her sleeve. "The mark was swollen and blue. Discolored."

Mr. Gasper begins to look frustrated. It's increasingly clear why Grace couldn't qualify as a teacher.

"What did you mean when you wrote that you saw Miss Pigot and Kali Churn Banerjee with their arms around each other? Were they wrestling?" Mr. Gasper asks sarcastically.

"No, they were standing side-by-side."

"If they wished to make it public, could they have chosen a better place?"

"No," Miss Gordon says.

I hear a ripple of laughter. My entire career is at stake and people laugh. Even the judge.

"Miss Gordon, are you quite sure they had their arms around each other? Were their arms around each other's waists?" Mr. Gasper asks.

"Yes." Miss Gordon blushes, *and so she should.*

"And they didn't know you were there?"

"I called to Miss Pigot and she came to me," Miss Gordon says.

"Did she seem put out?" Mr. Gasper asks.

"I didn't notice."

"What became of Kali Churn Banerjee? Did he jump out the window, or did he remain?" Mr. Gasper asks.

Justice Norris suppresses his own laughter and bangs his gavel for order.

Grace flinches at the sound. "I didn't notice."

"You wrote you saw Miss Pigot and Babu Banerjee in close conversation. Is this the incident when you saw them?"

"I'm not sure what you mean by close conversation." Miss Gordon's voice shakes slightly. "Do you mean when I saw Miss Pigot on her couch and Kali Churn Banerjee talking to her with his elbows on the couch?"

"Did you see this happen more than once?" Mr. Gasper asks.

"I saw it one time."

"This was in the drawing room that's accessible to everyone?"

"Yes." Grace looks down at her lap.

"When you saw them in close conversation, did you retreat again, or did you go up to them?" Mr. Gasper asks.

"I went away."

"And when you saw them on the lounge, did you speak to them?"

"No."

"What made you come away?"

"I was walking up and down the terrace with the children. The children called my attention to it," Miss Gordon says.

"Did you want to see what was happening?" Mr. Gasper asks.

"I tried not to see."

"Do you know the names of the children?" Mr. Gasper asks.

"I don't remember their names."

"Of course not." Mr. Gasper inhales deeply and clears his throat. "In the case of Bidu, did she receive a fearful caning?" Mr. Gasper asks.

Grace shakes her head. "I don't understand what you mean."

"Was the caning severe?"

"Yes, very severe," Miss Gordon nods.

"Which was worse, Bidu's or Joboni's?" Mr. Gasper asks.

"Bidu's."

Mr. Gasper begins slowly pacing in front of the box. He stops and looks at Grace.

"She couldn't get up for four days, I suppose," Mr. Gasper says.

"I didn't notice."

"Did you think her life endangered?"

"I don't think so."

"Do you remember whether Bidu had any marks on her face?" Mr. Gasper asks.

"No."

"Try," Mr. Gasper elongates the word.

"I think she had a mark."

"Where was it? Right side or left side?"

"I really can't remember."

Mr. Gasper returns to his table. "No further questions, My Lord."

I feel a flicker hope. Grace was a very bad witness for Mr. Hastie. I wonder if she wrote that letter herself or if someone wrote it for her. I'll probably never know.

Mr. Trevelyan stands behind our table. "What is your present age, Miss Gordon?"

"I don't know."

"Do you mean you've no idea?" Mr. Trevelyan asks.

315

"None at all," Miss Gordon says.

"You can't be serious," Justice Norris says incredulously.

"I am, My Lord."

"You must be able to say whether it's between ten and fifty," Justice Norris says. "You can't be fifty, can you?"

"No, not fifty," Miss Gordon smiles.

"Not forty?" Justice Norris asks.

"No, My Lord."

"How much under forty are you?" Justice Norris asks.

"I think I'm over twenty, but I don't know exactly," Miss Gordon says.

Justice Norris shakes his head and waves at Mr. Trevelyan to continue.

Mr. Trevelyan begins asking Miss Gordon about her acquaintance with Miss Leslie. She joined Miss Leslie's Sunday School and stayed with her after the school closed. She came to me about 1879. Mr. Trevelyan walks over to the witness box.

"Did you get in with Miss Pigot straight away?" Mr. Trevelyan asks.

"No, I had to wait," Miss Gordon says.

"What did she employ you as?"

"Matron," Miss Gordon says.

"Did you have any grievances while you were with Miss Pigot?"

"I didn't like the food, and the work was too hard," Miss Gordon says. "I didn't like it there."

"Did you dine with the teachers?" Mr. Trevelyan asks.

"No. I thought I was supposed to dine with them but I had to eat with the other matrons."

"Did you ever speak to Miss Pigot about it? Ever complain?"

"I don't think so."

"Why did you leave Miss Pigot's employment?" Mr. Trevelyan asks.

"I never liked it there."

"To return to Kali Churn Banerjee," Mr. Trevelyan says. "You say you thought you saw him coming out of the house. Did you think he stayed in Miss Pigot's bedroom from ten p. m. until dawn?"

"No, I didn't."

"You don't suggest any impropriety between Miss Pigot and Kali Churn Banerjee?"

"I never thought that," Miss Gordon says.

"Did you think Miss Pigot behaved indecently at any time?"

"Never."

"Did you think the same regarding the other incident—the one when the *durwan* was there and Kali Churn Banerjee had the slippers on? Do think there was any impropriety?" Mr. Trevelyan asks.

"I didn't think it was nice," Miss Gordon says. "I never thought about it."

"Was anyone else there that day? Was Mr. James there?"

"I never saw him, so I can't swear."

"Miss Gordon, did you see the *durwan* conduct Kali Churn Banerjee to Miss Pigot's room?" Mr. Trevelyan asks.

"No," Miss Gordon replies.

"What time did the bell ring for prayers? For instance, what time did you find Kali Churn Banerjee sitting on the cane lounge?"

"I think it was past six o'clock."

"Was that the usual time for prayers?"

"You want me to remember trifles." Miss Gordon's voice is strained. She clenches her fists. "It was either six or half past six."

"You call these trifles?" Mr. Trevelyan asks.

"It's a trifle to me."

"Did you see Kali Churn Banerjee in the courtroom yesterday?" Mr. Trevelyan asks.

"No. I'm shortsighted. I didn't see him," Miss Gordon replies.

"So, you went in and saw them on the lounge..."

"I didn't go in."

"You saw them from where you were."

"Did you forget they were on the veranda?" Miss Gordon asks.

"I'm asking if you said anything," Mr. Trevelyan says with exaggerated patience.

"I asked if she would come to prayers. She said she would," Miss Gordon says. "Babu Banerjee and I said 'good evening' to each other."

Mr. Trevelyan gazes at Grace. She looks shattered. "I have no further questions for this witness, My Lord," Mr. Trevelyan says.

"My Lord, I have some questions," Mr. Gasper says.

Grace's exhausted expression becomes bleaker.

"Miss Gordon, you said that when you saw Miss Pigot and Babu Banerjee, one with his or her arm around the other, that you stopped short and retreated. Why did you do that?"

"Because they stood in that position."

"But why, Miss Gordon?" Mr. Gasper asks. "What was it about their position that made you retreat?"

"I just thought I shouldn't go in," Miss Gordon says.

I wish you had, you silly girl. Then you might remember it never happened.

"And when you saw the scene with the lounge chair, why did you turn away?"

"Because if I looked at them, it would draw the children's attention."

"Miss Gordon, you said that from your window you could see across to the drawing room and Miss Pigot's staircase. Did you ever see anything from your room that drew your interest?" Mr. Gasper asks.

"One night I saw a figure go up the stairs, and I saw it go down again in the morning." Grace hangs her head.

"How do you know it was the same figure?" Justice Norris asks.

"I don't," Miss Gordon says.

"How was the figure dressed?" Justice Norris asks.

"In a white, loose dress. It looked like a sort of coat."

"Who did you think it was?" Justice Norris asks.

"I thought it was Kali Churn Banerjee."

Mr. Trevelyan stands. "I don't think this is evidence, My Lord."

"Quite so. Continue Mr. Gasper," Justice Norris says.

"Miss Gordon, do you remember a girl named Caroline Swaries?" Mr. Gasper asks.

"Yes, she was in the Upper School," Miss Gordon says.

"Did anyone come to see her?"

"Some people came to see her one Sunday. They wrote something on a slate and gave it to the *durwan* to take to Miss Pigot."

"Tell us what happened then," Mr. Gasper says.

"Miss Pigot came downstairs and told them to go away," Miss Gordon says.

"How do you know that? Could you hear them?"

"She pointed at them to go to the gate."

"Did they leave?"

"No, they started throwing stones at her until the servants came to her rescue," Miss Gordon says.

"Did anyone else come downstairs?"

"Babu Banerjee came down with his coat half on."

"How do you mean?"

"One arm was in the sleeve; the other was out."

"Did you see anything else of interest?" Mr. Gasper asks.

"His slippers looked like ones I saw in Miss Pigot's bedroom. They had a peculiar pattern."

Mr. Gasper smiles. "Nothing further, My Lord,"

I'm stiff from sitting and aching with mortification, but it isn't half past seven yet, so Mr. Gasper calls each of the Leslie women: Mary Eliza, who ran the Sunday School and sponsored Grace as my matron, and her sister Helen, who worked for me at the time I punished Bidu Grace. Why does he keep harping on that one incident? Bidu herself concedes it was necessary.

Mr. Gasper asks Helen Leslie about the day at Barrackpore Park, whether anything in my conduct was amiss. "Miss Pigot and Mr. Wilson sat supporting each other back-to-back. That's all I saw."

I like to think Mr. Gasper found the answer disappointing.

Now Mr. Gasper calls a woman named Eliza Mukherjee. The woman is short, her dark hair streaked with gray. I don't recognize her. She's wearing a yellow sari and bangles on her wrists and ankles. The charms make a ticking noise as she shifts from foot to foot in the witness box. Mrs. Mukherjee says she taught at Kidderpore School for sixteen years and was a matron at the orphanage in 1871. Mr. Trevelyan is on his feet.

"I object, My Lord," he says. "Nothing that happened in 1871 has any bearing on this case. If we allow this witness's evidence, where will Mr. Gasper's questions end?"

"My Lord," Mr. Gasper replies in his smooth voice, "it influences the question of damages. This witness's testimony demonstrates the plaintiff's general conduct the entire time she was at the Scottish Mission."

"Humph. I'm not prepared to decide this question now," Justice Norris says. "Proceed, Mr. Gasper."

"Mrs. Mukherjee, while you were matron, did people call at the orphanage?" Mr. Gasper asks.

"Oh yes. *Babus* visited constantly to see Miss Pigot," Mrs. Mukherjee says in a singsong voice.

"Did you observe anything that made a particular impression on you?"

"One evening I saw a carriage drive up and a *babu* going up the steps."

"Did you see the room he entered?" Justice Norris asks. "Was it a bedroom?"

"No. I saw him go up the steps," Mrs. Mukherjee says. "He was upstairs about an hour and a half. Then he came down and went away."

"Did you see Miss Pigot during the day?" Mr. Gasper asks.

"She was down to the *zenanas*. She came back and went to her room, saying she wasn't well," Mrs. Mukherjee says. "Even if I went to see her on business, she wouldn't see me."

"When was this?" Mr. Gasper asks.

"The very evening before the *babu* came," Mrs. Mukherjee says. "I saw him come that way two evenings."

"On the second evening, did Miss Pigot say she wasn't well?" Justice Norris asks.

"No," Mrs. Mukherjee replies.

"Did you go with Miss Pigot to a house on Coolootola Street?" Mr. Gasper asks.

"Yes, we visited a *zenana* there," Mrs. Mukherjee says. "We went in Miss Pigot's *gharry*. She left me there to teach the children and said the *gharry* would return for me."

"Did the *gharry* return?" Mr. Gasper asks.

"Yes. The driver took me to a house in Amherst Street," Mrs. Mukherjee says.

"When you went there, what happened?"

More innuendos. I can't believe Mr. Hastie stoops so low. Mrs. Mukherjee says she went into the house and saw me reclining on a *tuktaposh* bed in the men's sitting room with a *babu* seated next to me on the edge of the bed. After planting his seed, Mr. Gasper switches to the topic of Mrs. Mukherjee's daughter.

"When did you have a daughter in the orphanage?" Mr. Gasper asks.

"After I left," Mrs. Mukherjee says.

Justice Norris interrupts. "When did you put your daughter in the orphanage?"

"In 1873."

"And when did you see this incident of the *tuktaposh*?" Justice Norris asks.

"In 1871."

"So, you put your daughter in this orphanage after you saw this incident," Justice Norris says.

"Yes," Mrs. Mukherjee says.

"I put it to you, Mr. Gasper," Justice Norris says, "is it likely the witness would, after what she says she saw, entrust her daughter to Miss Pigot's care?"

"I ask Your Lordship not to look upon the matter in such a lofty way," Mr. Gasper says. "The moral atmosphere of this country isn't altogether pure."

"Perhaps not. As I said before, I don't see how this evidence has any bearing on the case, but I'm not prepared to rule on that now. Continue," Justice Norris says.

"Mrs. Mukherjee, did Miss Pigot punish your daughter?"

"Once," Mrs. Mukherjee says.

"What happened after you got to Miss Pigot's presence that day?" Mr. Gasper asks.

"I went to see my daughter and talk to the teachers," Mrs. Mukherjee says. "When I saw Miss Pigot, I asked her why she punished my daughter. She said my daughter sang bad songs, so she beat my daughter and locked her up." Tears flow from Mrs. Mukherjees eyes. She dabs at them with a frayed handkerchief. "After that, I went downstairs to the bathroom where my daughter was. One of the teachers unlocked the door."

Mr. Gasper asks about Nelly, Rachel, and Mary Anne, three *zenana* teachers who were sixteen or seventeen years old in 1871. I don't remember them at all. Mrs. Mukherjee says I punished them for not eating their dahl and rice. She says I beat Mary Anne with a cane, and she put mustard oil on the wounds. Finally Mr. Gasper is out of questions, and since it's half past seven, Justice Norris adjourns the court until Monday.

I can't believe people I employed when no one else would lied about me. They paint me as an immoral woman who beats children. I sit in stunned silence unable to move. Mr. Carruthers taps my shoulder. I unclasp my hands, so Mr. Trevelyan can shake hands with me and wish me a restful Sunday. Mr. Carruthers helps me get up and escorts me to my hotel.

"Miss Pigot, you must rest and eat tomorrow. Mrs. Mukherjee is one of the last listed defense witness, so we expect to begin our rebuttal on Monday. Think through everything you remember about anything in the testimony," Mr. Carruthers says.

"I don't know if I can. I've had a blinding headache for the past several days. It's taken all my effort to sit upright."

"I'm sure rest and food is all you need," Mr. Carruthers says confidently. "I'll leave you here in the hotel lobby."

A servant holds my arm as I pull myself up the stairs. In my small room I wet a cloth and throw myself on the bed. I dearly hope Mr. Hastie is as miserable as I.

Chapter 18
"I Can't Believe She Would Do Such A Thing"

Monday, 10 September 1883
William Hastie

I look at my pocket watch. Ten o'clock, precisely. I don't like Mr. Geddes's office. It's small, stuffy, and has papers stacked on every possible surface. His clerk had to remove documents from the chair I'm sitting in. I should have paid better attention and selected a solicitor more appropriate for my position. The door opens and Mr. Geddes walks in, his dark suit already crumpled.

"Thank you for coming to my office before court this morning. I need to speak with you about a witness." He finds an empty spot on his desk and places a small file on it. "First I must tell you our case remains unproven."

"What do you mean?" I ask. "Every witness speaks to Miss Pigot's poor management, free manner with men, and general indelicacy. There can be no doubt I had to forward the letters."

"Unfortunately, the witnesses aren't the best. Most have reason to dislike Miss Pigot, so their accusations become less compelling, and one is so ignorant she doesn't even know how old she is." Mr. Geddes shakes his head. "Mr. Trevelyan is a skilled barrister, and at the moment, the judge is sympathetic to him. After court yesterday, Mr. Gasper expressed concern that things aren't going as well as they should. He asked me to speak to you about a new witness."

I swallow. "Surely you don't think we could lose the case."

"That's a risk in any trial, but with a mercurial judge and no jury we face a bigger challenge. A few days ago, I received a note from your colleague Mr. Fish. Mr. Gasper and I think his testimony is just what we need to turn the judge against Miss Pigot."

I think of my supercilious colleague. "I can't think of anything he could contribute. If he knew anything of interest he would have told me."

"That was my opinion until Mr. Gasper and I met with him. Mr. Fish told us he observed shocking behavior between Miss Pigot and Mr. Wilson," Mr. Geddes says. "Activities so disgusting, his report can't fail to impress the judge's mind."

"He didn't mention anything to me."

"Mr. Fish didn't want to testify on this matter. He hoped the entire incident could be left in the dark where it belongs. But he's been following the case and recognizes it isn't as strong as it should be, and that his testimony could make a difference and turn the judge to our favor."

"Stop beating around the bush, man," I say. "What did Mr. Fish see?"

"There's no way for me to be delicate," Mr. Geddes says. "You must understand he only brought this to our attention out of his concern for you. Mr. Gasper and I think we must use his testimony, however indelicate."

"Out with it," I say. "What did he see?"

"Mr. Fish saw Miss Pigot's hand on Mr. Wilson's private anatomy."

"What! That's not possible," I say. "No. Never. Miss Pigot's free with men, but I can't believe she would do such a thing."

"Nevertheless, Mr. Fish saw the action," Mr. Geddes says.

I take my head into my hands. This cannot come out in open court. It will humiliate the entire Scottish mission, and I'll be held accountable. I feel frantic and lift my head.

"You may not bring this up," I say. "I forbid you."

Mr. Geddes shrugs. "Mr. Gasper has his instructions already."

"Countermand them," I say. "This cannot go forward."

"Mr. Gasper doesn't lose cases. He has his instructions, and will act upon them," Mr. Geddes says. "The only reason I mention the matter beforehand is to spare you the shock. Come, it's time to go to court."

Mr. Geddes saunters along as if he hasn't just dropped me into a vat of darkness. I lift up my face to the rain, not caring how it will destroy my appearance. I'm ruined. The mission is doomed. We'll never live down Mr. Fish's testimony. Fool! Doesn't he realize he'll be sacked as soon as the Mission Committee learns what he's about to do. They're already after me for allowing events to reach open court.

As we walk into the courtroom, I see Miss Pigot seated, as yet unconscious of what is about to happen. Mr. Trevelyan and Mr. Gasper enter from the judge's door. Mr. Trevelyan looks like thunder, and Mr. Gasper doesn't look too happy himself. He has to bring out the sordid business. Justice Norris appears about five minutes later, and we begin. I scarcely hear Mr. Trevelyan cross-examine Mrs. Mukherjee.

Mr. Trevelyan returns to his table and confers with Mr. Carruthers who appears as shocked as I feel. Miss Pigot looks puzzled by their agitation. Mr. Trevelyan whispers in her ear. Her mouth drops open.

Mr. Gasper rises. *No, don't do this. It's not too late.*

"The defense calls William Fish."

The judge raps his podium with his knuckle. "One moment, I can't allow ladies to remain in court during this testimony and will thank the lady at the plaintiff's table to leave the court."

"My Lord," Mr. Trevelyan rises. "As the plaintiff, she has a right to be here."

"No, Mr. Trevelyan, she does not," Justice Norris snaps. "I know enough about the upcoming testimony to remove all ladies from the court. And Mr. Gasper, I rely on you to put only those questions that are directly relevant to this case."

Mr. Trevelyan speaks briefly to Miss Pigot before she leaves. She glances in my direction, but I don't look up. Mr. Fish proceeds to the witness box with his head held high without looking at me. I can't think why he would give such testimony without discussing it with me first.

Mr. Fish raises his right hand and swears to tell the truth. Streams of sweat pour down my face. I let them fall on the table.

Mr. Gasper begins smoothly as if he isn't about to drag us all through the mud. "Mr. Fish, tell the court your position at Scottish College."

"I'm Professor of English. I also work with the Female Mission examining pupils," Mr. Fish says. He's very composed.

"Do you know Mr. James Wilson?"

"Yes, he's also a Professor at Scottish College," Mr. Fish replies.

"Have you seen him at the orphanage?"

I think Mr. Gasper would like to drag things out more, but Mr. Fish gets right to it. "I remember one particular occasion when I went with him the orphanage. I was engaged with examination work for the Upper School."

"What happened when you arrived?" Mr. Gasper asks.

"Miss Pigot took me upstairs to the class I was to examine and left me there."

"What was Mr. Wilson doing?"

Mr. Fish pauses a moment. "I don't know," he says. "We separated at the veranda."

"Did you see him again that day?" Mr. Gasper asks.

"I went to the dining room for *tiffin* about one o'clock," Mr. Fish says. "I should say the drawing room. I don't think there was a dining room. I found Miss Pigot and Mr. Wilson, and we took *tiffin*."

"Was alcohol served?" Mr. Gasper asks.

"There was a glass of beer poured out for me. I took a mouthful," Mr. Fish says. "As a rule, I don't drink beer in the day."

"And Mr. Wilson?" Mr. Gasper asks.

"He drank almost two quarts of beer, with the exception my glass," Mr. Fish says. "After the beer, Miss Pigot pressed Mr. Wilson to take a glass of whiskey."

"Did he?"

"Well," Mr. Fish pauses. "Miss Pigot took some liquor, and Mr. Wilson joined her."

"How long did you remain in the drawing room?" Mr. Gasper asks.

"I returned to my work about two o'clock and continued until four o'clock when I returned to the drawing room. I don't know what the others were doing."

"Was anyone else there?"

"No. I found the *durwan*, and he knocked at the door of a room that leads away from the drawing room."

"Did anyone answer?" Mr. Gasper asks.

"The *durwan* knocked a second time, and I heard a voice," Mr. Fish says. "The *durwan* opened the door for me, and I went through. Miss Pigot lay on a sofa with Mr. Wilson beside her on a chair."

Justice Norris leans over the witness box to hear better.

"What happened then?" Mr. Gasper asks.

"Mr. Wilson lifted a piece of ornamental wood off the table and directed it to my attention," Mr. Fish says. "I said it was pretty, and then told Miss Pigot I'd finished my examination work."

"Did Mr. Wilson say anything?" Mr. Gasper asks.

"Yes. He wiped his face, and said, 'Miss Pigot, you've made me drink too much beer today. I've scarcely done anything.'" Mr. Fish says. "Mr. Wilson said, 'Miss Pigot won't allow me to do much work. We've been engaged all day with these schedules.'"

"How long did you remain?" Mr. Gasper asks.

"After a few minutes, Mr. Wilson and I left together."

Stop right there, Mr. Fish. You've said enough. I want to stop the questions, but it's out of my hands. I stare at Mr. Fish. I shake my head. But he keeps his eyes on Mr. Gasper and doesn't see me.

"Do you remember any other interesting occasions?" Mr. Gasper asks.

Mr. Fish takes his time answering. "Once I was preparing lists of names for the distribution of prizes. I had to arrange the names in order of merit," Mr. Fish says. "I had to add up the marks opposite the students' names, and then put the names in order according to the marks."

"Was anyone else there?" Mr. Gasper prods.

"Mr. Wilson and Miss Pigot were there," Mr. Fish says. "I sat on a chair at the table, and Mr. Wilson and Miss Pigot sat on a bench."

"What was Mr. Wilson doing?"

"The same thing I was."

"Did you see anything unusual?"

"While Mr. Wilson added the marks, I noticed Miss Pigot leaning her folded hands on his shoulder," Mr. Fish says. "She said he was her dearest friend and she didn't know what she'd do without him. After that, she sat next to him and I observed Miss Pigot's right hand on Mr. Wilson's private parts. She moved her hand backwards and forwards."

I feel like I'm choking, but no sound comes out. *Mr. Fish, what have you done?*

"When this occurred, what, if anything, did you do?" Mr. Gasper asks as if Mr. Fish has said nothing indelicate at all.

"I didn't know what to do. I'd never seen any behavior remotely like this. I was shocked," Mr. Fish says. "I looked at my list until I collected myself. Then I asked Miss Pigot to spell the names of some of the pupils on my list. I thought my question would interrupt the process."

"Were you successful?"

"As a matter of fact, I wasn't," Mr. Fish says.

"What happened next?"

"After a few minutes, Mr. Wilson and Miss Pigot rose from the table and went into a room at the head of the stairs adjoining the drawing room," Mr. Fish says.

Justice Norris's face goes slack. He opens his mouth, then closes it.

"How long were they in the other room?"

"About twenty minutes. Mr. Wilson came out of the room alone. Miss Pigot came out a few minutes later." Mr. Fish looks down at his hands. "Mr. Wilson and I finished the remaining names and left."

"Did you speak to Mr. Wilson about this incident?" Mr. Gasper asks.

"Not directly. I spoke with him about this suit."

Mr. Gasper walks back to our table. "No further questions." I can't meet Mr. Gasper's eyes.

Mr. Trevelyan rises. He looks angry but controls his temper. "Mr. Fish, when did you speak to Mr. Hastie's solicitor?"

"I made a statement last week on Thursday or Friday. Not Saturday." Mr. Fish says.

"Did you speak with Mr. Hastie prior to meeting his solicitors?" Mr. Trevelyan asks.

"No."

"How often do you see Mr. Hastie?"

"I live with Mr. Hastie and see him every day," Mr. Fish says. "I have meals with him and professional communications."

"Has he consulted you about this suit?" Mr. Trevelyan asks.

"Yes, but I can't say he's told me what occurred each day in court," Mr. Fish says. "I read about the case in the papers."

"When did this incident you described occur?" Mr. Trevelyan asks.

"February or March last year," Mr. Fish says.

"And how long did you chum with Mr. Wilson?"

"Until this suit began last April."

"After such an incident, why did you continue chumming with Mr. Wilson?"

"I would have avoided it if I could without causing comment," Mr. Fish says.

"When did you mention the incident to Mr. Hastie?" Mr. Trevelyan asks.

"I told Mr. Hastie about it after I spoke to Mr. Wilson," Mr. Fish says.

"Did you go into all the particulars?"

"I don't think I ever told Mr. Hastie the details of this incident," Mr. Fish says. "I don't know whether he knows about it yet."

"I daresay, he does now," Mr. Trevelyan says. "Why did you discuss the incident with his solicitor?"

"It came out as I answered his questions," Mr. Fish says.

"Did you discuss the incident with anyone else?"

"When the case was about to come to court, I mentioned the matter to Mr. Wilson," Mr. Fish says. "I think I mentioned it to Mr. Hastie the day after."

"What did you tell Mr. Hastie?"

"I told him Mr. Wilson was distressed. Mr. Wilson asked me if he was likely to be drawn into the case, and I told him that if the case came to court, more than Miss Pigot would be ruined by it," Mr. Fish says. "Mr. Wilson wanted me to say whether he'd be involved. I said I couldn't say, because I might be accused of libel."

"In your opinion, did Mr. Wilson and Miss Pigot have sexual intercourse?" Mr. Trevelyan asks.

I wince at Mr. Trevelyan's language, but Mr. Fish is unaffected.

"I'm unwilling to say they had sexual intercourse," he says as if the subject is an ordinary conversational topic.

"Why?" Mr. Trevelyan asks. "Had you any doubt they retired to that room to have sexual intercourse?"

"That's a hard question," Mr. Fish considers his answer. "I thought it was wrong for them to leave the room together."

"I'll ask again. Do you have any doubt they went into that room to have sexual intercourse?" Mr. Trevelyan asks.

Mr. Fish sighs and shakes his head. "I have little doubt."

"Have you any doubt?" Mr. Trevelyan presses the point.

"I have no doubt," Mr. Fish admits.

"Then why didn't you say anything?" Mr. Trevelyan demands to know.

"Mr. Wilson and I are communicants in the church. I didn't say anything, because I didn't want to create a public scandal."

I wish you'd kept to your secrets.

"Wasn't Mr. Wilson appointed Session Clerk shortly after this incident?"

"Yes."

"And you think an adulterer is fit to be Session Clerk in the Church of Scotland?"

"No, I don't," Mr. Fish says. "You're using very harsh words."

"Are you sure you saw this incident you describe?" Mr. Trevelyan asks.

"I saw it plainly."

Now that he's described it, I see it too. Clearly Justice Norris also has an image in mind.

"What name did you ask Miss Pigot to spell?" Mr. Trevelyan asks.

"I can't remember," Mr. Fish says. "She spelt the name for me."

"And Miss Pigot never changed her position," Mr. Trevelyan says.

"She kept her hand where it was," Mr. Fish says. "I looked her straight in the face, and she still moved her hand."

"How was it you didn't leave the room?" Mr. Trevelyan asks. "One would think your first impulse would be to leave."

Answer the question, Fish. Don't stand there with your mouth open.

"Did you hear any conversation?" Mr. Trevelyan follows up.

"When they left the room, I heard Mr. Wilson say, 'Oh, Miss Pigot,'" Mr. Fish says.

"Did they give any reason for leaving the room?"

"They may have made some excuse."

"When they returned, was Miss Pigot's clothing out of order?" Mr. Trevelyan asks.

"I didn't notice."

"What did you do when they returned?" Mr. Trevelyan asks.

"I pressed Mr. Wilson to come away as soon as possible," Mr. Fish says.

"I have no further questions, My Lord," Mr. Trevelyan says.

"The witness may stand down," Justice Norris says. "Bailiff, invite that woman back into court."

Do my ears deceive me? Justice Norris called Miss Pigot "that woman." Mr. Fish's testimony shifted the judge's opinion, and I doubt she'll be able to reverse it. Miss Pigot comes back to her table. She gives her barrister a questioning look. He shakes his head and frowns. He'll have to work hard to erase the image of Miss Pigot with Mr. Wilson. I wonder if Mr. Fish's testimony is true. I'll never ask.

After that bombshell, we return to the original witness order. Mr. Gasper calls Eliza Humphreys and begins his questions. Another mousy woman trying to make her way alone. She looks composed as she takes her position and waits for Mr. Gasper to speak.

"When did you work at the Female Mission?" he asks.

"My employment began about 1871. It was a very long time ago," Miss Humphreys says. "Miss Pigot was Lady Superintendent then.

"Do you remember a girl called Hester?"

Mr. Trevelyan jumps up as if coming out of a trance. "My Lord, I object to any evidence from 1871. The libel doesn't refer to these years."

"My Lord," Mr. Gasper says, "it will show a pattern of behavior."

"I think," Justice Norris says, "upon the whole, it would be safer to admit it."

"Tell us about Hester."

According to Miss Humphreys Hester was not entirely in her right mind. Miss Humphrey uses the word "silly" to describe the girl. She testifies Miss Pigot whipped Hester with a cane and had the girl tied to a horse trough. Mr. Gasper has a more damaging point to make.

"Did you see anything it would have been better not to see?" Mr. Gasper asks Miss Humphreys.

"I saw a ship captain stretched on the couch in the drawing room at about nine o'clock. Miss Pigot was hanging all over him. Her face was almost touching his."

"Were there any other men in the orphanage?" Mr. Gasper continues.

"I remember Mr. Bomwetsch. He was a clergyman," Miss Humphreys nods. "Miss Pigot was sick, and he was in her room."

"Were there other visits from the captain?" Mr. Gasper asks.

"He called the day Mr. Bomwetsch was there. Miss Pigot said to send him up, so I did,"

When Mr. Trevelyan asks why Miss Pigot caned Hester, Miss Humphreys says it was because she ate some horse feed.

Reverend Chuckerbutty is the next witness. He's an impressive figure with his white hair and beard. He's in the orphanage at all hours, so his testimony can only support my statements about Kali Churn Banerjee. As he passes me on the way to the witness box, Reverend Chuckerbutty winks.

Mr. Gasper asks how often Mr. Chuckerbutty was at the orphanage.

"I used to go twice or three times a week," he says, nodding his head. "I used to examine the pupils in Bengali and Sanskrit. And I took my meals there every afternoon." He strokes his beard.

"Did you see Kali Churn Banerjee at the orphanage?" Mr. Gasper asks.

"Oh, yes, almost every time I went there," Mr. Chuckerbutty nods. "I saw him any time between four o'clock to almost nine o'clock at night. Sometimes on the veranda. Other times in the drawing room. And sometimes in Miss Pigot's bedroom. One time as I ascended the steps, I heard Miss Pigot and Kali Churn Banerjee talking. They were inside a room and came out about an hour later."

"Have you seen Kali Churn Banerjee go into Miss Pigot's bedroom?" Mr. Gasper asks.

"Oh, yes. I've seen him go into her room without any notice, and also coming out. And I've seen both of them coming out together. That is true."

"Do you remember any unusual incidents?" Mr. Gasper asks.

"Nothing of importance to me. There was one Sunday morning after service. Miss Pigot asked me to come to her house," Mr. Chuckerbutty says. "She wanted to speak to me about something. So, one day later in the week at about four o'clock in the afternoon, I went to her house and found the gate open. I went upstairs. No one was on the veranda, so I looked in the drawing room and saw Kali Churn Babu seated on a mat on the floor. He had on his trousers and shirt, but nothing else. No jacket or coat."

"Was he alone?" Mr. Gasper asks.

"No. Miss Pigot was lying on a sofa, and Kali Churn sat near her leg," Mr. Chuckerbutty gestures the length of the sofa. "He stood up immediately and invited me in. I asked Miss Pigot what she wanted to talk to me about. She looked confused and replied in a faltering, trembling voice. She asked me to come another day. So I came away."

"What else have you seen?" Mr. Gasper asks.

Mr. Chuckerbutty strokes his beard. "I've seen her lying on a rattan sofa, and Kali Babu seated near her leg. This I've seen on several occasions. Both on the same sofa and his body in contact with her leg."

"Did you mention this to anyone?" Mr. Gasper asks.

"I told Mr. Hastie when he asked me, after he received the letters from Miss Gordon and Mrs. Walker."

"I have no further questions," Mr. Gasper says.

Mr. Trevelyan doesn't look as confident as he usually does. His client is a trollop, and there's no way he can obliterate that impression from the judge's mind.

"What did you infer from Miss Pigot's behavior?" Mr. Trevelyan asks.

"It was my impression Miss Pigot was behaving improperly," Mr. Chuckerbutty says. "I thought there was a great deal more than mere familiarity."

Mr. Trevelyan clears his throat. "Really? What did you conclude?"

"I suspected Kali Churn Banerjee was committing adultery with Miss Pigot. Yes."

"When did you suspect this?" Mr. Trevelyan asks.

"In 1880," Mr. Chuckerbutty says.

Mr. Trevelyan looks surprised. "Do you give communion to a person you suspect of wrongdoing?"

"When I give communion to someone I suspect, I say something to them ahead of time," Mr. Chuckerbutty says.

"Did you say anything to Miss Pigot?" Mr. Trevelyan asks.

"I said nothing to Miss Pigot particularly," Mr. Chuckerbutty says. "However, before I give communion I say, 'We are all sinners, but if any person is particularly sinful, I ask him not to come near the table.' That is what I say."

"Did you share your suspicions with Miss Pigot?" Mr. Trevelyan asks.

"No, I never pointed out the sinfulness of her conduct."

"I have letters you wrote to Miss Pigot. Why did you write to her?"

"Whenever preparations were being made to baptize any female, I used to write Miss Pigot, and she instructed the females," Mr. Chuckerbutty says.

"Given your suspicions, was she an appropriate person to instruct candidates for baptism?" Mr. Trevelyan asks.

"No, I didn't think a lady who carried on an intrigue with a married man was a fit person to instruct a candidate for baptism."

I glance at Miss Pigot. She keeps her eyes forward, but I detect a certain rigidity to her posture. Considering her loyal attendance at the native church, she probably feels betrayed by her minister's testimony. Did she really think her behavior would go unnoticed?

Mr. Trevelyan passes two letters to Mr. Chuckerbutty. "Did you write these letters?"

"Yes, because so long as a person isn't found guilty by a court or church, I can't consider that person guilty," Mr. Chuckerbutty says.

"You sign them 'yours affectionately,'" Mr. Trevelyan says.

"I always write 'yours affectionately' to any person friendly to me."

"Even to a person you suspect of adultery."

"It wasn't proven," Mr. Chuckerbutty says. "She was friendly to me. That is the ordinary way of writing in this country,"

"Did you tell Mr. Hastie that Miss Pigot was an illegitimate Eurasian?" Mr. Trevelyan asks.

"I never said she was illegitimate. But she grew up here, and that is who a Eurasian is. Someone who is born here with a European parent. Most often the father," Mr. Chuckerbutty nods.

"When did you first suspect something improper between Kali Churn Banerjee and Miss Pigot?" Mr. Trevelyan asks.

"When I heard them talking in that room in 1879. But as a Christian I had to tolerate such things. What was I to do?" Mr. Chuckerbutty opens his hands.

"I'll tell you presently," Judge Norris responds waspishly.

"Wasn't Kali Churn Banerjee also Christian?" Mr. Trevelyan asks.

"He may be Christian, but he may also be addicted to vices. I consider him a weak Christian."

"Because he belongs to the Free Church, and not the established church?" Judge Norris asks.

"It has nothing to do with that," Mr. Chuckerbutty says. "I was afraid if I remonstrated with him, he would take proceedings against me for aspersions against his character."

"All I can say is that it was a very erroneous impression," Justice Norris says. "Instead of remonstrating with him, you had dinner with him. How long did you continue to have those dinners?"

"Until the end of 1880," Mr. Chuckerbutty says. "After that I was ill and took my dinner at home."

"Sounds like those suspicions didn't prevent you from filling your stomach," Justice Norris says.

Several people laugh. The judge glares at the seating area and the room becomes silent.

"When I'm asked to dine, I can't refuse," Mr. Chuckerbutty tilts his head to one side.

"Why not?" Justice Norris asks.

"They would ask my reasons."

"Yet you believe Kali Churn to be a weak Christian, and Miss Pigot a bad Christian," Justice Norris questions.

"I was helpless," Mr. Chuckerbutty responds, "and I couldn't well refuse them."

"I think the less you say about other people's weak Christianity, the better," Justice Norris says. "You're excused."

Surely this will end soon. After Mr. Fish and Mr. Chuckerbutty, why do we need more witnesses? What more is there to prove? The woman is an adulteress. She beats children. Her mission is a travesty. And my comments are entirely correct. No libel occurred. I write a note to Mr. Gasper to stop the proceedings, but he ignores me and calls another witness. Maud Mary Faulkner testifies she only worked as a *zenana* teacher for six months, because she and Miss Pigot didn't 'pull well together.' She didn't like her room, and she didn't speak Bengali. But she did see Mr. Wilson in Miss Pigot's bedroom. Mr. Gasper presses forward.

"I was reading the newspapers between ten and eleven at night," she says in a soft voice, "and the servant came to remind me he had to put the gas lamp out. When I passed the veranda door, I saw Mr. Wilson standing in front of Miss Pigot's bathroom door. He was wiping his hands on a towel."

Mrs. Faulkner testifies Miss Pigot had Mr. Wilson sit in a chair while she combed and brushed his hair. Shocking!

Next, Mrs. Palmer comes forward to tell us about her years as a *zenana* teacher with Miss Pigot. She went with Miss Pigot to Dr. Chunder's house on Amherst Street.

"I saw a *babu* with his hands out coming to greet Miss Pigot," Mrs. Palmer says. "He said 'Come, come.' She said, 'No, no.'" Later, Mrs. Palmer saw a *babu* lying on a cot and Miss Pigot sitting to the side of it. She might have seen more, but Miss Pigot sent her home. I don't see the point of that witness.

Dr. Cruden testified he was at the school prize distribution in April 1882. He saw Miss Pigot's fit of temper and heard her say she wouldn't distribute the prizes as long as 'that woman is in the house,' presumably Miss Smail. The judge wouldn't allow Mr. Gasper to proceed further. Mr. Gasper said that in that case he was prepared to close our case.

"This is an agreeable surprise," Justice Norris says. "I don't think I'll trouble Mr. Trevelyan to open his case tonight. We're adjourned until tomorrow morning."

Mr. Gasper shakes my hand. "We made excellent points today," he says. "I've no doubt we'll prevail."

"Thank you, Mr. Gasper," I reply. "I wish the suit was never filed."

"But it was," he says. "You may think my measures harsh, but they're for your defense. A few days more, and this will be a distant memory."

I make my way back to the College. After Mr. Fish's testimony, I don't see how I can chum with him anymore. The language alone was appalling. I'm not sure the Mission Committee will let him keep his position. During the entire day Miss Pigot stared straight ahead with her hands folded on the table. I can't help wondering how she'll respond tomorrow.

Chapter 19
"I Look Into My Heart For Courage"

Tuesday Morning, 11 September 1883
Mary Pigot

Yesterday evening Mr. Trevelyan and Mr. Carruthers told me about Mr. Fish's testimony. I burst into tears. The shame of it. Mrs. Wilson will never forgive me for this. And the things Reverend Chuckerbutty said. I thought he was my friend. He ate at my table. Now he accuses me of indiscretions with Kali Churn. I remember the day he came. It's true I was on the cane lounge but Kali Churn wasn't seated on the floor. I had one of my headaches. Kali Churn sat on a chair next to me and we talked. How could Mr. Chuckerbutty twist the situation like that?

I don't know how I got back to my hotel room. When I looked in the yellowed mirror this morning, my face was gray. I wish I could sink my head into my collar. I wish God would strike me with lightening. But he just sends rain, dark skies, and mud. I don't bother to lift my skirts any more. My boots leave puddles as I drag myself into the courtroom.

Mr. Trevelyan turns toward me when I arrive at our table. "Have faith, Miss Pigot," he says. I press my lips together.

We stand for the judge. He sits, polishes his spectacles, places them on his face, and reaches for his pen. "Mr. Trevelyan, are you ready to present your case?"

Mr. Trevelyan rises and places his notes directly in front of him on our table. I see broad strokes of black ink on good quality paper but can't make out the words. Mr. Trevelyan looks at the judge and tucks his fingers behind his lapels. "May it please the Court, I open by pointing out that prior to Mr. Hastie's arrival, not a breath of scandal ever blew against Miss Pigot's reputation. Her reputation both here and in Scotland was spotless. Her orphanage and schools rescuing increasing numbers of Calcutta's most vulnerable girls and women. But as soon as Mr. Hastie arrived, disputes arose. Mr. Hastie behaved maliciously beyond all manner of doubt in the way he circulated, repeated, and reasserted these libels, none of which has been proven."

Both the judge and Mr. Gasper take notes. Mr. Hastie drops his chin on his chest, not sitting erect as he usually does. Mr. Trevelyan reminds Justice Norris of my exoneration from Miss Smail's charges and the scurrilous leaflet her sister wrote.

"But Mr. Hastie couldn't accept the result. When Mrs. Walker fired yet another volley via letters she solicited against Miss Pigot, Mr. Hastie forwarded the letters with a personal endorsement. He hoped to keep Miss Pigot from returning to her position, thinking a woman with limited funds would never challenge him."

Justice Norris nods as if in agreement. I keep my face blank and look straight ahead.

"My Lord, Mr. Hastie didn't even arrive in Calcutta until January 1879. Yet without proper warning, he's dragged up all sorts of matters from the oblivion of the distant past, and Miss Pigot is expected to refute them. Whatever occurred in 1871 has no bearing on events ten years later and may never have occurred at all. Mr. Hastie and his barrister knew their case to be weak."

Mr. Trevelyan pauses and looks directly at Justice Norris until the judge returns his gaze. "Mr. Fish's dirty story yesterday was the Defense trump card. It alleged events which have nothing to do with the libels inflicted on Miss Pigot and only serves to deflect the Court's attention from the libels under consideration."

Mr. Trevelyan, why won't you say that Mr. Fish lied? He lied! Lied! Lied! Lied! The word is screaming in my head. Mr. Fish lied.

"Returning to Mr. Fish," Mr. Trevelyan continues. "Mr. Fish took an oath to tell the truth, but the obligation of the oath doesn't bind everyone."

"I think it more reasonable to believe he told the truth, than that he deliberately invented what he saw," Justice Norris says conversationally.

"I agree, My Lord," Mr. Trevelyan concurs. "It is difficult to believe someone would make up such a story, except for the close friendship of Mr. Fish and Mr. Hastie. And the fact that the evidence previously submitted wasn't enough to support the defense."

Mr. Hastie is leaning forward over the defense table. *Does he finally realize what he's done? Is he choking on remorse? I hope so.*

Justice Norris is speaking. "The most extraordinary part of it, Mr. Trevelyan, is that Mr. Fish testified they said nothing when they left the room for twenty minutes, and nothing when they came back."

"Indeed, My Lord," Mr. Trevelyan says, "and was it likely that after the incident mentioned, Mr. Wilson would return to the bedroom with Miss Pigot without so much as saying 'Excuse us for a few minutes'? If they were planning such an act, was it likely they would have so far forgotten themselves as to behave in an indecent manner before Mr. Fish?"

"It's difficult to believe it," Justice Norris responds, "but there is the difficulty of believing a man would invent something like that."

"The witness was either lying, or he was indecent," Mr. Trevelyan says. "Why would they do this in Mr. Fish's presence? There was no reason for it. People don't exhibit that sort of behavior in company."

"Then why didn't you question Mr. Fish on that issue, Mr. Trevelyan? You had the opportunity to bring this out during his testimony."

I sense Mr. Trevelyan is angry. He makes a choking sound, takes out a snowy white handkerchief and spits into it. He folds the fabric and puts it back into his pocket.

"My Lord," Mr. Trevelyan says with great dignity, "it's less than twenty-four hours since Mr. Fish testified. I had no instructions regarding his testimony yesterday and little opportunity to gather further evidence regarding his testimony. But as it turns out, there was a third person present that day."

"You didn't cross-examine on it," Justice Norris looks surprised.

"How could I?" Mr. Trevelyan asks. "I didn't have instructions then, but I have them now. We shall prove that Mr. Hastie has done nothing but spread unproven, malicious rumors and gossip about Miss Pigot since his arrival in 1879."

The judge calls a twenty-minute recess. The room spins. Mr. Trevelyan grabs my arm.

"Miss Pigot, are you ill?" He places me back in my chair and the spinning slows slightly.

"I'm fine, Mr. Trevelyan. I just wasn't paying attention."

Mr. Carruthers's clerk brings me a cool cloth. And quick as that, I have to stand again. Mr. Trevelyan calls James Wilson as our first witness. He walks by me without a glance. I wish I could tell him how sorry I am for all the trouble I have brought into his life. Mr. Hastie sinks down in his chair and doesn't look at his colleague. Mr. Wilson enters the witness box, raises his hand to take the oath, stands a moment as if he's praying, and turns his attention to Mr. Trevelyan who stands between our table and the witness box.

James Wilson

Mr. Trevelyan begins his questioning with a conversational tone. He asks how I heard of Mr. Hastie's illness shortly after he first arrived. I answer in the same tone of voice. I was at a prayer meeting when I learned about Mr. Hastie's illness. "Early the next morning, Mr. Steele sent his carriage with a letter. I went to his house and remained there four days."

"What did you do there?" Mr. Trevelyan probes.

"I lived there in case there was a crisis. That is to say, in case I had to resume my role as Acting Principal of the College."

Mr. Hastie's snaps up. Perhaps he didn't know how sick he was.

"Miss Pigot was also there, wasn't she?"

I glance at Miss Pigot. "Yes, she was there."

"What were your relations with her at the time of Mr. Hastie's illness?"

"They were friendly," I say in a flat voice.

"Do you remember when Miss Pigot came to nurse Mr. Hastie and how long she stayed?" Mr. Trevelyan asks.

"She came Thursday morning and remained until Monday."

"Where was Mrs. Briggs, now Mrs. Sharpland, when Miss Pigot undertook the night work?" Mr. Trevelyan asks.

"She slept in a part of the veranda that was made into a little room."

"Mrs. Sharpland testified you came into the sick room at twelve at night and four in the morning. Do you remember that?"

"I was never in Mr. Hastie's room after ten o'clock." I speak in a firm voice.

"Mrs. Sharpland said Miss Pigot put her hand on your thigh and lolled with her head on your shoulder," Mr. Trevelyan says. "She said Miss Pigot was bold, rude and in close conversation with you. Do you remember that?"

The very idea is an insult. "Nothing of the kind occurred. Miss Pigot and I spoke together, and she whispered to me when I happened to be in the room during the day but there was no physical contact or levity."

"Do you remember about this time there was a dinner party at Mr. Steele's?"

I remember. I was looking forward to the dinner party. Miss Pigot would be there and Mr. Steele always served good food. When I arrived, Miss Pigot wasn't there yet and I had to chat with Mr. Hastie. Mr. Trevelyan gives me a long look as if reminding me to answer the question.

"It was a small party on a Wednesday night after Miss Pigot returned the book to Mr. Hastie. Only Mr. Hastie, Miss Pigot, and myself attended."

"Did you notice anything in particular at the dinner party?" Mr. Trevelyan prods.

"Mr. Hastie was silent and sullen."

"After dinner, what did you do?"

"We went to the drawing room."

Mr. Trevelyan asks if Mr. Hastie was correct in saying that after retiring to the drawing room, Miss Pigot threw herself upon a sofa and put her legs up in a way he'd never seen a lady do. Miss Pigot never behaved like that.

"Miss Pigot lay down on the sofa," I reply, "but to say she flung her legs up is an exaggeration. And I may be allowed to say it was after a long day's work that she did this. The poor woman was exhausted."

"Were you struck by Miss Pigot's levity of conversation?"

Despite her fatigue, I remember she smiled and laughed, her face aglow in the candlelight. I tell Mr. Trevelyan I was struck by Miss Pigot's vivacity.

"Did you think there was anything improper with how Miss Pigot conducted herself?" Mr. Trevelyan asks.

"I considered her vivacity an antidote to Mr. Hastie's sullenness."

"Do you remember about this time a picnic at Barrackpore Park?" Mr. Trevelyan asks. "Who gave the picnic?"

"My cousin and I contributed to it. I can't say who else."

"What did you do at the park?"

"We went to the banyan tree and stayed there until *tiffin*," I say. "There was a mat spread on the ground, and we lounged on it."

"Mr. Hastie testified you were seated with your head in contact with Miss Pigot's shoulders. Do you remember anything like that?" Mr. Trevelyan asks.

"No. However, not being accustomed to sitting on the ground, we all felt awkward. Someone proposed we should sit back-to-back to support each other. I don't remember who."

"It wasn't Mr. Hastie, I suppose," Mr. Trevelyan says.

I wonder if Mr. Trevelyan is making a joke. The judge smiles slightly. I reply that many of us sat back-to-back.

"Who did you sit back-to-back with?"

"Miss Pigot."

"Was Mr. Hastie back-to-back with anybody?"

"He came and placed his back against Miss Pigot's shoulder." It was very awkward. She sitting with her back against mine, and Mr. Hastie's back on her shoulder.

"Objection," Mr. Gasper interrupts. "Mr. Hastie's sitting position isn't in evidence. This is highly irregular."

"There is nothing irregular, Mr. Gasper. It gives you an opportunity to recall Mr. Hastie," Justice Norris says. "However, Mr. Trevelyan, please avoid extraneous matter as much as possible." Justice Norris pulls out his watch. "As it's now time for *tiffin*; we shall adjourn." He bangs his gavel.

I exit the courtroom without glancing at Miss Pigot.

Mary Pigot
Tuesday Afternoon, 11 September 1883

Mr. Carruthers cajoles me into eating cheese and fruit at *tiffin*. I'm not sure that was a good idea. As the trial resumes, Mr. Wilson walks by me as if I'm not there—his shadow falls on the table as he passes. Mr. Trevelyan resumes his questions.

"Mr. Wilson, at Barrackpore Park, do you remember what happened after *tiffin*?"

"Everyone dispersed through the grounds. I walked with Miss Pigot, Mrs. Edwards and the children," Mr. Wilson says. "Afterwards we sat under a tree."

"What was Mr. Hastie doing?"

"He walked through the grounds."

"Mr. Hastie testified he once called for Miss Pigot," Mr. Trevelyan says. "and you came to him from what he thought was Miss Pigot's bedroom. Tell us about that."

"It occurred after the picnic. I called at the orphanage. Miss Pigot wasn't well. The *durwan* took me to her room. She was lying on a couch, and I sat on a nearby chair."

"When Mr. Hastie arrived, where did he go?" Mr. Trevelyan asks.

"The *durwan* announced him, and Mr. Hastie followed close on his heels into the room."

"And, when Mr. Hastie discovered he wasn't in a public reception room, was there any conversation?" Mr. Trevelyan asks.

"Nothing was said. He withdrew. I came out and joined him in the drawing room. I told him Miss Pigot would join us presently."

"What happened next?"

"I remained about ten minutes with Mr. Hastie until Miss Pigot came out, and then went away."

"Mrs. Faulkner testified she saw you in Miss Pigot's bedroom between ten and eleven at night, that you stood in front of Miss Pigot's bathroom door, and that Miss Pigot combed and brushed your hair. Do you remember this event?"

Mr. Wilson looks annoyed. "Nothing of the sort took place."

"Did you go to the orphanage in 1881?" Mr. Trevelyan asks.

"Many times."

"Did Mr. Fish go with you?"

"Frequently."

"Do you remember any work you did with Mr. Fish regarding the distribution of prizes at the orphanage?" Mr. Trevelyan asks.

"Yes."

Mr. Wilson looks uncomfortable. We both know Mr. Trevelyan is about to ask him about Mr. Fish's testimony.

"When did you do work related to a prize distribution?" Mr. Trevelyan asks.

"I believe it was the twenty-first of March."

"When you got to the orphanage, what did you do?" Mr. Trevelyan asks.

"Mr. Fish and I sat down at a large round table on the veranda. Miss Pigot produced large sheets containing marks from which the prize list was to be made out."

"Was anyone else there?" Mr. Trevelyan asks.

"Mr. Wetherill, treasurer of the Corresponding Board, came in. He sailed for England the following month." Mr. Wilson pauses.

"Was anyone else there?" Mr. Trevelyan asks again.

"Babu Nitya Gopal Mukherjee."

Mr. Hastie and I both look up at the same time. I want to see Mr. Hastie's reaction. He must be surprised that his convert will testify on my behalf.

"And who is Babu Mukherjee?"

"A convert of our mission."

"How long did you stay to prepare the prize lists?"

"Until seven o'clock."

"What was Nitya Gopal Mukherjee doing?" Mr. Trevelyan asks.

"He assisted in the same work," Mr. Wilson says.

"Have you read what Mr. Fish said?" Justice Norris asks.

Mr. Wilson blanches and wipes his hand over his forehead. His cheeks begin to color. Justice Norris watches him and waits for his answer. "Yes," Mr. Wilson says clearly. "I read it in *The Englishman* this morning."

Dear God, what must he think of me to put us into this situation? No wonder he won't look at me.

"Is there any truth in what Mr. Fish said about Miss Pigot's conduct with you?" Mr. Trevelyan asks.

A flash of color rises on Mr. Wilson's pale face before he answers. "None whatever. I never left the table."

"Have you ever been guilty of any misconduct with Miss Pigot such as Mr. Fish related?"

"Never," Mr. Wilson says with great emphasis.

"Either there, or anywhere else?" Mr. Trevelyan asks.

"Either there, or anywhere else," Mr. Wilson affirms, his face now fully flushed.

"Do you know whether Mr. Wetherill or Nitya Gopal Mukherjee remained or went away?"

"Mr. Wetherill left first. Nitya Gopal Mukherjee remained. I think we left together," Mr. Wilson says.

"You came home with Mr. Fish that evening?"

"Yes."

"Did you keep a diary at that time?" Mr. Trevelyan asks.

"I keep a scribbling diary for myself and so I can write my wife about my activities."

"Do you remember what you did the next day?" Mr. Trevelyan continues.

"Mr. Fish drove me to a prayer meeting at St. Andrew's."

"Did you go to Miss Pigot's again?"

"Mr. Fish and I went there the following day, the twenty-third."

"How did you write it in the diary?"

Mr. Wilson takes the diary from his pocket and reads from it. "With Fish at Miss Pigot's."

"Did anything happen at the orphanage on the first of April? Did you go there with Mr. Fish?"

"The distribution of prizes was that day."

"Do you remember dining at Miss Pigot's on the twentieth of April?" Mr. Trevelyan asks.

"Yes. The diary entry reads: 'Dined with Miss Pigot.'"

"Now look at the entry for the twenty-third of April. Whom did you dine with?" Mr. Trevelyan asks.

"That was a Sunday," Mr. Wilson says. "The entry reads: 'Dined with Mr. Fish and Dr. Valentine at Miss Pigot's.'"

"This is a fishy story," Justice Norris chuckles.

"So it would seem, My Lord," Mr. Gasper responds from the defense table.

Stop making jokes when our lives are at stake

Mr. Trevelyan ignores the comments and goes on. "Where were you on the third of May?"

"The entry says: 'At prayer meeting. Home with Mr. Fish.'"

"Where did you dine on the eleventh of May?"

"'At Miss Pigot's with Mr. Cruden, Mr. Fish, and my cousin.'"

Mr. Trevelyan takes the diary. "So you frequently saw Mr. Fish after the evening you prepared the prize lists." Mr. Trevelyan turns a couple pages. "On the thirteenth of May you write: 'After dinner went to see Miss Pigot off.' What do you mean?"

"On her departure for Scotland."

"What were your terms of intimacy with Mr. Fish during May and afterwards?"

"Most cordial," Mr. Wilson replies.

James Wilson

Mr. Trevelyan guides my testimony to highlight the impossibility for any gentleman, let alone a missionary, to remain on intimate terms with someone who behaved in the way Mr. Fish described. I've always been fair in my dealings with Mr. Fish. I can't think of any reason for him to testify as he did. I'm horrified that a fellow missionary could harbor such malice. For the sake of my family, I've no choice but to go down in the muck Mr. Fish deposited.

"Mr. Fish spoke of an occasion when you went to the orphanage,' Mr. Trevelyan reminds me. "He left you downstairs while he went to examine a class and returned to join you and Miss Pigot for *tiffin*. Mr. Fish testified you drank two quarts of beer, less a glass poured for him, and a glass of whiskey. He says he examined another class and came downstairs to find the drawing room empty. He summoned the *durwan* who opened the door to another room where he saw Miss Pigot lying on a sofa and you sitting in a chair beside her. Is this correct?"

"Certainly not," I say emphatically.

"Did you go and have this enormous *tiffin*?"

"I remember going to examine classes in the Upper School in December 1881."

"Did you drink two quarts of beer?" Mr. Trevelyan asks.

"Look at me." I gesture to my small frame. "I couldn't consume so much."

"Mr. Fish testified you drew his attention to a piece of ornamental wood, wiped your face, and said Miss Pigot gave you too much to drink. Now, Mr. Wilson, I ask you if on that day any impropriety occurred between you and Miss Pigot?"

I sense Justice Norris looming above me. "Is Mr. Fish's statement true?" he asks. "Did you say Miss Pigot gave you too much beer to drink?"

I remember the day was exceedingly hot, and Miss Pigot's anteroom has almost no ventilation. Miss Pigot gave me hill beer. As a rule, I don't overindulge. Is it possible that on that day I did? "I don't recollect drinking too much beer," I finally reply.

Justice Norris continues. "The suggestion is, you see, that you tried to divert Mr. Fish's attention with this piece of woodwork."

I don't remember anything about a piece of wood. I shake my head. "I don't recollect anything about a piece of wood."

"Humph." Clearly dissatisfied with my answer, Justice Norris leans back in his chair.

Mr. Trevelyan changes the topic. "You said Miss Pigot went away on the thirteenth of May 1882. Do you remember Miss Pigot visiting you at Scottish College?"

"She came several times."

"When you say several times, how often do you think she came?" Mr. Trevelyan asks.

"Perhaps half a dozen times. She drove to my steps, and I came down and spoke to her."

"Do you remember her getting down from the *gharry* and going to your room?"

"Yes," I say.

"What was her business?"

I shift my feet. "She called with a book and spoke to me about the entrance class which I'd undertaken to teach during her absence."

Mr. Trevelyan nods. "You state your relations with Mr. Fish during 1882 were cordial. Have they continued to be so?"

"Not since the end of March."

"What changed?"

"I received information he and Mr. Hastie went to the orphanage to collect evidence with reference to me, and I thought they wanted to drag me into this suit, which they have."

"At any time since you became acquainted with Miss Pigot, has there been any sexual intercourse between you two, any impropriety, or indecency such as should not exist between you?"

There it is. The question that will define my future. I look Mr. Trevelyan in the eye. "No. Never."

Justice Norris leans over the witness box. "And to that, will you pledge your oath to God now?"

"Yes, I swear it." What more can I do?

"Do you remember any conversation with Mr. Fish before April of this year in regard to this case?" Mr. Trevelyan asks.

I clear my throat "Mr. Fish came home late one evening in a state of great excitement. He said the suit would go forward and seemed quite put out about it. He rambled and said it wasn't Mr. Hastie who would suffer. I thought he meant Miss Pigot, but he left without being specific. So I followed him to his room and asked him whether I was to be brought into the suit."

"Why did you ask him that?"

"Because I knew Mr. Hastie's character, and he would drag me into the suit if it would injure Miss Pigot."

"No further questions, My Lord," Mr. Trevelyan says. His face is impassive.

I see Mr. Hastie say something to Mr. Gasper who shakes his head and proceeds to stand in front me. I prepare myself for his onslaught. "You and Miss Pigot often share carriages. When did you first go out in a carriage with Miss Pigot?"

What kind of question is that? "I can't possibly recollect the first time I went out with her."

"Did you go in the same carriage with Miss Pigot before the dinner at Mr. Steele's?"

"I can't recollect. I remember driving with her from the railway station to Mr. Steele's house when we returned from our trip to Barrackpore."

"How long were you there?"

"About an hour."

"Then what did you do?"

"Went home."

"With Miss Pigot?"

"Not to my knowledge." I look directly at Mr. Gasper.

Mr. Gasper looks at his manicured nails before he asks, "About the time of Mr. Steele's dinner party, were you on friendly terms with Mr. Hastie?"

"Yes."

"Did you know Mr. Hastie had a carriage to take him home?"

"I believe it was Mr. Steele's carriage." May as well clarify matters.

"Who dropped you home that evening?" Mr. Gasper asks.

"Miss Pigot dropped me."

"Didn't she go out of her way to drop you?" Mr. Gasper asks.

"Yes, but it was an easier route for the horses." I don't mention she needed fresh air.

"Have you driven with Miss Pigot since then?"

"Yes, I've been to places of business with her, to prize distributions, to schools, and to Mr. Joseph Cook's lecture."

"Have you been to an evening entertainment with her?"

I think a minute. "Once I met her at Mr. Gillan's, and she drove me back until our roads diverged. I left her and got in my cousin's carriage."

"Have you ever been to a *nautch* with Miss Pigot?" Mr. Gasper asks suggestively.

Justice Norris leans over his dais. "Where was this *nautch*?" he asks.

"The dance performance was at Sobhabazar Rajbari during the Durgā Puja festival." I emphasize the word 'dance.'

"Was there the slightest indelicacy at the *nautch*?" Justice Norris asks.

"No, My Lord."

"Didn't you go with Miss Pigot?" Mr. Gasper asks.

"No. She had her own *gharry* with another lady."

Mr. Gasper consults his notes. "How often have you been in Miss Pigot's bedroom?"

"I suppose about fifty times." I wait to see how Mr. Gasper will twist my words.

"That many? Who was in her bedroom when Mr. Hastie was announced?"

"Mrs. Tremearne was there. People went in and out. The day Mr. Hastie was there, I went up with the *durwan*."

"Do you mean to tell me you've never been inside the room alone with Miss Pigot?"

"I think not." I'm offended by Mr. Gasper's constant innuendos. "I may tell you the room is always open."

"Have you ever washed your hands in Miss Pigot's bathroom?" Mr. Gasper asks.

"Yes."

"Have you ever changed your clothes at the orphanage?" Mr. Gasper asks.

"Once," I reply. "In January, 1882."

"Do you remember the *tiffin* you had at the orphanage when Mr. Fish was there?"

"Yes," I say testily.

"When did you and Mr. Fish arrive?" Mr. Gasper asks.

"Between eleven and twelve in the afternoon."

"What did you do?"

"Mr. Fish examined some classes and, so far as I remember, I wrote out accounts."

"Where did you write out the accounts?" Mr. Gasper asks.

"In Miss Pigot's office, a sort of anteroom between the drawing room and the bedroom."

"Was the doorway generally left open?" Mr. Gasper asks.

"Not usually," Mr. Wilson says.

"Was it open that day?" Mr. Gasper asks.

"I don't remember."

"You can't say it was shut," Mr. Gasper says.

"I can't." I'm sure he brings this up for the judge's benefit, to demonstrate the possibility that Miss Pigot and I were alone together.

"Where was Miss Pigot while you were doing these accounts?"

"Moving about between that room, the bedroom, and the drawing room."

"Do you remember how much beer you took at *tiffin*?"

"No." I feel my temper rising. "I certainly didn't take the quantity Mr. Fish said I did."

"What is the latest hour you've been alone at Miss Pigot's?" Mr. Gasper asks.

"I've never been alone at Miss Pigot's. There are always teachers, or servants, or guests about the premises."

"How frequently did you dine at Miss Pigot's?" Mr. Gasper fires back.

"Perhaps twice a week."

"Did you sometimes dine alone with Miss Pigot?"

"Not precisely. We dined away from the teachers in the drawing room, but people were always passing through the room."

"On the occasion when you had *tiffin* there with Mr. Fish, did you draw his attention to some ornamental woodwork?" Mr. Gasper asks.

"I have no recollection," I say again.

"Will you swear to that?"

"How can I, when I have no recollection?"

"Did you say you drank too much beer?" Mr. Gasper presses.

I shake my head. "I have no recollection."

"Will you swear that?" Mr. Gasper asks.

"I will not swear to something I don't remember."

"Will you swear the door was shut between the drawing room and the bedroom?" Mr. Gasper asks.

"No."

"Will you swear nobody knocked at the door before Mr. Fish came in?"

"I can't say anything about it because I know nothing." I glance at Mr. Trevelyan and wonder why he raises no objections.

"What were you doing when Mr. Fish came in after his work?"

"I have no recollection." My temper goes up another notch.

"Then, as a matter of fact, you have no recollection of the incident," Mr. Gasper says.

"None at all," I blurt, "as I told you from the beginning."

Mr. Gasper clenches his jaw. "When these marks were being added up, were you seated on a bench?"

"I sat at a round table. I can't say in what seat."

"Was Miss Pigot seated near you at any time?"

"I don't remember." If I'd known the day would become so important, I'd have made notes.

"You can't say she didn't sit near you."

"I can't."

"Has Miss Pigot ever put her hand on any part of your body?"

"At various times Miss Pigot has placed a hand on my shoulders, on my head, or on my back as a way of emphasizing a point."

"On your thigh?" Mr. Gasper asks quietly.

"I think not," I say through gritted teeth.

"Will you swear?"

"No." I won't swear about such an indecent suggestion.

"Are you quite sure?" Mr. Gasper asks.

"I'm quite sure." Though Miss Pigot keeps her eyes straight ahead, I sense her disappointment that I don't deny such a thing could occur.

Mr. Gasper watches me closely. "When did Miss Pigot put her hand on your head?"

"Perhaps when I was seated writing, she came behind me, stood at the back of my chair, and put her hand on my head, or back, or shoulders."

"Have you ever been to Miss Pigot's bathroom to wash your hands?"

"Yes, during social gatherings."

"Besides social gatherings," Mr. Gasper says.

"I can't remember. You suggest an occasion and I'll answer you." I'm not going to bring up anything.

"When you washed your hands, whose brushes and combs did you use?"

"Such as were on the table."

"Are you sure Miss Pigot never brushed your hair?" Mr. Gasper asks.

"I'm quite sure of it. No such thing ever occurred."

"When Mr. Fish spoke to you about the case, did he say whether you'd be brought in?"

"I've answered that," I reply firmly

"I'd ask you to answer it again," Mr. Gasper says.

"I thought Mr. Hastie would take advantage of my warm friendship for Miss Pigot and bring me into the case."

"Has Miss Pigot had her hands upon your leg or thigh?" Mr. Gasper asks.

I inhale. "No, never."

Justice Norris raps his knuckle. "Court is adjourned for twenty minutes." He swooshes out the door.

Mary Pigot

I feel odd, as if I am seeing everything from a far distance. Mr. Wilson walks by me to sit next to Mr. Carruthers. They whisper to each other, but I can't make out what they're saying. Mr. Geddes and Mr. Gasper confer while Mr. Hastie fans himself with a piece of paper. I hold myself up from the table to stretch my legs, but I can't stand straight, so I slip back down just before we have to rise again for Justice Norris. Mr. Trevelyan holds my arm. Mr. Wilson returns to the witness box.

Mr. Gasper asks whether I told Mr. Wilson about a native missionary's wife being pregnant. Mr. Gasper seems to think it an indelicate subject. I don't see why. Where does he think children come from? Mr. Gasper moves to the outbreak of fits we had a few years ago. The girls had a terrible time, and we had to call for the doctor. Mr. Gasper tries to make something of Mr. Wilson suggesting to Mrs. Ellis that cold water and perhaps enemas would ease the situation. Again, Mr. Gasper infers Mr. Wilson was indelicate.

Now he questions Mr. Wilson's visits with me at Serampore. "Did you converse with Miss Pigot regarding this case before it began?"

"Yes. I knew she meant to institute some proceedings," Mr. Wilson says.

"Did you try to dissuade her?"

"I did."

"Were you present at the distribution of prizes when Miss Pigot lost her temper?" Mr. Gasper asks.

Justice Norris interrupts. "Mr. Gasper, there's no proof she lost her temper."

Mr. Gasper ignores him. "Answer my question, Mr. Wilson."

"I was present at a distribution when Miss Pigot spoke in anger."

I was justified. Mr. Gillan should never have brought Miss Smail after I threw her out of the mission.

"Do you remember Miss Pigot saying 'I won't allow this distribution to go on when that woman is in the house'?"

"I heard her say 'Unless Miss Smail goes away,'" Mr. Wilson corrects.

"To whom did she say this?"

"To Mr. Gillan."

"Do you remember Mr. Gillan saying, 'I can't stand this kind of scene'?"

Justice Norris interrupts. "Mr. Gasper, what has this to do with the case? It doesn't affect Mr. Wilson's case or any part of the alleged libel."

Mr. Gasper ignores Justice Norris a second time. I'm surprised the judge is letting him get away with this.

"Did you say to Mr. Gillan, 'You ought not to have brought her here'?" Mr. Gasper continues.

"I did say that," Mr. Wilson says.

"Thank you. No further questions." Mr. Gasper prances back to his table. Mr. Wilson takes out a handkerchief and wipes his forehead.

For a moment I think it's over. Then Mr. Trevelyan stands and approaches Mr. Wilson.

"To continue the thought, why did you say Mr. Gillan shouldn't have brought Miss Smail to the distribution?" Mr. Trevelyan asks.

"Because Miss Smail was in rebellion against Miss Pigot," Mr. Wilson says.

"Why did you urge Miss Pigot not to bring this suit?" Mr. Trevelyan asks.

"Partly to save this great scandal, and partly to save myself from Mr. Hastie's temper when he's aroused."

"I have no further questions," Mr. Trevelyan says and walks back to our table.

Mr. Wilson turns to face Judge Norris. "I wish to clarify an important point. I never suggested Miss Pigot quietly accept these libels. I requested she vindicate her character by a private inquiry."

I tried that. No one returned my notes. Even you wouldn't intercede with Mr. Hastie. I had to go forward any way I could. I press my fingers to my temples. My head feels as if it will explode.

"Thank you, Mr. Wilson. You're excused," Justice Norris says. Mr. Wilson leaves the box and walks straight past me, so close I could touch him. I hear the outer door close and he is gone.

"Do we have other witnesses, Mr. Trevelyan?" Justice Norris asks.

Mr. Trevelyan looks surprised. "We expected the court to rise at six o'clock, My Lord."

"I intended to sit until seven o'clock, and it's not yet six-thirty. I'm disappointed, gentlemen. I want this case concluded before Saturday, because if it isn't, I'll have to postpone my leave, which is short enough as it is. I'm prepared to carry on the case until next week, but I'll be very disappointed if that happens. Am I clear?" Justice Norris bangs his gavel. "Court is adjourned."

Mr. Carruthers takes my arm.

"Who is it tomorrow?" I ask.

"Babu Banerjee, and yourself," he says.

"I thought we had other witnesses. Nitya Gopal Mukherjee can prove Mr. Fish a liar." I'm desperate to avoid testifying.

Mr. Carruthers shakes his head. "Mr. Trevelyan and I want you to go after Babu Banerjee. Our case is built on your innocence, not how many corroborators we can find."

I turn to him. "I don't think I can do it."

"You can and you must. This case isn't just about you any longer. Two fine men could also lose their livelihood. Your testimony is vital to our case," Mr. Carruthers tells me. "You must go forward."

I nod. I don't know what forward means any more.

When I get back to my hotel, I pray as I've never prayed before. I beg God to give me a place in the world. I tell him he what He already knows. The charges are false. I didn't slip as many orphans do. I didn't fall into temptation and an easy life. If I had, I couldn't be more reviled than I am now. I pray and sob until I have no more tears. My mind wanders to the adulteress in John's Gospel. The scribes and the Pharisees want Jesus to say the woman should be stoned, and he said whichever of them never sinned should cast the first stone. Everyone left. Eventually Jesus asked the woman whether anyone still accused her. When she said no man condemned her, Jesus said, "Neither do I condemn thee: go, and sin no more." If Jesus could say that to a woman who was probably guilty, couldn't He say that to me when I am completely innocent? Why doesn't God drive away my accusers? I look into my heart for courage and fall asleep.

Chapter 20
"I Look Upon Her As A Mother"

Wednesday Morning, 12 September 1883
William Hastie

I thought Mr. Wilson a credible witness yesterday. Gasper never put him off his stride. I don't think his denials will make any difference to the judge, but they make a difference to me. It's unfortunate Mr. Wilson got dragged into this mess, but it's his own fault. Kali Churn Banerjee testifies this morning, and he deserves everything he gets and more besides—after those newspaper articles. "One Against Two Thousand," indeed.

Geddes and I arrive at the courthouse together. We have nothing to say to each other, except the usual banal pleasantries. Banerjee is waiting outside the courtroom when we arrive. He looks decidedly ill this morning. I fully expect him to collapse in the witness box.

Geddes and I walk through to the defense table. I shake hands with Gasper and take my seat. Miss Pigot arrives clutching her solicitor's arm. The woman appears shorter every time I see her. She has no one to blame but herself. Justice Norris opens the court day, and events take their monotonous course.

Banerjee looks uneasy as Mr. Trevelyan approaches the witness box. He clenches his hands around the rail. Mr. Trevelyan starts gently, confirming Banerjee is a *Vakil* of the High Court who received his legal training in India. He asks Banerjee what church he attends.

Banerjee's voice rings out. "I've attended the Free Church of Scotland since 1864."

Trevelyan takes the witness through his relationship with Miss Pigot—when they met, how well they knew each other. "When did you first send your children to the Upper School?"

"In February 1880," Banerjee says. "At first there were two children from my house, my daughter and my niece. Subsequently, three other children. Later, one more. I had six children there, five of them my own."

"And at that time, did you visit the orphanage?" Mr. Trevelyan asks.

"I stopped by almost every day."

"What did you do when you got there?" Mr. Trevelyan asks.

"Sometimes the children were ready to go home with me," Banerjee says. "Other times they weren't. I waited for one girl who attended a class in the afternoon."

"As a rule, what time did you go home?" Mr. Trevelyan asks.

"Sometimes five. Sometimes six," Banerjee says. "If I had meetings in the evening, I stayed until seven."

"What meetings did you attend?"

Get on with it Trevelyan. No one cares about Banerjee's social commitments.

Banerjee counts on his fingers as he recites the meetings he attended in the evenings. "Monthly Presbytery meetings with our church," he says, "and monthly Conference meetings with our missionary conference. And there were meetings of the Pension Fund and the Bengali Christian Conference."

"Were these the only occasions you stayed late?"

"Sometimes I did work for the Upper School. I drew up the program of studies. And Miss Pigot asked me to prepare certain government reports. Miss Pigot also held monthly social gatherings," Banerjee says.

"So you contributed services to the orphanage and school."

Banerjee drops his head to the side. "Yes. Miss Pigot had so much to do. It was a pleasure to assist her."

Trevelyan picks up a letter from the table, takes it to the witness box, and hands it to Banerjee. "Is this letter in your handwriting? Do you remember writing it?" Mr. Trevelyan asks.

"It refers to one of the reports. There's no date, but I see a reference to Mr. Fife's departure. He left early in 1880," Babu Banerjee says.

"To whom did you send this letter?"

"Miss Pigot."

"Allow me to read the letter aloud," Mr. Trevelyan reaches for the letter. *'Dear Miss Pigot, do you kindly excuse an undutiful son. I've put you to so much trouble in connection with the reports. I've put them right. Tomorrow is Mr. Robertson's meeting for taking leave of Mr. Fife. I shall try to see you. Yours affectionately,'"*

"At the time you wrote the letter, on what terms of intimacy were you with Miss Pigot?" Mr. Trevelyan asks.

"Since I first met her, I've looked upon her as a mother," Babu Banerjee says.

"'As a mother,'" Mr. Trevelyan repeats. "Tell me, did you do any other work for Miss Pigot in the evening?"

"I arranged the monthly social gatherings. And meetings for the Preachers' Association which sometimes met at Miss Pigot's," Babu Banerjee says.

"Did you do anything else?"

"In 1881, I taught the entrance class for about an hour in the afternoon. I taught it on my way home."

"When did you become acquainted with Mr. Hastie?" Mr. Trevelyan asks.

"In 1879 I called on him to arrange an address we asked him to give at the Free Church on the occasion of our anniversary."

You don't mention your complete inaccuracy in thinking your church had a fiftieth anniversary. Ask him, Trevelyan. See what he says about that.

"Do you remember in July 1880 certain articles in the *Indian Christian Record?* They were called 'One Against Two Thousand,'" Mr. Trevelyan asks.

"I do," Babu Banerjee says.

"Mr. Hastie thought you wrote the articles."

"So I supposed from the letter he wrote me."

Justice Norris leans over the box. "Did you write the articles?"

Babu Banerjee looks confused. "Does Your Lordship think I'm free to disclose it?"

"Mr. Gasper is sure to ask you," Justice Norris says.

"If Your Lordship thinks I'm free to disclose it, I'll answer," Babu Banerjee says.

"You are quite free," Justice Norris says, leaning back.

"Yes, I wrote the articles."

I knew it all along. Banerjee gives me a defiant look.

"Babu Banerjee, do you know from anything Mr. Hastie said or wrote to you what his feelings toward you were?" Mr. Trevelyan asks.

"I know it from something he did. He wasn't on speaking terms with me afterwards. And when it was his turn to issue invitations to the Mission Conference, he didn't invite me," Babu Banerjee says.

"Were you invited previously?" Mr. Trevelyan asks.

"Always."

Justice Norris asks, "Had the conference met at Mr. Hastie's previously?"

"Yes. I was there. Mr. Hastie presided, and I gave the address."

"When was that?" Mr. Trevelyan asks.

"Before I wrote the articles. It was in 1879 or the beginning of 1880."

Rubbish. I didn't know your true leanings then.

"When you went to Miss Pigot's in the evening, who else was there?" Mr. Trevelyan asks.

Banerjee starts listing names. Reverend Mr. Thomson. Reverend Mr. James. Reverend Chuckerbutty. Miss Pigot had them all doing her work. Now Trevelyan asks about the teachers in the Upper School and the *zenana* teachers. *Must we go through every person he's ever met?* Finally, he gets to the point.

"Babu Banerjee, did you ever dine at Miss Pigot's?"

"I dined sometimes with the teachers in the dining room. It's not a room exactly. It was a veranda used as a dining room. I often dined there the year I taught and had to wait for my children. That was in 1881."

"Where did Miss Pigot dine?" Mr. Trevelyan asks.

"As a rule, she wasn't at the dinner table."

"Did you sometimes dine in the drawing room?"

"Yes. I usually dined alone there."

"Have you been at Miss Pigot's in the early morning?" Mr. Trevelyan asks.

"Twice. Once, on my way home from Sealdah Train Station. I'd been to Krishnaghur and a friend sent his daughter with me to be left at the school."

"How old was the daughter?" Mr. Trevelyan asks.

"About thirteen," Babu Banerjee says.

"What was the other occasion you went to Miss Pigot's in the morning?" Mr. Trevelyan asks.

"One time, there was to be an all-day gathering. I was there to make arrangements around eight or nine o'clock."

"Now, when you say you dined first with the teachers, and then afterwards, sometimes alone in the drawing room...why did you stop dining with the teachers?" Mr. Trevelyan asks.

Babu Banerjee shrugs. "Whenever Mrs. Ellis was at the dining table, I went to the table. Otherwise I didn't. I didn't enjoy dining with just the teachers."

"At the time you went to Miss Pigot's, do you remember a Mrs. Oliver?"

"I do."

"I call your attention to the evidence she gave in this case," Mr. Trevelyan says. "She said Miss Pigot sat on a cane lounge on the veranda, and on one occasion she saw Miss Pigot reclining, and you seated on the lounge with her. Mrs. Oliver said this occurred when the prayer bell rang. Do you remember that?"

"I don't remember the prayer bell. I remember sitting on the projecting part of the cane lounge."

"What kind of chair was this?" Justice Norris asks eagerly.

"A cane lounge sold in the bazar with supports for the arms," Babu Banerjee says.

Justice Norris smiles. "And a little round hole for the person to put a toddy glass."

"Yes, My Lord. There are projecting parts at the extremities."

Justice Norris makes a note, or perhaps he's drawing a toddy glass.

"Do you remember a teacher named Miss Gordon?" Mr. Trevelyan asks.

"Yes, but she was a matron, not a teacher."

"Miss Gordon testified she saw you and Miss Pigot standing in the center window of the drawing room with your arms around each other," Mr. Trevelyan says. "She went to the drawing room to get medicine and stopped short when she saw you. Do you remember anything of the kind?"

"Nothing like that ever happened," Babu Banerjee says. "We might have stood there, but never in that position."

Not the strongest denial I've ever heard.

"The suggestion is that you were on terms of improper intimacy with Miss Pigot. Is that true?"

The color drains from Banerjee's face. He looks at the floor. "No."

Justice Norris breaks in. "Babu Banerjee, the suggestion is that at that time and antecedent to that, and subsequently to that, practically the insinuation is, that you had sexual intercourse with Miss Pigot. Is there any truth in that?"

I want to stand up and applaud the judge.

"It is absolutely false," Babu Banerjee asserts in a clear voice.

"At any time?" Justice Norris asks.

"It is absolutely false for all time," Babu Banerjee says with a bit more force.

Mr. Trevelyan waits a moment before he resumes. "Miss Gordon says she saw you and Miss Pigot in close conversation, and that she saw you with Miss Pigot while she reclined on a couch. You sat on a chair opposite her with your elbows resting on the couch. Do you remember any such circumstance?"

"I don't remember the circumstance, but it's possible." Babu Banerjee drops his head.

"Miss Gordon also said she saw Miss Pigot resting full length on the lounge, and you at the foot with your arms across her feet. Do you remember that?" Mr. Trevelyan asks.

374

"I've sat on the projecting part of that lounge."

"The suggestion was something more than that," Justice Norris breaks in again. "The suggestion is that you were sitting while this lady reclined on the lounge, and that you were cuddling her feet or legs."

Hooray for the judge.

Babu Banerjee raises his head. His face is flushed. *I don't think he has the gumption to be angry, so he must be embarrassed.* "If that's the suggestion, it's entirely false."

"Miss Gordon spoke of another incident," Mr. Trevelyan says. "She saw a figure go upstairs about ten o'clock at night and go down just before dawn. She thought it was you."

"It wasn't," Babu Banerjee shakes his head.

"Do you remember seeing a disturbance at the mission one Sunday afternoon when you had been on a preaching mission?" Mr. Trevelyan asks.

"Yes," Babu Banerjee says.

"What time did you go to the orphanage that day?"

"I believe it was early afternoon."

"Were you alone?"

"I believe Mr. James was with me."

"Do you remember anything about Miss Pigot's slippers while you were there?" Mr. Trevelyan asks.

"Miss Pigot gave me a new pair of slippers," Babu Banerjee says. "I had a pair of boots on. Very tight. I felt uneasy, and she went out of the drawing room and returned with a new pair of slippers which I put on, and then took home."

Justice Norris looks up from his notes. "Miss Gordon testified there was a girl named Caroline Swaries in the Upper School, and some people called for her on a Sunday. They wrote something on a slate and the *durwan* took it to Miss Pigot. She claims she saw you come downstairs with your arm in only one sleeve of your coat. I ask you, were you ever in the house in an indecent costume or a costume that a man shouldn't wear in a woman's house?"

"Never, My Lord," Babu Banerjee says.

"Humpf."

"When did you leave that day?" Mr. Trevelyan asks.

"We went away about four o'clock."

"Do you remember about the sleeve?"

"I always wear an inner coat and an overcoat," Babu Banerjee says. "I may have taken off the overcoat, but I've never been there without the inner coat."

"Reverend Chuckerbutty testified he saw you in Miss Pigot's bedroom. Have you ever been in Miss Pigot's bedroom with her alone?" Mr. Trevelyan asks.

"No."

"Will you swear that?"

"I swear." Mr. Banerjee sends me another defiant look.

"Mr. Chuckerbutty said he saw you seated on a mat on the floor of Miss Pigot's drawing room wearing nothing but trousers and a shirt, while Miss Pigot lay on a sofa in the same room. According to Mr. Chuckerbutty, when he went in, Miss Pigot spoke to him in a faltering voice and asked him to call another day," Mr. Trevelyan says. "He said you stood when he entered. Did he surprise you, sitting on a mat on the floor?"

"I never sat on a mat."

"You never sat on a mat by Miss Pigot?"

"Beside or without, I never sat on a mat in that room or any other room in that house," Babu Banerjee says clearly.

"Mr. Chuckerbutty said Miss Pigot spoke in a faltering tone," Mr. Trevelyan says. "Was that because he caught you and Miss Pigot in an impropriety?"

"The suggestion is absolutely false." Babu Banerjee looks directly at Mr. Trevelyan who pauses before continuing.

"Mr. Chuckerbutty goes on to say he saw you seated with Miss Pigot lying on the sofa and you sitting near her leg—that he saw you both seated on the same sofa, and the two of you seated on a long cane chair with your body in contact with Miss Pigot's leg. Is this a true description of your position with Miss Pigot?"

"I've sometimes been on the same lounge, but I would never consciously allow any part of my body to touch hers," Babu Banerjee says quietly.

"The suggestion is that her position was an improper one," Mr. Trevelyan says.

"If that's the suggestion, it's absolutely false," Babu Banerjee says a bit more loudly.

Banerjee's denials gain emphasis with each statement. He may be convincing himself, but he doesn't convince me. He was at the orphanage every day doing Miss Pigot's work. No man does that to pass the time.

"Did you have any correspondence with Miss Pigot while she was in Scotland in 1882?"

"I wrote to her once."

Mr. Trevelyan picks up a document from the plaintiff's table. "I have the letter here. There is a scriptural text from Isaiah 49:15: *'Can a mother forget her child? Yea, she may forget.'* How did you come to write that?"

"I hadn't heard from her since she left Calcutta," Babu Banerjee says.

Justice Norris reaches for the letter. "I see the word 'may' is underlined. I suppose if the scripture is true, a mother may forget." Justice Norris shakes his head and gives the letter back to Mr. Trevelyan.

"Since you became acquainted with Miss Pigot, has there been any improper intimacy or improper intercourse between you whatever?"

"Absolutely not," Babu Banerjee asserts.

Justice Norris leans over the witness box to enhance the question. "Do you understand Mr. Trevelyan's question? Improper intimacy isn't just about conversation. Do you say there was no fondling or even touching—manipulations that ought not to go on between any two people: nothing which you, as a man, would have been ashamed of; nothing that you would not have your wife and daughters know?"

Miss Pigot loses what little color she had.

Babu Banerjee blanches. He opens and closes his mouth several times before he replies in an almost hysterical voice. "Nothing, My Lord. I think of Miss Pigot as my mother."

"Humpf. Babu Banerjee, you appear to be in some distress. We'll take a ten-minute recess before Mr. Gasper begins his cross-examination." Justice Norris bangs his gavel.

You did well enough, Banerjee, but wait until my man starts asking questions. You won't escape the truth of the matter. There's no doubt in my mind your intimacy with Miss Pigot was improper, and perhaps other things as well. We've got you dead to rights.

Mr. Carruthers helps Babu Banerjee from the witness box and takes him to a seat. His clerk passes Babu Banerjee a cool towel. Babu Banerjee keeps shaking his head. I decide to remain in the courtroom rather than relieve myself.

Miss Pigot keeps dabbing her eyes and seems to have the hiccups. She shakes her head when the clerk offers her his arm. She'd better collect herself in case she has to testify today.

Mr. Gasper looks like he's just won at the horseraces.

Justice Norris returns in exactly ten minutes, his wig somewhat askew. Perhaps he took it off to wipe the sweat from his head. "Are you ready to proceed, Mr. Gasper?"

Mr. Gasper bows. "Yes, Your Lordship."

We watch Babu Banerjee return to the witness box and steady himself. His eyes look like they're going to fall into the back of his head. Mr. Gasper strolls towards the witness box and sets his trap. "Babu Banerjee, how long have you been a *Vakil* in this Court?"

"I've been practicing since 1877," Babu Banerjee says calmly.

"Just so. I see you in court quite often. You must have a large practice." Mr. Gasper looks as if he's interested.

Babu Banerjee falls for the bait. "I do have a large criminal practice. I've probably cross-examined hundreds of witnesses."

"Then you'll know how witnesses are prepared for their testimony and how we barristers compile our questions in order to bring out the truth. May I take it that before you came into the box this morning you knew, generally speaking, all the allegations against you stated by witnesses under oath?"

"Yes," Babu Banerjee says. "I'm aware of what has been said about me."

Mr. Gasper moves to his first sequence, confirming Banerjee went up for his Entrance Examination to Calcutta University too early and signed a declaration that he was sixteen years of age when he was, in fact, only thirteen.

"Mr. Gasper," Justice Norris asks, "how did this defraud anyone?"

"I don't say it did, My Lord," Mr. Gasper says. "I only wanted to know. Babu Banerjee, are you Clerk of the Sessions in the Free Church?"

"Yes," Babu Banerjee says.

"I believe you oversee the minutes notating church business. Do you know whether minutes from any year are missing?" Mr. Gasper asks.

Babu Banerjee glances at Mr. Trevelyan. "There's a certain book I can't get ahold of."

"Did you hear there was anything about you in that book?"

"Yes," Babu Banerjee says reluctantly.

You broke through his reserve. Well done.

"Do you know a person named Obhoy Dutt?" Mr. Gasper asks.

"I did," Babu Banerjee says.

"What religion did he follow?"

"He was a Christian when I knew him, and a member of the same church as myself" Babu Banerjee says. "He was a student when I knew him."

"Was it ever alleged that you were guilty of immorality with his wife?"

The trap snaps.

Babu Banerjee looks surprised. "Not to my knowledge."

"Have you ever slept in the same room with Obhoy Dutt's wife?"

"I've been in the same room."

"On the same bed?"

"If I say on the same bed, it wouldn't describe the actual circumstance," Babu Banerjee says. "It was on the same bedding, on the same carpet. There was a bed on the floor."

Mr. Gasper's voice takes on an accusing tone. "As a matter of fact, weren't you brought up before the Kirk Sessions in connection with a matter concerning Obhoy's wife?"

"I was." Babu Banerjee drops his head.

"Was there a suggestion you were guilty of immorality?" Mr. Gasper asks.

"No suggestion was made in my presence."

"Do you know the gentleman seated over there, The Reverend Lal Behary Dey?" Mr. Gasper gestures towards the spectators' gallery. "Wasn't he the Moderator who reprimanded you?"

Banerjee looks at a man wearing a minister's collar. The man nods. "Reverend Dey admonished me."

"What were you admonished for?"

"He said I was too familiar with the Dutt family and advised I shouldn't be so familiar."

"Do you consider admonishment merely to mean you were advised?" Mr. Gasper asks.

"I understood they didn't approve," Babu Banerjee says. "They thought the situation might lead to evil and advised me not to be so familiar with that family."

I lean back in my chair and glance at Miss Pigot. Her dark eyes look larger against her pinched white face. Her hair is dark with sweat.

With the judge primed in this pattern of immorality, Mr. Gasper moves to the heart of the matter and begins questioning Banerjee about his relations with Miss Pigot—the friendship, the teaching, the dining, his children, and his activities at the orphanage.

"Have you frequently sat on a cane lounge with Miss Pigot?" Mr. Gasper asks.

"On very few occasions," Babu Banerjee says. "When I was in a hurry to come away, and another chair wasn't sent for. As a rule, I didn't sit on the lounge."

Mr. Gasper won't be deflected. "How often?"

"Twice, thrice, perhaps four times."

"Did you try not to allow any portion of your body to be in contact with hers?"

"I can't recollect. I made no special effort," Babu Banerjee says.

Justice Norris shakes his head and makes another note. He has a sheaf of them now, the ink running on the damp paper.

Mr. Gasper moves on to proper clothing when ladies are present. "Is it considered wrong for a native gentleman to be in the drawing room wearing only his shirt and trousers?"

"I've seen people dress this way. I personally consider it indecent and improper," Babu Banerjee says.

"Is there any harm for a son to be in his shirt and trousers before his mother?" Mr. Gasper asks. "Any harm in you wearing shirt and trousers before Miss Pigot?"

"No harm, but I wouldn't do it," Babu Banerjee says.

"Have you ever heard you were talked about with regard to Miss Pigot?"

"Never until this case."

"How often have you seen Miss Pigot since her return from Scotland?"

"Before this case, perhaps three or four times. My friends advised me not to see her."

"Have you been in Miss Pigot's bathroom?" Mr. Gasper asks.

"Perhaps half a dozen times."

"And in her bedroom?"

"At least that many times."

"Was she present?"

"Not always."

"Have you called when Miss Pigot was ill and confined to her bed?" Mr. Gasper asks.

"I was there once," Babu Banerjee says.

"Was she reclining against anything?" Mr. Gasper asks.

"Yes. She reclined on her pillows and taught her class."

"How long did you stay in the room?"

"Perhaps five minutes until the class finished," Babu Banerjee says.

"Did you make any effort to avoid being alone in the bedroom with Miss Pigot?"

"No. I had no occasion to avoid it," Babu Banerjee says. "I've been to the house, and if she was in the bedroom, the *durwan* took a message, and she always came out."

"Did anyone tell you not to go to 125 Bow Bazar?" Mr. Gasper asks.

"I had a letter from Mr. Hastie," Babu Banerjee says.

"Do you know why you had to stop doing work in the orphanage?"

"I heard there was correspondence with the home authority," Babu Banerjee says. "But I'm sure they wouldn't interfere with Miss Pigot's private friendship."

"Then why—"

Mr. Trevelyan interrupts. "Does Your Lordship think this is evidence?"

"I don't think it is," Justice Norris says. "But if I stop Mr. Gasper every time he goes off topic it will prolong the trial."

Mr. Gasper allows himself a slight smirk. "Babu Banerjee, did you know Mr. Gillan told Miss Pigot you shouldn't go to the orphanage?" Mr. Gasper asks.

"I understand he didn't want me at the dinners," Babu Banerjee says.

"Don't you think it would've been better if this intimacy between you and Miss Pigot ceased?"

"No, I thought Miss Pigot persecuted. She was alone without friends and I saw no reason why I should withhold my company and assistance."

"How generous. Tell me, has Miss Pigot ever put her arm on you?"

"Never." Babu Banerjee looks slightly horrified.

"Not on your shoulders?"

"She might have, to draw my attention to something," Babu Banerjee says.

"Did she put her hand on your shoulders?" Mr. Gasper asks.

"I think so. At a social meeting, she put her finger or fingers on my shoulder."

Instead of pursuing the issue, Gasper returns to the subject of Banerjee's many meetings. We adjourn for *tiffin*. I do wish Gasper would get to the drawing room scene and be done with it.

2:00 Wednesday Afternoon, 12 September 1883

When we resume, Mr. Gasper assumes a friendly manner. "Babu Banerjee, I'm puzzled. Are you aware the orphanage is connected with the Church of Scotland?" Mr. Gasper asks.

"Yes."

"But you're a member of the Free Church, correct?"

"Yes, I am."

"Isn't there a first-rate girls' school connected with the Free Church?"

"There is now, but not when I sent my children to the Upper Christian School," Babu Banerjee says.

"I see. I wonder, did you buy the boots you said were too tight?"

"No. They were a gift from my wife."

"When did you first wear them?"

"I wore them several months, and then the weather changed and I didn't use them for some time before I put them on again," Babu Banerjee says. "The leather was cracked and hard."

"That day when you ran downstairs with the slippers on your feet, where did you come from?"

"The bedroom."

Mr. Gasper gets to his point at last. "Do native gentlemen sit on the floor?"

"Yes, often."

"I understand not every native establishment has chairs."

"No," Babu Banerjee agrees.

"Would it be improper or derogatory to sit on the floor?" Mr. Gasper asks.

"If there are chairs and sofas, it would be," Babu Banerjee says.

Mr. Gasper lets the answer hang in the air. "I have no further questions for this witness."

Wait. You didn't ask about the drawing room with Miss Pigot in only shirt and trousers. You didn't ask if they had their arms around each other. You've left things hanging. What's wrong with you?

Babu Banerjee starts to step out of the witness box

Mr. Trevelyan rises. "I have a question, My Lord."

Babu Banerjee turns back into the box with a sullen expression.

"Babu Banerjee, how did you manage to sleep with Obhoy Churn and his wife?

"I paid them a visit one morning, took a fever that night and had a fit. Fearing that I might have another fit, Obhoy Babu proposed that he wouldn't sleep. He and his wife took me into their room."

385

"Did you continue your friendship with Obhoy Babu?" Mr. Trevelyan asks.

"Up until he died."

"What became of his wife?" Mr. Trevelyan asks.

"She and the children came to me and are still living with us," Babu Banerjee says. "The elder girl is the one I describe as my niece."

"Thank you, My Lord. No further questions," Mr. Trevelyan says.

Babu Banerjee limps out of the witness box and through to the door out of the courtroom. He and Miss Pigot don't look at each other.

Justice Norris looks at the witness list. "Call your next witness, Mr. Trevelyan. I believe it's Miss Pigot."

Chapter 21
"Did You Employ Immoral Agents?"

Wednesday Afternoon, 12 September 1883
Mary Pigot

I take special care this morning: polish my boots, brush my hair until it crackles before putting it up. My dress is pressed and my fichu white. Today, I testify. There's no way around it, so I must go through it. Mr. Gasper will find nothing to criticize. No reason to think I'm faint or unsure. I shall stand firm...I hope.

I speak to Mr. Trevelyan before court begins. He tells me to be brave and trust him. He says I must speak out clearly and without hesitation. Unfortunately, I'm not the first witness. First, Kali Churn testifies strongly on my and his own behalf. But by the time Mr. Gasper is through with him, Kali Churn's testimony doesn't ring true. It's too desperate. As Kali Churn leaves the stand, my courage seeps away.

Mr. Trevelyan turns away from the judge and calls me forward. The distance between my chair and the witness box seems like a great chasm. The *punkah* fan stirs up the dust overhead. I walk past Mr. Hastie's table and glance at him. He looks drained, which is odd, because it seems to me he's winning the case. I reach the witness box and walk deliberately behind the rail. I focus my eyes on Mr. Trevelyan and don't think about anything except answering his questions.

Mr. Trevelyan stands before me, gives me an encouraging look and asks me my name.

"Mary Pigot," I say. My voice echoes in the now silent room.

"State the details of your birth."

"I was born on the sixth of September 1837. My father was Julius Pigot, an indigo planter by profession and later, a hotelier. My mother's name was Desirée Casubon."

Mr. Trevelyan reaches into his jacket pocket, withdraws a document and unfolds it. "My Lord, I tender Mr. and Mrs. Pigot's marriage certificate." He hands the fragile paper to the clerk who passes it to Justice Norris. I watch the judge read the document that proves my legal birth.

Mr. Gasper rises to object. His pettiness knows no bounds. "If a parent is alive, it's for he or she to come forward to say whether there was a marriage," Mr. Gasper says.

I don't wait for Mr. Trevelyan. "My father is dead," I say flatly. "My mother lives at Dacca and is too frail to make the journey."

Justice Norris looks at me over his spectacles. "I'll allow the certificate."

"My Lord, I also enter Miss Pigot's baptismal certificate into evidence," Mr. Trevelyan says. "The Reverend Mr. Bray of St. John's Church signed it."

"Objection," Mr. Gasper says. "It has no relevance."

"I'll allow it," Justice Norris rules. "It clarifies the question of which church claims Miss Pigot as a member and her father's standing with that church."

Mr. Trevelyan nods so I know he's changing the topic. "When did you make Mr. Hastie's acquaintance?"

I think back. "I met Mr. Hastie about two days after his arrival and invited him to breakfast to see the Mohammedan procession pass our house," I say. "The next time I saw him, he was ill with cholera."

"Did you nurse him?" Mr. Trevelyan asks.

"I nursed him for four nights."

"Did you see Mr. Wilson there?"

"I saw him late in the afternoon the first day I was there."

"How long did Mr. Wilson remain?" Mr. Trevelyan asks.

"He was there the entire time I was."

Mr. Trevelyan walks near Mr. Hastie's seat and asks me "Is it a fact that in Mr. Hastie's sickroom you continually leaned and lolled against Mr. Wilson?"

As many times as I've gone over this claim, it never fails to shock me. "Never," I say firmly.

"Did you do so anywhere else?" Mr. Trevelyan asks.

"Never." I shake my head.

"Did you laugh with him?"

"It's hardly possible I would laugh in a sickroom," I say, "especially considering the seriousness of Mr. Hastie's illness."

"Were you rude or bold to Mr. Wilson? Did you do anything unladylike?"

"No," I pronounce clearly.

"Did you put your hand on Mr. Wilson's thigh?" Mr. Trevelyan asks.

I feel my cheeks warm. "No."

"Have you ever done so?"

"Never."

Mr. Trevelyan nods. "Did you meet Mr. Hastie at a dinner at Mr. Steele's?"

"Yes," I say calmly.

"Who was at the dinner party?" Mr. Trevelyan asks.

"Mr. Hastie, Mr. Wilson, Mr. Steele, and myself."

"What did you do after dinner?" Mr. Trevelyan asks.

"I went into the veranda to look at some furniture Mr. Steele offered to lend me. Then I came back into the drawing room."

"What did you do there?" Mr. Trevelyan asks.

"I sat for a little while," I say. "We played cards and talked. I told Mr. Steele I was tired and reclined on the sofa."

"Was there anything indelicate in the way you reclined on the sofa?" Mr. Trevelyan asks.

"No. It was a reclining sofa open on one end and with a back support on the other."

"Whose carriage did you leave in that evening?" Mr. Trevelyan asks.

"The mission *gharry*," I say.

"Did anyone go with you?"

"I took Mr. Wilson to Scottish College in Cornwallis Square, and then went home." I remember that night. Mr. Wilson told me I had nothing to fear from Mr. Hastie. He couldn't have been more wrong.

"Do you remember having *tiffin* at Barrackpore Park?"

"Yes." Amazing how such a harmless picnic could become so problematic.

"Who sat next to you?" Mr. Trevelyan asks.

"Mr. Hastie."

"Did you recline against Mr. Wilson?" Mr. Trevelyan asks.

"No. He was at the other side of the park," I say.

"Did Mr. Wilson sit near you at all that day?" Mr. Trevelyan asks.

"Objection," Mr. Gasper says. "Irrelevant."

Justice Norris turns to look at Mr. Gasper. I fall silent.

"I see nothing irregular," Justice Norris says. "Carry on, Mr. Trevelyan."

"Did you sit down next to Mr. Wilson that day?" Mr. Trevelyan asks.

"Yes."

"Do you remember sitting on the mat?"

"Before *tiffin*."

"Was your conduct improper that day?"

"No."

"Was your head ever in contact with Mr. Wilson's shoulder?"

"No."

"How did you sit on the mat?" Mr. Trevelyan asks.

"We all sat back-to-back," I say.

"Against whose back did you sit?" Mr. Trevelyan asks.

"Mr. Wilson's."

"How did Mr. Hastie sit?" Mr. Trevelyan asks.

"He leant against my shoulder."

Mr. Trevelyan nods. Another change of topic. "Do you know Mrs. Monomohini Wheeler, the Inspectress of Schools?"

"Yes."

"Do you remember a conversation with her about a teacher who was dismissed?"

"I don't."

Mr. Trevelyan frowns. Did I give the wrong answer? Mr. Trevelyan asks if Mrs. Wheeler told me anything about a *box-wallah* and one of the teachers. A peddler? Why would I remember that?

"No," I answer.

Mr. Trevelyan raises his eyebrows and looks directly at me. "Do you remember her telling you the upper part of the teacher's body was so insufficiently covered it was indecent?"

"No." I'm doing something wrong. I can tell Mr. Trevelyan is cross with me but I don't know why. My heart pounds.

"How do your native teachers dress?" Mr. Trevelyan asks.

"They wear an undergarment and a white sari with a dark blue border," I say.

Mr. Trevelyan gives me a long look and then nods. "Do you remember a girl named Bidu at your school?" Mr. Trevelyan asks.

I remember her testimony. She said I treated her well. "Yes."

"Did you chastise her?" Mr. Trevelyan asks.

I hated having to punish her, but I had to set an example. "Bidu stole a pair of gold bracelets," I begin.

Mr. Trevelyan asks if the bracelets were the only things missing.

"No. We had constant thefts."

"How did you chastise Bidu?" Mr. Trevelyan asks.

"I carefully caned her on the back. I wanted to set an example for the others, but I didn't want to cause her unnecessary harm."

"Did you punish her in any other way?" Mr. Trevelyan asks.

"I isolated her. We had so many thefts. Bidu stole a dress belonging to another girl. Other girls were more fearless. Bidu didn't confess to—"

Mr. Gasper interrupts from the defense table. "This is a very long story," he comments to no one in particular.

"It is a long story," I say, holding my ground. My voice rises. "I had to isolate Bidu, because she wouldn't confess what she did with the bracelets." I glare at Mr. Gasper's now blank face.

Mr. Trevelyan clears his throat. "That will do, Miss Pigot, about Bidu." He pauses while I collect myself. "Do you remember a girl called Joboni? Did you chastise her, Miss Pigot?"

Joboni? "I chastised some children for quarreling and throwing away food," I say. "I don't doubt Joboni was one of them."

"How did you chastise her?"

"My usual method is a hard smack on the hand," I say.

"Could you have chastised her elsewhere? Might you strike her face or her head?" Mr. Trevelyan asks.

"No," I say. "Only the hand."

Mr. Trevelyan consults his notes and asks if I know a person named Eliza Mukherjee.

"She was at my school for a short time," I say. "I dismissed her in 1871 under unfavorable circumstances. I engaged her on the condition she wouldn't leave the orphanage without permission. She broke the rule."

"She didn't come back in 1875 or 1876?"

"By no means. My rules are clear and I don't allow any deviation." I think a minute. "I had her children in the orphanage."

"Do you know anyone living on Amherst Street?" Mr. Trevelyan asks.

"I know Dr. Kumar Chunder Dey. I used to know him very well," I say. "I remember his sitting room."

"When you were in his sitting room, what did you generally do? Did you sit or lie down there?"

"No, never." How can he make such an implication? I imagine the judge's ears picking up.

"Is there any truth to Mrs. Mukherjee's evidence about your visit to this house on Amherst Street?" Mr. Trevelyan asks.

"Not the slightest." Warm flush creeps up my neck and onto my face.

"How was the room furnished when you used to visit?" Mr. Trevelyan asks.

Mr. Gasper interrupts. "What room is this?" he asks.

"The sitting room," Justice Norris snaps. "Pay attention."

I continue. "The room has a marble table and three sofas."

"In European fashion?" Justice Norris asks.

"Quite."

"Not with a *tuktaposh* or cushioned couch?" Mr. Trevelyan asks.

"Not that I saw." A vision of the room appears in my head. The European sofas with carved mahogany trim and velvet upholstery stand out in my memory.

"Did you ever go this house on Amherst Street with Mrs. Palmer?" Mr. Trevelyan asks.

"I really don't know what she was talking about. I have no memory of going there with her."

Mr. Trevelyan frowns. "You heard what Mrs. Palmer said with reference to a *babu* lying on a couch and you sitting by him," Mr. Trevelyan says. "Was there any truth to her observations?"

"I may have sat on a bed in the house with a *babu* when his whole family was there, but alone with a *babu* would be impossible," I say. "Especially in that house, because the rooms opened into one another, and the family was there."

"Was there any impropriety between you and Dr. Dey?" Mr. Trevelyan asks.

"Most solemnly no," I say clearly.

"I suppose you know what Mr. Fish said regarding you and Mr. Wilson. Is there any truth to his statement?"

The question stops me cold. For a moment I can't think. I grip the rail.

"Mr. Fish's statement is a great falsehood," I say firmly.

"Miss Pigot, you had a bedroom in the mission," Mr. Trevelyan says.

"Yes, it was a study and bedroom combined," I say.

"Has Mr. Wilson been in that room?" Mr. Trevelyan asks.

"Several times."

"On what sort of occasions has he been in that room, and at what hour?"

"When he comes to examine the school and needs to wash his hands before *tiffin*, and on other occasions," I say.

"Have you been alone in your bedroom with Mr. Wilson?"

My heart skips a beat. "I'm not aware of ever being alone with Mr. Wilson." I think a minute. "It's possible I might have been for two or three minutes when one person has gone out and another come in, but never longer than that."

"What is the latest he's been in your bedroom?" Mr. Trevelyan asks.

"Before sundown."

Justice Norris leans over his desk like a large red bird. "You say Mr. Wilson was never been in your bedroom later than sundown?" Justice Norris asks.

"Not with me," I say. "I may have been with a large number there, and he amongst them."

"Besides being your sleeping room, what was the room used for?" Mr. Trevelyan asks.

"I used it for every purpose. It was the first chamber. I had classes in it, and the lady teachers and delicate orphans slept in it," I say. "When there were entertainments, I had it spread with Bengali sweetmeats."

"Did you ever brush Mr. Wilson's hair either in your bedroom at ten or eleven o'clock at night, or in any other place?" Mr. Trevelyan asks.

"What a ridiculous notion!" Mr. Trevelyan sends me a warning look. "No, never at any time, or at any place, or on any day of my life."

"Do you have friends among seafaring men?" Mr. Trevelyan asks.

"I knew the Seamen's Chaplain, the Reverend Mr. Alcocks. He and Mrs. Alcocks lived for several months with me," I say. "During that time, I allowed them to invite a few of their pious officers and captains."

"Did you get on familiar terms with them?" Mr. Trevelyan asks.

"No."

"Did they come to your drawing room?" Mr. Trevelyan asks.

"No. They had no reason to be there."

"Did you bend over them?" Mr. Trevelyan asks.

"No."

"You heard Miss Humphrey's statement about the sea captain in your drawing room," Mr. Trevelyan says. "Was it true?"

I shake my head vehemently. "No."

"Did you receive any ship captain in your bedroom while you were in bed?" Mr. Trevelyan asks.

"No, I did not." Outrage is starting to replace my lack of confidence. I feel stronger with each answer.

Mr. Trevelyan looks at me intently. "Do you know Reverend Mr. Bomwetsch?"

"Yes."

"Did you receive him and a sea captain in your bedroom while you were lying in bed?" Mr. Trevelyan asks.

"No," I say. "Mr. Bomwetsch was a particular friend of mine, but I have no recollection of his coming under those circumstances."

"Has there been any impropriety of any kind between you and Mr. Wilson?" Mr. Trevelyan asks.

"No." How many times must I say it?

"Do you remember the day the lists were made out for prize giving? Who was there that day?"

"Nitya Gopal Mukherjee came first, then Mr. Wetherill. Mr. Wilson and Mr. Fish came afterwards."

"Where did you receive them?"

"I usually received guests in the drawing room. Then, we went to the veranda."

"Is there a table there, Miss Pigot?"

"Yes, a round table. It's actually a telescopic table, but I keep it round."

"Did everyone stay together? Who went away first?"

"Mr. Wetherill went somewhat early. The other three remained and went away together."

"How long did they remain after Mr. Wetherill left?"

My mind goes blank. "I don't remember."

"You went home in May," Mr. Trevelyan says. "Did you see Mr. Fish in the interval between this occasion and your departure?"

"He came to my house. He dined about three times and called at other times."

"Do you remember going to see Mr. Wilson in 1882?" Mr. Trevelyan asks.

"I went occasionally."

"Did you go alone?"

"I usually went with one or two native teachers."

"And sometimes alone?"

"Possibly." I'm not sure what Mr. Trevelyan wants.

"Did you get out of your *gharry*?" Mr. Trevelyan asks.

"Very seldom," I say. "I usually sent for Mr. Wilson. He came downstairs and I saw him at the carriage door."

"On what occasions did you get out of the *gharry*, Miss Pigot?"

"Twice, once when I went with Reverend James Thomson," I say. "Reverend Thomson went to remove his things, and I saw Mr. Wilson once...so twice."

"What did you see Mr. Wilson about?" Mr. Trevelyan asks.

"He objected to my leaving Calcutta on a particular day," I say. "I went to speak to him about my passage."

"Besides the passage, was there anything else?" Mr. Trevelyan gives me a pointed look.

I concentrate until I remember. "I ran up to give him the class books I brought," I say. "And I wanted to see his rooms, so I could tell his wife I'd come fresh from them and what the room was like. I wasn't there five minutes."

Bang. Justice Norris hits his gavel on the dais. "We'll take a fifteen-minute recess."

Everyone stands.

Mr. Trevelyan escorts me to our table, so I can sit. My knees are stiff from standing. I ask if my answers are what he wants me to say. He draws himself up.

"Miss Pigot," he says, "it isn't a matter of what I want you to say. You must tell the truth."

"I am," I assure him. "Will it take much longer? It's exhausting trying to remember so many details."

"You must steel yourself. We have a long day ahead," Mr. Trevelyan says. "And you must listen carefully to the questions so I don't have to repeat myself."

I promise to do my best. Fifteen minutes passes quickly. The judge is in his seat, and I'm back in the box.

"Do you know Kali Churn Banerjee?" Mr. Trevelyan asks.

"I've known him seventeen or eighteen years. I met him when I lived with Dr. and Mrs. Roberts at Bethune School."

"Did you see him continually?" Mr. Trevelyan asks.

"Yes, until I took a position at Calcutta Girls' School."

"When did you next see him?"

"Two or three years after I joined the Scotch Mission," I say. "It was on Circular Road then, not Bow Bazar."

"Did you become intimate with him?" Mr. Trevelyan asks.

"I resumed the old friendship. When we began to have social gatherings with native Christians, I saw him frequently."

"Who introduced those social gatherings?"

"It was done at the suggestion of Miss Bernard of Pune," I say. "A great many missionaries and clergy attended."

"And this brought Babu Banerjee to your house more frequently?" Mr. Trevelyan asks.

"I had a committee for social gatherings, and he was a member."

"Did he come for any other purpose?"

I think a minute. "When I had the Upper School, he taught for me. I consulted him on every detail of the school and took his advice on social questions. He also came to take his children home."

"Anything else, as far as you remember?" Mr. Trevelyan asks.

What else could there be? "Will you put it directly?" I ask. "I'm not here to deny anything."

"Did Babu Banerjee call on his way to any meetings?" Mr. Trevelyan asks, looking slightly annoyed.

I stand for a minute trying to figure out the question. "The manner of his coming was this," I eventually say. "He came from the Court for his children, and when he had a meeting later on, he stayed. That was our arrangement."

"What was the latest hour he was in your house, alone or with company?" Mr. Trevelyan asks.

"I suppose about eleven was the latest," I say. "That was at the Native Conference Feast."

"And the latest when he was alone?"

"Those were the occasions when he had meetings. I suppose about eight o'clock."

"Were you ever alone with him in your bedroom?" Mr. Trevelyan asks.

"Never at any time." I shake my head.

"Did he go into your bedroom?" Mr. Trevelyan asks.

"Yes. Sometimes when he had meetings, he wished to wash his hands before he went. And also when the Bengali sweetmeats were there, or on other social occasions. I don't remember anything else."

"How did he dress when he came to your house?" Mr. Trevelyan asks.

"I suppose in a *chupa*, which is a sort of inner jacket. And he wore a long overcoat."

"Did you ever see him in only shirt and trousers?"

"No, he would never be so informal. I never saw him dressed that way," I say, "not in my house or anywhere else."

"Do you remember Reverend Chuckerbutty coming into the drawing room when you and Kali Churn Banerjee were there?" Mr. Trevelyan asks.

"Yes. He frequently arrived while we were there."

"Do you remember any particular occasion?"

"Stop being so timid, Mr. Trevelyan," Justice Norris breaks in. "Miss Pigot, do you remember a specific occasion on which Kali Churn Banerjee sat on a mat in your drawing room near your feet with only shirt and trousers on? And Chuckerbutty coming in, and Kali Churn Banerjee getting up and appearing surprised at being disturbed with you, or anything of that sort?"

I turn to look up at the judge. "No," I say clearly. "I never saw Kali Churn sitting on the floor under circumstances like that."

"Did Mr. Chuckerbutty leave you and Kali Churn Banerjee alone as late as he stated?" Mr. Trevelyan asks.

"He never stayed that late himself," I say. "He always went away before the teachers had their dinner."

"You heard what Mr. Chuckerbutty said about Babu Banerjee speaking to you in your bedroom. Was there any truth in that?" Mr. Trevelyan asks.

"He might have spoken to me in the bedroom along with other people, but never alone."

"Did you speak to Mr. Chuckerbutty in a faltering and trembling voice, and say 'come another day'?"

"I never speak to anyone in a faltering voice."

"Miss Pigot," Justice Norris breaks in again. "Do you remember the incident when Mr. Chuckerbutty said you asked him to come see you, and he came and went upstairs. And you told him in a faltering tone that you couldn't speak to him on that occasion?"

I object to the inference that I'm weak. "I consider that the most extraordinary invention I've ever heard. There's not the slightest truth in it."

"Humpf."

"Did Babu Banerjee use your slippers?" Mr. Trevelyan asks.

"I gave him a new pair of slippers because he told me he had to take his shoes off and preach in his stockings. His boots were too tight. I had a large pair of slippers someone gave me. I often have those sorts of things and then give them away."

"Was anyone else present then?" Mr. Trevelyan asks.

"Mr. James, the Baptist missionary," I say.

Justice Norris leans over the box. "Why was Babu Kali Churn Banerjee in your bedroom that day?"

Why so much focus on my bedroom? I wasn't in it. "After *tiffin*, I told them to go and wash their hands, and rest a few minutes before they went on their next preaching expedition."

"Why did Babu Banerjee take meals at your house?" Mr. Trevelyan asks.

"It was when he had meetings."

"Where did he take his meals?"

"For a long time, he took them with the teachers. When Mrs. Ellis began going to the *zenanas*, his dinner was sometimes brought into the drawing room, and sometimes to the veranda."

"How long did this last?" Mr. Trevelyan asks.

"When he first began to help me, it was almost every day. But as his legal practice increased, his visits became fewer."

"Do you remember a time when Babu Banerjee sat at your feet on a lounge with his arms across your feet?"

"I can't identify any occasion," I say. "He might have reached his arms to the other side without touching my feet. I've allowed him, occasionally when a chair wasn't to hand, to sit at the foot of the lounge. I gave the seat to my teachers or any particular friends. I put my feet aside and left room to sit."

"Has there ever been any impropriety of any description at all between you and Babu Kali Churn Banerjee?"

I look Mr. Trevelyan directly in the eye. "Never at any time. I considered Kali Churn like a son in all my connections."

"You heard Mr. Hastie's charge regarding Babu Banerjee. Is there the smallest truth in it?"

"It is the cruelest imputation any man could have made." I take a deep breath.

"When Babu Kali Churn Banerjee came, were the doors ever closed to the room he was in?"

"The doors are never closed in that house," I explain. "In my two rooms, the doors were open at all times. During the day the drawing room was partly closed during the Hot Weather, but there was always a door open. There's a great deal of dust on the road, but after four o'clock, everything was thrown open."

"Is it a fact that when you and Mr. Wilson were in that room, the door wasn't kept open outside?" Mr. Trevelyan asks.

"Certainly not."

"The suggestion is that the *durwan* was placed outside to prevent you from being surprised," Justice Norris explains.

"That is the most absurd statement of all," I tell the judge.

"Do you remember the occasion when the *durwan* brought up Mr. Hastie, and Mr. Hastie found you and Mr. Wilson there?"

"Yes. It was soon after Mr. Hastie arrived."

"Was anyone else there?"

"Mrs. Tremearne was there. I was ill, lying on a couch, and Mr. Wilson sat on a chair. The doors were open."

"Did the *durwan* need to knock twice?"

"He didn't need to knock at all."

The room is very still with just the sounds of the *punkah* fan and the judge slapping at mosquitos. I take a handkerchief out of my sleeve and dab the perspiration off my face. Mr. Trevelyan watches me pull my sleeve back down and resumes his questions.

"It's been suggested you employed immoral agents. Is that true?" Mr. Trevelyan asks.

What's he talking about? "Please explain."

"Did you employ immoral agents?" Mr. Trevelyan asks.

What does he mean by immoral agents? I take a guess. "Do you mean did I employ women who led immoral lives?"

"Yes."

"On no account."

"Is there any truth to such a suggestion?"

"It's the grossest falsehood."

"Do remember resigning from the Female Mission in 1879?" Mr. Trevelyan asks.

"Yes."

"Did Mr. Hastie come visit you then?"

"Yes."

"What was his manner?"

"I thought him overbearing," I say. "He told me he represented the church and set forth great claims."

"Did you ever put your arms around Kali Churn Banerjee?" Mr. Trevelyan asks.

I wasn't expecting that question. I thought you wanted to know about Mr. Hastie.

Judge Norris restates the question. "Did you ever stand facing a window with your arms round Babu Banerjee's waist, or his arms round your waist?"

I don't know how to answer. "No," I finally say. "I may have touched his shoulder as I would a young person, but he never attempted to take any liberties with me. He treated me with great respect."

"Has there been anything you've ever done that warrants the imputations made against your character?"

"No, never."

"No further questions at this time, My Lord," Mr. Trevelyan says and leaves me standing as he walks back to his chair.

"Mr. Gasper," Judge Norris nods, "I'm sure you have something to say.

Chapter 22
"I Refuse To Be The Goat"

Wednesday Afternoon, 12 September 1883
Mary Pigot

Mr. Gasper takes his time getting up. He bows to the judge, taps his papers, and strolls to the witness box. I feel like a goat that's been tied to attract the tiger. The goat bleats mournfully, but no one takes any notice. I pull myself up. I refuse to be the goat.

Mr. Gasper smiles at me and speaks slowly as if he's still thinking about his question. "Miss Pigot, in your judgment, have you ill-treated any girl?"

"I've only done what is necessary to maintain order and discipline."

"Do you consider it ill-treatment to beat a girl who isn't in her right mind?"

"It depends on the occasion," I say. "If she were taking her life, I would use all necessary means to prevent her."

"So you think under certain circumstances a girl who isn't in her right mind should be beaten," Mr. Gasper presses me.

I know it's a trap, but I can't avoid it. "Yes, depending on the circumstances."

"Did you beat a girl named Hester?" Mr. Gasper asks.

Hester. I think back to the child with the vacant eyes. "Yes, I punished her once that I remember."

"Did you beat her, because she asked for horse feed?"

I shake my head. "I don't remember beating her for that."

"Then why did you beat her?"

"She threw herself into a water tank on Circular Road. She could have drowned."

"Was the child tied up after that?" Mr. Gasper asks.

"Not by me."

"Will you swear it wasn't done?" Mr. Gasper asks.

"I'll swear I'm not aware it happened," I say. "Hester was a difficult child. She got ill because she constantly stole horse feed and ate it. I thought she'd outwitted me, so I made a childish scene of it. I told her if she ate horse feed again, I would treat her like a horse, because I couldn't keep her with the other children. But I never tied her up."

"Did you beat Joboni anywhere but on the hand?" Mr. Gasper asks.

"I always beat on the hand."

"Then, it's your practice to cane the girls for faults," Mr. Gasper says.

"No. Very seldom."

Mr. Gasper's eyes glitter. "How often have you done it?"

"Only on serious occasions. I can't remember how often."

Mr. Gasper places himself in front of me. "In your thirteen years as superintendent, how often have you beaten the girls?"

"I can't remember." My voice begins to crack.

"Miss Pigot, did you beat Joboni on any part of her body except the hands?"

"It wasn't my practice to strike anywhere but the hand." I stop. "I may have given her a cut on the back."

"Might you have given her a cut on the face?" Mr. Gasper asks.

"Not consciously," I say. "I'd never strike a child on the face."

"You said you don't consider Bidu's caning severe," Mr. Gasper says.

"I tried to make it appear severe."

"Was the flesh cut open?"

"No."

"Will you swear to that?"

"I do swear. Most vehemently." I speak firmly.

"The child herself said that, Mr. Gasper," Justice Norris says.

"Do you remember any other girls you've beaten?" Mr. Gasper asks.

That's a low question. "I couldn't identify the girls," I say.

"How long did you confine Bidu?"

He's made me feel so bad about the punishments I can't think. "I don't understand what you mean by confinement."

"How long did you isolate her?" Mr. Gasper asks.

"She was in my room most of the time, and for two days in the loft."

"How long did you confine her after the beating?" Mr. Gasper asks.

"She was never confined absolutely."

"Well, without absolutely. How long was she confined?"

"About a fortnight in my room."

"After that, how long did you isolate her elsewhere?"

"I put no great restrictions on her."

Mr. Gasper gives me a look of exasperation. "Miss Pigot," he says. "Are you saying you don't know Bidu was isolated after she left your room?"

Mr. Gasper asks me so many questions about staff and students, I can't keep them straight. He wants to know if the matron Mrs. Balthazar was respectable. She was in the school. Do I remember punishing Regina Shircore by tying her hands for two hours? I have no idea what he's talking about. And do I remember locking Julia Twiddle and Emily

Funnel in the bathroom? That's highly likely. Emily was a naughty girl. But I never kept a girl locked up all night away from her bed.

Then he wants to know why I resigned from Calcutta Girls' School. "Did you resign because you were told if you didn't resign, you'd be dismissed?"

"No, that is a great untruth," I say with what dignity I can gather. "I had a better offer elsewhere."

"Why did you leave Bethune School?" Mr. Gasper asks.

"I resigned," I say. "There was a conflict between the Committee and myself on the one hand, and the government on the other. The Committee and I both resigned."

"Why?" Mr. Gasper wants to know.

"I offended the Director of Public Instruction because I consulted his subordinate and overlooked him."

"Were there any other issues?"

"There was a set of charges against me," I say. "One was for teaching Christian songs, and another about the sewing classes."

"Wasn't the charge regarding the sewing class that you collected funds when there was no charge for sewing materials?"

"That is utterly false, Mr. Gasper," I say. "I claimed the money charged to the government each month wasn't paid to me."

"And wasn't the reason they didn't pay you because they found, on inquiry, you acquired no materials?"

"Because I had no money to purchase them," I blurt.

"What was the exact charge?" Mr. Gasper asks.

"That I neglected to teach sewing," I mumble.

Mr. Gasper smirks. "Did you expect any questions about this matter?"

"I never had the slightest idea, or I would have come prepared," I say.

Justice Norris intervenes. "Mr. Gasper, I don't think she thought proving malice would come to this extent. I don't suppose she expected the whole of her past life would be raked up this way. If you fail to prove this, nothing could be more cogent evidence of malice."

"Yes, My Lord," Mr. Gasper says. "Miss Pigot, as a matter of fact, were your services dispensed with?"

"The Lieutenant-Governor said I might be asked to resign, as the others were." I look at Mr. Trevelyan. His face is blank.

Mr. Gasper walks back to his table and looks at his notes. "Do you remember the names of those sea captains who came to your house?"

"Very few. There were a great many of them," I say.

"I think you said they were all pious captains."

"So I understood."

"If you didn't think that, may I take it you wouldn't have asked them to your house."

"I never asked them," I say. "I allowed Mrs. Alcocks to ask them. They may have called after. I can't recollect."

Mr. Gasper fires questions at me about the various sea captains who came to call on me after the Alcocks left. Did they dine? Did a son or daughter accompany them? Was I alone with them? He concludes by asking me if any captain ever lay on the sofa in my drawing room. I find the question appalling. No gentleman would ever do such a thing.

Now Mr. Gasper goes after the teachers. "Was Miss Humphrey well-behaved when she was with you?"

"She had an exceedingly bad temper, couldn't do her work, and quarreled with the teachers. She was a great trial to me, overall."

"Was there any occasion when you found Miss Humphrey untruthful?" Mr. Gasper asks.

This is too much. "I can't believe you want me to go through such a long history."

"Do you remember any incident in which you thought Miss Humphrey untruthful?" Mr. Gasper asks again.

"Yes. She related things about other teachers."

"Do you remember when Mrs. Faulkner was at the school?" Mr. Gasper asks.

"Slightly."

"Did you doubt her truthfulness?" Mr. Gasper asks.

"No."

"Was Mrs. Palmer ever untruthful?" Mr. Gasper asks.

"Yes. There were complaints from the *zenanas* against her. She ran down the other teachers and extolled herself."

"How long have you known Reverend Mr. Chuckerbutty?" Mr. Gasper asks.

I take a breath. Mr. Gasper fires names like a Gatling gun. "I've known him since I joined the mission."

"How do you view his character as regards his truthfulness and veracity?" Mr. Gasper asks.

"I never suspected him of falsehood."

"How long have you known Mr. Fish?" Mr. Gasper asks.

"Since he came out," I say.

"Did you believe him to be a truthful man?" Mr. Gasper asks.

"In all but one instance, I did at the time before this trial. When I asked if he was coming to see me off to Scotland, he said Mr. Edwards was likely to go to Govindpore. He was going to tell Mr. Hastie he was seeing Mr. Edwards off, and come see me off instead."

"You heard Mrs. Wheeler's evidence," Mr. Gasper says. "Did you engage a woman you knew lost her position for gross immorality?"

What on earth? The air is humid. I can't get a good breath. "I never heard that."

"Did she tell you any teachers you engaged were dismissed for gross immorality or suspicion of immorality?" Mr. Gasper asks.

Did she? I don't know. I don't think so. What shall I say? I feel like I'm suffocating. "No," I say.

"Did she tell you not to allow your teachers to dress the way the one she saw stooping over the *box-wallah* did?" Mr. Gasper asks.

"No, she never told me that. She just reported how the teacher dressed."

Mr. Gasper looks incredulous. "Are you saying the whole of Mrs. Wheeler's evidence is false?" Mr. Gasper asks.

"That isn't an admissible question, Mr. Gasper," Justice Norris says.

"Very well, My Lord." Mr. Gasper goes back to his notes, but I think it's a ploy. He doesn't forget things. "Miss Pigot," he says. "Do you remember a great intimacy between yourself and Babu Kali Churn Banerjee?"

"Yes, so far as intimacy can be with a young boy," I answer.

"Do you know how old he is now?" Mr. Gasper asks.

"I haven't the slightest idea. I should think he's well over thirty."

"Have you read reports in the papers about this case?"

"Not all of them. I didn't have time to look at yesterday's."

"Then you didn't review what Mr. Wilson said," Mr. Gasper says.

I remember enough. "I don't know everything."

"What paper do you read?" Mr. Gasper asks, conversationally.

"The *Indian Daily News*, but I had a fever this morning and was unable to read the paper."

"Did you see the *Supplement* of the *Daily News*?" Mr. Gasper asks. "Did you read it to review what Mr. Wilson said?"

"I didn't read it carefully."

"I repeat, did you take up the *Supplement* to read what Mr. Wilson said?"

"Yes."

"Why couldn't you tell us that five minutes ago?" Justice Norris snaps.

The room starts to tilt.

"Did you read it?" Mr. Gasper asks again.

"I glanced at it." *Please stop.*

Justice Norris drums his fingers on his desk, pulls out his watch, and snaps it shut. "Mr. Gasper, have you completed your cross-examination?"

"No, My Lord. I have more questions."

"Very well. Court is adjourned until ten o'clock tomorrow." Justice Norris bangs his gavel and departs. Mr. Gasper turns his back on me as if he hasn't tried to crush me beneath his feet. I remain standing, unable to move until Mr. Carruthers takes my hand.

"Come, Miss Pigot," he says. "It's over now. I'll take you back to your hotel so you can rest."

I can't say anything. I think I'm going to faint. If I do, would anyone notice?

A storm came up during the night. I couldn't sleep for the thunder. I drink morning tea and try to eat a *chapatti*. It doesn't stay down. I dress slowly and twist my hair into a bun. I don't know how I'll face Mr. Gasper this morning. He hammers questions at me as if he wants to destroy me. Mr. Hastie only wants to ruin me. I don't understand why he lets his barrister be so cruel. I do everything in slow motion. I go downstairs to find Mr. Carruthers in the hotel lobby.

"I was just about to send for you," he says. "Are you strong enough to continue?"

"I suppose."

"Come along," he says and helps me into his *gharry*.

At the High Court, Mr. Carruthers takes me into a small room. Mr. Trevelyan is there already. "Miss Pigot," he says. "Come, take a chair."

I let him guide me.

"Miss Pigot, are you listening?" Mr. Carruthers asks.

"Did you say something?"

"Miss Pigot, I must ask you to be prepared for harsh questions," Mr. Trevelyan says. "You did very well yesterday, but today's examination will be more intense. I believe Mr. Gasper's gambit will be to tarnish your reputation in order to prove the libels are true. And he will pressure you relentlessly to break you down."

"What shall I do?"

"Do what you did yesterday," Mr. Trevelyan says. "Listen to the question. Answer clearly and speak up. Don't let Mr. Gasper's questions or demeanor alarm you. It's important you remain in control of yourself. No tears. You understand?"

I nod. We stay in the room until quarter before ten when Mr. Carruthers escorts me into the courtroom. I glance at Mr. Hastie in his clean suit, his eyes on the floor. Mr. Geddes and Mr. Gasper confer until Justice Norris comes in. I manage to walk into the witness box without assistance.

Mr. Gasper walks forward and smiles. "How are you this morning, Miss Pigot?"

"I'm well," I reply in my firm voice.

"Good," Mr. Gasper says. "Now then, how often during the week did Kali Churn Banerjee dine at your place?"

"At first he came every other day or so, and sometimes on successive days," I say in a calm, flat voice. "Sometimes there was an interval. Gradually, it became less and less."

"Why did he start dining at your place?"

"When he arrived, I asked if he'd had anything to eat."

"Every time?" Mr. Gasper asks.

"I can't say it was every time."

"Why did he dine at your place so often?"

"It was the hospitality of the house," I say. "I offered it to everybody."

"When he dined in the drawing room, didn't he dine alone and you generally join him?"

"Not always."

"Generally?" Mr. Gasper asks.

"I can't say..." My throat closes, and I feel my voice drop off.

"What?"

"That I was with him as often as that," I repeat.

"Did he stay after dinner?"

"He stayed until the entrance class girl was ready to go, or if he had a meeting," I say. How many times will I be asked the same thing?

"Besides Kali Churn Banerjee, did any other man sit on the cane lounge while you were in it?" Mr. Gasper asks.

I pause to think. No one comes to my mind. "Perhaps Mr. James Thomson did. I don't remember anybody else."

"When Kali Churn Banerjee sat on the lounge, did you remove your feet?" Mr. Gasper asks.

"I always moved my feet a little on one side to make room," I say, "and very often slipped them down. I took care to avoid contact with him."

"Why did you do that?"

"To make room. I wanted to give him a seat. That's all I thought of."
What is he inferring?

"Did he ever have his arm over your feet?" Mr. Gasper asks.

*He couldn't have, could he? I don't let anyone touch my feet. But I
can't focus.* "I don't remember."

"Will you say there wasn't such an occasion?" Mr. Gasper asks.

Surely I'd remember, but my mind is blank. "I have no recollection,"
I say.

"Did Kali Churn Banerjee ever work in the drawing room with the
door closed?" Mr. Gasper asks.

"What door?" Justice Norris asks.

"The door leading from the veranda into the drawing room," Mr.
Gasper says.

"I suppose they're glass doors?" Justice Norris asks.

"No, My Lord, Venetian doors."

"But with glass?" Justice Norris asks.

"With glass behind them." Mr. Gasper sounds slightly strained. "Was
the door closed, Miss Pigot?"

"I've never known the doors to be closed."

"How often has Kali Churn Banerjee worked on papers in the
drawing room?"

"He's been there often," I say. "He helped me a great deal with all my
writing."

"I understand that for some time you didn't enjoy good health," Mr.
Gasper says.

That's not true. "I wasn't strong, but I had no ill-health."

"Have you ever been ill when Kali Churn Banerjee called?"

"I must have been on some occasions."

"On these occasions, did Kali Churn Banerjee see you?" Mr. Gasper asks.

"Not if I were very ill," I say. "If I could move about the house, he saw me."

"When you were indisposed, or not up to the work, did Kali Churn Banerjee see you?"

I can't grasp the question. "Everyone saw me unless I was confined to bed."

"Yes or no," Justice Norris demands in a sharp voice.

Why is he so emphatic? What does it matter? "I don't remember," I say. I really don't.

"Besides social gatherings or prize distributions, have you been in your bedroom with Kali Churn Banerjee?" Mr. Gasper asks.

"Not alone."

"I didn't ask if you were alone. I asked if you've been in your bedroom with Kali Churn Banerjee."

"Yes."

"You said, 'not alone,'" Mr. Gasper says. "Name any other person or persons present in the bedroom when Kali Churn Banerjee was there."

I feel as if I'm drifting above the courtroom. There's a parade of white ants walking on the rail beside the witness box. They seem so sure of themselves. I snap my mind back on the question. *Focus.* "I've been at private examinations, and I think he was beside us when the Principal of the Sanskrit College was examining in the room. And perhaps when I had a class. My memory is indistinct."

"When you saw Kali Churn Banerjee while indisposed, where did you see him?"

"I saw him in the drawing room and in what we called the anteroom or office room," I say.

"Did it ever happen," Justice Norris asks, "that during the time you were Lady Superintendent your indisposition confined you to your room?"

"Not unless I had headaches. Then I saw no one," I say.

"Did you see Kali Churn Banerjee or any other man in your room alone on such occasions?" Mr. Gasper asks.

"I can't remember Kali Churn Banerjee."

"Anybody else?"

"One day Mr. Wilson saw me," I say. "I was lying on a couch. Mr. Gillan came once while I was there. He came to say good-bye to me."

"You say you can't remember about Kali Churn Banerjee?" Mr. Gasper asks.

"I can't remember."

"He may have."

"He may have," I sigh softly.

"Have you ever put your hand on any portion of Babu Banerjee's body?" Mr. Gasper asks.

Why would I do that? "I may have, on his shoulder," I say. "I have no recollection." I think a minute. "I shouldn't have thought I was doing anything wrong, if I wanted to emphasize something, in just touching his shoulder, but I don't think I did."

"Have you ever put your arm round his neck with your hand on his further arm?" Mr. Gasper asks.

"I suppose I might have," I say. "I wouldn't hesitate to say so if I'd done so, but I haven't the slightest recollection."

"Was your relationship with Kali Churn Banerjee one that would or wouldn't make it wrong for you to have your arm round his neck?" Mr. Gasper asks.

I know the answer to that. "I've never been on such relations with anyone."

"You heard it said Kali Churn Banerjee addressed you as 'mother,'" Mr. Gasper says. "That being so, would you consider there would be any harm putting your hand on his arm?"

"I've never been given to endearments," I say.

"Would there be any harm if Kali Churn Banerjee sat near you without his coat on?" Mr. Gasper asks.

"It wouldn't be respectful. Kali Churn is always polite." I nod.

"You told Mr. Trevelyan you never spoke in a 'faltering voice' to anyone. Do you mean you've never done so, even when ill?" Mr. Gasper asks.

"Faltering," Justice Norris interjects to explain the word, "implies there's a consciousness of guilt, not a weakness."

I look at the judge. I don't think he understands Mr. Gasper's question any better than I do.

"When you've been ill," Mr. Gasper continues. "When one is ill, one may speak with a faltering voice. Have you done so?" Mr. Gasper asks.

"I've never been that ill."

"These slippers that were given to you," Mr. Gasper asks. "Do you remember who made them?"

"Mrs. Tremearne's mother. She makes them in all sizes and sends them to me."

"How long did you have them before you gave them to Kali Churn Banerjee?" Mr. Gasper asks.

"I can't tell." *How does he expect me to remember that?*

"How long ago did you give these slippers to Kali Churn Banerjee?"

"It must have been 1880 or 1881. I don't remember the date."

"Did gentlemen who lived in the Mofussil put up at your house while in Calcutta?"

"Yes. I keep an open house."

"Do you know if they had any male acquaintances with whom they could have put up?" Mr. Gasper asks. "For instance, they could have put up at the Scottish College. People who knew Mr. Wilson, or Mr. Hastie, or Mr. Fish?"

"Not all of them. Perhaps one," I say.

"Who stayed at your house?" Mr. Gasper asks.

"Dr. Valentine, a medical missionary at Agra," I say. "He was with the United Presbyterian Mission. There was Reverend James Thomson of the Scotch Church, and Dr. Roy, a civil surgeon. Dr. Bose of Serampore also stayed."

Mr. Gasper gives me a sly look. "Do you know anyone named Cockburn?"

I search my memory. The name Cockburn sounds vaguely familiar, but I can't connect it to anyone. I tell Mr. Gasper I don't remember the name. He looks at me in surprise.

"You don't remember Laura Cockburn?"

I think again. I recollect an association with the name. *Oh dear.* "I didn't know her personally."

"Have you heard of her?"

"Yes," I answer reluctantly.

"When you say you don't know her personally, what do you mean?"

"I don't remember speaking to her."

"Will you state positively that you haven't spoken to Miss Laura Cockburn?" Mr. Gasper asks.

"I state positively that I don't remember speaking to her."

"Isn't it a fact that this person was a notorious person in Calcutta?"

"In that relation, I remember her," I admit.

"Then, she being a notorious person, surely you'd remember if you spoke to her."

I hear blood rushing in my ears. I wonder if I'll faint. I tell Mr. Gasper I can't remember speaking to Miss Cockburn.

"You must remember whether you've spoken to her," Justice Norris says.

"No. I saw her at a distance," I say.

"Where?" Mr. Gasper pounces.

I want to slam my fists on the rail. "I don't remember. It may have been at a house in Royd Street."

"Do you remember the number of the house in Royd Street?" Mr. Gasper asks.

"No."

"Wasn't it No. 24?"

"I've no idea."

"Aren't you aware that Laura Cockburn used to keep a school under which she cloaked the most notorious doings in Calcutta?" Mr. Gasper asks.

The roaring in my ears gets louder. "No," I burst out.

Mr. Gasper leans forward. "Do you hear that now for the first time?"

"So far as I recollect," I say.

"Yes or no, Miss Pigot," Justice Norris says. "Do you now hear for the first time from Mr. Gasper the suggestion that the woman Laura Cockburn kept a school in a house in Royd Street under which filthy practices were cloaked?" In his red robes the judge looks like the devil.

I fight down an urge towards hysterics. "Yes, this is the first time I've heard it with reference to that period."

"I didn't limit it to any period. Do you hear that suggestion now for the first time?" Mr. Gasper asks.

"No," I mumble as the room spins.

"When did you first hear it?"

"After I came back to Calcutta," I say, "and after I went to this house in Royd Street."

"Isn't it true that for years and years Miss Laura Cockburn's school was simply a house of assignation?" Mr. Gasper asks.

"Yes," I say softly. "It is a fact."

"And wasn't it a rendezvous for the most disreputable characters in Calcutta?" Mr. Gasper asks.

"I don't know."

Justice Norris leans over me. "Who were you, a Superintendent of this mission, on such terms with, that you could discuss the character of such a woman? Answer that question, please."

"I heard it from one of the pupils of the Normal School." My voice sounds like a whisper.

"What was her name?" Mr. Gasper asks.

I shake my head. "I can't remember."

"What do you think her name was?"

"I think it would be the teacher, Miss Berry," I say.

"Do you think, Miss Pigot, that you heard from Miss Berry that the house was a house of assignation?"

"I never heard the particulars."

"You said that under the cloak of keeping a school, she allowed practices to go on which ought not to have gone on," Justice Norris says.

"I heard that report," I say.

"Did you hear she was a common prostitute?" Mr. Gasper asks.

"I heard she was free with people, and that she went to Barrackpore with some gentlemen."

"Did you hear at any time that she was a person of immoral character, that she kept a common brothel, and that instead of being school girls in the school, they were prostitutes?" Mr. Gasper asks.

"I never heard that," I say. *I didn't.*

"Did you hear it was a house of assignation?" Mr. Gasper asks.

A house of what? "I don't understand the expression. I've never heard the word before."

"When you were asked whether it was a house of assignation, you said it was."

"I... I didn't understand it as a house of assignation. I understood it as an individual living in the house."

"Have you heard of Surrut of Burtollah?" Mr. Gasper asks.

I shake my head. "No."

"Do you know where Burtollah is?"

"Yes, I do. It's part of Calcutta."

"Do you know anyone there, or whether you visited a house there?"

I take a breath. "We have several *zenanas* in that district. I dare say I've been to more than one house there," I say in a normal voice.

"Have you ever been into any woman's house in Burtollah?" Mr. Gasper asks.

"I haven't known it as a woman's house. I've known it as a *zenana*."

"Are you aware that the woman Surrat, whom you went to see, was a common woman of the streets?" Mr. Gasper asks.

"No," I say.

"Will you swear your teachers never taught women of this class?"

"Not if we knew them to be such."

"Have you given Scripture cards to any women of this sort?"

You would deny them Scripture? "I gave Scripture cards everywhere I went."

"But have you given them to women of this sort?" Mr. Gasper repeats. I hear him in my mind repeating over and over again.

"Surely there can be no wrong in that," Justice Norris says.

Mr. Gasper is trying to trap me. I think a moment. "If I knew a woman to be immoral, I didn't give a Scripture card to her."

"Have you ever given Scripture cards to people you afterwards learned were immoral?" Mr. Gasper asks.

"Not to my recollection." Mr. Gasper looks annoyed, but I can't remember the answers to his questions.

"Do you remember the first incident Mr. Fish described, the matter of the lunch?" Mr. Gasper asks.

Mr. Fish. I suppose we have to talk about his lies now.

"I remember the lunch."

"How much beer did Mr. Wilson drink?"

"I don't really know. In general, if it were *tiffin*, he seldom took more than a glass. I didn't take any notice." *Why is this so important?*

"Will you say that he didn't drink nearly two quarts?" Mr. Gasper asks.

"I could swear he didn't," I say.

"Were two bottles opened?"

"No, I don't think so."

"Have you a distinct recollection that two bottles weren't opened?"

"I have no recollection." Mr. Trevelyan is giving me an odd look. *Have I got it wrong?* "Perhaps it was a quart bottle and a pint bottle."

"And you say two bottles weren't opened," Mr. Gasper says.

"No," I correct him. "I meant two quart bottles weren't opened. In fact, I never knew of two men at my *tiffin* table drinking two quarts of beer, or a pint and a quart." Mr. Trevelyan looks impassive again.

"Did anyone drink whiskey after drinking beer?" Mr. Gasper asks.

"No."

"Will you pledge your oath that after *tiffin* on that occasion, whiskey wasn't drunk?" Justice Norris asks.

"Yes, My Lord," I answer.

"Did you have whiskey in the house?" Mr. Gasper asks.

"Yes."

"For whom?"

"For any guest who came."

"As a matter of fact, weren't you in the habit of giving whiskey to Mr. Wilson?" Mr. Gasper asks.

"Yes."

"Did you give liquor after *tiffin*?"

"I think I had some myself."

"And you didn't give Mr. Wilson any?" Mr. Gasper asks.

"I don't know," I say. Mr. Trevelyan is giving me an odd look again. *How do they expect me to remember what happened at tiffin over a year ago? And what does it matter?*

"After *tiffin*," Mr. Gasper says, "what did Mr. Wilson take that day?"

"I can only tell you what I've heard," I say.

"Then, may I take it you haven't the slightest idea from your personal knowledge what Mr. Wilson did that day after lunch," Mr. Gasper says.

"He did some writing for me," I say.

"How do you know that?"

"Because I always have a great deal of writing going on, and Mr. Wilson assists me with it."

Mr. Gasper gives me an exasperated look. "Where did you have a great deal of writing that day?"

"I'm sure it was in the office room."

"Did you do any writing that day in the office room?"

"I don't think so, because my writing is very bad."

"Were you in that room after lunch?"

"I don't remember. I won't swear I wasn't."

"Then how do you know Mr. Wilson was writing?" Mr. Gasper asks.

"Because I was writing letters and preparing accounts that day," I say. "I didn't write letters myself. Mr. Wilson wrote them for me. I haven't the faintest recollection what I was doing that day."

"If you remember the occasion on which there was *tiffin*, can't you say what were you doing after *tiffin*?" Mr. Gasper asks.

"I couldn't tell."

"You have, I suppose, tried to think what you were doing," Mr. Gasper says.

Why would I do that? "No, I haven't."

"Not at all?" Mr. Gasper asks in surprise.

"No," I say, because it's true.

"Do you know what Mr. Wilson said occurred after *tiffin*?" Mr. Gasper asks.

"Yes. I read the newspaper report."

"When you saw what he said in the newspaper, did you try to think whether you agreed or differed?" Mr. Gasper asks.

"I didn't try to reconcile it," I say. *What would be the point?*

"Will you state positively that after Mr. Fish came up, Mr. Wilson didn't say, 'Miss Pigot, I've had too much beer today,' or something to that effect?" Mr. Gasper asks.

"I can't. I don't remember." *I wish I could remember.*

"Do you recollect now what Mr. Wilson was writing that day?" Mr. Gasper asks.

"Yes," I say. *It was the accounts.*

"If you recall that, try to recall what you were doing," Mr. Gasper says.

"I can't." *Why does he keep asking this question?*

"How do you know Mr. Wilson was writing for you that day?"

"Because I had writing for him to do."

Justice Norris leans over the dais. "If you can't remember where you were, how do you remember he was sitting at the writing table all afternoon, and never reclined on the sofa?"

I consider the question. There could only be one reason. "I must have been there myself for a time," I say. "I must have come in and out."

"You remember being there for a time," Justice Norris says.

"Yes."

"What were you doing?" Justice Norris asks.

My mind is blank. "I can't remember."

"What took you into the room?" Justice Norris asks.

I shake my head. "I can't say."

Mr. Gasper returns to his list of questions. "Do you remember Mr. Fish coming up after lunch?"

"No." *I can't remember anything now. The entire day is blank.*

"Will you swear that when he came up, he didn't find you lying on the sofa?" Mr. Gasper asks.

"But he may have." My voice catches. "I don't know. I don't think so."

"Will you swear that when he came up, he didn't see Mr. Wilson either in contact with or sitting on, or rising up from a chair?" Mr. Gasper presses me.

"I don't know."

"He may have?" Mr. Gasper asks.

I close my eyes to think. "No, I don't think so."

"If Mr. Fish might have seen you lying on the sofa, couldn't he have seen Mr. Wilson rising from a chair?" Mr. Gasper asks.

I can only repeat what I know. "I have no recollection of Mr. Wilson doing anything but sitting at my desk."

"Could Mr. Fish have seen it?"

"I won't state it." *How can I state what I can't remember?*

"Just to clarify," Justice Norris says. "If you have no recollection, you can't say whether Mr. Fish may have seen it or not."

"It's clear in my mind that Mr. Wilson sat at the desk writing."

"Do you remember the day of adding up the marks?" Mr. Gasper asks.

He watches me as I think. That was in March. "Yes."

"How long did it take to add up the marks?"

"Perhaps an hour or two."

Mr. Gasper steps back with a surprised look. "Aren't there about a thousand girls who had been examined?"

"No. The number of students was just over two hundred."

"And the marks for two hundred students were added up in an hour or so?" Mr. Gasper asks.

"No. Nitya Gopal took some papers home."

"When this adding was going on, what were you doing?" Mr. Gasper asks.

"Moving about," I say.

"Do you have any recollection what you were doing?" Mr. Gasper asks.

"I watched what was going on," I say.

"You couldn't have watched while you moved about," Mr. Gasper says.

"I did. My writing is very bad, and I often had to tell them how to spell a girl's name," I explain.

"Where did you sit while those marks were being added up?"

"I don't know. I might not have been sitting at all."

"Have you ever touched Mr. Wilson on the head, or the arm, or the back?" Mr. Gasper asks.

"Very likely," I say with confidence.

"Did you put your crossed hands on Mr. Wilson's shoulder?"

"I might have. It's possible, but rather improbable."

"Why improbable?"

"Because it wasn't my habit to do that."

"Did you consider the action too free, not quite ladylike?"

"It would be unnatural for me to do it."

"Then, if it would be unnatural, how is it possible you did it?" Mr. Gasper asks in an exasperated voice.

"I'm not saying I didn't do it. I just mean, it wasn't my way of doing things."

"If you say it was an unnatural behavior, how can you say it was possible that you did an unnatural thing?" Mr. Gasper asks.

I try to visualize myself doing such a thing. "I can't understand that I could have done it in the form you describe."

"Did you say it wasn't possible because the expression unnatural has been joined to it?" Mr. Gasper asks.

He's twisting my words. I don't know what to answer. "I don't know if that's the reason."

"What's the difference between saying 'You're my best friend' and saying 'I don't know what I'd do without you?' as indicating familiarity?" Mr. Gasper asks.

"If you're referring to Mr. Wilson, I wouldn't make either statement," I say.

"Have you touched Mr. Wilson's knee when speaking to him?"

"I'm sure I have not."

"Will you swear you've never done it?" Mr. Gasper looks into my eyes.

I look away. "I will swear."

"What made you nurse Mr. Hastie?"

"Because I was distressed that he was ill."

"Did you sit up the whole night for four nights with Mr. Hastie?"

"Three nights, I sat up the whole night," I say. "The fourth night, I started at twelve o'clock."

"Did you ever go into the sickroom with Mr. Wilson during that time?" Mr. Gasper asks.

"He came into the sickroom when I was there."

"Did you go into the room with him?" Mr. Gasper asks.

"I don't think so," I say.

"Did you sleep in the day?"

"I slept in the mornings at the mission house."

"How long did you sleep?" Mr. Gasper asks.

"Two or three hours," I say.

"So during the whole of these four days, you slept only two to three hours in the day. What was the necessity of that?" Mr. Gasper asks.

"I was anxious," I say. "Mr. Hastie was very ill."

"Wasn't Mrs. Sharpland a perfectly competent nurse?"

I think of Mrs. Sharpland's impersonal demeanor. "I thought a paid woman wouldn't care as much as I cared. Mr. Hastie was part of our mission family."

Mr. Gasper picks up the pace, firing questions until I can't breathe. "During that time, did you ever sit on the same sofa in the sickroom with Mr. Wilson?"

"I don't remember," I say.

"Can you say you didn't sit on the sofa with him?"

"No, I can't."

"Did you ever whisper to Mr. Wilson in the sickroom?"

"I don't remember."

"Do you remember laughing in a way that would be audible?"

"I can state positively that I didn't."

"Was there a sofa in the sickroom?" Mr. Gasper asks.

"Yes."

"How far from the bed?"

"The distance from here to the table I sit at," I say, pointing at the plaintiff's table.

"Did Mr. Wilson come in at night to see how Mr. Hastie was?" Mr. Gasper asks.

"Not at night," I say. "He came after dinner. We had dinner at eight o'clock. He and Mr. Steele and I dined together." I bite my lip until it bleeds to keep myself from screaming. Mr. Gasper's questions are relentless.

"Did Mr. Wilson ever come to see how Mr. Hastie was after you took up your duties?"

"He never came," I say.

"Can you suggest why Mr. Wilson didn't come in with you to see how Mr. Hastie was?" Mr. Gasper asks.

"No reason that I can think of." *How would I know?*

"Who sat next to you at Barrackpore Park?" Mr. Gasper suddenly asks.

What? I pause and wait for my heart to slow down. "Mr. Hastie."

"What was this business about sitting back-to-back?"

"A little nonsense on someone's part."

"When did you give up sitting back-to-back?"

"We couldn't sit so at *tiffin*. It was another part of the ground."

"You were tired that day at Mr. Steele's dinner. Were you unusually tired?" Mr. Gasper asks sympathetically.

"Yes, I was extremely tired."

"If you were so tired, how do you explain your vivacity at dinner?"

"Because I thought it was my fault the dinner was so dull. I tried to talk as much as I could."

"Is your regard for Mr. Wilson intense and warm?"

Is he trying to trap me? "It's warm."

"Is it intense?" Mr. Gasper asks.

"No."

"Are you aware that Mr. Wilson spoke of his regard for you as intense and warm?" Mr. Gasper asks.

Did he? "I don't know what he said."

"Have you been alone in the same carriage with Mr. Wilson?" Mr. Gasper asks.

"Often," I say.

"Going where?"

"On different errands."

"What errands?"

"To look at a carriage, or see a horse, or select books."

"Ever been with him to an evening party?"

"Not that I remember."

"After an evening party, have you been in the same carriage with him?" Mr. Gasper asks.

"I never went to evening parties," I say.

"You've not been out to dinner with Mr. Wilson?"

"Only to Mr. Steele's."

"Didn't you go with Mr. Wilson to a dinner at Mr. Gillan's and then come back part of the way with him?"

I don't understand what he's talking about. I shake my head. "I have no recollection."

"Isn't it true that when you dined with Mr. Gillan, Mr. Wilson's cousin was there. And after dinner, Mr. Wilson got into the same carriage with you until your ways diverged, and Mr. Wilson got into the other carriage?"

Did I? The rushing in my ears comes back. "I don't recollect."

Justice Norris clears his throat. "Surely if such a thing took place, you'd remember it."

"I haven't a good memory," I say.

Justice Norris looms over me. "I'll rephrase Mr. Gasper's question. You were at dinner at Mr. Gillan's house. Mr. Wilson and his cousin were also there. They live in the same place, but after dinner Mr. Wilson drove with you until there was a turnout. Then he shifted to the other carriage. Do you remember that?"

"I can't remember." I smile at him weakly. "I'm sorry."

Mr. Trevelyan looks at me like thunder. I'm doing my best, but everything is so far away.

"Will you swear the incident I described didn't take place?" Mr. Gasper asks.

I clutch the rail. "I can't remember."

"How often have you been in the same carriage with Mr. Wilson at night?" Mr. Gasper asks.

"Very rarely," I say.

Justice Norris glares down at me and turns to my barrister. "Mr. Trevelyan, at any given time, this witness is unable to recall where she was or what she was doing. She appears unable to comprehend the simplest question. Her testimony is useless. I think it best to adjourn the court and call the next case, so the witness can organize her thoughts. Perhaps tomorrow she'll be in a better frame of mind."

Yes, please adjourn.

Mr. Trevelyan stands. "Thank you, My Lord. That won't be necessary."

Mr. Trevelyan walks over to the witness box and stands before me. He looks quite angry. "Miss Pigot, focus on Mr. Gasper's questions and answer them correctly. Do you understand?"

I nod. Mr. Trevelyan gives me a long look and walks back to his seat.

Mr. Gasper stands behind his table. Next to him Mr. Hastie examines his manicured fingernails.

"Let's try again," Mr. Gasper says walking towards me. "Miss Pigot, how often have you been in the same carriage with Mr. Wilson after dark?"

I inhale and shift my feet to release a cramp. The response floats forward in my brain. "I think perhaps three or four times."

"Has Mr. Wilson ever dressed at your place?" Mr. Gasper asks.

"Once."

"Did he put his evening clothes on?"

"Yes." My voice sounds mechanical in its flatness.

"Why did he put his evening clothes on at your house?" Mr. Gasper asks.

"I asked him to stay and help me with a letter about Miss Smail. He had to go home to dress, so to save time, I asked him to send for his clothes and help me with the letter."

"Have you been to Mr. Wilson's quarters alone?" Mr. Gasper asks.

"Only once."

"When was that?" Mr. Gasper asks.

"I went to look at his room, so I could write to Mrs. Wilson that I'd just come from there."

"How long were you there?" Mr. Gasper asks.

"Five minutes."

Justice Norris breaks in. "Mr. Gasper, I don't think you need to continue this cross-examination. It's taking far too much time. Allow me to get to the crux of the matter. Miss Pigot, did Mr. Wilson ever kiss you?"

I gasp. "No!"

"Do you swear that?" Justice Norris asks.

"I swear it!"

"Good, that's settled. You may sit down, Mr. Gasper. Mr. Trevelyan, have you any questions?" Justice Norris asks.

"Just a few points to clarify, My Lord," Mr. Trevelyan stands. He picks up a paper and walks forward. I lock my eyes on him. "Miss Pigot, did you tell Mrs. Wilson about going into Mr. Wilson's room?"

"Yes."

"What did you say to her?" Mr. Trevelyan asks.

"I told her I'd been there."

"And when did you know Miss Cockburn?" Mr. Trevelyan asks.

"I didn't know her to speak to."

"In that case, when did you see her?"

"Perhaps in 1860."

"When did you hear about her character?"

"It was a long while after. I knew nothing about it at the time I saw her."

"No further questions, My Lord," Mr. Trevelyan says.

"Then you are excused. Mr. Trevelyan, will you finish today?" Justice Norris asks.

"I expect to," Mr. Trevelyan answers.

I wobble back to the plaintiff's table. Mr. Carruthers takes my arm. When we get outside, the rain has stopped. Mr. Carruthers's clerk takes me back to the hotel. Someone helps me to my room. I begin to shiver. My teeth chatter. I get into bed with my clothes on. I want to die.

Chapter 23
"I Want To Wrap This Up Today"

Thursday Morning, 13 September 1883
William Hastie

Mr. Carruthers's clerk leads Miss Pigot out of the courtroom. The woman can hardly walk. I think we're almost done. Trevelyan calls Mr. James to the witness box, probably to bolster Banerjee's claims. He doesn't swear an oath like the rest of us. He "affirms." Another one of the strays frequenting Miss Pigot's house. He's simply dressed in a crumpled linen suit. I think he's Baptist.

Trevelyan asks him about the day Miss Pigot gave Banerjee the slippers. "When did you arrive at the orphanage that day?"

"I was there with Kali Churn Banerjee," Mr. James says. "We were on our way to Beadon Square to preach when we stopped in. Miss Pigot invited us to rest. I rested on a sofa,"

"Did anything unusual happen?" Mr. Trevelyan asks.

"Half an hour later, we heard a row in the courtyard below," Mr. James says. "Both of us looked out the window, and then went down to see what was going on. Babu Banerjee wore the slippers you mentioned."

"Do you remember what sort of coat he had on?" Mr. Trevelyan asks.

"I'm almost sure it was a black coat."

"What did you do then?" Mr. Trevelyan asks.

"I went back to the drawing room and had something to eat. We left shortly afterward," Mr. James says.

"Did you attend social gatherings at Miss Pigot's?"

"Several."

"Do you remember the bedroom being used?"

"It isn't denied," Justice Norris breaks in impatiently. "Do you have further questions? I want to wrap this up today."

"No further questions," Mr. Trevelyan says.

Justice Norris looks at my man. "No questions, My Lord," Mr. Gasper says.

Nitya Gopal Mukherjee comes forward next. I haven't seen him since he left the College. He's lost weight. He seems a bit hesitant as he takes the oath. I don't see how he can testify for the plaintiff after I took him in for so long. Treated him like my own son, and now he turns his back on me. Trevelyan hands him a document.

"I wrote this report in 1882 on the veranda in Miss Pigot's house," Babu Mukherjee says. "This is the prize list."

"Do you remember when the prize distribution took place?" Mr. Trevelyan asks.

"Mr. Trevelyan, that fact is proved. The distribution occurred on the first of April," Justice Norris snaps.

"Where did you write the report?" Mr. Trevelyan asks.

"He said he wrote it on the veranda." Justice Norris waves his hand. "Do move on."

"Tell us what happened when you arrived at Miss Pigot's house," Mr. Trevelyan says.

"The drawing room was empty when I arrived, as was the office room," Babu Mukherjee says. "Miss Pigot came in. We went out to either the drawing room or the veranda. I don't remember which."

"Was anyone else there?" Mr. Trevelyan asks.

"No."

"Did anyone come upstairs?"

"Mr. Wilson and Mr. Fish."

"Where did you sit on the veranda?" Mr. Trevelyan asks.

"On a chair," Babu Mukherjee says.

The judge gives Trevelyan an exasperated look and taps his knuckle on the table.

"What did you do on the veranda?" Mr. Trevelyan asks.

"We sat around an oval table and added up the marks," Babu Mukherjee says. "I added up the marks of girls with Bengali names. Mr. Fish and Mr. Wilson added up marks for girls with English names."

"What was Miss Pigot doing?" Mr. Trevelyan asks.

"She moved about. Sometimes helping me, sometimes Mr. Wilson, and sometimes Mr. Fish."

"Did anyone leave the veranda?" Mr. Trevelyan asks.

"No. Miss Pigot may have left for a minute or two, but I don't know."

"How long did you remain there, adding up these marks?"

"We were there about two hours," Babu Mukherjee says. "Mr. Wilson and Mr. Fish finished their portion. I hadn't quite finished, so they asked me to take the papers home with me and send them back the next day."

Justice Norris holds up his hand. "Let me understand this. You all left?"

"Yes," Babu Mukherjee says.

"Together?" Justice Norris asks.

"Yes."

"Was anyone else with Mr. Wilson and Mr. Fish?" Justice Norris asks.

"Mr. Wetherill came for a short time. He must have gone before us."

Justice Norris adjusts his spectacles. "Did Mr. Wilson and Miss Pigot leave the room together and return after twenty minutes?"

"No," Babi Mukherjee says with some heat. "It isn't true. I read the testimony in the papers."

"What did you do when you read it?" Justice Norris asks.

"I read it aloud to a Christian gentleman and told him it was a lie."

I hardly know what to think. Either Mr. Fish is wrong, or Mukherjee is covering up for Miss Pigot and Mr. Wilson. Mr. Fish didn't mention Mukherjee's presence, an odd omission on his part. I stop following this line of thought.

Mr. Trevelyan asks, "Is there any truth in what you saw in the papers about Mr. Wilson and Miss Pigot?"

Mr. Gasper bounces up, "I object to the question."

"Allow me, Mr. Gasper," Justice Norris says. "Did you, when adding up the marks, see any act of impropriety between Mr. Wilson and Miss Pigot?"

"No, My Lord," Babu Mukherjee says. "Nothing at all."

"Anything else, Mr. Trevelyan?" Justice Norris waves him back to his table and nods to Mr. Gasper. "I'm sure you have questions."

Mr. Gasper walks up to cross-examine. "When did you make a statement to your solicitor?"

"Yesterday at eleven o'clock," Babu Mukherjee says. "Mr. Wilson wrote my statement down for him."

"Was there any jogging of the memory by Mr. Wilson?" Mr. Gasper asks. "Did he tell you anything you didn't know or had forgotten?"

"No. I asked Mr. Wilson about Mr. Wetherill," Babu Mukherjee says. "He told me Mr. Wetherill isn't in India. Then he asked if I read Mr.

Fish's statement in the paper. I said I had. And he asked if I agreed some of the statements were false. He asked me what paper I read. I told him *The Statesman*. He said, 'Oh. There's very little there. Read it in the *Indian Daily News.*'"

"And he said this before he began to write?" Mr. Gasper asks.

"Yes."

"Did you read Mr. Wilson's entire statement?" Mr. Gasper asks.

"No. I read the portion of Mr. Fish's evidence relative to Mr. Wilson and Miss Pigot," Babu Mukherjee says.

"How do you remember Mr. Fish, Mr. Wilson and you went away together?" Mr. Gasper asks.

"Because after they finished their work, they told me to take my papers home." Babu Mukherjee leans his head to one side.

"You swore just now that you wrote a portion in the veranda," Justice Norris says. "It is no laughing matter. You seem to think it is a trifle. Did you say you wrote a portion on the veranda?"

"I didn't say that."

Justice Norris consults his notes. "You said, 'this is my writing. In 1882 I wrote it. A portion of it was written in Miss Pigot's veranda.' Did you say that?"

"If I swore it, I was wrong," Babu Mukherjee says.

"You needn't go through these explanations. Why, if you wrote it at your house, did you swear to me you wrote it on Miss Pigot's veranda?" Justice Norris asks.

"I must have been wrong." Babu Mukherjee shrugs.

"How many girls' marks did you add up?" Mr. Gasper asks.

"I don't remember. There were a great many names."

"Do you remember a serious quarrel with Mr. Hastie?" Mr. Gasper asks.

"Yes," Babu Mukherjee says. "He opened my letters."

"When you fell out with Mr. Hastie, did you go to Miss Pigot? Did she befriend you?" Mr. Gasper asks.

"No."

"Do you remember Miss Pigot sympathizing with you?" Mr. Gasper asks.

"Yes. Miss Pigot was there when I spoke to Mr. Thomson," Babu Mukherjee says.

"Did she show you any outward demonstration of sympathy?"

"She sympathized with me in a general way."

"Did she put her hands on your shoulder?"

"Yes."

"Did she touch your head or your cheek?"

"No."

"Where did you go after you left Scottish College?" Mr. Gasper asks.

"I teach two classes at Bishop's College," Babu Mukherjee says.

"How many students have you?" Mr. Gasper asks.

"Only twelve. Seven students in the first class, and five in the second."

"Are you a member of the Church of England?" Mr. Gasper asks.

"Yes."

"But you began as a member of the Church of Scotland?" Mr. Gasper asks.

"I was baptized in the Scotch Kirk."

"Why did you leave the Church of Scotland?" Justice Norris asks. "In your astute Bengali mind, what was the difference between the Church of Scotland and the Church of England?"

"I've discussed this in the newspapers," Babu Mukherjee says quietly.

"I don't read the newspapers," Justice Norris says.

Babu Mukherjee turns to look at the judge. "In the *Christian Herald*."

"I don't read that," Justice Norris frowns.

"The Church of England is more primitive, more apostolic. It has more order," Babu Mukherjee says. "It suits my idea of devotion."

"Had you any professorship in the Church of Scotland?" Justice Norris asks.

"Yes."

"How much did you get per month?" Justice Norris asks.

"When I became a professor, my pay was between seventy and eighty rupees per month," Babu Mukherjee says.

"And now you teach seven students in the first, and five in the second class at Bishop's College, what do you get?" Justice Norris asks.

"One hundred thirty rupees per month."

"Then decency, unity, and increase of salary have gone together." Justice Norris laughs at his own joke.

"No further questions," Mr. Gasper says.

Mr. Trevelyan comes forward with another set of questions. He asks what work Babu Mukherjee took home.

"Names written by Miss Pigot, figures written by the pundits, and names and figures jotted down by Bengali examiners," Babu Mukherjee responds.

"Any other questions?" Justice Norris asks.

"No, My Lord.

"Babu Mukherjee, you're excused. I recall James Wilson."

Mr. Wilson enters from the hallway, looking a bit apprehensive. Justice Norris motions him into the box.

"You said Babu Mukherjee was there the afternoon when the marks were added. Can you say where you next saw him?" Justice Norris asks.

"I could conjecture. As he was living at Scottish College, I may have seen him there."

"If Babu Mukherjee said anything to you about the paper with the marks, would you recollect it?" Justice Norris asks.

"Not unless there was something extraordinary," Mr. Wilson blinks. "I've no recollection of any kind. I considered it trifling work then. Now it's assumed importance."

"Did he tell you he took work home, finished it, and gave it to you to take to Miss Pigot?" Justice Norris asks.

"I've no recollection," Mr. Wilson says.

"You're excused," Justice Norris says crossly. "We're adjourned for *tiffin* until two o'clock."

Gasper turns to me. "It's over, Mr. Hastie," he says. "They have two minor witnesses of no consequence." When I ask if he thinks we've won, he looks clearly affronted and leaves the table. I'm gratified I'll soon be about my own business. I've a translation due at the publisher, and government reports to oversee. I don't know if Mr. Wilson will still be on the faculty or not now that his unhealthy indiscretion is revealed. I'll consult with Mr. Edwards about staffing.

Gasper is right about the last witnesses. They brought Robson over from Hugli College. Strange to think he was the cause of my first altercation with Miss Pigot. She insisted on taking his side against the Corresponding Board. He has nothing to contribute, as Gasper points out.

The last witness is even less relevant. Dr. Anderson testifies Chunder Kumar Dey is unable to testify, because he isn't in a fit state of mind. So we'll never know what happened on Amherst Street. Not that it matters. Gasper made Miss Pigot out to be nothing but a strumpet and an imposter. It's a sad state of affairs. She presented herself to everyone as a pillar of our mission, and all the time her feet were made of clay.

444

Finally, Trevelyan says, "The Plaintiff rests."

Justice Norris calls a ten-minute recess before Trevelyan sums up his case. I wonder how he'll gild this lily.

Mr. Trevelyan stands behind his table with his hands on his lapels, spectacles on his nose, and notes before him. Justice Norris tells him to proceed.

"I draw Your Lordship's attention to one or two salient points. In the first place, Mr. Fish made a heinous charge against Miss Pigot. This charge must be addressed, though it has nothing to do with the original case of malicious libel. Everyone concerned denies the charge. In addition, Nitya Gopal Mukherjee was present on that occasion. I therefore submit, Mr. Fish's story is just that: a story."

Trevelyan looks at his notes, and then returns his gaze to the judge.

"With reference to Miss Pigot's testimony, I believe the thing operating most in Your Lordship's mind is her confusion about the questions. I ask Your Lordship to consider my client's position. Mr. Hastie's allegations preyed on her mind for many months, resulting in an extremely nervous mental state."

Trevelyan spreads his hands. "Miss Pigot has never been in a courtroom before. A woman doesn't have the same self-possession as a man and the questions were difficult. When Miss Pigot heard a circumstance, she magnified it. A touch on the shoulder or head might be innocent or something else. To a lady's mind, it was unclear how to answer. If she said yes, it might be charged against her. Naturally, she hesitated and became confused when badgered in cross-examination.

"My Lord, Miss Pigot knew this suit was the most important circumstance in her life. She knew her occupation, reputation, and everything of any value to her depended on the result of this suit. Under such circumstances, even a strong witness would be cautious. Mr. Hastie himself, a man who studied law, had difficulty giving direct answers under cross-examination."

Miss Pigot knew exactly what she was doing when she reinstated the suit, and if the results aren't to her liking, that's the chance she took. Trevelyan drones on about Miss Pigot's inability to remember anything of consequence because she's a shy, sheltered woman. He tries to say the courtroom was a threatening place for a woman of her sensibility. None of this is true. The judge nods along.

"Mr. Gasper attacked Miss Pigot. Your Lordship attacked her. Miss Pigot said yes and no. And then the question was put about Miss Cockburn and a house of assignation. Just because a man would recognize the word's meaning doesn't mean Miss Pigot knew a house of assignation was used for immoral purposes."

Trevelyan moves on to Mr. Fish's allegations. "None of these charges have anything to do with the libel but were brought after Mr. Fish's testimony. Mr. Wilson was bound to deny the charge but consider whether there was anything in his demeanor from which Your Lordship could conclude he wasn't truthful. If Mr. Wilson's reference about persons present at the time the prize lists were made up is true, Mr. Fish's story has no merit."

That's a big "if." I doubt the judge will accept the word of an Indian over that of a Scotsman.

"When Miss Pigot went to Scotland, there was no charge regarding Kali Churn Banerjee. This allegation first appeared in the anonymous letters. When she was away, Kali Churn Banerjee wrote to her one time. Was that the letter of a man guilty of impropriety? Even Mr. Hastie charged Mr. Wilson with nothing more than a flirtation.

"Based on the evidence I've presented and the original tenets of this case, I ask Your Lordship to say the charge of malicious libel is justified, and that those alleged acts weren't committed by Miss Pigot, Mr. Wilson, and Kali Churn Banerjee. I ask Your Lordship to rule a verdict on Miss Pigot's behalf."

Gasper listens to Miss Pigot's man with absolute stillness. At this point the worst charges have nothing to do with my alleged libel, but I don't think the judge is clever enough to pick through the details. He strikes me as a man who goes with his impressions, and Gasper played that to the hilt.

Trevelyan goes back to his seat. The plaintiff's table looks empty without Miss Pigot's tiny figure. Gasper stands and waits for the judge's attention.

"Mr. Gasper," Justice Norris says, "before you begin. I may have been a little premature when I stopped your cross-examination of Miss Pigot. I ask you not to draw any inference from that. I simply didn't think it desirable to continue the questioning. The woman had nothing useful to say."

"My Lord, the plaintiff's case had broken down already. I simply wanted to bring further matters to Your Lordship's attention," Mr. Gasper says graciously. "Speaking for myself, I wish Your Lordship could come to any conclusion except the one you must make."

Mr. Gasper approaches the bench. "The issue in this case is simple. Whom shall Your Lordship believe? Shall Your Lordship believe the number of witnesses who have no interest in the outcome of this case, or those whose minds must be influenced by self-preservation?"

"My learned friend pleas Miss Pigot had a severe cross-examination and was unaccustomed either to a courtroom or giving direct answers.

The same could be said of the ladies who testified on our behalf. If Your Lordship believed the veracity of their testimony, then that's an end to plaintiff's plea."

Gasper goes through every iota of evidence we presented, highlighting that of Mrs. Faulkner, Miss Humphrey, and Mrs. Palmer's testimony about Chunder Kumar Dey. And why hadn't Chunder Kumar Dey come to court? Plaintiff's witness said his intellect was weak.

"If forgetfulness and repeating questions is a sign of intellectual weakness, then it applies to nearly every witness. The real reason they didn't call Chunder Kumar Dey is that he couldn't deny the facts," Mr. Gasper says.

"Mr. Trevelyan makes the point that Miss Pigot put her entire life's course on the outcome of this suit. I ask Your Lordship to remember that Miss Pigot counted the cost before she filed and knew she must deny everything or the suit would be ineffective."

I wonder if she did count the cost. She probably thought I would withdraw my comments to avoid the publicity. I expected her to back off when I refused. It appears we're both too stubborn for our own good. But only one of us can prevail.

Gasper turns to Mr. Fish's testimony. "There's the suggestion he perjured himself to protect Mr. Hastie. If Mr. Fish planned to invent his testimony, he could easily say he was going out to smoke a cigar and coming back sooner than expected found Mr. Wilson giving Miss Pigot a kiss. Your Lordship is asked to believe Mr. Fish invented an unnatural story. If this is true, death wouldn't be too bad for Mr. Fish.

"But if the story is false, why wouldn't Mr. Wilson swear he hadn't taken two quarts of beer, or that he asked Mr. Fish to look at the woodwork, or that he didn't say to Miss Pigot he'd had too much beer. He did what becomes a man. He didn't deny anything but sailed close to the wind. Nitya Gopal Mukherjee's evidence was supposed to demolish Mr. Fish, but it's fallen through."

Gasper brings up an interesting question about the time I was ill. "Why were Mr. Wilson and Miss Pigot at Mr. Steele's house for four days and four nights? Dr. Charles is one of the ablest physicians in Calcutta. He appointed a nurse, and Miss Pigot took her place."

"I ask Your Lordship to contrast the evidence Mrs. Sharpland gave with the demeanor of Miss Pigot. Mr. Trevelyan, the most eminent cross-examiner in Calcutta, questioned Mrs. Sharpland. There was no contradiction, no hesitation, not a single occasion when Your Lordship had to tell her to answer the question. Compare this with Miss Pigot who couldn't answer any question without a prevarication. When asked whether she sat on the sofa with Mr. Wilson, she said 'possibly.' This is not a denial. Anything is possible. Likewise, on the question of touching Mr. Wilson's thigh."

Gasper goes on to other witnesses and points out a significant exchange. Mrs. Wheeler asked Miss Pigot why women dismissed from their positions for immorality came to Miss Pigot, and she replied they looked upon her as friend. Gasper rightly reminds the judge of the adage, "Tell me who your friends are, and I'll tell you who you are." And then he focuses on Miss Pigot's proclivity to be in the company of men and reminds the judge she wasn't always forty-six years old as she is now. From there he jumps into Miss Pigot's relationship with Cockburn. In short, Gasper paints Miss Pigot as an immoral woman throughout.

"My final point is Miss Pigot's harsh treatment of the children under her care. The girl Hester..."

"Stop there, Mr. Gasper," Justice Norris says. "If you wanted the court to accept the story of her ill-treatment, you should have produced her in court."

"Yes, My Lord," Mr. Gasper says. "There are also the cases of Bidu and Joboni. In both cases the punishment inflicted was unnecessarily severe. Bidu's treatment was worse than she said it was."

"I questioned her myself on that point," Justice Norris says.

"I hope Your Lordship won't put too much weight on her answer. She knew once she left the witness box, she'd have no protection. A beating might be justified for a theft, but how can Joboni's punishment be justified? I submit that if in the case of Joboni, the beating was unjustified, the plaintiff shouldn't receive any damages."

I thought Gasper had more to say, but he returns to our table. Justice Norris announces he'll pass judgment Saturday, the day after tomorrow. I don't know what will become of Miss Pigot now. But as the Bard said, *"Frailty, thy name is woman."*

Chapter 24
"I Think This Concludes Our Business"

Friday, 14 September 1883
Mary Pigot

"Mary, open your eyes. Open them now."

For a moment, I think it's Mama but she's in Dacca. Who's calling? I turn my head. A woman in a summer dress with her dark hair drawn back sits by the bed.

"Who're you?" I whisper.

"A friend," says the woman. "Do you want to speak Bengali or English?"

"English. We never speak Bengali at home. Are you real, or am I dreaming?"

"I'm real. You can pinch me if you like." The woman smiles. "I've been reading about you in the newspaper. You need a friend, and I've nothing else to do, so I came. You were in a bad way last night."

"You stayed with me all night? Why?"

"My husband is a Salvationist, like Mr. James. They called your story to my attention, and suggested I come to you. I've been here since nine o'clock last night. I think you should sit up now."

The woman arranges pillows behind my head. I realize I'm wearing the same clothes from yesterday.

"I wasn't expecting to see anyone," I stutter.

"I know. I sent for sambar, rice, and tea. After you breakfast, I'll send for a bath, if that's agreeable," the woman says. "I also sent for this morning's newspaper, so you can read what happened after you left court."

"I'm sure it's nothing good," I say.

The woman shrugs. "My name is Margaret. Call me Meg. It's shorter."

"I'm pleased to meet you, Meg," I incline my head. "It's kind of you to visit me."

"No more kind than your work with children and women in the *zenanas*," Meg says. "God calls us where we need to be."

A servant taps at the door and brings in a tray. "Leave it on the table by the window," Meg orders. "Come, my dear, it's cooler by the window."

I'm relieved I at least removed my shoes before I got into bed. Meg pours tea and joins me in the meal. I'm famished.

"You look better now," Meg says. "Shall I read the newspaper to you?"

She doesn't wait for a reply and relates what Mr. Trevelyan and Mr. Gasper had to say yesterday.

"I don't think Mr. Trevelyan did a very good job for you," Meg says. "Justice Norris isn't the type to worry about women's sensitivity to courtrooms, especially in this type of case."

"Why do you say that?" I ask.

Meg shrugs. "The problem is everyone's fascinated by indiscretions in the mission community, but no one's comfortable discussing them."

A man comes in carrying a fairly large metal tub, which he places on the floor. As he leaves, women bring jugs of water. The man comes back to set up a screen around the tub. Meg claps her hands and shoos them away.

"Here, I have glycerin soap for you," Meg says. "Now, go behind the screen, throw those awful clothes to me, and wash. There should be enough water for your hair as well."

I do as she instructs. The water feels amazingly cool, though that must be my imagination. I wash my hair and wring it out. Meg throws me a sheet to use as a towel.

"I brought you new underthings, a corset and a dress," Meg says and hands them over the screen.

The dress is a plain muslin walking dress like hers. I put it on as best I can and come out so she can adjust the laces.

"That will do nicely. You shouldn't wear black all the time," Meg says. "I think the color black accounts for a great deal of melancholy." She fluffs my hair until it's dry enough to arrange. "It's too wet to walk in the Maidan, so we're going to the Indian Museum in Chowringhee. Have you been there?" Meg asks.

"I never go to public exhibits. Couldn't we just stay here?"

Meg shakes her head. "You need fresh air and exercise. I didn't help you dress so you could mope in the hotel lobby. And it will get your mind off your troubles for a few hours."

A few hours? I feel like she's abducting me.

"Why are you doing this? Surely you have better things to do," I say.

"There is no higher commandment than loving one's neighbor. Today, you're my neighbor. Think of me as a small blessing," Meg smiles and pushes me out the door.

It's a magical day. The rain isn't too heavy, so we take the longer drive to the museum. We walk, talk, and gaze at Mughal paintings and different temple artifacts. We come back in time for tea at the hotel. Mr. Carruthers waits in the lobby.

"Mr. Carruthers," I say extending both hands. "I'm sorry I made such a terrible witness yesterday."

"You did your best, which is all one can do. Don't brood over it," Mr. Carruthers says. "Mrs. Monroe, thank you for looking after Miss Pigot."

"You two know each other?" I ask.

"I sometimes assist in her husband's work," Mr. Carruthers says.

He looks a bit embarrassed, so I don't ask anything more.

"I've reserved a table for tea," he says.

We walk into the foyer and spend a lovely hour conversing about everything but the case, until Mr. Carruthers places his napkin on the table.

"Miss Pigot, I'm delighted to see you looking better. I'll send my clerk to escort you to court tomorrow. Justice Norris will make his ruling, which will end your active participation in the case. In all likelihood, we'll appeal to get a fair judgment, but you're not to worry about that now."

We shake hands.

Meg cocks her head to one side. "I think you're much better than you were this morning. You take things too seriously."

"My entire life is on the line."

"Your life is in God's hands, and justice will come in good time. I suggest you look through your psalter tonight and rest comfortably. You've nothing to fear," Meg says. "I must leave you now."

I nod. "Thank you." It seems such a small phrase for the service she did for me today. Yesterday I wanted nothing more than to die in my despair. Today I have a glimmer of hope. I might be able to build a new life, after all.

I sleep deeply and wake to see a break in the clouds. My black dress hangs on the screen, looking more presentable that I thought it would. My collar is starched. My shoes are polished. I pinch my cheeks in the mirror and go downstairs to meet my escort. I don't have a spring in my step, but I'm not shuffling either. When I arrive at the courtroom, I wish Mr. Trevelyan a good morning.

"Don't get your hopes up, Miss Pigot," he says. "One never knows how or why Justice Norris rules."

"I apologize for the other day."

"If you were more definitive, our case would be stronger," Mr. Trevelyan says. "However, my colleague's manner was shocking, to say the least. Don't think about it anymore. I'm not."

Justice Norris comes in with a flash of red robes. "Good Morning, everyone," he says. "I now pronounce my ruling in the case of *Pigot vs. Hastie*. And may I say what a travesty it is we weren't allocated a jury. I think it deplorable that the task of deciding a case such as this is left to one man, however experienced, competent, quiet, self-possessed, and reticent. But we must carry on."

Mr. Trevelyan stifles a laugh. I think the judge has an inflated opinion of himself, but I don't know if a jury would make things better or worse.

Justice Norris adjusts his spectacles and begins reading.

"Plaintiff Mary Pigot brought this action against William Hastie to recover damages for libel in the amount of twenty thousand rupees. The plaintiff's statement sets out certain facts, many of which were proven in evidence. Miss Pigot was for many years superintendent of the Scottish orphanage in Calcutta. In December 1881, a Miss Smail came from Scotland to work with and under Miss Pigot. She forwarded certain complaints to the Scottish Ladies' Association..."

Justice Norris drones on. He has a rather nasally voice as he reviews the history of my relations with Mr. Hastie. He agrees Mr. Hastie thought too much of his position and wanted to seize control of the Female Mission. Justice Norris explains my exoneration in Scotland, Mrs. Walker's anonymous pamphlet and overtures for the incriminating letters. Justice Norris notes Mrs. Walker sent the letters to Mr. Hastie, who endorsed them and sent them to Dr. Scott.

"I wish to make some observations about Mr. Hastie's comments during his conduct of the case," Justice Norris says. "He seemed under the impression that a party in his position wasn't liable for the publication of libels he received. Legally, the letters are libels of the grossest character. One letter suggests that the orphanage over which Miss Pigot presided was a brothel. Could there be a viler or more outrageous libel?"

Justice Norris looks towards the defense table. Mr. Hastie keeps his eyes straight ahead, while Mr. Gasper makes notes.

"Mrs. Walker sends these letters to Mr. Hastie. I hope and believe Mrs. Walker had a real desire to see the Female Mission managed as she thought it should be and see a person she thought unfit for her position removed. But I can't believe the whole of her motive was pure. She had to be annoyed her sister's charges were put to one side.

"Neither was Mr. Hastie animated with a pure motive when he sent the letters on. There is evidence of malice. He wanted to remove Miss Pigot and put Miss Smail in her place. At the very least, he wanted Miss Pigot subordinate to the Corresponding Board. He had a bad opinion of Miss Pigot, smarted from her rebuffs, and felt his efforts thwarted. He had every reason to want Miss Pigot removed or placed in a position of subjection. When he recommended the Corresponding Board have the power to dismiss any employee not of Scotch nationality, he aimed that suggestion at Miss Pigot."

I glance over at Mr. Hastie. His back is rigid. For the moment, he's the one under scrutiny.

Justice Norris begins talking about Mr. Hastie's comment that the letters took him by surprise and he'd long been suspicious of my misbehavior.

Justice Norris says, "The things stated were acts of deliberate cruelty to children suffering from fits, an ill-regulated supply of food, insufficient clothing, mismanagement, and a lack of oversight which allowed the institution to become a brothel. As well as suggestions Miss Pigot was too familiar with a native pleader and flirtatious with a married Scotchman. Yet he took no action until he received these letters. Clearly there is evidence of malice, and a jury might have found a verdict for the plaintiff. But…"

But? There's a but? I don't understand. You just said the statements constitute libel. And he sent them on, so he's guilty. How can there be a but? I feel myself stiffen.

"The matter has assumed a totally different complexion," Justice Norris continues.

No. Libel is libel. You said so.

"The defense brought out four basic matters to justify the alleged libel: allegations of relations between Miss Pigot and Mr. Wilson and between Miss Pigot and Kali Churn Banerjee. Also the alleged ill-treatment of the girls and Mr. Hastie's concern with the disregard of social proprieties. The latter point he based on a picnic at Barrackpore Park, Miss Pigot's unladylike conduct at Mr. Steele's house, and Miss Pigot's visits to Mr. Wilson. Initially, I thought this too flimsy to prove impropriety.

"But if the evidence leads me to conclude Miss Pigot is an impure woman, that is another matter. Her relations with Mr. Wilson and Babu

Banerjee appear trivial until viewed in light of Miss Pigot's character and the later revelations.

"I was struck by Mrs. Wheeler's testimony that Miss Pigot employed teachers she knew to be immoral women. Miss Pigot's explanation wasn't satisfactory. She couldn't remember what Mrs. Wheeler told her."

Mrs. Wheeler complained about everything. How was I to remember one complaint more than another? And now he's going on about Kali Churn. Yes, he visited frequently. He helped me. Justice Norris thinks there was an opportunity for us to engage in immoral relations. We never did anything questionable. But the judge believes Mrs. Oliver and Miss Gordon, women from nowhere. He doesn't believe me or Kali Churn. I feel lost in a sea of words. Large ones. Small ones. Thank God the judge believes Mr. James about those silly slippers.

But truly, the judge wants to believe the worst of me. The judge thinks there was something wrong about my visits with Chunder Kumar Dey. That he didn't testify because he couldn't deny they occurred. That his wife didn't testify because she couldn't either. But there was nothing inappropriate. Everything is twisted.

"There's no doubt Mr. Hastie's evidence concerning Kali Churn Banerjee should be taken with modification," Justice Norris intones. "It's evident Mr. Hastie is, as far as a Christian man and a clergyman may be, indignant at Babu Banerjee's language towards him. For the same reason Mr. Hastie's evidence regarding Babu Banerjee should be received with caution, so ought Mr. Chuckerbutty's, because he is, to a considerable extent, under Mr. Hastie's control.

"Mr. Hastie has been unwise in much he has done, but he hasn't been dishonorable. On the question of Mr. Chuckerbutty's evidence about Miss Pigot and Kali Churn Banerjee, I must ask if it is true or a fabrication. I believe that substantially, the evidence is true.

"Miss Pigot denied the incident took place, but she wasn't asked if she'd actually requested Mr. Chuckerbutty to visit her. Her denial related to Kali Churn Banerjee's dress in shirt and trousers, and it seems to me she protested too much.

"Mrs. Palmer and Mrs. Mukherjee both said Miss Pigot went to Dr. Chunder's house on Amherst Street. I find this the strongest possible evidence that extreme familiarity existed between Miss Pigot and this *babu*."

I've lost. The judge wants to believe the worst of me, and there's nothing I can do.

"On the question of whether Mr. Hastie made any effort to verify the letters, I'm satisfied he conferred with colleagues, though I'm not saying his queries proved the letters to be true. I think it a great pity Mr. Hastie sent the letters to Dr. Scott, a person he wasn't asked to send them to, and who had no concern with them. There is evidence Mr. Hastie surreptitiously opened another man's letter and sent it to his ecclesiastical superior in Scotland. A man who would violate one of the fundamental rules of the Code of Honor is a man on whose evidence no jury should rely."

The judge slaps Mr. Hastie on the hand and calls him a bad fellow. Me, he excoriates on the basis of false evidence.

"We now come to Mr. Fish's evidence. I approach this with hesitation and not a little disgust. But it must be dealt with, because it's become the keystone of the case, the pivot upon which everything must stand or fall. Both Mr. Trevelyan and I pressed him on how a professed Christian could witness such indecency, and yet remain in familiar, even intimate, relations with the man and woman he saw commit indecent acts. Mr. Fish replied he was the only witness, and it was more important to maintain the peace and harmony of the mission. This seems unsatisfactory, but I'm sure most people would do the same.

"Astounding as Mr. Fish's conduct is and in need of explanation, I'm faced with this: it would be more extraordinary if he invented the story. I've struggled hard and earnestly to disbelieve it. I would to God I could disbelieve it. But there was great force in Mr. Gasper's comment that if Mr. Fish was going to invent the incident, he could've created something far simpler.

"I've said harsh things about Mr. Hastie. But I don't think him a man who would conspire with Mr. Fish to invent this story, and then commit perjury of the most wicked and malignant description in the witness box."

I sigh. I think Mr. Fish would do anything to ingratiate himself with Mr. Hastie.

"There's the question of who else might've been present. When Mr. Trevelyan cross-examined Mr. Fish, nothing was said about Babu Mukherjee's presence. Nothing was said until Mr. Wilson was in the witness box. Mr. Wilson said he couldn't remember if he sat on a bench or a chair, but this is a matter of importance. In addition, there seems to have been unnecessary social intercourse, visiting, and familiarity between Miss Pigot and Mr. Wilson. I can't bring myself to believe this friendship was purely platonic. This business of Miss Pigot going to the house that last time so she could have a photograph of Mr. Wilson's room in her mind, I'm bound to say, I don't believe it."

Having cast my friendship with Mr. Wilson in the most scurrilous light, the judge moves to my relations with Kali Churn Banerjee. He thinks it strange neither Kali Churn's wife nor his niece were called to corroborate our friendship, and that no one ever saw him with his children.

"The evidence of Babu Banerjee going to the orphanage and into Miss Pigot's bedroom satisfied me that his relations with Miss Pigot weren't of a proper character. At first, I was struck by the way Babu Banerjee testified, but this faded in view of his cross-examination, and was almost entirely removed by the piteous spectacle Miss Pigot presented in the witness box. I would expect a talented Bengali pleader of the High Court to do well in the box, but I did notice a certain unwillingness to meet my eye."

Justice Norris picks up his last sheet of paper.

"I think the defense has substantially succeeded. The evidence of Mr. Wilson and Babu Banerjee broke down during cross-examination, and what little superstructure remained was entirely removed by Miss Pigot's testimony. I can't attach any importance to it. It was given in a deplorable manner that left no doubt it my mind it was false.

"The charge of cruelty toward the children wasn't proven, therefore I order the defendant to pay damages amounting to one *anna*, and each party bear their own costs."

One *anna*? One-sixteenth of a *rupee*? I'm destroyed. Mr. Hastie shakes hands with Mr. Gasper and Mr. Geddes and walks towards me. He reaches into his pocket and pulls out two coins, which he lays on the table.

"I think this concludes our business," he says, and walks away.

Chapter 25

"The Entire House Of Cards Will Fall"

Mary Pigot

I pick up the copper coins, each valued at one-half an anna. I examine one, rubbing the grime off with my fingers. Queen Victoria in her imperial crown graces one side. The other spells out *'Half Anna India'* with the date 1875, the same year we moved to Bow Bazar. A wreath twines around the coin's edge. My reputation is worth two of these coins. I roll them in my hand before putting them in my pocket. I pick up the valise I brought today. I'm going back to Serampore on the next train.

Mr. Trevelyan shakes hands. "I know this is a blow. Rest assured, we'll appeal. The judge completely disregarded the actual libel."

I look at him and shake my head. "I don't see the point."

"The point is justice," Mr. Trevelyan says. "The ruling is in error and must be corrected. Leave it with me."

"Very well," I say. "So long as I don't have to testify."

"Appeals are based on the law and recorded testimony. It's most unusual to call witnesses."

Mr. Carruthers's clerk takes my valise. "I have a *gharry* for you, Miss Pigot," he says.

I take a final look at the site of my betrayal and leave the courtroom.

The newspapers are quick to comment on the verdict. To my surprise, they express support for me and vilify Justice Norris. *The Statesman* is kind enough to say they can't decide what the most remarkable aspect of the trial was—Mr. Fish's story or the judge accepting it as evidence. That's something, I suppose. One writer cleverly points out that if any improprieties took place in my bedroom, every *ayah* and servant within a mile of the orphanage would've gossiped about it, eliminating any need for the defendant to interview witnesses from ten years before.

I take no comfort in this, nor the local community's outrage. Why didn't they come forward to testify to my generosity and efforts to bring everyone together? Perhaps I should've gone about like my opponent and found witnesses.

I'm offered a position as European Headmistress at Victoria College for Women. It's a new school for the Brahmo reformer community. Students study at home except for a weekly lecture. It will be like visiting *zenanas,* except I won't be able to share the Bible. Still, I'm grateful for the opportunity to hold my head up and earn my way.

William Hastie

I walk out of the courtroom a vindicated man, only to find enemies surround me. The Foreign Mission Committee at home takes the case up with a vengeance, aggravated by what they see as the great humiliation of having our mission dragged through the public mud, and denying the fact they brought it on themselves.

If they'd done as I advised in May, Miss Pigot would've been unable to bring such a suit. If they hadn't exonerated her from Miss Smail's accurate observations, she'd have been out. And if Mr. Scott had kept a private correspondence to himself, Miss Pigot would never have known about the letters. The Committee erred in every way, and now calls on me to account for it.

I can't fathom their calumny. I'm under review. Mr. Wilson, has been suspended as one would expect, but Mr. Fish as well? For what? Telling the truth? Mr. Chuckerbutty is also under investigation. And I'm supposed to explain how it all happened. What can I say beyond what's in the transcripts?

Six weeks later, the Foreign Mission Committee declares that after reviewing correspondence since my arrival in Calcutta, they find unmistakable proofs of temper and disposition that make me unsuited for my position. I'm to transfer control of the College to Mr. MacFarlane and walk away with six months' salary. The cheek. I've raised the College to the highest academic level in its existence, and this is their thanks.

As news spreads, the response is great indignation. The College is in an uproar over my removal. My students in the advanced classes are very upset, and even teachers protest the way I've been treated. Two large public meetings are planned to protest my departure. I'll speak in my best style. It may be the last chance people have to hear me.

The congregation at St. Andrew's Kirk sent a strong memorial asking that my service continue, as has Mr. Chuckerbutty's Bengali church and even some leading Hindus. The response is a great consolation.

Mr. MacFarlane arrives in Calcutta and stays with Mr. Steele. To think he and I were once friends. Now I could have no greater enemy.

Today, 17 December 1883, is perhaps the greatest test of my endurance. I sit in my study for the last time. Falak sent my things to Mr. Gregory's house. Scottish College passes from me to Mr. MacFarlane. I've no pang of regret, because it cannot stand. Every member of the Corresponding Board thinks the Mission Committee is wrong to dismiss me without giving me an opportunity to rebut the charges. They resolve to send a final appeal to Edinburgh and swear to resign if I'm not reinstated. I hope it doesn't come to that. It's in God's hands.

Mary Pigot

Mr. Trevelyan is true to his word. He's filed the appeal. The document says I'm dissatisfied with the judgment and decree. That's putting it mildly. According to Mr. Trevelyan, in addition to his verdict, Justice Norris erred in just about everything he did. He gave more weight to Mr. Hastie's evidence than mine. He admitted evidence that had nothing to do with the case. His conclusions were wrong.

To all of this, I agree. But it no longer makes any difference. Any vindication can only be hollow for me, though it could make a great deal of difference to Mr. Wilson and Kali Churn Banerjee. Kali Churn has his advocates, and, as far as I'm aware, continues with his church and profession. I hear Mr. Wilson is cast out of the College and no longer part of the mission. Yet he stays and teaches. I'm sure he believes everything will work out in the end. Besides, his very presence must infuriate Mr. Hastie.

I go about my duties. I bought a pair of birds in the bazar yesterday. I like to watch them dance in their bamboo cage.

William Hastie

Unbelievable! The wench is appealing the decision. Whining that the judge was wrong. Wrong? I'll show her wrong, and the Mission Committee too.

I sit at a table on Mr. Gregory's veranda and begin writing. It's true the judge erred. He should've ruled my communication with Mr. Scott was privileged. That would've stopped the entire, tawdry spectacle. I had absolutely no malice towards that abominable woman until she filed suit. The judge wouldn't let me prove her behavior was a pattern. He was wrong in dismissing charges about how the children were treated.

My pen scratches across the paper. Now I've got my teeth into things. The entire house of cards will fall. I'll be reinstated at the College, and after an interval, resign without notice.

Chapter 26
"I'll Not Pay A *Pice* To That Woman"

Appellate Court, February 1884
William Hastie

Since I've no pressing matters, I decide to sit in on the Appellate Court arguments. Mr. Gasper somehow arranged for Gregory Charles Paul, the Advocate General, to argue on my behalf. He takes little notice of me, as if my presence is of no consequence. I should think my insights would be helpful. Perhaps he'll call upon me later.

Chief Justice Garth takes his seat at the high table. He's not a young man any more. He has a baleful countenance. His colleague Justice Wilson sits to his right. Justice Norris lamented he had to decide the case alone. But I don't imagine he's pleased two justices now go over his decision. I expect them to note my complete lack of malice in this matter. I simply did what I had to do, with the result I've been unfairly treated by almost everyone involved.

Mr. Paul is more eloquent than Mr. Gasper as he delivers his opening statement, but he lacks passion.

"My Lords," the Judge Advocate says in a matter-of-fact voice, "our appeal consists of twelve points, the most important of which is that Justice Norris should have ruled the documents in question were privileged, and that Mr. Hastie didn't forward them with any sense of malice. Had he done so, we wouldn't be here today."

467

So very true. See where Justice Norris got us. The mission is disgraced. And I... who can say how long it will take to restore my position to its former respect?

Mr. Paul reminds the judges that my only interest was for the good of the mission. "Mr. Hastie knew things weren't right at the Female Mission. Mismanagement can't be kept secret indefinitely. From the time of his arrival, Mr. Hastie became aware that all wasn't as it should be. Indeed, the Foreign Missionary Committee at home specifically requested he restore harmony within the mission. Mr. Hastie had no ill feeling towards Miss Pigot. He simply tried to bring about reconciliation."

My mind wanders to the Old Testament prophets. So many of them were disregarded when they tried to reconcile the Hebrews to God: voices crying in the wilderness. Mr. Paul drones on until Chief Justice Garth interrupts him. "With regard to the passage referring to Miss Pigot as an illegitimate half-caste. If that was Mr. Hastie's position, why did Mr. Gasper object in the court below when Mr. Trevelyan wished to introduce her parents' marriage certificate?"

Mr. Paul looks surprised. "The certificate is irrelevant, My Lord. It didn't affect anything regarding the alleged libel."

Chief Justice Garth doesn't look convinced but he tells the Advocate General to continue. Mr. Paul notes that Miss Pigot and Kali Churn Banerjee admitted they were on intimate terms, implying a greater intimacy than they said occurred. Justice Wilson leafs through the transcript as if checking the testimony. The Advocate General says he's prepared to show Mr. Fish's evidence was true. I'm not sure he should've brought that up. Mr. Fish already lost his position over it. I've no desire to see my reputation similarly tarred.

March 1884
Mary Pigot

Six months after the trial, I begin to enjoy my new life. Every day I visit my young charges at their homes. Though I don't mention the Bible, it's hard to escape the Christian message when reading English literature, so I'm content with my work. I attend the Danish Church now. Officially it's St. Olave's Church after the man who built it, but Baptist missionaries conduct the services. To add to the irony, it looks like St. Andrew's and is in the Diocese of Calcutta. The members don't seem to mind much about my case.

My adversary prowls around Calcutta awaiting the result of my appeal. Perhaps he'll gift me with another *anna*.

It's a pleasant day in March. I've been in the *zenanas* today and just returned to my residence when Mr. Trevelyan's messenger brings me the decree from the Appellate Court. He bows, hands me the documents and leaves me standing at the door with my mouth open in surprise. I take the envelope up to my rooms and set it on my writing table, not sure if I want to open it. Finally I offer a small prayer for courage and slit the thick paper. I'm impatient and go directly to Chief Justice Garth's conclusion.

I'm vindicated: The lower court judgment is reversed. God granted my prayer. Breath rushes out of me and sounds like a sob. I read the liberating words several times and hug myself: "My learned brother and myself are agreed in finding that the defendant has published this libel upon the plaintiff without any justification whatever, and that he was influenced in publishing it by malice."

Chief Justice Garth notes my enemy communicated a libel calculated to do me serious personal and professional injury. He grants me a judgment of three thousand *rupees*, plus court costs.

My Psalter open at Psalm 30, I repeat the words:

"I will extol thee, O Lord; for thou hast lifted me up,
and hast not made my foes to rejoice over me.
O Lord, my God, I cried unto thee, and thou hast healed me.
O Lord, thou hast brought up my soul from the grave: thou has kept me
alive, that I shouldn't go down to the pit."

Sunday, 6 April 1884
William Hastie

I watch Calcutta recede into the distance and shake the dirt off my shoes. A pox on all of them. I'll not pay a *pice* to that woman. Let her whistle up the wind for her money.

Chapter 27

"India—My Glory And My Humiliation"

Edinburgh
Wednesday, 28 May 1884
William Hastie

The General Assembly is the highest governing body in the Church of Scotland, and my last court of appeal if I'm to return to my position as Principal of Scottish College. I watch the opening ceremonies from the Assembly Hall gallery. The procession into the hall below engages my spirits in the solemnity of the occasion. For a moment, I believe I will finally receive justice.

The Lord High Commissioner, Queen Victoria's personal representative, sits on a throne to observe the proceedings. Moderator Peter M'Kenzie poses in the chair once occupied by John Knox, the founder of our church. Would that he had the fortitude of that great man. Below him the Clerks, the Agent, and the Procurator take their places. Then comes the Circumtabular Oligarchy, those supposedly wise men of the church who control everything that happens in the Assembly.

The scene reminds me of a Spanish bullfight. Soon, I'll take the place of the bull, while they flex their powers to throw darts at me from protected positions behind church barricades, and the audience bays for blood. I count my enemies.

Dr. John Tulloch, Principal of St. Mary's College and Moderator of the General Assembly is *Jupiter Olympus*, with his white hair and beard, descends from his great height to settle the church's quarrel with me. The Very Reverend Kenneth Phin, a moving force on the Foreign Mission Committee, sits like an almost extinct volcano, ready at any moment to jump from his chair and shout down unwary opponents. The Very Reverend Dr. Archibald Scott, Convener of the Foreign Mission Committee, at whose feet I lay blame for everything in Calcutta. I forwarded those letters to him privately. If he hadn't given them to Miss Pigot she would never have filed the lawsuit. Finally, there's Dr. Robert Story with his own long white beard, Principal at Glasgow University. All of them are humiliated by the Great Calcutta Scandal and looking for a scapegoat.

After luncheon the clerk calls my case, and I enter the pit. I nod to the newspapermen and center myself before my clay-footed superiors. I won't raise my voice. Let them lean forward if they wish to hear.

I look at each of my judges. "I present two petitions. First, I request that you reverse my dismissal as Principal of Scottish College. Second, I demand that this Assembly rule the Foreign Mission Committee failed to discharge its duty to defend an agent in the field and be ordered to reimburse me for my legal expenses."

The judges look at me with stone faces. Ministers from the parishes, however, lean forward in attention. Referring to my first petition, I point out the Presbytery of Edinburgh ordained me, and my appointment as Principal of Scottish College gives me the same standing as any parish clergyman in Scotland. Only the Presbytery or the Superior Court of the Church of Scotland can sever my appointment, not a mere Committee.

"And even if the Foreign Mission Committee had the right to dismiss me," I say, "they must give me an opportunity to refute their charge that my temper and disposition are unsuited to my position as Principal. The letters used to prove this misbegotten allegation were private, addressed to Dr. Scott alone."

I take a few steps forward and then back to relieve the pressure on my knees. They haven't been the same since my ordeal in the witness box last year.

"They charge me with having a temper," I smile. "I admit the Old Adam still lives in me, and God puts it to good use. Fighting for justice demands certainty." I look around the assembly room. "Was St. Paul a soft-spoken person? Or John Knox? Was *he* a quiet person in the defense of righteousness?" I shake my head. "Our founders weren't subservient in discharging the duty God laid upon them, and neither am I."

I look again to the expressionless judges. "I've no desire to smite prominent men such as yourselves. I won't launch thunderbolts. But neither will I hesitate to do so, should it become necessary. I suggest that if Dr. Story and Dr. Scott took up my task, they would quickly discover their own true tempers."

Cries of *'hear, hear'* and *'go on'* rise from the Assembly.

Dr. Scott stands to quell the enthusiasm. He knows I'm right and have the clergy on my side. "I ask the Assembly to hear me," he says. "The decision to dismiss Reverend Hastie resulted from long and regretful deliberation. Judge his letters for yourselves."

Dr. Scott begins reading my letters, a clear attempt to slow the momentum of my case.

"I place this last letter on the table. I can't take responsibility for reading it. Anyone here may read it for himself," Dr. Scott says.

"It must be something terrible, though I have no idea what," I riposte. "Perhaps I charged Dr. Phin with heresy."

Lord Balfour of Burleigh moves that ladies be excluded so the letter can be read.

Such a kerfuffle. When Balfour reads the letter aloud, there's nothing in it but College business that could be heard by anyone. I continue my discourse until the dinner break, after which I resume the floor to defend my second petition.

"What you call the Great Calcutta Scandal is entirely due to the Dr. Scott and the Foreign Mission Committee. They refused my advice and showed my private correspondence to Miss Pigot, never thinking a woman bold enough to file a legal suit. I assure you, Miss Pigot is nothing if not bold.

"When Miss Pigot's accusations fell upon my head as an agent of the Church of Scotland, the Foreign Mission Committee accepted no responsibility and offered no funds for my defense—a defense I successfully mounted with the exception of one point; a defense that wouldn't have been necessary if Dr. Scott had kept the communication to himself as intended."

I focus directly on Dr. Scott. "Justice Norris held that Dr. Scott erred in showing the letters to Miss Pigot—clear proof he is responsible for this unfortunate lawsuit." He doesn't even have the grace to look embarrassed.

After speaking eight hours with only a break for dinner, I sit down at two o'clock in the morning thinking we'll adjourn. Dr. Scott, however, demands to be heard and carries the Assembly further towards the dawn.

"I ask this Assembly not to be swayed by oratory," he says, "but to confirm the actions of the Foreign Mission Committee. Allow me to point out a different side to the petitioner, who has been less than honest in his presentation. A native gentleman with whom I correspond, says that when he told Mr. Hastie he wouldn't receive any more impertinent letters from him, the Principal of our College responded that any further reply would be delivered from the tip of his boot. Is this the man to lead our missionary enterprise in Calcutta?"

That can only be Kali Churn Banerjee. Scott must have initiated the correspondence. I'm shocked that he should stoop to such methods of obtaining information. And to what end? Was he looking for evidence against me?

Dr. Scott continues his attack. "Mr. Hastie claims a resemblance between himself and St. Paul. Can you imagine the apostle in Athens speaking with an Epicurean or a Stoic philosopher who asked him why he came to their city, and St. Paul delivering his answer from the tip of his apostolic sandal? I think not."

Ridiculous! He twists my words.

Dr. Scott turns to our correspondence. "Gentlemen, Mr. Hastie wrote offensive notes and letters throughout his service. He laced them with silly jokes and quotations from Shakespeare, Robert Burns, the Book of Job, and even nursery rhymes. One note appended to a quotation from Homer stated that it was originally in Greek, as if to say, 'I'll translate it for you poor ignoramuses at home, but we in Calcutta read the original Greek.' In my opinion, Mr. Hastie resembles that charmer in Butler's *Hudibras* who spoke Greek as easily as a pig squeaked."

There's uneasy laughter from the representatives, at least those who remain awake.

Dr. Scott's voice booms through the room. "Mr. Hastie is a man with a fractious nature hidden under an erudite exterior. This lawsuit made his inappropriateness for his position clear beyond any doubt. I move this Assembly support the decision of the Foreign Mission Committee to dismiss Mr. Hastie with six months' salary and no payment of the legal expenses he brought upon himself."

Friday, 30 May 1884

I don't know why I bothered to state the truth. The majority of the General Assembly follow the wise old men of the church like the sheep they are. They approve the Foreign Mission Committee's actions. They confirm Reverend Chuckerbutty's dismissal and Mr. Fish's termination. On the basis of the Appellate Court decision, the Assembly reinstates Mr. Wilson. Reasonable enough, I suppose. And now they come to me. The Assembly denies my petitions and confirms my services are no longer required.

I will not be dismissed like a common layman. "Moderator, allow me the final word. I herewith tender my resignation from all official connection with the Church of Scotland."

I turn and walk out the door into the free air of Edinburgh.

November 1884

If the General Assembly thought the Calcutta Scandal would die down after they dismissed me, they were mistaken. The entire missionary enterprise is about to crumble. Donations are down, and the episode is discussed in churches all over Scotland. I'm gratified to find I have many supporters.

The Foreign Mission Committee scrambles to restore their position and decides to send an Investigative Commission to report on the current state of affairs in Calcutta. But I've yet to hear from them. If they won't see me here, perhaps I should go to Calcutta to meet them.

In any event, I'd like to get the Appeal Court's decree off my head. I can't live in peace, comfort, or honor if Miss Pigot can take action against me whenever she has the whim. I decide to return to the scene of my disappointment, testify to the Commissioners, and vindicate my good name.

I take the steamer to Bombay in January 1885. When I arrive in Calcutta, there's a deputation to greet me. My best students are there, and Mr. Gregory again offers hospitality. People are impressed at my return, because I risk jail for failing to fulfill the court's decree.

I owe eleven thousand, two hundred *rupees* for court costs and three thousand *rupees* in damages to Miss Pigot. This amounts to one thousand, two hundred fifty pounds. I'll never pay it. I can't. I transferred my assets to Mother and my sisters before I left Edinburgh. I barely have enough funds for expenses.

Thursday, 12 February 1885

This afternoon Mr. Gillan and I sit chatting when Mr. Brown, Bailiff for the High Court, arrives with a summons and warrant for my arrest.

I laugh. I've expected this since I disembarked last Saturday.

"If you'll come with me, sir," the bailiff says. And takes me to court.

To my surprise Justice Cunningham commits me to the jail for non-payment of the decree as if I'm a common criminal.

Mr. Gregory came to court with me and drives the bailiff and I back to his house, where I eat a very nice dinner. Friends come to wish me well.

We conclude the sentence is an attempt to intimidate me. No doubt I'll be out tomorrow morning.

Mr. Gregory and the bailiff drive me to jail. I step inside the gate as the sun sets, an unfortunate symbolism. Everyone is courteous, the jailor a bit flustered to have a guest of my standing. I go to my cell, meet my fellow prisoners and settle down for the night.

The jail has two stories. The poor native prisoners stay in the lower level. The upper level, where I stay, is subdivided by a partition. On the eastern side there are four cells. The western half has four cells and two bathrooms.

My cell is about ten and a half feet by seven feet. Not spacious, but adequate. There's a table, a bedstead with a poor mattress, a barred window and a barred gate. I have the use of another cell for my meals, and a veranda.

The day after my arrival Mr. Gillan comes to visit, and to my surprise, the Commissioners arrive to take evidence. They bring Mr. Macfarlane who now leads Scottish College, and Mr. Edwards, my former colleague, to testify as witnesses. My incarceration has done what my requests failed to achieve.

"I should like Mr. Gillan to stay," I say. "I've no confidence in any of you and want an unbiased witness."

Naturally, the Commissioners refuse my request. Edwards declines to answer questions, especially from me. When I ask Rankin to put Edwards under oath, he replies no evidence in India will be taken under oath. *So why would anyone testify honestly*, I wonder.

Macfarlane also declines to answer my questions.

I look over the commissioners. Rankin has a cantankerous demeanor and is as unfair as the Mission Committee could desire. He's also soon to be Scott's brother-in-law. Not much I can expect from him. Gray clearly can't be counted on for an unbiased opinion, and Marshall won't take a stand against them.

That being so, there's no harm in speaking my mind. "Gentlemen," I say, "I'm tired of this mock trial. Your very presence is a sham. I wouldn't be in a Calcutta jail if you'd had the decency to meet with me in Edinburgh. But you refused. And here we all are to no purpose."

I suddenly realize I may have misread the situation. The commissioners have no interest in the truth. I have no funds to pay the court decree. I might be here for weeks or even months. The enormity of my position affects me, and I have to stop the discussion. I need quiet to reflect. Rankin and Gray don't bother to say farewell. Marshall shakes my hand. I'm snared in my own trap with no funds and no clear way forward.

I've been in jail for two weeks. My jailers give me every courtesy and bend the rules to admit my friends, but I crave freedom and fresh air. Mr. Gregory and Mr. MacNair come daily with legal advice. My students, my colleagues, and even ladies visit. Watching them leave my cell, I realize I have no idea when I'll be released. Friends offer to pay my costs, but I refuse to be in their debt. I'm advised that if I declare myself insolvent, the judge may release me. I'm told this is the only other path open to me, but I'm reluctant to take it. A decree of insolvency would be my final humiliation. But the prospect of remaining in jail for months or even years is unacceptable. I swallow my pride and appeal to the judge.

My enemies make things as difficult as possible. The woman's cat's-paw, Judge Wilson, requires I recover the money I transferred to my mother and sisters and wants a statement of my future prospects. How should I know? It's in God's hands.

Eventually, I'm a free man. Mr. Gregory takes me to his house. Spending a month in jail has depressed me—not just the surroundings, but my inability to prevail against my enemies. Before my final departure to Edinburgh, there's a public assembly at St. Andrew's. Gratifying, but I'll never return. I depart before the monsoons set in. India has been both my glory and my humiliation. My faith has been sorely tested, and I wish God had not sent me here. But who am I to question God's mysteries?

Edinburgh
Thursday, 28 May 1885

Never have I been so moved by the pile of rock called Edinburgh Castle. Seeing it's towers over the city assures me I'm home again. I arrive in time for the General Assembly and sit in the gallery as it considers the Report of the Investigating Committee. It is, of course, a whitewash.

The existing state of all the missions is satisfactory.

The charges made against Miss Pigot are ruled to be without foundation. If there were faults of mismanagement, it was due to her being given more to do than anyone should have been allowed to attempt. She either fooled them, or they just want a graceful exit from the entire matter. Probably both. I join Walter Scott in saying:

Women's faith and Woman's trust,
Write the characters in the dust.

Chapter 28

"Calcutta Will Always Be My Home"

Serampore, June 1888
Mary Pigot

The rain beats down in sheets and splashes in my window. I'm happier now than I've ever been. No pressure. No expectations. When I was young, I thought *zenana* teaching less important than superintending an institution, but now I see its true value. Where better to drive out darkness? And the ladies have much to teach me about harmony and respect. God didn't give me the answer I wanted—He gave me a better one.

Not only that, but I have a pension of sixty pounds a year from the Ladies' Association. Guilt money I'm sure, but I'm happy to have it. And Mr. Sen's daughter, the Maharini of Cooch Behar, guarantees me a pension and a home in the mountains when I can't work. Once I tutored her, and now she tends to me.

Another circle closes today. Mr. Wilson asked to call. I wait for him in the drawing room, refreshments laid out between the sofas.

"Miss Pigot," he says. "You look well."

"Thank you," I say. "Please sit." I can't tell him he looks well. He's tired, pale, and stooped. He stayed in India too long, and now his health fails.

"Please." I gesture to the fruit, and he takes a few pieces on a small plate. "It's poor fare compared to what I once served."

"Any food shared with you nourishes." Mr. Wilson looks at me through thick spectacles. "Miss Pigot, my sojourn here is at an end, and I didn't want to leave without..."

I hold up my hand to stop whatever he has to say.

"How many years has it been?" I ask.

Mr. Wilson gazes over my head. "Katy and I arrived in 1863. Such a long time ago."

"Twenty-five years," I smile. "I saw in *The Statesman* there was a farewell event at the College. Everyone spoke well of you, as they should. You'll be missed. Mr. Wilson, you didn't let me apologize before, but do me the honor of accepting my regret for the difficulty my troubles placed on you."

"No, Miss Pigot," Mr. Wilson says. "It was I who failed you. I was proud and left you friendless in your hour of need. It is I who am in your debt."

"I have a good life," I smile. "A simple life that suits me surprisingly well."

"I'm glad to hear it," Mr. Wilson says. "Miss Pigot, I..."

I interrupt. I don't want to revisit the days of our close friendship. In my mind's eye, I see Mrs. Wilson's welcoming face. "Will you return to Crieff?"

"Er, yes," Mr. Wilson says.

"I'm sure Mrs. Wilson will be glad to see you."

"Eh, well, she'll have to have me, whether she will, or no," Mr. Wilson says. He puts down his untouched plate and picks up his *topi*.

"No sun today," I remark.

"No, but after so many years, I can't be without my *topi*. I'm going to throw it on the waters when the ship departs, in case God allows me to return," Mr. Wilson says. "Calcutta will always be my home."

He rises and I escort him to the door. Mr. Wilson walks through the rain to his waiting *gharry*. I watch him depart from my life and remember the years we worked together for the Female Mission. I picture him trying to make sense of my accounting. No matter how much I tried his patience, he always had a kind word and gentle smile. Now he returns to Crieff and Mrs. Wilson. The *gharry* moves out of my sight.

"Farewell," I whisper to him and the moments we shared. The damp air is chilly. I go back inside. It's time to feed my birds.

Author's Note

In 1869 when Miss Pigot became Lady Superintendent, the Female Mission had an orphanage housing forty girls, a school at Kidderpore, and about four *zenanas*. When Miss Pigot left the position, the Female Mission had increased to twelve Hindu Girls Schools with eight hundred thirty-four pupils, an Upper Christian School with eighty-four students, and one hundred fifty-seven *zenanas* with four hundred fifty-three pupils.

Emily Bernard who succeeded Miss Pigot as Lady Superintendent on January 16, 1884 found that every time she thought she was changing a management policy, she was returning to Miss Pigot's methods. Miss Bernard found Miss Pigot's trainees to be superior teachers. She wrote that *"in all our female schools, our best teachers are the girls who have been trained in [Miss Pigot's] orphanage."*

After losing his appeal before the General Assembly in 1885, Reverend Hastie continued his pursuit for justice by filing a lawsuit against the Foreign Mission Committee in the Court of Session. Mr. Hastie repeated the arguments he made before the General Assembly. The first phase of the case went against Mr. Hastie, but before the second phase began, the Foreign Mission Committee offered Mr. Hastie one thousand, two hundred fifty pounds and an apology to clear his personal character, provided Mr. Hastie withdrew his suit. Mr. Hastie accepted.

The Reverend Hastie became an examiner at Edinburgh University, which awarded him the degree of Doctor of Divinity in 1895. The following year The Reverend Hastie became Professor of Divinity at Glasgow University, thereby achieving his goal of a University position. One writer described Reverend Hastie as the *"most preposterous professor in the history of the University of Glasgow."*

Reverend Hastie's obituary in *The Scotsman* observed Mr. Hastie seemed in good health and was *walking across the room when he fell as if in a faint and immediately expired.* Reverend Hastie died in Edinburgh on August 31, 1903.

I encountered the case of *Pigot vs. Hastie* in secondary sources focused on missionary work in India. Most authors attributed the dispute to the alleged relationship between Mary Pigot and Babu Kali Churn Banerjee. However, as I dug into the original source materials, I concluded the case centered more on politics, power struggles, and patriarchy. I chose to tell Mary Pigot's story as one of triumph over social oppression. Mary Pigot was a remarkable woman, not only for her professional accomplishments but because she stood up for her rights against all odds, and prevailed.

In 1884 an anonymous pamphlet appeared: *The Pigot Case: Report of the Case Pigot vs. Hastie as Before the High Court, Calcutta.* The pamphlet contained official documents filed with the suit, testimony, and judgments in the original and appellate courts. It doesn't show attorneys' statements or the questions posed during direct or cross-examination. These were faithfully transcribed and published in the *Indian Daily News* during the trial. *The Statesman* and other newspapers also provided coverage or reports, including newspapers in London and Edinburgh.

I also consulted the *Minute Book of the Foreign Mission Committee, The Church of Scotland Home & Foreign Missionary Record,* and *Female Mission Home and Foreign.*

Research travel took me to the British Library in London, Scottish National Library in Edinburgh, and to Kolkata where many structures from the British colonial period remain.

Two Coins is a work of historical fiction. I made adjustments to simplify the story. James Wilson's brother Robert Wilson resided with him in Calcutta. James and Robert Wilson contributed funds for the picnic at Barrackpore Park. I substituted a cousin named Robert Douglas for Robert Wilson.

Until 1908 Scottish Church College was known as the General Assembly's Institution relating to the Church of Scotland General Assembly. To simplify matters, I used the name Scottish College.

Magic lantern shows such as the one Mary Pigot held were a popular way for missionaries to illustrate Bible stories in the field. The lantern is a simple slide projector with images painted on glass, or photographs.

Narendranath Dutta took up The Reverend Hastie's challenge and visited Sri Ramakrishna. After completing his degree at the General Assembly's Institution in 1884, Dutta became known as Swami Vivekananda. He introduced Hinduism as a World Religion at the 1893 Chicago Parliament of the World's Religions. Swami Vivekananda died in 1902.

Transforming research into a book is not a solo occupation. Many thanks to my husband and son for reading through my original draft, and to Susan Forbes who went through more than one version. All contributed pertinent comments and encouragement.

I invite you to visit my website at sandrawagnerwright.com. You'll find my weekly blog, information on all my books, a gallery of pictures related to British Calcutta, and a chance to sign up for my weekly newsletter. Your contact details will never be shared, and you can unsubscribe at any time.

You can also find out what I'm up to on my Facebook page—facebook.com/SandraWagnerWright/ —and follow me on Twitter @SandraWWright

The best way for new readers to find books is by reviews. If you enjoyed *Two Coins*, please leave a review on Amazon.com or Goodreads.com.

If you're looking for another book about a strong woman of India, check out *Rama's Labyrinth*, my biographical novel about Pandita Ramabai, social reformer, world traveler, Christian convert and founder of Mukti, a still functioning ashram for women and children. Available at Amazon, Barnes & Noble, iBooks, and Kobo.

Reading Group Questions & Topics For Discussion

1. Who were your favorite characters? Why?

2. What was the Church of Scotland mission in Calcutta like before Reverend Hastie arrived in 1879? Were relations between the College and the Female Mission cordial?

3. Why did William Hastie accept a call to Calcutta? What did he hope to accomplish?

4. Did you like William Hastie? Was he a good person for the position of Principal at Scottish College?

5. Did your opinion of William Hastie change during the course of the book?

6. What was Mary Pigot like? How did she interact with the Scottish and Hindu communities?

7. Did Mary Pigot make good professional choices? Or was she impulsive?

8. Did your opinion of Mary Pigot change during the course of the book?

9. Why did Mary Pigot need so much assistance from the faculty at Scottish College?

10. Was William Hastie's assessment of Mary Pigot's qualifications and behavior accurate?

11. What caused the feud between William Hastie and Mary Pigot? What does it reveal about the politics between the Church of Scotland's two missions?

12. What type of relationship did Mary Pigot have with James and Katherine Wilson?

13. What type of relationship did Mary Pigot have with Babu Kali Churn Banerjee?

14. What do you think was the root cause of Mary Pigot's difficulties?

15. Did the Foreign Mission Committee, the Investigating Committee, and the Ladies' Association act appropriately when charges were made against Mary Pigot?

16. What do you think of the witnesses who testified for William Hastie? Were they unbiased, or did they have grievances against Mary Pigot?

17. Why do you think William Fish came forward with his testimony?

18. Would Mary Pigot have received more payment in damages if William Fish hadn't testified?

19. What do you think of Mary Pigot's testimony? What about William Hastie's testimony?

20. If you were in Justice Norris's place, how would you have ruled?

21. Was Justice Norris a fair judge? How does he interact with the witnesses during the trial?

22. After Justice Norris gave his verdict, do you think the Foreign Mission Committee made the correct staffing decisions?

23. Why didn't the Church of Scotland grant William Hastie's petitions? What made them change their decision?

24. What do you think the trial was about?

25. Should *Pigot vs. Hastie* have gone to trial? Did anyone win?

1863

- February. Mr. James Wilson arrives to serve as Senior Lay Missionary at Scottish College.

- Mrs. Wilson takes charge of the Female Orphanage.

1869

- Mary Pigot appointed Lady Superintendent of the Female Orphanage at the 72 Upper Circular Road location.

1870

- Babu Kali Churn Banerjee takes his law degree and enrolls at the Bar.

- Mr. and Mrs. Wilson go home on furlough.

1871

- Mr. Wilson meets Miss Pigot when he returns from furlough.

1872

- Reverend Bipro Churn Chuckerbutty ordained on 8 September at St. Andrew's Church, Calcutta.

1875

- March. Miss Pigot leaves on furlough to Scotland.
- 6 October. Female Mission moves from 72 Upper Circular Road to 125 Bow Bazar.

1876

- November. Miss Pigot returns from furlough.

1877

- January. Foreign Mission Committee appoints James Wilson as Officiating Principal of Scottish College when the current Principal, The Reverend Robert Jardine, returns to Scotland 1878.

1878

- 16 October. The Reverend Hastie ordained by Presbytery of Edinburgh and appointed Principal at Scottish College.

1879

- 2 January. The Reverend Hastie arrives Calcutta.
- 27 January. Picnic at Barrackpore Park.
- 8 February. Dinner Party at Mr. Steele's house.
- 22 February. James Wilson goes home to Scotland on furlough.
- April. Miss Pigot sends her resignation to Ladies' Association.

1880

- February. Mr. William Fish arrives.
- 17 May. Nitya Gopal Mukherjee baptized at St. Andrew's Kirk.

- July. Babu Kali Churn Banerjee's article "One Against Two Thousand" appears in *Indian Christian Herald*.
- 6 August. The Reverend Hastie bans Babu Kali Churn Banerjee from Female Orphanage.

1881

- 18 January. James Wilson returns from furlough.
- 8 December. Georgiana Smail arrives at Female Mission.

1882

- 21 March. Mr. Fish, Mr. Wilson, Mr. Wetherall, & Babu Mukherjee meet at the Female Mission to add up student marks for the prize distribution.
- 1 April. Prize Distribution.
- 13 May. Miss Pigot departs for Scotland.
- August. An anonymous leaflet relating to matters at the Female Mission in Calcutta appears in Scotland.
- 10 November. The Reverend Hastie forwards letters he received from Mrs. Walker to Dr. Archibald Scott.

1883

- 21 March. Miss Pigot files a lawsuit charging The Reverend Hastie with malicious libel.
- 21 April. The Reverend Hastie files his Written Statement.
- May. Miss Pigot suspended from Female Orphanage for mismanagement
- 28 August-13 September. *Pigot vs. Hastie* trial.

- 15 September. Justice Norris issues his verdict.

- 18 October. Mr. Wilson suspended.

- 29 October. Mr. Fish suspended.

- 6 November. The Reverend Hastie dismissed as Principal of Scottish College

1884

- 8 January. Mr. Fish dismissed with six months' salary.

- 14 January. The Reverend Bipro Churn Chuckerbutty suspended from the Bengali Church.

- 16 January. Miss Emily Bernard becomes Lady Superintendent of Female Mission.

- 13 March. Arguments heard in Appellate Court in the case of *Pigot vs. Hastie.*

- May. Church of Scotland General Assembly dismisses The Reverend Hastie's petitions.

- 19 November. Foreign Mission Committee appoints a Commission of Inquiry to review events in Calcutta.

1885

- 7 February. The Reverend Hastie arrives in Calcutta to clear his name.

- 13 February. The Reverend Hastie arrested and jailed.

- 11 March. The Reverend Hastie released from jail.

- 5 May. The Reverend Hastie departs Calcutta.

- 26 May. Church of Scotland General Assembly again dismisses The Reverend Hastie's petitions.

- 17 September. The Church of Scotland General Assembly accepts The Reverend Chuckerbutty's resignation.

1888

- June. Mr. Wilson retires from service in India.

1894

- The Reverend Hastie receives Doctor of Divinity Degree from Edinburgh University.

1895

- The Reverend Hastie appointed Professor of Divinity at Glasgow University.

Glossary Of Names

Banerjee, Babu Kali Churn. Barrister, Pleader in the High Court. Accused of intimate relationship with Miss Pigot.

Carruthers, Arthur St. John (1821-1895) Mary Pigot's solicitor.

Chuckerbutty, Reverend Bipro Churn. (b.1823) Baptized, 1843. Ordained minister in Church of Scotland Bengali Church, 1872. Witness for The Reverend Hastie.

Faulkner, Maud Mary Bartlett (Mrs.) Teacher at Female Mission, January-June 1879. Witness for The Reverend Hastie.

Fish, William. Arrived in Calcutta in February 1880 as Lay Missionary of the Church of Scotland, Junior Professor of English at Scottish College. Accused Miss Pigot of immoral relations with James Wilson. Witness for The Reverend Hastie.

Garth, Richard (1820-1903). Chief Justice of Calcutta High Court 1875-1886.

Gasper, Malcolm Peter (1848-1890) Leading Barrister of the High Court. First Armenian to pass the Indian Civil Service Examination. Barrister for The Reverend Hastie.

Geddes, Charles Turner. Solicitor for The Reverend Hastie.

Gillian, The Reverend George Green. Senior Chaplain at St. Andrew's Kirk.

Gordon, Grace (Miss). Matron at the Orphanage. Miss Pigot employed her 1879-1881. Wrote one of the libelous letters in response to Mrs. Walker's questions. Witness for The Reverend Hastie.

Hastie, The Reverend William (1842-1903) Appointed Principal of Scottish College 1878. Dismissed 1883.

Humphreys, Eliza. Employed by Miss Pigot for about two and one-half years, commencing 1872. Witness for The Reverend Hastie.

Mukherjee, Eliza. Taught at Kidderpore School for sixteen years and employed by Miss Pigot for a few months as a matron. Miss Pigot dismissed her in 1871. Witness for The Reverend Hastie.

Mukherjee, Nitya Gopal. Baptized May 17, 1880 at St. Andrew's Kirk. Witness for Miss Pigot.

Norris, Justice John Freeman. (1842-1904) Judge of the High Court 1882-1905. Presided over *Pigot vs. Hastie.*

Oliver, Lucinda Mary. *Zenana* Teacher and Matron at the Orphanage. Employed by Miss Pigot 1879-1881. Wrote one of the libelous letters in response to Mrs. Walker's questions. Witness for The Reverend Hastie.

Palmer, Emma Margaret. Worked for Miss Pigot as a *zenana* teacher 1871-1872 and 1875-1876. Witness for The Reverend Hastie.

Paul, Gregory Charles (Sir). (1831-1900) Advocate General of Bengal. Argued The Reverend Hastie's case on appeal.

Pigot, Mary Henrietta (b. 1837) Baptized at St. John's Church. Appointed Lady Superintendent of Ladies' Association Female Mission in 1869. Dismissed from her position in 1883.

Scott, Archibald (Dr.) (1837-1909) Convener of Foreign Mission Committee in Scotland.

Sharpland, Caroline Alice Briggs (Mrs.) Engaged as a nurse when The Reverend Hastie ill with cholera. Witness for The Reverend Hastie.

Smail, Georgiana Frances Downie Cullen (Miss). Arrived in December 1881 as Assistant Lady Superintendent of Female Mission. Writes letters critical of conditions at mission. Sister of Mrs. Walker.

Steele, Octavius (1840-1893) Merchant and senior partner of O. Steele & Company. Member of Corresponding Board and Elder of St. Andrew's Kirk. Hosted The Reverend Hastie when he first arrived in Calcutta.

Trevelyan, Ernest John (1850-1929) Advocate before the High Court, 1875-1885. Miss Pigot's barrister in original and appeal case.

Walker, R. Alexander. Lieutenant-Colonel in the Royal Artillery at Dum Dum (Retired 1892). Elder of St. Andrew's Kirk. Member, Corresponding Board. Husband of Mrs. Walker. Miss Smail's brother-in-law.

Walker, Amber Yewdale Lambert Smail (Mrs.) Wrote anonymous leaflet and solicited libelous letters The Reverend Hastie forwarded to Dr. Scott. Married to Colonel Walker. Sister of Georgiana Smail.

Wheeler, Mrs. Monomohini. Employed by Government of Bengal as Inspectress of Girls' Schools. Retired 1901.

Wilson, James. Senior Lay Missionary and Professor of English at Church of Scotland Scottish College. Served in Calcutta from 1863 to 1888. Accused of intimate relationship with Miss Pigot.

Wilson, Katherine (Mrs.) Wife of James Wilson. Lady Superintendent of Female Orphanage from 1863 to about 1867.

Glossary Of Terms And Places

Anna – Denomination of money used in British India. One *anna* equaled one-sixteenth of a *rupee.*

Ayah – Indian female servant who could be a housemaid, lady's maid, or nursemaid.

Babu – In British India a *babu* was often a native clerk. A term of respect.

Barrackpore Park – Founded in 1775 as a summer residence for British Governors-General. Government House and Government Estate built at Barrackpore to provide Viceroy with a suburban residence. About fifteen miles from Central Calcutta.

Butler's *Hudibras* – Seventeenth century poem by Samuel Butler about a knight named Hudibras. Reference is to Part I, Canto I, Line 51: *"Beside, 'tis known he could speak Greek as naturally as Pigs squeak."*

Chapatti – Unleavened flat bread.

Cholera Pills – Originated in British India. One-part opium; two parts black pepper; and three parts asafetida administered with calomel and quinine.

Chum – Close friend with whom one might share a chummery.

Chummery – Shared household, usually of bachelors.

Chupa – Men's sleeveless, inner jacket

Dahl – Preparation of lentils with onions, garlic, ginger, and various spices.

Dhoti – Traditional men's clothing in India.

Dum Dum -- Location of the Royal Artillery's Dum Dum Arsenal. Eighteen miles from Central Calcutta.

Durwan – Doorkeeper.

Gharry – Horse drawn cab or carriage.

Hugli River, also known as Hoogly River. A distributary of the Ganges River that eventually enters the Bay of Bengal.

Khansama – Head of the kitchen.

Khitmutgar – Chief table servant.

Mofussil – Rural countryside.

Mohurrum – First month of the year on the Islamic Calendar. Commemorates death of Husayn, grandson of Muhammad.

Naan Bread – Flat, leavened bread.

Nautch – Traditional dance performed by professional dancing girls known as *nautch* girls.

Peg – English term for a mixture of brandy and soda.

Pice – In British India, one *pice* equaled one-quarter of an *anna*.

Punkah – large swinging fan

Punkah Wallah – person who pulls the rope to make the *punkah* move

Sambar – Lentil based vegetable stew or chowder.

Serampore -- Became a center of English missionaries with the arrival of William Carey, Joshua and Hannah Marshman, and William Ward in early nineteenth century. They established the Serampore Mission Press. Under Danish control until 1845 when British East India Company purchased it. About twelve and a half miles from Central Calcutta.

Tiffin – Light meal served mid-afternoon. Word derived from the English "tiffing" which meant eating and drinking out of mealtimes.

Topi – Also called a pith helmet, safari helmet, or sun helmet.

Tuktaposh – Wooden platform or table covered by a mat, mattress, sheet, and cushions.

Vakil – Authorized pleader in the Indian court.

Zenana – Area of the house where women were secluded.

About The Author

Sandra Wagner-Wright holds the doctoral degree in history and taught women's history at the University of Hawai'i for over twenty years. She lives in Hilo, Hawai'i. *Two Coins: A Biographical Novel* is her second novel of historical fiction.

SANDRA'S BOOKS
Historical Fiction
Rama's Labyrinth

Non-Fiction
*The Structure of the Missionary Call to the Sandwich Islands 1796-1830:
Sojourners Among Strangers*

*History of the Macadamia Nut Industry in Hawai'i:
From Bush Not to Gourmet's Delight*

*For Beer and the Bible: One Hundred Years at the
Lutheran Church of Honolulu*

Edited Journal
*Ships, Furs, and Sandalwood:
A Yankee Trader in Hawai'i 1823-1825*

CONNECT WITH SANDRA

Website: sandrawagnerwright.com

Facebook: facebook.com/SandraWagnerWright

Twitter: @SandraWWright

Google+:   plus.google.com/+SandraWagnerWright

Pinterest: pinterest.com/sandrawagnerwri

Goodreads: goodreads.com/sandrawagnerwright

www.ingramcontent.com/pod-product-compliance
Lightning Source LLC
Chambersburg PA
CBHW051203120726
47905CB00004B/970